PRAISE FOR
Women's Intuition

"I inhaled *Women's Intuition* like a plate of barbecued chicken from the Eastern Shore and cannot wait to tell every woman I know, 'Honey, you have to read this!' All novels have characters, but *Women's Intuition* has people, the kind you really care about. Quirky, edgy, wonderful people… Christian fiction has waited a long time for a voice like Lisa Samson's: disarming, honest, funny, painful, triumphant, real."

—LIZ CURTIS HIGGS, author of *Bad Girls of the Bible* and
· *Mad Mary*

"Lisa Samson is one of my favorite authors! Her novels are artfully crafted, and her characters are complex and delightful. *Women's Intuition* is a 'must read' for anyone who appreciates fiction."

—TERRI BLACKSTOCK, author of *Cape Refuge* and the
Newpointe 911 series

"Lisa Samson has one of the most unique voices in women's fiction today. Never has that talent been more evident than in *Women's Intuition*. Come meet the delightfully quirky Summervilles. You're going to love them!"

—ROBIN LEE HATCHER, author of *Firstborn*

"*Women's Intuition* isn't just a book; it's an intimate conversation with friends. Having developed a style all her own—both humorous and touching—Lisa Samson is quickly becoming a world-class novelist."

—JACK CAVANAUGH, author of *Postmarked Heaven*

"A heartfelt exploration of family relationships, the need to heal old wounds, and the courage it takes to move on."

—VINITA HAMPTON WRIGHT, author of *Velma Still Cooks
in Leeway*

"In *Women's Intuition,* Lisa Samson uses outrageous hilarity and insight to gently peel back the layers of dysfunction in one multigenerational family to reveal a treasure at the center. I want more novels like this!"
> —HANNAH ALEXANDER, author of The Healing Touch
> series

"Insightful, delightful, mirthful, and thoughtful. *Women's Intuition* serves up characters we long to call friends."
> —NANCY MOSER, author of *The Seat Beside Me* and *The Invitation*

"Lisa Samson takes us on another excursion deep into the heart of sticky family relationships in *Women's Intuition.* This gentle story shows how God works under the surface to bring us face to face with the things we fear most—and to bring us out the other side with His healing balm applied to our hurts. This is a story you won't soon forget."
> —COLLEEN COBLE, author of *Wyoming*

"The women in Lisa Samson's *Women's Intuition*—Lark, Leslie, Flannery, and Prisma—leapt right off the page and into my heart. Delightful and honest reading!"
> —ANGELA E. HUNT, author of *The Shadow Women*

"Fresh in style, beautifully realized in character, *Women's Intuition* will greatly please Lisa Samson's faithful following. Another delight from a truly original voice."
> —JAMES SCOTT BELL, author of *The Darwin Conspiracy*

"With characters as crisp and recognizable as Jan Karon's and with the depth and detail of a T. Davis Bunn, *Women's Intuition* is sure to capture the hearts of all who allow themselves to be found inside the strength of Samson's women."
> —JANE KIRKPATRICK, award-winning author of *All Together in One Place*

"Join a new sisterhood where women grow and survive and sometimes even triumph...all while they drive each other crazy. I love Lisa

Samson's writing, and I can only think of one word for her new book: SUPERB."

—STEPHANIE GRACE WHITSON, Christy Award finalist
and author of nine inspirational novels

"*Women's Intuition* is an enthralling, introspective journey into the lives and hearts of four unique, vividly drawn women battered by life but never defeated.... Lisa Samson is a spellbinding talent in the field of Christian women's fiction."

—KATHLEEN MORGAN, author of *Embrace the Dawn*

"Reading [*Women's Intuition*] was like opening a box of fine chocolates. I couldn't decide whether to gorge myself on the entire story in a single sitting or portion it out to be enjoyed over as many days as I could make it linger.... This is a gem of a story!"

—JANELLE BURNHAM SCHNEIDER, author of "More Than Tinsel" in *Homespun Christmas*

"Lisa Samson shines in *Women's Intuition*! A jewel of a novel with multifaceted characters so real that I missed them the minute I turned the last page. In my opinion, Samson is the freshest literary voice in the industry today."

—DEBORAH RANEY, award-winning author of *Beneath a Southern Sky* and *After the Rains*

"Lisa Samson's eye for understanding the mysteries of family life is acutely tuned in *Women's Intuition* with characters deftly drawn by her benevolent imagination. Samson offers a village peopled with deliciously flawed characters all revolving through a credible milieu that makes the heart believe that grace and mercy are free for the picking.... Delightful!"

—PATRICIA HICKMAN, author of *Sandpebbles* and *Katrina's Wings*

"The characters in *Women's Intuition* are so real, so strong, so memorable that I keep hearing snippets of their conversations in my mind, like recalling a chat with a close friend. I find myself wondering how they're doing, expecting to see them, and being able to ask. If women's intuition is at the heart of how we naturally think, love, and operate with those closest to us, this book reveals how it's done."

—SANDRA BYRD, author of The Secret Sisters Series,
The Hidden Diary Series, *Girl Talk,* and *Inside-Out Beauty Book*

Women's Intuition

Other books by Lisa Samson

Indigo Waters

Fields of Gold

Crimson Skies

The Church Ladies

Women's Intuition

a novel by

LISA SAMSON

WATERBROOK
PRESS

WOMEN'S INTUITION
PUBLISHED BY WATERBROOK PRESS
2375 Telstar Drive, Suite 160
Colorado Springs, Colorado 80920
A division of Random House, Inc.

The characters and events in this book are fictional, and any resemblance to actual persons or events is coincidental. Scriptures are paraphrased or quoted from the *King James Version*.

ISBN 1-57856-596-0

Library of Congress Cataloging-in-Publication Data
Samson, Lisa, 1964-
    Women's intuition / Lisa Samson.— 1st ed.
        p. cm.
    ISBN 1-57856-596-0
    1. Women—Maryland—Baltimore—Fiction. 2. Parent and adult child—Fiction.
3. Mothers and daughters—Fiction. 4. Runaway husbands—Fiction. 5. Baltimore
(Md.)—Fiction. 6. Divorced women—Fiction. I. Title.
    PS3569.A46673 W66 2002
    813'.54—dc21

                                                    2002006908

Printed in the United States of America
2002—First Edition

10 9 8 7 6 5 4 3 2 1

This book is dedicated to the memory of my mother,

JOY EBAUER,

July 23, 19– to August 6, 2001.

She never told her age, so neither will I.

Good-bye for now, dear.

I love you.

Acknowledgments

A lot of writers will tell you that it's poor form to list family and friends in your acknowledgments. To which I respond, "Oh yeah? This is the one chance I get to be totally me!"

I'd like to thank two very cool women with great intuition: my editor, Erin Healy, and my agent, Claudia Cross. Thanks for picking me up and strapping the running shoes back on. Lori York, LSCW-C, thanks for reading the manuscript and making a difference on the front lines of heartache every day. Thanks to you, Marty Ehrhardt and Mike Polischeck, for your firsthand info on Hamilton and to you, Loretta Ebauer, for our drives in Guilford, along Greenway Avenue, and into Hamilton.

My prayer ladies—Celestine, Tanzel, Freida, and Lori—thanks for bringing me daily before the throne. Patty, Jim, Liz, Deb, Colleen, Till, Angie, Nancy, Terri, Robin, Cheryl, and Jane—you all are such a source of encouragement. Eric Wiggin, thanks especially to you. It was a hard year as a writer for me. Your enthusiasm for my work kept me going at times. Jack, what would I do without your friendship and concern?

Thank you to all my family and friends, but, in particular, to my sister, Lori Chesser, and my friends Jennifer Hagerty, Heather Gillot, Chris Burkett, Marty Ehrhardt, and Karen Mortimer, who make my life as a woman rich. To Gloria Danaher, I'd like to say thank you for being a wonderful example of true womanhood and for your open-door policy! I couldn't have made it through my mother's illness without you. To my family—Will, Tyler, Jake, and Gwynnie—what a life we have been blessed to share. Thank you for giving me a broader heart from which to write.

Thank you, Jesus, for giving me this job to do and equipping me to do it. Your graciousness astounds me daily.

To my reading sisters who have been so supportive, who love stories with hope and a happy ending, I'm so thankful for you all. Thanks for the e-mails! Write me at lesamson@hotmail.com. Or visit my home-grown Web site, www.lisasamson.com.

To anybody I've forgotten (and that's the risk of making a big list like this), forgive me! The gray matter ain't what it used to be.

June

Lark

FLANNERY DESERVES TO KNOW THE TRUTH about her father. One day I'm going to have to tell her. But not tonight. I am worn out.

It's a tiredness of years.

You know how those ladies' magazines pretend women can do it all and still appear fresh as a sweet-smelling daisy by a clear Swiss spring? Wearing cute loafers, tweed miniskirts, and a camel cashmere twinset, they deposit their kids at soccer in sleek silver cars, green vans with television screens, or gargantuan white SUVs. Drive-through windows constitute meal planning. They see the best doctors because they don't mind going across town. Malls and boutiques bark their clothing on glitzy, stylistic posters. They instantly rid themselves of the nasty Flair inserts in the Valu-Pak coupon collections I look forward to each month. And they throw them into a recycling bin they bought from some woodsy, catalog-driven company.

They adroitly embroider their own existence with the silk threads of others' lives as though the fabric of their day-to-day duties was spun of gossamer and not the heavy mail plates that make up mine.

Was I ever like that?

Once upon a time, I suppose.

Really, though? Perhaps even then my fears festered deep down like mushrooms, and I chose to concentrate on the grass above the soil.

But one activity I do share with most women is this: I love coming home. I rarely leave it except to go play the organ at the local parish, or run down to the CVS for a gallon of milk or a loaf of bread. The priests at St. Dominic's laugh at me, and I just let them.

"If you didn't come here and play for mass," Father Charlie says from between his full, sweetheart lips, "you'd be a hermit, Lark."

"I'm a good organist, Father. Besides, a lot of holy men were hermits."

"That was then, this is now. You need to live a little."

Always the same.

Now, when a priest tells you to live a little, that spells trouble or, at the very least, a musty lifestyle. But I love my little home. My refuge. My relief. Ever since I signed the small mortgage. My very own consolation and sometimes insulation.

When I lie down, exhausted from trying so hard, I talk to Jesus. Now, I'm very thankful for the Resurrection, because if Christ had remained in that dark tomb, where would I be? I'm not just talking about my eternal destiny, I'm talking day by day. I know how it feels to be forsaken by someone you love more than yourself, and I know the love of Someone who loves you more than His own life.

I cry out to Him in the nighttime.

I imagine Him sitting there on the end of my bed and saying, "Come on, Lark. Give me your cares. All of them."

As far as I'm concerned, Jesus was the only man who ever walked the face of the earth that a woman could count on.

Home feels good on nights like tonight, cool and soothing, like freshly washed sheets on freshly shaved legs. I usually read on Friday nights or watch movies with Flannery, but Father Charlie called me earlier and asked me to meet with Marsha Fortenbaugh, our cantor. "I know it's late, but I've got a great new responsive piece for you to do."

I gripped the phone. "It's ten o'clock at night, Father!"

"I know this is short notice."

My heart started racing. "You're telling me, Father. You actually want to do it for Saturday evening mass? Tomorrow night? This had better be an easy piece."

"Wait till you hear it! And come on, Lark, you're the best organist we've ever had."

Which, according to Marsha, who grew up at St. Dominic's, says absolutely nothing.

So, feeling the ants of anxiety milling about beneath my skin, I yanked on my black pants and rose-colored blouse, brushed my brown frizz back into a headband, and headed over to the church. I wanted to make them wait for me, but who knew what lurked out on Harford Road this time of night?

There is no fear in love. There is no fear in love.

As I entered the sanctuary, I looked down and realized I had run to St. Dominic's in my slippers.

Soon people will whisper behind their hands, "There goes the Crazy Woman of Hamilton." I refuse to get a cat, though, for fear that once I do, more and more will litter my yard, eventually landing me in a mental institution somewhere as the Crazy Cat Woman of Hamilton.

A bit of pride lingers somewhere down with the mushrooms, I believe.

So I scanned the sheet of staff paper on the music rack before me and sank into the instrument that has cradled me for years, my fingers easing down onto the keys, pressing forward, lifting up.

Marsha gripped the lectern with bratwurst fingers supporting more Service Merchandise–type rings than any woman in Hamilton has a right to wear.

But who cared about rings, because right then, a refrain that proclaimed that all the ends of the earth have seen God's power streamed like a warm rainbow from the pipes. Father Charlie, running a knobby, ebony hand over his slicked-back, tweed hair, belted it out with his usual African-American gusto, only tone-deaf. Thank goodness Marsha held the microphone.

Goose bumps stippled my arms and drove away the ants.

So majestic. So beautiful.

And such a strong melody.

Some church songs really wander around. Drives me crazy. But not this one.

"What do you think?" Father Charlie pushed his Buddy Holly glasses back up on the bridge of his forthright nose. He puffed his black-shirted chest forward, the white square of his collar gleaming like a beacon of priestliness in the night gloom of the church.

"I love it!" I cried from a place deep within.

There is no fear in love.

Father Charlie raised his fine, winged brows. "See, I told you, didn't I?"

We rehearsed for the next ten minutes. Very straightforward chords, softly played for Marsha's verses, royally rendered for the chorus. Those goose bumps returned.

Every single time.

God gave Marsha that kind of voice. Imagine if ice felt as warm as it looked clear.

Yep, Father Charlie nailed this one, all right. Definitely worth leaving home for. It was why I played here at all. I mean, Mother and Daddy baptized me a Methodist, for heaven's sake. But something pulls me back week after week to St. Dominic's. Catholic churches cloister within them an attractive mysteriousness to Protestant types like me. After all these years here, I still am no exception. But praising God at St. Dominic's, accompanying Marsha and the parishioners, well, I know God desires me to use my gift right here. And sometimes I feel more at home here than anywhere else.

Maybe it's the scent of the candles.

Maybe it's the altar.

Maybe it's watching people kneel, watching people humble themselves in a way Protestant churches fail to expect, that humbles my heart.

Maybe it's because Father Charlie reassures me at my loneliest moments that one can get along fine in life without a member of the opposite sex confusing things. "You'd make a great nun, Lark," he keeps saying. But becoming a nun? No. The whole Mary thing unsettles me.

You'd make a great nun, Lark.

Oh my word.

"How about coming down to the kitchen for a milkshake?" Father Charlie asked when we finished.

Marsha, who happens to be my best friend, tightened her porous, bleached-blond ponytail, dividing it in two and pulling the sections apart in a painful-looking manner toward her purple zebra-print scrunchy. "Great. What flavor did you get this week, Father?"

"Butter pecan. How about it, Lark? You look like you could use some ice cream."

"I'll pass. I've got to get home."

"Oh, come on. Your answering machine will pick up the calls, and you can call them back."

I swung my feet around to the side of the bench. "No, really. I've got to go."

The ants go marching one by one.

There is no fear in love.

Marsha shoved her music into a satchel. "She's on a no-sugar kick now anyway, Father."

He turned to me with surprise. "You don't say? How come?"

Marsha jumped right in, thank you very much. "She saw a special on one of those health news spots on WJZ that sugar is actually a poison."

I shook my head. "Marsha, come on."

"It's true, Lark."

I almost said something about cellulite so profound it actually displays its topographical contours through purple Lycra leggings—hint, hint, Marsha—but Father Charlie just laid a hand on my shoulder and squeezed. "It's okay, honey."

"Thanks, Father." Thank heavens he interrupted before I voiced my thoughts. "I'd better go."

"See you tomorrow for five o'clock mass."

"I'll be here."

"I know you will."

I scurried down the main aisle, the real live church mouse.

"I'll call you!" Marsha hollered.

"I'm sure you will, sister!" I pushed on the front door and found myself in the night street, right there on Harford Road, streetlights ineffective in the fight against crime. Somebody once called Baltimore's streets "the mean streets." Pretty apt.

Just breathe, Lark. Just breathe.

Remember, you're in Hamilton, not Patterson Park.

Right foot. Left foot.

Forget about the guys that held up your father all those years ago. Just like that.

What about that stickup in the Hutzler's parking lot down on York Road when you were thirteen?

Perfect love casts out all fear.

They only got five bucks from Aunt Joy.

There.

And a pamphlet on the laetrile miracle cure from Uncle Bill.

See.

You can do it.

See?

Only gone an hour, I thought about my answering machine and the many voices now trapped on its tape. People tend to call after ten. And from eleven to midnight one call rings right after another. I know from experience that eleven to twelve is the loneliest hour of the day.

"Is this 1-777-IPRAY4U? I saw your ad in this magazine…and well, I feel a little silly now. Should I just leave my request? Should I call back later? Well…"

Or, "Hi, Prayer Lady, it's just me, Gene. I was calling to let you know what happened today at work. You won't believe…"

Or, "Help me. Is this for real? I need prayer real bad…"

And they all did. Everyone that dials my toll-free line needs prayer. And I pray with them. Right there over the phone. It's the least anybody can do, right?

A fire truck blared its horn.

No fear. No fear.

I jumped back to the doorway of St. Dominic's with a small scream.

Father Charlie slammed through the door. "Lark! You okay?"

"The fire truck."

"It's okay, child."

I just love Father Charlie. And we watched together as it barreled over the hill.

"I've always hated fire trucks." I laughed that tin-can laugh that grates on even my own nerves.

"Go on home and don't fear, Lark."

Fear not. Fear not.

"There is no fear in love, Father Charlie."

"John the Beloved couldn't have been wrong, child."

"Perfect love casts out all fear."

"You remember that, Lark."

He squeezed my shoulder with an oven mitt–sized hand.

Good thing the roster of shepherds on Christmas morning didn't include me is all I can say, because those angels might have been a little miffed at me, Lark Summerville, sitting there with all the sheep, frozen with fright and unable to even hear the most wonderful announcement ever made.

I stepped back out onto the sidewalk, passed Mo the Friendly Drunk, the most honest drunk alive.

"Hi, I'm Mo the Friendly Drunk, and I need some money for a drink. Now, I'll be honest with you. That's what I want the money for." He smiles politely and nods, his eyes diminished by the quarter-pound lenses in his wire glasses.

I shouldn't have handed him the fifty cents in my pocket, but I did. Mo the Friendly Drunk and Lark the Recluse.

There but for the grace of God, they say.

I headed down the street. The 3 B's Restaurant, sealed up and ready for the morning, displayed a chrome-lined counter, coffee cups facedown in their saucers. I'm talking some great chili in there. And the crab soup? Wonderful. Except I always worry a little bit when I spoon the flesh of bottom-feeding scavengers into my mouth. Babe Babachakos, the waitress and owner's wife, worries over a grand-nephew down at Hopkins in the pediatric oncology ward. She calls the prayer line but never reveals her name. I find it impossible to mistake the voice that scrapes over tobacco-stained vocal cords that way. I don't let on that I know.

The door from one of the dark Irish bars on Harford Road opened up, spilling the stink of stale beer and men's hairy underarms and two drunk guys wearing yellow CAT hats onto the sidewalk. Peering inside for the instant the door spread-eagled onto the sidewalk, I tried to fuse my backbone with the light pole, willing my heart to calm itself.

What is it with men anyway?

There they all sat in a row, talking, watching television, their big behinds spreading like melted cheese on barstools miniaturized by their overabundant flab. There they sat, drinking their booze, watching their sports, yuk-yukking at the inane, while most probably a wife at home who made dinner, did the dishes, bathed their four children, put them to bed, then threw in a load of laundry and made lunches for the next day, fell with exhaustion into an empty bed at 10:30.

And then beer boy in there will stagger home, expect a little hanky-panky, and wonder why she doesn't feel like it, will sulk, be a typical, selfish male, maybe even smack her around if he's the abusive type, and then fall asleep and snore so loudly in his drunkenness she won't even be able to get a wink of sleep.

Men.

Men. Men. Men.

If they could just be more like Jesus the world would be a better place, and that's the utter truth. Why do the best men always take a vow of celibacy?

Shoot. Forgot the milk.

I crossed Harford Road and skittered back to the twenty-four-hour CVS. We needed a loaf of bread for toast in the morning, and some extra milk wouldn't hurt a bit. Two percent. Can't forget the arteries while looking out for osteoporosis.

Behind the counter, in front of all those cigarettes I still craved twenty-three years after I gave them up, stood Rots DiMatti. How a man ever comes by a nickname like Rots is beyond me. At first I imagined all sorts of devilish escapades. Soap on windows. Eggs on shutters. Flaming bags of dog doo on doorsteps. But Babe at the 3 B's told me he was called Rotten Tomaters as a kid back in the thirties.

Huh?

"DiMatti-Tomaters, DiMatti-Tomaters. Get it?"

I set my purchases on Rots's counter.

"Hi, Mr. DiMatti."

"Hey, Doll."

I love that. Doll.

"How's Mrs. DiMatti?"

"In Florida! I says, 'Sweetie Pie, now's not the time to pick up and go to Florida.' It's hot there now.' And she says, 'Rots, I'll go to Florida when I please.'" He waved a bony, polka-dotted hand. "So off she went."

"How long you batching it?"

"A month."

"Lucky you."

He winked and handed me the change. "And stop giving your money to that bum, Doll."

"I don't give him much, Mr. DiMatti."

"Would you buy him a drink?"

"Well, no." I apologized. "And I know, I know it's the same thing."

"You're too nice."

Oh my word. How wrong could somebody be?

"'Night, Doll."

It looked so dark outside those doors.

"'Night."

Go on out, Lark. Go ahead, you can do it, sister.

The three-block walk seemed like a mile with two gallons of milk hanging in blue plastic bags about to cut my forearm in two. Not to mention the two-liter bottle of Coke for Flannery, my sweet daughter, or the bag of Nutter Butters. I figured I'd show Marsha.

I can eat Nutter Butters with the best of them. And I would.

Maybe tomorrow.

But now the early summer dew settled sweet and soft, and the streets of Baltimore hummed their tune above the silent strains of a dormant energy building up for tomorrow's city life. The scent of life waiting patiently in the wings coated my nostrils. Still. Sweet. Large.

I absolutely couldn't wait to get home.

I pictured my bed with that frequently laundered old quilt my Grandma Summerville stitched for my wedding all those years ago, a wedding with a hailstorm, a power failure, a leaning cake, two fainting bridesmaids, a ring bearer that pooped in his pants during the vows, and a flying urn of Béarnaise that burned my left hand—a wedding, had I known it, that was nothing more than a sinister harbinger.

My chuck roast of homes may not look fancy, but it tastes good. I grew up in a filet mignon, so I know the difference. Home isn't much, honestly, but it's warm. I love my little yellow house in Hamilton. Maybe one day I'll paint my bedroom pink and green and save up enough for that canopy bed I saw in the Domestications catalog. But all those paint fumes? Who knows how many cancer cells someone builds up per coat of paint?

Yes, home is good. It belongs to me.

Better than anything Bradley and I ever lived in all those years ago, that's for sure. Oh, Brad. If I hadn't yelled like that, maybe you wouldn't

have gone speeding off on that motorcycle like you did. The loud rever-
berations of that Harley engine stab me over and over to this day. Who
did I think I was back then? What right did I have to make the demands
I did?

Life is better this way, right? Easier.

And poor Flannery. She deserves none of this.

Eleven P.M. Timex time.

I turned off Harford Road by the Jiffy Lube right onto Bayonne
Avenue, where I live. I pictured my daughter, Flannery, who had just
graduated from college and moved back in a few days ago, at home
waiting for me. She planned on renting an old movie to play on the
television set she brought back with her from Chicago, and I said,
"Don't forget about popcorn." And she won't forget the popcorn. Not
Flannery.

I really am blessed, when it all comes down to it.

One day I'm going to have to tell Flannery the truth about her
father, and then even this blessing may wither in the heat of the out-
come. I wonder at least five times a day how much longer I can put it
off. I wonder how someone who walks with Jesus can perpetuate a lie
like this?

Oh, Jesus, Jesus, my Jesus.

Another fire truck breezed around the corner.

The peculiar smell of fire prickled my scalp then, and though I
couldn't see it, I just knew—just like I just knew at eighteen I was pregnant—I just knew the problem belonged to me and most likely me
alone. And so I ran toward the smoky sky, the smell, the destruction.
There it blazed, the fire, a living thing, hot and hungry. I dropped my
bags and I lurched toward the flames, hoping my eyes deceived me.

"Flannery!"

Fear not, fear not. Fear not.

Leslie

MY GRANDDAUGHTER FLANNERY CALLED from her car phone an hour ago. "The house is on fire, Grandy!" she shouted above the cacophony of sirens and firemen yelling back and forth.

"Your mother, Sweet Pea?" I shouted too, even though my house lay still in the quiet of early morning. "Is Larkspur all right?"

"She's at a late practice at church," she hollered, and I pictured her there with her fine black hair sticking out all over her head in copious, curious little ponytails, her pale skin gilded by the flames consuming the forlorn little Dutch Colonial. "Don't rush down here, Grandy."

"But—"

"I'm telling you, Grandy! It's a zoo."

Naturally. It was Hamilton, mind you.

"But your mother."

"I'll take care of her when she gets here. You know I'm good at that."

"Come back here when you finish up. I'll have Prisma make up your rooms."

"We got no place else to go, Grandy. I gotta run."

And we hung up after our good-byes.

Dear Lord. Poor Larkspur. I can't begin to think what I can say that will make her feel better. But then, I never could.

Flannery

I SEE THE LOOK ON MOM'S FACE as she runs up and sees the house on fire, and I wish I could die. Her eyes are sort of darting around, and I see her staring through the crowd gathering in the street. I used to love those scary-type teen movies, and I thought the looks of terror on the actors' and actresses' faces were real. Believe me—*believe* me—terror is never so big or so bold as that. It's pale and kinda thin. Purplish gray if I had to paint it.

I've never come face to face with terror before. But then again, I've never seen anyone's entire world being licked clean by flames. Piranhas. They remind me of piranhas.

Mom stands there so helpless, her hands out at her sides as if singing a broad, aching note, and all 110 pounds of her melts into further insignificance in the face of what stands before her.

"Flannery!" she screams. "Flannery!" And she gulps air and mutters, "Oh, God, oh, God, oh, God, oh, God. Oh, Jesus, help me. Oh, God. Flannery! Where are you!"

I am on Mrs. Dickerson's porch drinking a Coke and talking with her son Tommy about the fire—how I managed to get out so easily—when she runs up. I jump right over the edge yelling, "Mom!" as soon as what's happening computes.

I trip over the pink azalea, but I'm A-Okay.

Now, let me tell you that true relief is a lot bigger and bolder than in the movies. Mom throws herself at me, and we tumble down onto the grass in between the sidewalk and the street, her black slippers flying like bats against the smoky sky, and she heaves sobs so big she ends up throwing up all over Mr. Cahey's new Reeboks.

"I saw your car, and I didn't see you. Oh, God. Oh, thank God."

"I'm here," I say, and I am glad I am more for her sake than mine. 'Cause I could be sitting around at Kim's Ceramics or something, oblivious to the fact that everything we own is caught in a fiery furnace with no miracle to save it. She's always been a really good mom, and I'm not going to make up some bogus complaints because those stupid talk shows tell me that it's cool to be dysfunctional and that 98 percent of the homes across America are dysfunctional.

So she's a loner. But it's always been her and me together. And to be honest, I think God used me to keep her sane after Daddy died.

From over her head I watch the house burn. "It's all gone, Mom." I don't know why I say it. You can see that by just looking at it.

She pulls away from me and sits up in the grass, wiping off Mr. Cahey's shoes with a tattered Kleenex I hand her. He told her to stop, but she just can't seem to listen to him. "How did it start?"

"They won't know until it's been put out and the fire inspectors do their job."

But they sort of do know it started somewhere in the basement. Not that I would say that out loud! Not that my silence makes a difference because, bingo, she guesses it.

"I knew I should have had all that wiring replaced! I've just been waiting for the tax refund. And you might have been still inside, and I would have killed you because I kept putting it off! Oh, Jesus."

That tax refund is nowhere in sight. Mom filed two extensions already. Organists don't make much money, let me tell you, and the donations to IPRAY4U are only enough to keep the actual phone number going and pay for the heat in the house. I tell her I saved her Bible, her shoebox of photographs, and her answering machine, and she cries some more and throws up again. "What about your stuff? All your artwork…when I think about those canvases in the basement…" And she heaves once more.

She is right though, my paintings from high school—gone! The body of work from college, thankfully, hasn't arrived yet from UPS. But I'm choosing to look at it this way, like, sometimes it's just better to put the past behind you. And believe me—*believe* me—when I tell you, some of those paintings were "ghastly" as Grandy would say. Definitely compositions only a mother could love.

So in the meantime we're going to have to go stay with Grandy at the medieval monstrosity on Greenway. Speaking of green, that's what color Mom is at the thought of leaving Hamilton and going back to Stoneleigh House where she grew up. I've always liked the place though.

Still, poor Mom. I figure I'll fling a prayer up to God because only He knows how to get Mom out of this one.

Lark

I SUPPOSE ABSURD THOUGHTS HIT MOST OF US during horrible moments like house fires. But after I located Flannery on the neighbor's porch, regurgitated, and reacted as I imagine the normal woman reacts when she sees her dear house on fire, I thought, "Man, what's my brother going to think about this?" Crazy, I know. Bigger worries consumed me just then. But Newly's superior-looking grin and his normal "God help you, Lark—" prologue that invariably began his verbal missives drifted through the smoke. And even though Newly is an albino, he did far more with the two pair life dealt him than I ever did with the full house it handed me.

I should have been nicer to him when we were little. But his annoying qualities inbred to produce toothless, chinless children in the form of his equally annoying friends. I tried to tell him about Jesus a few years ago, after praying for months and finally building up the nerve. He just looked at me askance and quit calling me after that. Was I wrong? Insensitive? I mean, I pray with people all the time that need Jesus to lift them up, heal them, help them make it through. I thought I knew what I was doing.

But he threw a barb that day. "You need God more than I do, Lark. The way you messed up your life so young." And then, because the Summerville genes built him in the first place, said, "I'm happy you've found what you need. Let's leave it at that, shall we?"

And yet, despite my fornication with Bradley and the resulting disastrous marriage, despite my quiet existence, I still feel sorry for my brother Newly, CEO of my father's Fortune 500 company and pride and joy of all who once taught him, bless him, and bless his Mercedes, his striped ties, his Manhattans, and his condo at the Inner Harbor.

However rude her conception, the greatest kid in the world loves me, and I refuse to think Flannery, the love of my life and my reason for living, enjoyed no initial blessing from the Father's heart. That she was merely an allowance, not a plan, is unacceptable. The theology of it confuses me, so I ignore it and chalk it all up to the fact that God created the world in the first place.

What will Mother say? Probably not much. Mother prides herself on her lack of interference.

All gone. Not that it was much to begin with. But oh, Jesus, my Jesus. It's all gone. My home is gone.

And it hit hard once more. The previous fleeting thoughts of Newly and Mother tried desperately to pad my brain from reality, but Leslie and Newly Summerville proved inept at such a pitiful task.

The tears dripped quickly, like rushing droplets of heavy rain down a clean windshield, collecting upon each other, rolling, growing, eating each other alive.

Flannery held me as we stared at the rolling flames and just said, "It's all right, Mom. It's all right, Mom. Don't be afraid. I'm right here."

Leslie

WHAT'S LARKSPUR FEELING RIGHT NOW? Impossible to imagine. Fortune has certainly never smiled upon my daughter as it has upon my son, Newly. And the fact that she has remained single for the past twenty years just aggravates her situation. Well, as my mama down in Charlottesville, God rest her soul, always said, "It only takes one scoundrel to ruin a girl for good."

Enter Bradley del Champ.

I can't blame the fellow for zeroing in on Larkspur the way he did. That long, wavy brown hair of hers the color of a glistening caramel. Those serious butterscotch eyes. And nougat skin. Larkspur always appeared so tan and healthy in those days. A choker in an opera-length world, she's a bit diminutive. A bit diminutive? Well, actually, we even took her to a Hopkins growth specialist years ago and returned with the insightful answer, "She's just short."

Well!

That's what I deserve for sticking with my Charles, I suppose. His mother, even shorter than my daughter, reminded me of an apple dumpling. And sickeningly sweet, to boot. She never cared for me, and I never cared for her, but we both tried to at least act like it for the sake of all involved.

The mystery remains as to how long it took Bradley, tall, blond, and fine looking, to induce my daughter's moral compromise, but in those days when a girl found herself pregnant, the boy married her. We thought we were doing the right thing. He hailed from a better family than the Summervilles, not as well bred as us Strawbridges, mind you, as my mama, God rest her soul, always reminded me ad nauseam, and certainly Charles and I thought we were doing the right thing. We thought it was the right thing.

Bradley and Larkspur shared so much with their music and all. And his folk rock band experienced little success until Larkspur, a poetic soul, revamped his lyrics and sometimes his melodies and began playing whatever type of keyboard the song needed. She could sing background too. Unfortunately, he seduced the beatnik out of her, his presence magnifying her artistic-sensitive nature, painting over her good roots and stable background like the black goop my groundsman uses to gussy up the driveway.

After Bradley's final departure, just after Flannery turned two, I think we all breathed a sigh of relief. Bent on spending his yearly trust fund dividends by April on musical instruments, sound equipment, and all those wiry things, Bradley forced poor Larkspur to rely on the money Charles mailed all the way to San Francisco to feed and clothe our granddaughter. Not that we minded supporting Flannery and Larkspur.

Heavens, no!

In fact, I never said a thing about it to her. A woman must keep her pride, and the last thing she needed was a harping mother. Charles and I discussed it more than our marriage could sometimes bear. At least we realized we belonged to the same team.

Well, imagine our relief when we heard the news of Bradley's demise. I did feel a smidgen of guilt at that. But, naturally, I invited Larkspur and Flannery to move back home to Guilford. Our Greenway Avenue is such a lovely street. And our Stoneleigh House? Definitely the pick of the litter. It still amazes me that I assimilated into city society as well as I did. We're a tad more genteel in Virginia, mind you. Not that I'd ever say such a thing out loud! Of course not! Mama always told me a lady keeps her mouth shut and never compares herself with others.

Well, Larkspur flatly refused to come back home, but she did return to Baltimore, living in an old carriage house for a while where the good, clean horse smell lingered, and being from horse country, I find that a lovely aroma. Finally, after a year of not visiting or even picking up the phone, she rented to own a little yellow two-bedroom bungalow, two blocks off Harford Road, on Bayonne Avenue, right down the street from a little church-run elementary school where she sent Flannery. Larkspur's life, a pedagogy of penurious survival, has taught me all sorts of things I never knew: rent-to-own, layaway, and monthly APR financing. Not sure what that one means. I do know the poor thing still pays on a car she totaled four years ago, having let the insurance lapse due to finances. She refuses to accept even one penny from me to pay it off.

Where did I go wrong? She could have been anyone, done anything. She planned on becoming a concert organist, you know. Enter Bradley del Champ, if you please.

The rat.

Regrets. Womanly regrets.

We all have them. In fact, I wonder at times if conception itself gifts us with them. If they lie in wait there in the middle of our ovaries, ready to pounce at our most vulnerable moments.

Larkspur must know I understand about mistakes.

She's not getting any younger, and I fear her life of loneliness will sidle up unawares, set her on his lap, and bind arms of unbending steel around her midsection in a death grip, then shoot up and fly away with Lark to an unknown planet in the cold, wide universe. Never to return.

Oh my, but I'm waxing emotive today! And so touchy lately too! Just call me Lady Vesuvius. Ever since I started on this new medication—thank you, Dr. Medina, a sadist to be sure—the top of my skull steadily wears away! Toprol, Rocaltrol, and four other prescriptions. Not to mention the Metamucil, the Ensure, the glucosamine, and for good measure and because youth never makes U-turns, a little ginkgo biloba. If you popped me with a pin, a stream of tablets and capsules would fly out with the air!

The simple days of a little Geritol are gone for good, I'd say.

But Larkspur's coming home! With only the clothes on her body and my Sweet Pea granddaughter at her side. I'm sorry she lost the house. She made her life there on the corner. A paltry life, but one of her own making, which I admire. Running that religious phone service, singing with the Catholics.

Now, I try to be ecumenical with the best of them, but the Catholics? Oh my. What would my parents think about that? Thank

God they never lived to see it. I'd wager that Henry VIII got rid of the
whole religion for a very good reason, not that I know my history all
that well, but someone as memorable as Henry VIII would surely have
a good reason for getting rid of an entire religion from my family's country of origin. And all those statues simply give me the willies. But then,
statuary always has, whether it's St. Joseph or one of those garden
nymphs with nary a piece of clothing on their reedy frames.

Lark reminds me of a garden nymph actually—skinny, ill-clad, and
scraping along penny to penny unnecessarily. Looking so sad all the
time. I've tried so hard to uplift my daughter but find myself acting
"perky." I know I wouldn't find myself at all reassuring. Will I be able
to pull her up out of this one? I doubt it. But I have to try.

Antidepressants are much better these days.

Well, no sleep will be forthcoming the rest of the night, so back to
work on my photo album. Prisma dragged it out for me several weeks
ago and we looked over the photos of Larkspur as a baby. I hate to admit
this, but the thing moldered in the dark attic for thirty-five years.
Thirty-five years!

What kind of mother am I?

I thanked my lucky stars when I opened up my box of snapshots
and they hadn't grown hair.

I flipped to the page where Larkspur turned four. Oh, the party
Charles dreamed up that year. Like something out of a movie. That's
what Charles said he wanted. "Les, I want a carousel, ponies, and
clowns." Charles always got what he wanted, and in a way that the giver
was glad to bestow it on him.

Embarrassed me to no end, staging a show like that. Ostentatious,
my mama would have said. Garish. Nouveau riche. But now that I look
back on the pictures and see the utter expressions of joy on Larkspur's
and Charles's faces, it made the embarrassment worth it completely.

Flannery

IT IS ALL I CAN DO TO GET HER TO STOP SHAKING. She won't stop staring at the house. The flames died awhile ago, but the ruins smolder. "Mom? How 'bout if I go get you a cup of warm milk? Mrs. Cahey said to just knock on the kitchen door if we need anything."

"I don't know, Flannery." Her teeth chatter despite the fact that it's June. "It's so late. And she probably doesn't really want us to bother her."

"In fact, why don't you sit in their kitchen and I'll talk to the firemen and take care of things out here."

She doesn't respond except to nod, and I go into action. Ushering her into the Caheys' place, I feel relieved to see a teakettle already on the stove. Mom loves tea. Mrs. Cahey folds Mom in her big, jiggly arms, even though Mom never once initiated a conversation between the two since Mrs. Cahey moved here when I was four. She kisses her forehead. "Tea's almost done, hon." And she sits her gently on one of the captain's chairs swiveling at the head of the kitchen table.

Poor Mom. Living proof that Jim Morrison was right about the whole "people are strange" thing.

Well, anyway, Miss Prisma will sure be glad to see us when we arrive at Stoneleigh House. Someone else will eat her Congo bars besides her and Asil Smitzer. Not that she needs any help in consuming sweets.

I punch my Uncle Newly's number into my cell phone around one in the morning. Mom is asleep on the Caheys' brown Colonial-print couch, guys with wheelbarrows and ladies with flowers in their aprons, and I figure I'll give her a couple more hours to sleep in oblivion.

"Um, hello?" Uncle Newly clears his throat.

"Uncle Newly, it's Flannery."

He clears his throat again. "Buddy. Do you realize the time? Are you drunk? Have you no designated driver?" As he speaks his voice slowly inches back to life.

"I'm fine. Mom's house just burned down."

"Oh my! You don't say! Horrible! You don't say!"

"I do say."

"How awful."

Uncle Newly went to Oxford and talks like one of those fancy-pants Englishmen. It drives Grandy crazy! "For heaven's sake, you're an American, Newly Summerville!" she says every time she hangs up the phone from one of his calls.

"I say, is she all right? Are you all right?"

"Yes, we're fine."

"Well, then, you just called to give the news?"

"Uh-huh."

Silence. I love making Uncle Newly uncomfortable. He thinks he's so continental and suave, but how suave can someone that white really be? Can you imagine him on the beach in the south of France?

Yikes.

"Can we come over to your place to sleep tonight?"

"Uh…"

More silence.

"Just kidding!"

Oh, he's so much fun, Uncle Newly.

"I just thought you'd like to know."

"Thank you, Buddy. Are you going over to Greenway then?"

"Yeah. I'm sure Prisma is already laying out plates for breakfast."

"Naturally."

"So when are we going out for lunch?"

"How about Saturday next?"

"You got it."

I hear his smile as he finally begins to warm up. It takes awhile with Uncle Newly. If we didn't love each other so much, I doubt he'd have any contact with the family. He's always been a great uncle though.

"How about a game of pool afterward?" I ask.

"All right, Buddy. We'll do that, too."

"And I'll wipe up the floor with you, Unc."

He chuckles.

We say good-bye.

He and mother have the weirdest relationship I've ever seen. They haven't talked in two years, and I don't think either of them even realizes it.

I know I should be more upset about the house and all, but to be honest I'm happy to see it burn down. Maybe God is finally pushing my mom out into the big wide world.

Leslie

THE SOUND OF THE PHONE AWAKENED ME around 4 A.M. My stars. I fell back asleep!

"Grandy?"

"Sweet Pea?"

"We're leaving now. We'll be there in twenty minutes or so."

"Do you need Asil to come around with the car?"

"No thanks. I've got mine."

"How's your mother?"

"Like Jell-O."

I sighed. "Oh dear. I might have guessed."

"I'd better go."

"All right, dear. The side door will be unlocked."

I hurried down to Prisma's rooms off the kitchen and knocked on the door. The pleasure of Prisma's company, not to mention her cooking, has belonged to us since before I married Charles fifty years ago. Even older than myself, Prisma lies about her age with the best of us! Truth be told, Prisma is my best friend. Not a soul knows that. Not even Prisma Percy.

So the little house in Hamilton burned to nothing more than a charred pit. Sweet Pea, as I call Flannery—quite a ghastly name despite its literary connotations—said once she heard the smoke alarm screeching she grabbed a few things of her mother's and her own laptop. The child performed well. Of course she inherited my ability to keep one's head firmly attached during a disaster.

I'll never forget the rogue tornado that barreled down on our farm one year when I was fourteen. I had to almost drag my mama down to the cellar by her hair. She cold-shouldered me for a week she was so angry. But that typified Libby Lee Strawbridge, pride as thick as the sole of a dirty old boot.

Ah, but my Charles. He deserves credit as well. Now, that man kept his wits in any situation. I miss him so.

I rapped on the door to Prisma's quarters, and I heard her shuffle her wide feet into the pair of the gold Daniel Green slippers I had tucked in her stocking last Christmas. I own a pair just like them. "What is it this time, Mrs. Summerville?" she grunted. "Four A.M.? You all right?" The volume of the suede bottoms of her mules soft-shoeing it across the dull wooden floor increased.

"It's about Larkspur and Sweet Pea."

The Daniel Greens steamed at full speed now. And the door opened, Prisma's face blending at first with the shade of middle night. "They all right?" She stepped into the light, her golden maple skin, neither peach nor brown, illumined by the brass sconce on the wall of the mud room, which separated her apartment from the general house.

"The house is gone. Burned to the ground."

Prisma slapped both hands over her heart. "Are they safe?"

"Sweet Pea is fine. Larkspur's been trembling like a leaf ever since."

"How did it start?"

"Why, Prisma, I don't really know. I didn't think to ask."

This naturally disgusted Prisma, thorough as an IRS agent and twice as particular. "What am I going to do with you, Mrs. Summerville?"

"I was just so relieved they were safe, is all!"

She threw a heavy, ropy braid the color of aged hemp over her shoulder. Silver flashed along the strands of the wiry coil. "Like I said, I don't know what I'm going to do with you."

Now, you may think I've lost control of my housekeeper, the way she browbeats me, but truthfully, she only does it because she knows I love her. "You don't need to do anything with me, Prisma Ophelia Percy, with you sticking your nose into all of my business and making all my decisions without telling me!"

"Hmmm. Well, somebody had to follow up at the doctor's for you!"

"I had planned on calling the very next day!"

"Like I even believe that, Mrs. Summerville."

"H'm."

"M'm."

Argument ended nicely as usual.

What a pair we make! My stars.

She pulled on her braid, hand over hand. "Let me get dressed. You didn't wake me up just to tell me the news. So they're coming here?" She shuffled over to the bed on her gilded platypus feet.

"They've got no place else to go, do they?"

Prisma opened the door to her closet and pulled down a tweed skirt and a white blouse the size of a clipper ship's mainsail. "Lark could go live with Newly."

We laughed so hard we couldn't keep from crying.

L a r k

I GRIPPED THE HANDLE OF THE CAR DOOR, a primordial burble of nausea threatening to pop down in my throat. "Oh man."

Shove it down, Lark. Shove it down.

Flannery pulled two sticks of gum out of her backpack and handed one to me. "It's not like going back to Greenway is the end of the world, Mom. Right?"

Easy for you to say. "I don't know about that, Flannery."

"Hey, I just moved back in with my mother, and I don't think it's all that bad!"

But she's wrong. Because I say, if life comes full circle at my age, then you know trouble's sidled up beside you and tapped you on the shoulder with a smarmy chuckle. It means you failed at snipping the cord like you thought you did, that you left a small stringy bit of sinew, a stretchy thread that connected you more than you ever imagined to those from whom you desperately wish to separate yourself.

I folded the gum twice. "At least there will be the insurance money."

"See? It won't be forever."

I placed the gum back on my right bottom molars. "And then maybe I can build that little cabin I've always wanted, right there in Hamilton."

M'm, Juicy Fruit. I love Juicy Fruit. How bad can a world in which Juicy Fruit exists really be?

Wait! What about the insurance money? Had I paid that bill? Or put it off?

"See there? It's not so bad." Flannery latched on to my optimism like a nursing infant who slept through the night for the first time. "I'll bring home a log home magazine tomorrow from Barnes and Noble.

Although I gotta tell you, Mom, I can't picture a log cabin in the middle of the city."

"Why are you going to Barnes and Noble?"

I watched her pretty face smooth as she forgot the family tragedy and centered on herself. Good for her.

"I've got a job interview at Starbucks, to be a Barista."

Naturally I needed a definition.

Blathering on about espresso machines and foamed milk, regular, skim, or 2 percent, chai tea, whatever that is, and extra shots—"Some people call them Depth Charges, some call them Red Eyes, and others call them a Shot in the Dark"—we blazed a homeward trail through the city, cutting over North Avenue and on up Charles Street. The pools of light illumined no activity save the wild, jerky mazurkas of bugs and moths. The city rested quiet. All the once-potential hangovers having been achieved, only *Sunpaper* trucks, bakery vans, and the occasional cop car stirred the misty soup of predawn air.

"Can you get just a cup of tea there?" I asked.

"Oh, Mom, you crack me up!"

"Can you?"

"Actually, you can. All sorts of tea."

"What about just plain old Lipton or something?"

"There's no plain old anything at Starbucks." She reached into her backpack again and dug up a tube of lip gloss. "Want some?"

"No thanks. We'll be there in just a few minutes, sweetie. I'm sure you're tired." I felt the tears sting my eyes, and I quickly looked out the side window.

Blink, Lark. Blink.

But Flannery knew because she sighed.

"Don't worry, Mom, it will all be okay. And I promise I won't say anything about the wiring to Grandy."

"You always come through."

You know how they say that like a good cook God wastes nothing? Well, it remains a mystery what He's cooking up with all of this. What changes are ahead? And are they broiled, fried, or fricasseed? Because, I can tell you this, having all your worldly goods snatched away does not bode well for the comfort-food life I've lived these past few years. Did

He have plans for a gourmet spread, or, heaven help me, grilled shish kebab?

John the Beloved could easily talk about "no fear in love" because he rested his head directly on the actual bosom of the Savior. I wonder if he would have been so confident if he'd never had that experience, if he'd muddled around in faith alone wondering if he'd be delivered only on the other side of heaven.

"Should I call Marsha?"

"I already did," Flannery answered. "She said she'd call Father Charlie so he could start praying."

That sounded fine with me. When God appoints a prayer warrior like Father Charlie to guard you spiritually, you're not only grateful, but totally relieved. He'd better go overtime on the supplications, I reasoned, because soon I would be getting pretty miffed at the entire situation.

PRISMA

YOU'LL ALWAYS GET THE TRUTH FROM ME, whether it's about myself, the Summervilles, or the president of the United States. So when I tell you that this big old house needs the bodies of Lark and Baby Girl around, you know I speak straight. I call Flannery "Baby Girl," because nobody deserves a name like Flannery. Her mother thinks she likes it, but I know for a fact she went by Fanny in Chicago.

Fanny del Champ.

Goodness me!

You know if someone would rather be called Fanny over something else, that something must fall into the same category as used shoes. I know they called her Fanny because I'm the only one that ever traveled up there to see her during all four years of college. I owed that to Mr. Summerville's memory. Mrs. Summerville refuses to fly anymore with her poor heart. Lark refuses to even leave Baltimore City since she totaled her car. That poor girl meets life with all the ferociousness of a lima bean. Been like that ever since living in San Francisco with that rascal Bradley del Champ. Lord forgive me, but I never could stomach the boy.

But the sight of my Baby Girl in her cap and gown made every awful sandwich I consumed in the train canteen car worth it! I cried enough tears to swell the Susquehanna River. And a woman my size can cry more than her fair share of tears.

Along with Mr. and Mrs. Summerville, I raised Lark, which, by all rights, makes Baby Girl my grandchild. And as Flannery grew up, well, I drove over to Hamilton in the Duster, and we had us all sorts of fun. Bowling. Miniature golf. Fishing. Sometimes Mrs. Summerville came too. Just not in the Duster. And not bowling, either. Or fishing, actually.

During those times Asil drove us up to Loch Raven Dam to feed those big ugly carp, or out to Westminster for lunch at Baugher's and their hot turkey sandwiches made to put a shine in your eyes and an extra inch of bulge over your waistband.

Lark never joined us. "You all just go on and have fun," she'd say with a wave from behind one of her library books. Someone like Lark should not read the crime novels she does, I can tell you that.

I looked out the kitchen curtains to our back lawn. Not much acreage here in the middle of the city, but we do own one of the larger lots. Almost an acre. Our gardener, who doubles as the chauffeur, possesses a green thumb that causes the whole neighborhood to break the "covet not your neighbor's house" commandment. I know Asil will want me to rouse him so he can welcome the girls with flowers in their rooms. That man. Honest to Pete, one day before his rheumatism started flaring up on a regular basis I found him asleep in the greenhouse. I shoved his shoulder with my foot, and he started mumbling something about Easter lilies. What a fine way with flowers. And a fine way with womankind, other than we who live here on Greenway at Stoneleigh House. Asil Smitzer wears a bow tie with more business than any man I've ever seen, including my late Mr. Percy, who only wore a bow tie twice that I knew of—the day I married him and the day I laid him in his grave with one of Asil's Easter lilies for company.

Asil lives above the garage and keeps the main house pretty much at bay. Mrs. Summerville says she can't stand two things—dirty fingernails and white shoes after Labor Day. Asil hasn't a prayer with either thing, because he's always digging in the dirt and hasn't bought new dress shoes since 1975 during his Earth, Wind, and Fire phase. We all keep praying he'll wear a hole in those platforms, but so far God's been silent.

My mind wraps itself around a list of things to do.

Open the windows. Hopefully that surly, chain-smoking old house painter with the low-slung pants and only three fingers on his left hand who took more breaks that I think decent didn't paint them shut four years ago.

Change the sheets. No visitors up there in almost a year. Now what does that say?

Give the bathrooms a good wipe down with a Lysol rag.

Though I feel my age more each day, I still take pride in a clean-smelling bathroom.

I figure by the time they get here they'll want breakfast, so I'll get the sweet dough rising first. Nobody can make a sticky bun like Prisma Percy. And with a cup of my good, strong coffee for Baby Girl, a nice pot of tea for Lark, and a hug or two or ten, they'll realize that more sorrow might have been heaped on their plates.

Four-thirty A.M.

Mrs. Summerville sleeps quietly on the sofa in the den. Lord help her, she had the best of intentions with that old photo album this morning. But she needs her sleep. I don't like the look of her these days. Kinda tired and gray around the mouth. Ever since that heart attack a few years ago she worries me along those lines. Not that she'll let me go with her to the doctor's office. "It was a mild heart attack, Prisma," she always says. As a first-class meddler, I do know when to quit attacking on the battlefield and initiate the guerrilla warfare.

First things first though. I stand by my sitting room window and look up at the thinning sky and I pray to Jesus. I picture His face there against the night, same color as mine, Him being Jewish and me being a potpourri of racial DNA, and I see His eyes and His love and feel the arms of eternity embrace me, and I see Him smile at me. And I think, "You're up to something with all this, aren't You, Lord?"

And He nods and says, "You up to it, Prisma, My girl?"

And I say, "It's always been You and me, Lord. You and me."

And Jesus says, "You got that right."

Lark

SOMETIMES GOD RISES ABOVE AND BEYOND the call of duty. Okay, most times. Case in point: when I walked into Stoneleigh House to find Mother snoring like Elmer Fudd on the couch in the den. The scritch of Prisma's fork across the pan as she fried the bacon in the kitchen defined my escape route. And I ran before the ants caught up with me, depositing them right there with Mother. Or tried to.

My life circled home to Greenway. To Stoneleigh House.

The ants crawled all over me anyway, my skin burned and my heart raced. Oh, Jesus.

Stay asleep, stay asleep, I silently ordered Mother as I tiptoed toward the flip-flop door leading into the kitchen. A thousand questions accompanied me, and I wanted to run away, to keep going. But where? Home no longer existed. Huge old, drafty old Stoneleigh House stood in its place. And how would I get to St. Dominic's now? My license lapsed last year, and the thought of letting Asil chauffeur me around in the Bentley slightly abraded me, like wearing jeans with no underpants.

All I have left to wear on my feet are these stupid slippers too.

At times like this people say they feel like the carpet has been pulled out from under them. Right then, I felt as if the whole world had tumbled away from beneath my feet. And there I dangled on some swaying trapeze, gripping the bar but feeling the pain in my arms as my adult weight hung from fingers grown weak.

How do I describe my childhood here in Greenway with Mother? How do I describe wearing saddle shoes and plaid headbands while everyone else clunked around with wooden-heeled sandals strapped onto their feet and peacock feathers and leather held in their hair with roach clips?

And those sweaters Mother used to knit. She meant well. She said, "My mama never made a thing for me, Larkspur. Not one thing."

The permeating feeling left over from my childhood lies there in a single word. Embarrassment. "Hi, Lucy!" the neighborhood kids would yell. "Where's Linus?"

Get over it, Lark.

But walking through the door to my childhood home brought back those things forgotten for years. At least Jeff Siebert, who lived three doors down and told me to pull down my pants when I was five and he was nine, moved away years ago. Jerk.

I remembered my mother's words over the phone the day she called to try and convince me to accompany Prisma to Flannery's college graduation. "Larkspur, you never do anything halfway. First you're in a rock-'n'-roll band, then you're a hermit. My stars."

Home again, home again, jiggity-jig.

I hesitated by the door, figuring out a suitable angle from which to explain all this to Prisma.

Faulty wiring! Faulty wiring! Not a new problem. Did I think they somehow healed on their own? Grew scabs? Regenerated their rubber housing? Had my maturity calendar stopped flipping in 1978? Would I ever learn?

I pictured the night I got pregnant with Flannery. The night before I left for college, the night I succumbed to Bradley's pleading blue eyes. Sleep with me. Sleep with me. Actually he said, "Let's seal the deal, Lark." What a tip-off! And I placed my shaking hand in his, wanting to feel him closer than ever before, wanting him to have the sweetest of memories to cling to after we parted. Maybe I wanted to trap him.

But I'd be lying if I said it was wonderful. It hurt. It felt gangly and clumsy and all wrong. We improved during Thanksgiving and Christmas breaks, but it wasn't until years later that I realized I'd danced upon sacred ground in mud-caked shoes. That I defamed myself in the process. After Jesus' love rained down upon me, I realized the problems between Bradley and me festered like splinters beneath the skin, but as usual, I hoped they'd just work out on their own.

So upon finding Mother asleep and the morning breeze sifting in through the kitchen windows and with Prisma pulling me into her robust arms and saying, "Aren't you glad your postcard collection got too big for your little place?" I realized that maybe I should learn from Flannery and Prisma and grab a handful of optimism.

"I'll have to go up and get it. I got some new ones the other day."

"I already got it down from the attic. It's in your room waiting for you."

That absolutely did me in. "Oh, Prisma!"

"I know, baby, I know."

"It's all gone."

"I know that, too."

Prisma might have said something like, "You still got Flannery and all the things that matter." But she didn't because Prisma is Prisma. Loss is loss. And your own loss is your own loss, and it hurts.

"You're shaking like a leaf. Come sit down at the table, baby. I do believe the sky is just beginning to lighten. You should have seen Castor and Pollux last night. Just a sight they were!"

She led me to the old square table that lay hidden beneath a yellow-and-white checked cloth that matched the orange juice. A plate of hot sticky buns without raisins awaited us, as well as a bowl of scrambled eggs in cream, a plate of bacon, and a dish of sliced bananas, sugared and swimming in milk. When Prisma released me after yet another hug, she turned around and whipped a cup of tea off the counter and handed it to me. The china cup matched the plates at the table. I noticed only two place settings rested there.

My insides began settling, finally, after hours of this feeling, and this room, with nary a change since my childhood, calmed me. I prayed to Jesus. *Lord, please calm me down. I need to rest in You, and I just can't do it on my own right now.*

Prisma placed the kettle back on the stove. "I'll bet you'll want another cup."

"Always room for tea."

Ah. The sip of homey liquid inched its way into my torn spirit. Surely only momentarily soothing, but welcomed nonetheless.

I settled my cup onto the saucer. "Come on, Prisma, set up a place for yourself. Mother's snoring, and you know that means she won't be awake for at least another hour."

Prisma wrinkled her nose, her fawn eyes practically disappearing in the marshmallow folds of her face. "I'm just going to have another cup of coffee, Lark. To be honest, I've already eaten a bunch of that stuff as I went along. I couldn't eat another bite if someone put a gun to my head."

"There's always room for coffee, too."

"You got that right, girl." Prisma pulled me into her big arms again, her motherly bosoms soft and comforting against my upper chest. I reached around and settled my arms across her back, laid the entire weight of my head against her, and just stood. Oh, I just stood, so loved and supported by all that warm flesh she owns, and she kissed my hair and said, "You're all right, baby. You are definitely all right." And I stood some more and wondered why I didn't come home to her more, why I hadn't spent more time with Prisma, and she kissed me again, this time on my forehead as she swiped a hand over my head and pulled my face back to look into her glowing eyes, and she said, "I said, you're gonna be all right."

And Prisma always tells the truth.

"Here she is!" Prisma smiled as I straightened up to my towering, gargantuan four feet ten inches and turned to watch as willowy Flannery of the sweet, Celtic face and copious ponytails walked in. I sat down, and she joined me, her fair features and hands scrubbed free of the black streaks that had striped them earlier.

She sniffed the underarms of her T-shirt. "Man, I need a shower! I'm going to make your kitchen chairs filthy, Miss Prisma."

"They needed a fresh coat of red lacquer anyway. I'll get Asil to start on that this afternoon after he finishes pruning the azaleas."

I sipped my tea. "Prisma, could you ask the blessing? I'm too tired."

"Too many questions too, I'll bet," Prisma said.

I nodded.

"Bless the food, Jesus! And restore Lark's life tenfold, amen."

Tenfold? Lord, no! Don't listen to her. Just like before is all I can handle.

I spooned some eggs and cream in my mouth, experiencing for the thousandth time Prisma's heavenly gift of helping people accept their troubles, of easing their load. I suspect she believes in a direct correlation between blood flow in your arteries and the troubles of life.

Comfort. Prisma in a word.

Prisma poured herself some more coffee. "I'll wash your clothes while you sleep, baby."

"Are you sure? You don't have to treat me like a regular around here, Prisma. Hopefully I won't be around for long anyway."

She set her cup onto her saucer. "You know, there could be worse things than coming home."

"I can't think of what. I'm forty-one years old, Prisma. I'm tired. I'm worried."

"Then you don't need to be worried about cooking your meals. Not with all the playing you do and the prayer line. And think about how nice it's going to be to eat a good, hot supper before you get to the evening callers."

"I need to get that phone line installed here. Temporarily at least." Right?

"I'll call today. You can count on me to get that up and running by Monday!"

Did desperation heighten her voice? "Prisma, you're the last person that needs to be afraid of atrophy."

She pointed two fingers at me, raising her brows above the rim of her cup as she sipped. "Your mama doesn't eat much, Lark, and since the doctor went and put her on that dictatorial 'heart smart' plan, old Prisma has been a ship without a shore!"

Prisma adrift? Never! "It sounds like you're missing Daddy. Cocktails after work, little meatballs in sweet and sour sauce, pickled onions, and a bowl of cashews."

"Every day, 6:30 spot-on he'd walk in that door. And he left his cares behind when he ate my food!"

Daddy was a good man, born and raised in Highlandtown, a neighborhood with blue-collared necks of Continental European descent. Polish, German, Irish. How someone named Summerville settled down there on Fait Avenue still mystifies me.

But Daddy always loved beautiful things, which explains why he swept my mother right off her feet, off the horse farm, and straight to Baltimore and his newly constructed house on Greenway. Charles Summerville, fifteen years older and wearing a suit with more distinction and grace than anyone had a right to, told a bushel basket of lies to convince her to even look his way. He claimed he hailed from an old family with old money. Indeed, "the Baltimore Summervilles" earned a fair share of renown in the railway boom, and Leslie just assumed. But my daddy built Summerville Machine Parts up with a thousand-dollar loan from Maryland National Bank and a million-dollar brain. The only reason she stuck with him after the golden band hugged her finger was the fact that he gave her carte blanche in decorating the mansion. And Paris twice a year to buy clothes to boot! Well, what self-respecting female could resist?

Daddy told Prisma once that marrying a Strawbridge topped the list of the best investments he'd ever made. A classy girl from a classy family. Oh, and so slim and pretty. And he didn't mind the nutty accent either. "I'm surprised she stuck around with this old fool!" he used to say.

One lesson I glean from this story is that even a man as good as my father told one doozie of a lie. Like father like daughter, I guess.

I laid a hand on Flannery's bony arm. "We'd better get to bed."

"Are you kidding? I just got my second wind, Mom. I'm going to shower and get ready for my interview."

Prisma touched my shoulder blade. "Come on, baby. I've got everything ready."

She accompanied me up to my bedroom.

Oh, there it all lay before me. My window seat. My bed. True, Mother redecorated a bit, employing shades of mint and peach and pink and yellow, but everything was arranged just the same, and my bookshelf, now painted white, still cuddled my childhood books ranging from Little Golden Books' *The Three Bears* in their Russian outfits to my first couple of Barbara Cartlands. What a dame! On top of the dresser rested a stack of four albums of the circus postcard collection I've been assembling ever since I found some in an antique shop in London on a trip Daddy planned for my thirteenth birthday. It would save though. At that point I just wanted to crawl between the sheets.

"This stuff's been waitin' for you." Prisma fluffed the beautiful arrangement of peonies and larkspur Asil had placed on the dresser. That man. "You just sit, Lark. I'll go get one of your mother's old night-shirts for you to wear. I meant to do that earlier."

Probably a Puritan, scratchy gown. Fine by me.

I perched on the window seat. My window overlooks the walled garden on the east end of the house. Though the sun had not yet risen, I pictured the entire back of the lot. Walled by stone with gateways on either side of the house, the gardens softened the exterior of this place.

"We're a tough lot, us Summervilles," Daddy always said. But a ten-derness, like Asil's gardens, surrounds us, I think. The house suits us.

Keep talking, Lark. Maybe you'll convince yourself everything is going to be okay. Maybe you'll convince yourself that you're a Sum-merville at heart, enough to start acting like one again.

Through a freshly baking dawn, I could see Mother's fruit trees dis-played a few ornery petals, but the peonies cast their delight in an aro-matic net of pinks and lavenders. Usually Mother arranges glorious bouquets of them all over the house by now. Why not this year? Her complexion looked positively Madame Tussaud as she slept there on the couch. And this "heart smart" thing Prisma talked about? Why did Mother need "heart smart" anythings?

I turned away and pulled down the comforter, vibing Prisma to come back soon. All I really wanted to do was cry. This wasn't home, and sometimes I don't feel like it ever was.

Oh, Lord. Oh, Lord.

Oh, Jesus.

All sorts of Bible promises flared up, assuring me this would all end up for my good, but right then I just couldn't see how. Sometimes those promises burn when first applied like any effective wound cleaner. Heavenly peroxide. Divine Bactine.

Personally, I think God could have used a little Neosporin on me this time and saved me from this pain I felt. God bless ointments.

Prisma paddled in with a pair of silk pajamas in cherry red.

My word, Mother! Red silk p.j.'s?

She placed them in my hands. "Now you slip these on while I go heat up a cup of milk for you."

"With a little cinnamon on top?"

"Just a tad."

We smiled into each other's eyes, and I watched her until the door shut behind her. Why can't I be like you, Prisma?

I slid into Mother's pajamas, the silken fabric cooling me to a quivering mass, the arms flowing down past my fingertips, the legs four inches too long. And I flapped my arms, feeling foolish and small.

Flannery

GRANDY AND I ARE IN NEW YORK to shop for new clothes at Saks 5th Avenue. Not a moment too soon either, the fire being a week behind us now. We traveled by train yesterday and are staying at the Plaza. She sleeps so late these days so I'm doing something that would horrify her if she found out. Right now I am sneaking down to the NBC studios at Rockefeller Plaza to get my face on the *Today* show.

Sometimes I just crack myself up!

These two ladies park themselves directly in back of the railing, clutching a poster that says, "Mom's on Vacation in the Big Apple." The names of their kids are written all around on the cardboard.

I smile at them. They smile at me, and we talk about the street vendor coffee. I probably don't have to tell you, but bad coffee brings people together just as efficiently as good coffee.

The crew in the studios wave to us from behind the plate glass, giving thumbs-up to my new lady friends.

I feel sorry for men sometimes. They don't make friends nearly as quickly as we women do.

Grandy is getting her hair done at her favorite salon, and I'm bored. "How 'bout if I meet you at Saks just before lunch, Grandy?" I say.

"That's fine, Sweet Pea. I'll meet you by hats at one o'clock. I've been needing a new hat for church."

"Okay then." And I kiss her cheek, which feels like a deflated velvet balloon. The dryer warms my ear and neck.

Oh, wow. There are my *Today* show ladies. I see them in Saks buying barrettes.

They greet me enthusiastically, and I ask them how the vacation is going, telling them, "I'd like some specifics."

"Great! We had dinner last night in Little Italy, lunch at an Irish pub, and we're going down to Chinatown tonight." The lady who speaks is a fake blonde, and she's wearing these crazy, skewed glasses held together with glue. But she seems so happy, like, really different from my mother. She looks like one of those bird-looking ladies. A beaky nose and these piercing blue eyes. If she was a color, she'd definitely be Robin's Egg Blue even though she has on nothing but black. "It's not a good vacation if the food's no good."

The dark-headed lady laughs really loud, and she is very pretty and natural, more like a girl cat. I peg her as Golden Mustard with overtones of Olive. "We measure all our good times by the food we've eaten."

"If we don't have to cook it, we love to eat it!" the other lady says.

And then they ask all sorts of questions about me, oohing about my art hopes and saying how my hair is great and don't they wish they still had the glossy hair and pert breasts of youth?

Um. Okay then.

"We've nursed seven babies between us," says the dark-haired lady.

To be honest, the thought of breast-feeding gags me out, but I don't want to besmirch that which makes them so obviously proud.

We are eating dinner at the Rainbow Room looking out over the monoliths of the city. I ask Grandy if she nursed my mother.

"Oh yes. It's much better for the babies."

"Wow, Grandy. Did Mom nurse me?"

"Yes. You were a good little nurser."

It is nothing I've ever thought to ask before, but I'm sort of glad I'm finding this out. I don't think mothers should be far from their babies while they're still babies. But I know that's not a progressive way to think; I just know from experience. And most of my friends can hardly remember how long ago they had been given a key to the house either.

But a lot of their moms have a choice. Lark Summerville bowed and swayed under the tragedy of my dad's death. But she never buckled. Not until I had gone off. There were times I bet she thought her knees would bend too far and she'd fall over and take me with her. I look at her now and am amazed she was able to keep from going into the deep end for so long. I mean, she tries. And she makes herself do the basic-necessity things outside the house.

Mom wanted to be a concert organist when she went off to college, before she married Daddy and then got pregnant with me right away. I guess I ruined it for her, but she's never said that. She says at least once a month, "You're the best thing that ever happened to me." And I believe her.

I hate to see what's been happening to her since I went away to college. Don't get me wrong. She's always been a reclusive sort, but she used to have a real job too, before she started receding into herself even further. Mom had been a manicurist since I was four because it gave her time for me even if we had to scrape along.

Then the organist job came along too, and I'd go with her and feel so proud, the notes running over, under, and through her as she glistened under the intensity of the song. Even now she is transformed from a childlike woman to a musical entity all her own. You almost forget she's there, her sound is so all-consuming. I'm so proud of her.

I wish I could convince her of it. And in my deepest, craziest dreams I imagine someone from Carnegie Hall coming in, hearing her play, running up to her after the service and saying, "You must audition. I've never heard anyone play like you!"

Like Carnegie Hall sends people around even saying anything, let alone something like that!

But I hope that happens or something like it. I really do. Mom deserves that. She deserves something, that's for sure, especially since the fire last week. But if widespread musical success came her way, I'm scared she either won't recognize it or will go running off in a fright. After "San Francisco," as we call the brief years with my father, I think she believes she cashed in all of life's chances.

And then when she totaled the car, I think she took it as a direct sign from God or something that she needed to stay put in the neighborhood as much as possible. That's when she quit her job at the nail salon too.

But who knows with Mom?

Sometimes I think I've got her sort of figured out, and then I realize my mother is one of those mysterious people no one can ever really know.

I don't remember much about my father except a vague memory or two of him racing his motorcycle down the parking lot of our apartment complex in California, looking like a greaser. Really, really blond hair tangling like silken strips in the wind. Nobody wants to talk about him now and his parents, my other grandparents, never made an effort to keep in contact after he died, so I just say "poop on them." And anyway, they moved to Pittsburgh years ago.

Mom's never even taken me to his grave.

"Why bother with that, Flannery? Why go all the way out west to see a square of land that might be anywhere?"

She doesn't say that with bitterness but with sadness and regret, and because of that, I forgive her for not realizing how important that is to me.

See, forgiveness is a big deal with me. I mean, years ago, when I was in kindergarten, I had this nice teacher named Mrs. Danaher. She taught me all about God forgiving us of our sins and how that is all really basic if you have any sort of faith. And all these years later, I've found her to be exactly right about it all. Someday, though, I'll sit next to where my father lies and tell him all sorts of things.

Over dessert I fill Grandy in on the news Prisma gave me when I called home earlier today.

"Well, I got that job at Starbucks over in Towson."

"Did you? That's a coffee shop, isn't it?"

"Sort of. They call them coffee bars now."

"Oh my. Terrible when a bar becomes more admirable than a shop."

I laugh. "Grandy, only you would have thought of it like that."

"Why, thank you, dear."

Leslie

PRISMA FINALLY STOPPED PESTERING ME regarding my drives out to the wooded hills of Dulaney Valley to ride every day this week. "What about your heart, Mrs. Summerville?"

My stars. I love riding, and I refuse to lay aside the reins. Virginia horse-country girls refuse to give it all up at the first ache or pain. My father, John Clarence Strawbridge, rode as usual the morning he died of a massive stroke at age eighty-seven. Larger than life, that man! Not that I knew him all that well, really, the way he spent most of his time on the thoroughbred circuit, but my genetics render a bit of hope for this seventy-one-year-old body.

Not that I'd admit that out loud!

You know those ghastly, silly women who clam up when the conversation rolls around to age? Count me among them.

"Leslie Lee, for heaven's sake," I can hear Mama say, "when the subject of age rolls around, excuse yourself from the room, or do your best to change the subject!"

And so I sit there like some foolish Mona Lisa, hoping to be taken for mysterious, but realistic enough to know the main thought in the back of the other people's minds. "Who does she think she's kidding?"

A beautiful man named Jacob Marley, as in *A Christmas Carol*, works at the stables. A bit younger than me—actually, quite a bit younger than me, truth to tell—this forty-nine-year-old doesn't look a day over forty.

"Let me help you up, Leslie." His voice, raspy from all the Lucky Strikes he's smoked over the years, abrades my memory. Frankly, it surprises me they still make that brand. Seems utterly World War II if you ask me. And why ever did they not return to the green pack? The white pack projects an utterly flaccid appearance to me. Namby-pamby, in Charles's terms.

I've been climbing onto horses since I was big enough to walk, but when Jacob cupped his hand, my boot found it gladly. Jacob's large, strong hand provided surprisingly solid footing, and up I went! I must say, the little thrill that tripped along my spine reminded of the time a furiously courting Charles patted my hindquarters as we climbed into the seats of the Ferris wheel at the Virginia State Fair. Beneath Charles's businesslike exterior churned nothing but Marshmallow Fluff and peanut butter.

Now Mama would surely wonder about my attraction to men beneath my class. Not that Jacob Marley presents anything more than a pretty face, truth to tell. I played quite the game of charades, a year-long game of charades, to keep up Charles's lie, over on the *Mayflower* and such. For if I had made Libby Lee Strawbridge aware of the truth back then, well, her grave would have welcomed her gracious bones long before the lung cancer escorted her there two decades ago. She puffed to the end, my mama, refusing treatment, lying at home in her blasted boudoir with her two best friends Misters Daniel and Smirnoff. Prisma related just yesterday that Larkspur ate half a gallon of lime sherbet at one sitting. At eleven o'clock on a Saturday morning! And she watched that ghastly *Baywatch* all the while. Living up to her fullest potential? Surely not.

Larkspur assumed that role years ago though, not long after Newly arrived.

Oh, the parent-teacher conferences I endured, the comments on the bottom of report cards.

"Lark seems bored."

"Lark could do so much better if she applied herself."

"Lark is a bit of a loner but participates quite well during playtime."

"Cheerful but quiet, Lark is very well behaved. Could work harder during class time."

She should have achieved every inch of Newly's success. More so, actually, without the albino aspect working against her. I remember the day Charles and I waved good-bye when she left for Brown. Unable to stomach the thought of her leaving home by plane, Jimmy Percy drove

her all the way to Rhode Island. Prisma found the perfect mate in
Jimmy, I tell you. I probably should have gone too, but Larkspur's eager-
ness to be out of the house, up at the dorm, and leaving it all behind,
had her fairly shaking with excitement. I really thought she'd appreciate
our extending her some independence. Charles didn't think it was right.
He wanted to get in the Bentley with them and make a fine day of it.
"Come on, Les," I can still remember him saying. "We'll have us a grand
day out."

Grand. Grand. Charles loved that word.

Larkspur sent me a lot of letters from Brown, actually. Which surprised me. She told me all about her classes and her grades and the boys
who asked her out. Not one word about Bradley del Champ, whom she
had been dating for over a year. So much promise there—studies in
music and singing, the student concerts and women's field hockey. Not
to mention what she used to look like in those days all fixed up with her
hair so long and thick. Pretty, feminine clothes. But she had to go and
fool around with that Bradley del Champ. All it takes is one.

Tomorrow is going to be busy. The fashion show for cystic fibrosis at
the Hillendale Country Club begins at eleven. And I must remember to
check the silent auction for stocking stuffers for Sweet Pea and Larkspur.
Yes, I'm early in thinking about Christmas, but that's just the way I am.
When somebody cooks and cleans for you, you must fill your life with
something. Riding next, then my appointment with Dr. Medina, my
cardiologist. I suppose he deserves to know about that little blackout
incident a week ago. But then he'll insist on the ridiculous catheterization procedure that Prisma calls a Roto-Rooter, giving me no comfort
whatsoever. And then dinner at home with all of us girls. I mustn't forget to tell Prisma to buy some more lime sherbet for Larkspur and call
the health insurance company to see if payment has been made for next
year. And for heaven's sake, if I fail to get some yarn and start knitting
again, I deserve whatever's coming to me! Too many years have passed
since my hands busied themselves like that. I wonder if Larkspur remembers those sweaters I used to make for her? It took me forever to learn
that cable knit stitch, but she always admired cable knit as a little girl.

Does she still prefer cable knit?

For heaven's sake, I have no idea!

Flannery

I HAVE TO SAY I'M SORT OF A HIT AT STARBUCKS. I've already developed myself a cool little following of high-school boys who trample all over the hems of their pants. The manager feels relieved to have someone back there who actually knows how to smile. Sometimes workers in coffee bars can be so uppity. Like, if you're so cool, then why are you fixing beverages for $6.50 an hour? Nobody really chooses that for a life, do they? I do have to say that for the most part, my coworkers are pretty cool.

So June is almost over now, and two months remain until I have to start my master's in Fine Arts at the Institute. My paintings arrived a few days after the fire. I still like them, which is a relief. Sometimes when you're away from your work for a while, you come back to it and go, "Whoa! Yuck!" And other times you say, "Wow. That's pretty cool. Even cooler than I remembered. I can't believe I actually did that."

My high-school stuff all fit into the yuck category once I got over myself my junior year of college. Burned to a crisp, which is GREAT! Good riddance to bad rubbish, as Grandy would say. It's sort of sad to think about our little house all gone now.

All these thoughts and more like them buzz around my head as Prisma and I drive back in the Duster to that corner on Bayonne tonight.

I reach for her hand. "It just looks so wrong, sort of like a black moon crater there, like a puckered kiss mark made by a vampire or something."

Prisma nods and looks at the moon. "Desolation."

"I know."

"You doing okay with all of this, Baby Girl?"

We still hold hands.

"Sort of. I mean, I haven't really lived at home for four years."

"But all your stuff."

"All the important stuff I shipped."

Prisma shakes her head. "It's just sad, isn't it? That house sure wasn't much, but it did have a spindled front porch. And I do love a spindled front porch. You got your camera, baby?"

"Just a disposable one. That is one thing actually I regret losing in the fire, my camera."

So I take a picture of it for future artistic reference.

"These things are mile markers in our lives, Baby Girl. It's good to have a record of a happening that changed things for good."

"You think that's what's happening?"

"It sure wasn't a garden variety electrical fire, I can tell you that. Jesus is afoot."

I sure hope she's right. And if Jesus is getting Mom's attention, dear Lord, I pray He's giving her ears to hear as well, because my mom is sure stuck in her own little insulated world.

"Let's go now, baby. This is making me too sad."

I put my arms around Miss Prisma. "I'm with you."

So we drive back to Greenway and see Asil's light on in the little turret in the apartment over the garage, and Prisma had left her desk lamp on in her room behind the kitchen, and it just seems inviting and right. It feels like coming home.

L a r k

REMEMBER AUDREY HEPBURN in *Sabrina*? I tried to achieve that look as a youngster—pretty and thin—and if I failed to get it then, well, a middle-aged Audrey Hepburn seems unattainable. The small, slight thing weighs the scale in my favor, that waifish wispiness. However, what rendered Audrey ethereal just proclaims a woman like me insignificant and undernourished.

Mother thinks I'm trying to make myself as unattractive as possible because I wear so much polyester. Of course, if I found myself in a sudden sky's-the-limit mode, now that youth's blush has faded, I'd be a butterfly woman in flowing rainbow silks, soft and fluttery. An artistic beauty with a gleaming black bob, Egyptian eyes, and exotic slippers on my feet. That might bring back the roses. But, too short for that, I'd look downright silly in such a getup, seated at my bench at St. Dominic's. Like a character in some way-off-Broadway production. Perhaps I'd even be mistaken for a small transvestite. If only Mother had imparted her feminine ways.

Unfortunately, due to my current financial ineptness, Mother's hand-me-downs, which are much too long to begin with, constitute my narrow wardrobe.

As it stands, even in Mother's conservative, tasteful clothes, I'll be laughed right out the door at the 3 B's. Since the fire, I travel to St. Dominic's just for mass, bless Prisma, who goes Saturday nights and all three masses on Sunday so I can pull up in her Duster and not that Bentley.

But today she said she wouldn't mind running to Frank's Nursery and Craft up the road in Parkville because Mother declared some homemade summer wreaths for the outside doors of Stoneleigh House a needful thing. I just needed to haunt the old neighborhood, play in the silence of the church, practice, and feel. Just feel. I feel sorry for people who don't have music to express their emotions.

Prisma dropped me off by the chain-link fence surrounding St. Dominic's schoolyard. "I'll be back in three hours. That long enough?"

I nodded.

"Okay. I'm going to Harold's to get fresh produce, and I'm also going to stop and get some scrapbook pages for your mother. You need anything at the craft store?"

"Not unless you see something you think I should take up as a hobby, Prisma."

And I shut the car door. She zoomed off. Now, why did I offer such an open, cavalier invitation? I imagined Prisma sailing down the craft store aisle, an intrepid explorer in search of the perfect pastime for a troubled soul.

I could only pray it had nothing to do with plastic needlepoint sheets. That particular craft would, indeed, send me over the edge.

Playing the organ for a long spell always makes me thirsty, so I decided to pop down the block into the 3 B's for a carry-out cup of tea.

I love the 3 B's. No ants here. Not anymore.

Deke Babachakos waved from the grill. "Hi, sweetheart!" He reminds me of a used-car salesman from the sixties with his slicked-back, receding hair, his loud shirts, and his too-tight pants. Born and bred in Miami, Florida, once a cook to the mob in a club restaurant with gold lamé drapery behind the stage, Deke lit up a cigarette despite the Maryland nonsmoking laws. "Got a guy on the inside that tells me when the Health Department is comin' over," Deke explained.

Yeah right, Deke.

Last week he asked, "How you doin' since the fire, Lark?"

I said fine.

Deke never brings up the same thing twice if it's your thing. So he started right into the obvious topic at hand, something he and Babe thought worthy of prior discussion. Bared by his smile, his gold tooth gleamed in his hound's-tooth face, a beacon of dental self-expression.

The custom trim on his '75 Lincoln Continental glimmers gold, as well. "What're you gonna do with your lot there in Hamilton, sweetheart? Gonna sell it?"

Babe Babachakos, Deke's wife, the chain-smoking waitress, jumps right on in. "Of course she isn't. Right, Lark? I can think of a thousand reasons you'd be crazy to start over anywhere else."

Babe fluffed up the part of her fluorescent red Mrs. Frankenstein hair that crackles out of the top of her waitress cap. Actually the feline older face, childlike and kind, supporting all that hair gentles the monstrous coiffure. And the way Babe lines her eyes like Endora on *Bewitched* lends her a nostalgic air. "I'd bet money you'll rebuild a house right there. The lot's already paid for. You'll have insurance money, right? So it will just be a matter of finding the right house for the lot. And since the land is already free and clear, you can go extra nice with the kitchen. There are a billion reasons."

"Just don't go and name them all, Babe, okay?" Deke scratched the little bowling ball belly, the only body-extra the man possesses, that slowly accumulates beneath his full apron. From what Babe says, he never did sport a derriere, even when they met at fifteen down at an Orioles game in the hot dog line.

Babe shook her head, pointed up, then crossed herself. "By the way, I lit a candle for you at church this morning."

"Thank you, Babe."

"Glad to do it."

Deke grabbed a pot of hot water from the Bunn. "Your usual tea, hon?"

"Yeah, thanks. I'm going to go practice at church."

He grabbed a plastic foam cup. "So, what're you gonna do about Hamilton, Lark? Stayin' or goin'?"

"Man, Deke! How do I know? The truth is, I haven't thought much about it yet. Look at me! I'm sitting here in a periwinkle boiled-wool skirt of Mother's. Do you really think I care right now about the house?"

That sounded good, right? I mean, people would think me a nut case if they realized how much I really did care.

"Okay, okay." He stubbed out his smoke in the ashtray hidden behind this crazy statue of a Hawaiian hula girl. "Now see, I have an idea. You can just throw out everything Babe here has said—"

"Deke!"

"Well, sure, hon. You know Lark's been fond of Harford County for a while now. Right?" He hoisted his brows in my direction, full with the winds of expectation. "Right?"

I shrugged. They always placed me in the middle. Without any kids, they distribute all those latent parental urges right on my shoulders. As if I'm capable of bearing something like that. Ha! Little do they really know me.

"Come on. It's true," he said. "You were telling me in May that you love Bel Air."

"Yeah, I guess. I'd like a bungalow right in the town. Like my house now."

"But you could build that on your lot in Hamilton!" Babe said with triumph. "Or buy another bungalow right here. There somethin' wrong with us that you need to go traipsing all the way to godforsaken Harford County?"

Deke laughed.

"Who the heck would build a new house in Hamilton?"

I wasn't about to tell them I had let the homeowner's insurance lapse. Any of their plans seemed silly and reminded me of my own foolishness. I vowed to utter not one word. He shook his head and jerked a thumb at his wife. "You gotta love Babe."

What a woman. She speaks her heart.

"It would be much simpler my way," Babe said. "You know you and that quiet life you lead."

"What's wrong with that?"

Deke reached behind him, nabbing two packets of sugar.

"I'll take sweetener," I said.

"Suit yourself."

Babe sat beside me and lit up a cigarette.

Deke snapped the lid on my tea and slid it over. "Maybe you should enter a nunnery. You'd never have to set foot on the street again."

The nun thing. Again?

Babe turned on her stool, grinding out a laugh that all of Maryland could hear, then hacked her post-laugh smoker's cough. "There's the Carmelite's place right out there on Seminary Avenue."

Deke said, "Would make things easier in the long run and get you out of Guilford all the sooner."

"Oh, come on, you guys. Give me a break."

"You got it." Deke pretended to karate-chop my arm.

Off to church now. Off to absorb the almost holy silence of a quiet, de-peopled sanctuary. Off to absorb the caressing notes of the sacred tunes that lift me beyond my unholy self.

Oh, Jesus, I prayed that night after a nice meat loaf supper at home, Obviously my previous path has been tried, found wanting, and cast into the flames. I'm trying to be thankful in all things here—for the beautiful roof over my head, Prisma's good food, the delightfulness of Flannery—but all I can do is yearn for my own little place again.

And yet, heaven is my ultimate home. Is my longing really for that and not a place of my own?

While I had God's ear, I figured it wouldn't hurt to pray that the meat loaf contained only traces of hormones.

The prayer line rang.

"Prayer lady," I answered.

"Hi there. I saw your ad in *StarTrackz* magazine. You for real?"

"I sure am."

Prisma had arranged for the installation of the toll-free line in my bedroom and in the small den tucked off the family room. My father's old haunt—oak-paneled, naturally. Gloomier than Queen Victoria. Unable to face that room this evening, I lay back against my bed pillows and crossed my ankles. She also got me a headset. Which I love. And it freed up my hands for the Christmas stocking project she discovered at the craft store. Which I don't love. Whoever heard of embroidering with ribbon?

"So, like, you just pray for people?" The caller's voice jerked me back to the present.

White male, under thirty. Sounded blond, but one never knows.

"And with people, if they like."

"Right here on the phone?"

"It's what I do."

"Dude."

Make that under twenty-five.

"So what's on your mind? You want to give me a name to call you by?"

"Butch. It's my real nickname."

Yeah, right. No problem.

"So what can I pray about, Butch?"

"Well, see, I think I'm gonna make it big in music, see."

"What do you play?"

"Bass guitar."

"Great."

"Oh yeah. Keeps it all going, ya know?"

"Sure."

"Anyway, it's like this, my mom is big-time into God, you know?"

"Uh-huh."

"Right, like you are, I guess." Butch chuckled high in his throat. "I mean you wouldn't pray with people if you didn't think God was listening."

Sometimes I stay silent.

"Right, so anyway, it's my mom. She can't stop crying. Says all sorts of things about how I'm going to be sucked into that world like it's a big pit of quicksand and I'll never get out. I try to say things like, 'Whoa, Mom, you raised me better than that,' which I think is a pretty good comeback, but she takes this list she's made up of stars and musicians that have become what she calls dissipated. She says, 'All of these people were innocent babies at one time.'"

"Uh-huh?"

"So like, I know she's right about that. And well, I don't know what I'm asking you to even pray for."

"Your mother's blessing?"

"Maybe. And like, what if she's right?"

"About the quicksand?"

"Yeah. You know. Is it worth it?"

"Hey, I'm not a pastor." I sought to warm up my voice, trying to ease things up a bit. "I'm just a prayer lady. Those are questions you'll have to answer on your own."

"Then I don't even know what to ask you to pray for."

I fiddled with a length of burgundy ribbon. "Can I make a suggestion?"

"Yeah. I'm feeling kinda lost. You know."

"I do. Why don't we pray that God will give you a venue to use your talents and protect you from harm?"

I think he reached into a bag of chips or something because the crackling of cellophane tickled my eardrums. "You think?"

Maybe he unwrapped a candy.

"Sure. You want me to pray with you right now?"

"Nah. You got some kind of list going there?"

"Yep. I keep you on for a week, unless you call back with an update."

"People do that?" He crunched in my ear now. Definitely chips.

"Absolutely. I have a nice-sized list of regulars."

"Okay. Put me on your list."

"Gotcha down, Butch. Feel free to call back anytime."

"Thanks. And if I tell my mom I've got some prayer lady praying for me, she might not be so worried."

Make that under twenty. Definitely under twenty.

"Well then," I said. "I've got you on the list."

"Thanks, Prayer Lady."

"God bless."

"Yeah, uh, you too."

And he hung up.

I pulled the receiver away and stared at it. At least he wasn't some crank, obscene caller. I hate those more than anything.

PRISMA

LOVE EQUALS TIME. That's why I've never bought a store-made loaf of bread in my entire life! If you can't get down in the dough and work it until it's silky and satisfying, well, what can you do? My mother started teaching me to bake when I turned five, and I still lift my eyes up every day and tell her thank you. Honest to Pete, that's the truth. And you know me and the truth.

I don't know why I went into domestic service. Not many options existed for a woman like me back in those days. Always I told myself something extra-ordinary lay in wait beneath my exterior, like a hard kernel of corn needing only some high heat to turn it into something usable, something explosively unique and wonderful, like a Ph.D. in medical research and the cure for cancer or maybe even the lecture circuit for medieval history. But I graduated from Dunbar High, speaking fancy because my mother told me I wouldn't get anywhere if I couldn't be understood. I took some abuse from my schoolmates over that, but I don't regret it. Yes, Mama knew. But my schoolmates were bona fide African-American for the most part, and I'm a Heinz 57 human. Years ago I stopped looking back into my ancestry because the Lord knows, if I find one more race, a scream the likes of a factory whistle might rise from my lungs and, unable to work its way from my mouth fast enough, might just blow the top right off my head. That's right, clean off, like a dandelion head. Pop goes Prisma. My mama was black with a little something Irish on the side. And Daddy, a white boy with a bit of American Indian, Jewish, and all sorts of other things blended in for good measure, really confused things for me. Maybe too much, I think.

But for utter certainty, we weren't the most popular family in the neighborhood. My parents sought to fit in, Mama told me, but after a while gave up and lived their lives as best they could, providing a stable home for myself and my younger brother, Tony, who died in Korea.

If the Lord didn't whisper the name "Prisma" in Mama's ear, I'd be shocked. Because that's what I am…a human prism. I am neither Jew nor Greek, bond nor free, although I am a female, praise the Lord. At least I can claim something. And God did make us second, which means He practiced already.

O, Lord, You know I'm just teasin'. I love You, Lord.

So, years ago, without the money to go to college I only had a few options, and I figured I'd go where it was the most luxurious, the most warm. I worked at several homes in Guilford before Mr. Summerville built our house, and when these stone walls started accumulating, looking straight out of fifteenth-century England, I began living out of a suitcase.

The memory of my interview with Mr. Summerville, the way we started debating about the Orioles and the Yankees, still brings on a chuckle.

I never met a kinder man than Mr. Summerville. He sponsored my entire college education, got me into Johns Hopkins University during the days when skinny young multiracial women still "knew their place." On the day I graduated he merely sat next to my parents, in a black coat, sunglasses, and a bowler. Mr. Summerville always wore a fedora. He refused to take any of the credit so that my day of glory be seen as a feather in Charles Summerville's cap. But he wanted to witness my triumph, and his presence calmed my nerves. He treated us to Haussner's restaurant afterward. We all got stares, I don't mind saying. But we also got sauerbraten and spaetzle, and a piece of strawberry pie crowned the occasion. Thin as a noodle in those days, I ate two pieces.

Never heard a word about it in the papers either! And everything Mr. Summerville did was in the papers, unless it was his private business, and he considered anything on 724 Greenway Avenue his private business. It may not be the end of the world there on Greenway, but Mr. Summerville thought so, and I vowed to make sure it always felt like a real, honest-to-goodness home. Mrs. Summerville, sure as fog in the morning, had no training for such a task, and I don't believe she ever really forgave him for his fib, really. At least Mr. Summerville never saw it that way. Of course Leslie festered her own lie, but she never told Mr. Summerville. She never told me. Silly me just happened to open the wrong piece of mail one day!

Libby Lee Strawbridge deserved to die the way she did. Alone and dissipated. I try not to even think about the emotional havoc that woman's mother must have wreaked. It amazed me Mrs. Summerville turned out as well as she did. She sure loves those kids.

I stopped at Haussner's yesterday on my way home from church. Not that it's really on the way, truth be told, but certainly worth the extra drive! Two napoleons, three éclairs, a strawberry pie, and a box of lemon bars accompanied me home. Sharing the lemon bars would be the Christian thing, but I stuck them in the freezer in case the women of this house ever decide to go on vacation.

I know the Bible says "Do unto others," but so far, I haven't brought that lemon bar part of my sin nature under submission. Some folks have a sweet tooth. I have a sweet fang.

That Oprah girl tells people on her show that writing thankful lists at the end of each day brightens their lives. I find that a fine idea. It would be even finer if she said just whom we should be thankful to, but I guess I won't write a letter of complaint because Jesus knows what He does all over the earth. So today I give thanks to God for: fine baked goods, the fact that Mrs. Summerville still drives, the check sent out from the Days of Summer Charitable Trust today to that Romanian orphanage, and oh, Jesus, help those poor children, good knees despite my heft, and Jesus, Jesus, Jesus.

My lifelong companion.

"Lord, how much longer do I have here on Greenway?"

My, the stars burned clear this evening.

"Do you really think your work is done here, My girl?"

"Nope."

"Then why do you ask?"

"I miss my family. I miss my son."

"He's doing just fine. You raised him right. He knows Me, and he talks to Me all the time."

"They miss me."

"I know."

"Well, what about it, Lord? Will my time ever come to be with my family?"

"Just who is your family, Prisma, My girl?"

I smiled into the heavens. "I know what You're saying, Lord."

"I know you know."

"I love You, Jesus."

"I know you do. You listen with your heart, My girl. You've always been tender."

"Thank You, Lord."

"Just awhile longer."

"All right, Jesus."

"And you know that I love you, too."

"I certainly do."

See, me and Jesus straightened out that fact years and years ago.

Lark

THE AROMA OF THE DAY MY FATHER DIED permeated my life for good. Like the converted carriage house I rented after Bradley, one of the places Flannery and I haunted until I bought my little house-which-is-no-more. Horses deserted that place at least fifty years before. Despite the new plaster walls, new wooden floors, bathrooms, bedrooms, and kitchen, the day I moved into the apartment upstairs I still smelled horse. Not unpleasant, it just reminded me of the muscular beasts that worked the farm for over a century, without complaining, content to do their job, well rewarded with good oats, water from the spring, and a gallant run over the most beautiful fields in Maryland.

My dad was like that. He worked hard and good. After he made his fortune, he hired John Drexler to "run the Whole Darn Thing" as he called it at Summerville Machine Parts. And then he went around and "saw fit to do good," and I'm not talking giving to the opera either, which he did, because Mother found herself on the board for a while.

"Seeing fit to do good." That's what Prisma always called it. And I've scoured my Bible for years in search of that saying because I know it's in there since Prisma speaks in Bible terms frequently. Prisma is a God-fearing woman, but she fears Him in her own way. She believes that religion is about loving the One who made you and obeying Him because of that. I remember her telling me in my childhood, "Lark, you love Jesus because of who He is, and you don't give to God to get. You commit your life to God because He is love and His ways are best, not because you need a list of dos and don'ts to get by or want to escape hellfire and damnation. It's about redeeming the time."

Oh, Daddy. I miss you.

I wished I had listened sooner to Prisma about love and commitment and honor and optimism and all the things she tried to pass on down to me, all the things my own mother never quite managed to say.

Why did I ever leave my parents' church? Daddy, not your strict-Christian type, I'll admit, came back every Sunday with a clear spiritual insight that led eventually to the Days of Summer Charitable Trust. I remember it vividly. The sermon had been on the widow's mite, a story, I'll admit, I've come to love more with each passing year. And Daddy got out of the Bentley, slipped into his private den, and shut the door behind him. Prisma knocked an hour later, real soft like she did with Daddy, and said, "Sunday dinner, Mr. Summerville."

"Just put it in the icebox, my dear."

I sat on the couch. Eleven years old, leggy, toothy, and reading *Are You There, God? It's Me, Margaret,* and getting grossed out over the entire book the way it talked about menstrual periods, bust development, and all, I welcomed the diversion. "He's not joining us, Miss Prisma?"

"Honey, he and Jesus are in deep conversation. I'll guarantee it."

Nobody knew my father like Prisma. Not me. Not Mother. Not Newly.

I think they truly loved each other, Daddy and Prisma. In a different land, a different time, and under different circumstances…well, who knows? I could be wrong, and it isn't something I'd ever say out loud.

And nobody at Stoneleigh House loves and worships Jesus like Prisma. The day she ushered me into the kingdom, ten years ago this past April, she wept. Her tears, and not just the feeling of a cleansed heart, helped me understand what a truly joyous occasion it was.

Prisma took over Daddy's funeral arrangements. It reaped her the only real fight with Mother I ever heard. Loud and long and enough to frighten me, a woman in her early thirties. Prisma Percy stood there with her arms crossed, her golden eyes glowing inside a crucible of pain and loss, and she stood strong and firm against a formidable adversary. "Mrs. Summerville, he told us both expressly as he was lying there in that hospital bed that he wanted to be cremated! You can't go and bury him whole! I won't allow it!"

Mother barked back that Prisma had nothing to do with it, she was only hired help. But Prisma wasn't put off, even though neither of us ever heard Mother bark before.

"I was his best friend." Prisma's retort, very quiet, stunned me. And my mother raised her hand in the air, her palm flat out, and opened her mouth. Then she froze. Her face, still and expressionless, like a statue of Diana, lost all color. I dropped the teacup I was drying as I stood in the kitchen door, my black funeral clothes absorbing the quietness of fresh death. Neither my mother nor Prisma even jumped at the sound, they just stared at each other, both thinking and thinking and not speaking.

Finally Mother's flat hand turned into a pointed finger. "Fine then. But you'll watch that casket being shoved in the oven, Prisma. You'll watch it with your own eyes. I won't have him going off all by himself."

I watched Prisma nod.

"I'll be there, Mrs. Summerville."

Oh, Daddy.

He realized as he lay dying that even before he knew the Savior, God's hand guided him. He wished he'd loved Christ earlier, but he praised God for preserving him from a wasted life. Lives all around were changed because my father invested in humanity itself.

And then Jesus' love shone like a warm beam into his heart, and He ushered him home to heaven not long after. But I have to wonder if Jesus hadn't entered his life a long time before that due to the promise of faith, if sometimes we beggar down our very beliefs by making faith more complicated than God does.

After Prisma introduced me to an honest-to-goodness living Christ, I really started listening to Father Charlie's homilies. Why two years of such insightfulness washed over me like oil across cellophane, I don't know. And Father Charlie's influence still bolsters me to this day. There's another person filled with a working, beautiful faith in God. A bold faith. A walk-out-on-the-street-during-a-gang-war kind of faith.

Prisma loves Father Charlie, and even before the house burned down she'd visit St. Dominic's every once in a while. But then, Prisma always accompanied Mother to our sports games and concerts. Talk about a mismatched pair yelling and clapping there on the hard wooden bleachers!

Fact is, Prisma has always been there, for all of us. She could have gone on to a professorship somewhere, but she chose to stay on Greenway. I'll tell you this much, Prisma Percy made my father the great man he was. Without Prisma Percy there to make a home for him, he might have become just another rich, overachieving workaholic. Moreover, she kept a finger on the pulse of heartache all over the country. She had papers delivered from cities everywhere, and when checks arrived from Days of Summer to pay for an operation, open a school, buy a pair of shoes, or feed a neighborhood for Thanksgiving, it was all due to Prisma Percy's heart and her ability to do fine research.

Talk about your true working woman!

And she's not worried about how she appears either. I love that about her.

But even now she stays on, baking bread and rolls and subsisting on her small domestic salary and banking the stipend she gets from Days of Summer. Prisma has never taken kindly to change. My father proved himself a wise man by hiring Prisma. A very wise man.

I feel him beside me a lot. Or rather, I'm always aware of his legacy. And I fall so short of it. Why couldn't I have grown up to be like him?

Flannery

"UNCLE NEWLY?"

"Flannery! How are you, Buddy?"

"Great."

"Enjoying Starbucks, are we?"

"Love it. Well, it's not art, but it's not a bad way to make some money for the summer. How's your new girlfriend? Oooo-ooooh."

Silence.

"Come on, Uncle Newly, tell me everything. I saw you guys go into Barnes and Noble."

"She's lovely, Buddy."

"As lovely as me?"

He chuckles. "Nobody is as lovely as you."

"Okay, just checking. So am I going to get to meet her soon? Are you going to bring her around to Greenway?"

"And give her the fright of her very life? Not on your life, my dear. Not on your life."

What a crackup!

"So when's our next date, Uncle Newly?"

"How about this weekend?" Only he says it "this week*end.*"

"Let's go out to the shooting range."

"First pool. Now guns. Really, Buddy, what are you trying to do to me?"

"Get you to broaden your stuffy horizons."

"I'm only thirty-six, dear. How stuffy can I really be?"

"Oh, you'd be surprised."

Another chuckle.

"I'll meet you in your lobby at noon on Sunday, Uncle Newly."

"I'll see you then."

That man cracks me up! If I had to paint Uncle Newly, I'd make him Navy Blue on the edges and Puce, Magenta, and Sky Blue tie-dye in the middle.

Lark

MARSHA FORTENBAUGH WOULD TELL ANYONE she's been my best friend for eleven years now. The type of woman who calls private parts by their anatomically correct names, Marsha views life, and God, at face value. In fact, it was Marsha who invited me to St. Dominic's in the first place after we met at the mall on Flannery's eleventh birthday. Having saddle shoes fitted for her first year in private school, I was a bit put off to begin with. I had always resisted Daddy's offer to pay her way at Roland Park Country Day School, a place I could never in a millennium of millions of years have afforded on my own, but I finally agreed to St. Dominic's Parochial. She was learning some pretty unsavory things with bananas at public school, and I wasn't about to let my pride send Flannery down the path of sexual experimentation, not to mention relativism.

I may be a hermit type, but that doesn't render me unintelligent. I know what relativism really means. And I know what it really does.

It was that kind of stuff that landed me in trouble in the first place.

Any woman who tells you the sexual revolution freed women to call the shots is an idiot. It just gave men the opportunity to use us with even less responsibility than before.

I remember explaining it all to Marsha, right in the middle of Stride Rite. Flannery started to get involved with eyelinered fillies on the cusp of losing their virginity before they even started their periods. I felt radical and reactionary, one step away from asking Jerry Falwell out on a date, and I stumbled over my words and apologized, and I finished up with, "I don't know why I'm telling you all this. Maybe I'm wrong about it all. Maybe I shouldn't try and shelter my daughter like this. I mean, you can't choose their friends, can you?"

Marsha picked at the coral-colored polish on her nails, real quiet, and then looked up with a feverish stare. "The heck you can't!" Only she didn't say "heck."

She freed me.

When she invited me to church while I paid up, it surprised me, with the mild profanity and all. But sometimes situations exist where no words are strong enough to describe the pain. Some may call her verbiage tasteless, but Marsha's only daughter died of AIDS one year before we met, and she wishes now she had known the value of extreme motherhood when her motherhood remained. She's an instrument of grace because she receives so much of it from God.

Leslie

"Newly?"

"Yes, Mother?"

"How are you?"

"Very well, thank you."

My goodness. And I thought I was formal.

Silence.

Perhaps I hope too much to think he may actually ask how I am doing in return.

"Anyway, Son, I was wondering if you might come up for dinner on Sunday after church? Flannery told me you had a wonderful time playing pool together."

"Yes, we did. She beat me soundly."

"Did you let her?"

"What do you think?"

I honestly didn't know what to think. I barely know Newly anymore. He changed so drastically at school. "You let her win."

"You don't know me well, do you, Mother?"

Oh dear. Wrong again.

"Well, that wasn't why I called. So can you come for Sunday dinner or not? I'll have Prisma roast a fresh ham. You love fresh ham, don't you?"

"I used to."

"But not anymore."

"No. I gave up pork five years ago."

I shook my head and rolled my eyes like a grade-schooler. At least my record as the mother most likely to utter the wrong thing stood like the Rock of Gibraltar.

"Well, we'll have whatever you like then."

"I can't make it anyway, Mother, so don't worry."

"Oh."

"I have a date."

Glory be! "You do?"

"Don't get too excited, dear. You'll pop a vein."

"Who is she?"

"Nobody that you'd know. She's not from our stratosphere."

"Oh, Newly."

My children categorize me neatly as a social snob. Perhaps they know better. But it's what I know. I'm not exactly the kind of woman that branches out. I'm not at all like my children.

"Better run, Mother. Thanks for the call."

"Lark would be glad to see you."

He chuckled. "Oh, that's a good one. Talk soon, dear."

Click.

Click. Click. Click.

Click.

In the past eighteen years, I've never once been the first one to hang up.

Lark

MARSHA—BENEDICT ARNOLD—FORTENBAUGH promised to take me right home after practice. Instead she parked her real-estate mobile in front of Mick O'Shea's Irish Pub.

"What's this about, Marsha?" I held for dear life on to the door handle of her old white Riviera.

She tightened her ponytail. "You need to go someplace else to eat besides the 3 B's. I mean, come on, Lark. How long has it been since you've eaten at a restaurant besides the 3 B's?"

"Nobody's business."

"See?"

"Oh, Marsha. Come on." Stop sounding like a little kid, Lark! I pictured myself begging my mother to stop talking to an acquaintance at the grocery store so I could get home and go to the bathroom. I even jiggled my leg. "Let's just go back to Greenway. I'll ask Prisma if she'd fix us something Irish if you have a hankering for that sort of thing."

"Nope. We're going in." She began rummaging through a straw purse the size of Slovenia.

Just walk right on up Charles Street, Lark. Just go right on home.

But some pretty rough parts lay between there and here. "I can't afford it. You know I don't make a lot of money, and now there's clothes to buy, and I'll need to replace my furniture when I move out of Greenway."

Hand now frozen inside the purse, she turned, displaying trooper-on-the-doorstep eyes. "You let the homeowner's insurance lapse, didn't you?"

I nodded, willing dry all tears congregating behind my eyes. Stupid. Stupid.

A sigh blew from between her lips. "Oh, girly. What are you going to do?"

"Not think about it?"

"Good grief, Lark! When are you going to learn? Problems like this don't just go away."

"Sometimes they do."

"No, Lark. They don't. We all make decisions."

I hate that saying.

She had me right then. That was the thing. Incapable of getting out of the car on my own, I possessed no ability to start walking north. Marsha Fortenbaugh made me her prisoner. Marsha and the ants who returned at the first sign of weakness.

Think, Lark. Think.

Do as she asks and stop fussing, or she'll detain you that much longer. And you need to get back to the prayer line. "Let's go in."

"See? I knew you'd see sense."

There were a lot of things I wanted to say right back, but I clamped my mouth shut. We all make decisions, right?

Couples milled around this area of Charles Street where a world of restaurants sat behind the sidewalk. You name it; Charles Street claims it. Afghan, Thai, French-Japanese, Italian, Irish. Youngish couples waited in line at the Thai place, and an older couple wielded chopsticks behind the front window at Shogun. The way the sun shone up the street on the marble tower that supported a raging statue of George Washington and the way the flowers bobbed about in the wind created one of the loneliest moments of my life. Even the smells shut me out.

I know we're supposed to be complete as we are, little human beings encapsulated within our very own coping mechanisms. I've even tried to become that. But if that's true, why do I feel lonely at suppertime, and why do I cry for myself every time a bride and groom say their vows at a St. Dominic's wedding?

Honestly, for the first time in years I wanted to get good, old-fashioned toasted, like Brad and I used to do at this very same pub years ago. I ordered a pint of Guinness, just like the old days, and a flood of memory enveloped me. Brad's Dresden eyes. His saucy smile. His hand on mine. The menu frayed behind a rising tide of tears. Consumed by loneliness, disillusionment, and disappointment, Lark Summerville dis-integrated further, degenerating to Lark Summerville minus five, a sad, wanting equation no matter how I added it up.

Twenty years I've been jerking and popping like an out-of-joint skeleton, wondering which skin to choose, because none of them fits comfortably anymore.

And now the skin of the four years since Flannery left for college shrinks and shrivels and granulates, blown away by the winds of change as though it were nothing more than talcum powder.

I stared at my Guinness. If Queen Marsha, well-meaning or not, granted herself the privilege of dragging me out, I refused to be her court jester. I stayed mum.

So there.

Of course Marsha, being Marsha, banished my silence to an unseen dungeon in some far corner of her kingdom.

"So here's what I think, Lark." She fiddled with her drink napkin. "Since you didn't have insurance, you're just stuck with the lot, right?"

I said nothing.

"Because the house was paid off, right?"

I nodded. Bought for a song back in those days, it only devoured fifteen years of my life until payoff. In fact, I'd just paid it off three years ago. Figures.

"So sell the lot."

"Who would want a lot in Hamilton?" I broke the silence. Darn it!

"Maybe your next-door neighbors. It would mean a bigger yard."

"True. But then what? Where would I go?"

"Stay at home on Greenway."

"Oh yeah, right, Marsha. It's right in a residential section. How would I get what I needed? I can't walk down to any store, there's no CVS, and I need to be near St. Dominic's."

"Why?"

"It's my job?"

"Take the bus."

Marsha, Marsha, Marsha. "I'll pick up all sorts of things on the bus. Strep. Shingles. Some kind of venereal disease. You name it."

Of course, the waitress arrived right when I said "venereal disease."

"You can't pick up a venereal disease on a bus."

My face grew hot, and I tried to smile at the waitress as she set down my plate of bangers and mash.

Marsha picked up her fork as the waitress walked away. "A horribly apropos-looking meal considering the conversation, Lark." And despite the circumstances, we burst into laughter.

I jerked awake as if some antagonistic puppet master had yanked my strings.

"Hello?"

"Lark?"

"Yes?"

"How are you?"

Ten P.M.

"Who is this?"

"You don't recognize my voice anymore, babe?"

"Oh, dear Lord."

"That's right, babe. I'm guessing you're seeing the light."

I hung up the phone.

I don't think I meant to really hang up the phone, and if I'd given myself time to think about it, even for two seconds, I might have worked against the urge. I might have gripped the phone until my palms sweated and I turned nauseous, I might have smiled on my end to complete the act, I would have done something other than slam the phone down.

So I stuck my head between my legs and sucked in as much air as possible. Breathe. Breathe.

But not too much. Hyperventilation will not redeem this situation, Lark.

If he called back, I wouldn't hang up this time.

Don't let him call back.

He called back.

I yanked it before the ring had completed itself. "You promised me you'd never come back, Bradley."

"I'm not back. I'm just making a little phone call. Come on, babe, it's been twenty years. Come on."

Help me, Jesus.

There is no fear in love. There is no fear in love.

I tried Lamaze breathing. Come on, Lark. Breathe. Talk. Pretend a normal lady lives inside your skin. Think PTA, think dinner parties with friends, think hanging baskets of geraniums. "What do you want, Bradley? I know you must want something."

"I figured I'd get your mom or something. I tried to call you at your house in Hamilton, but the number rang and rang."

"How'd you get that number?"

"Information. I got it years ago."

"You did? Really?"

I didn't know whether to be happy or sad. Yeah, he kept track of me by getting the number, but he never once bothered to call.

"So what made you actually call the number?"

"Well, it's been so long."

"Yeah."

"Like, a really long time."

"And so?"

Man, I was doing great. Just like Newly would have done if he were a woman in my shoes. Not that Newly would have ever found his lily-white self in my shoes.

"I want to see my daughter."

He didn't say "Flannery." He said "my daughter." Laying a claim. Driving in a stake at the get-go. Right? Think, Lark. Think. Pretend you're Leslie. Or even Newly. Newly never experienced a loss for words. Newly never took anything off of anybody.

"Not on your life, buddy. The hard part is done. Besides, she thinks you're dead."

And I hung up the phone again because I wanted to, because I said something completely Summerville.

It rang again, and rang and rang. And then rang and rang and rang thirty minutes later.

And I sat by the phone and shook, praying to the Lord that he'd never call Greenway again.

"Larkspur!"

"Yes, Mother."

"Should I answer the phone next time?"

"No, Mother. It's one of those telemarketers."

"This late?"

"I think he was calling from the West Coast."

Please, God, let him be calling from California.

"All right then. Good night, dear!"

"Good night."

So I took the phone off the hook and sat up in bed. After all these years, Bradley del Champ steps back into my life. I ran to the bathroom and threw up. Shaking, feeling sweaty and cold, I scooted back and leaned against the tiled wall.

Wasn't the fire enough, Jesus?

Thanks ever so much.

A bug rammed his armored body over and over against the fluorescent sink light.

Leslie

OH MY. I THOUGHT WHEN A WOMAN reached my age the frantic worry she experienced as a young mother dissipated a bit.

Not so.

Something is afoot with those phone calls! I'm not a nincompoop. But the thought of asking Lark gives me goose bumps. Maybe she'll sigh a lot tomorrow like she used to do as a young teen, her cue for the inevitable question that would blossom from my lips. "Is there something wrong, dear?"

Yes, perhaps she'll sigh several times in a row, then I'll know for certain that she wants to talk.

Oh, for heaven's sake, I forgot to slurp my fiber again this evening! Well, no time like the present.

Darkness fills the rest of the house. Flannery arrived home a little while ago and kissed me and said, "Grandy, I love you!"

The air-conditioning unit below my window just whirred to life, and I find that a comforting sound. Certainly better than Charles's snoring, but what I wouldn't give to hear that buzz saw again.

I click on the bathroom light, avoid the mirror, and mix up a glass of that sandy nightmare.

Hold your nose when you drink, Leslie Lee, and make the going down a whole lot easier.

I'm going riding again tomorrow. I do believe I'll sleep in and head out in the afternoon. Riding never felt like exercise before this, I'll admit. But looking at a man like Jacob Marley all the while gives me a little gumption, and eyes like that go a long way in putting a little heart back into a woman!

PRISMA

POOR, QUIET LARK. No longer the fun child of yesteryear, busy cutting and pasting gum wrappers, toilet-paper tubes, strings, and construction paper and assembling them into what she called her "machines." Busier than a short-order cook and singing church songs all the while. And always too fast. But that was Lark, going too fast at whatever she set her mind to.

She composed her first song at seven, her first choir piece at thirteen, and won a statewide award for it. She learned piano first, then added organ to the mix at sixteen. Heaven lives in her music, I can tell you that, and I tell you the truth, angels already sing her songs in heaven.

Lark has enabled the devil to steal almost everything from her over the years. I know Jesus lives inside her, and I know He allowed her to retreat like she did. And now He's taken away the last little bit Himself. Kind of like fighting fire with fire, I'd say.

At least no one stole her ability to play. And at least she came back home, gifting me and Mrs. Summerville with a house full of music again. Mr. Summerville actually had a pipe organ from Germany installed all those years ago! Just for Lark.

The other day as I made bread and she sat working a crossword puzzle at the kitchen table, I told her I liked what she had just been playing. "Who wrote that, baby?"

"It's just something I put together last night as I was falling asleep."

"You did that in your head?"

She nodded. "It's the first piece I've composed in twenty years."

What troubles these artist types so? What tortures their spirits and shreds their psyches to bleeding ribbons? What thins out their dignity exposing wide their emotional turmoil?

It's hard to see someone implode like she did over the years since Bradley was killed. I don't know where she'd be without Jesus, and I don't even want to guess.

Thank the good Lord I love what I do and wake up each morning thinking, "Let's go, Jesus! Let's redeem the time!"

We drank a cup of tea together last night on the screened porch at the back of the house. Not Jesus and me, Lark and me, and she confided in me the heartache of coming home again, of living with her mother.

"I don't know why you don't just get an apartment until you buy a piece of property for your cabin, Lark."

"I can't afford it. Doggone it, Prisma, I'm forty-one years old, and I can't even afford an apartment."

Poor baby. "Any chance of getting another job to supplement your income?"

Call me cruel, but Lark needs a little stirring up.

"I let my license lapse. There's not much around here within walking distance."

Nice try, baby.

"You know, if you decided to just stay on here at Greenway, you'd be able to play the organ right here. Maybe Marsha would come down here for practice and you wouldn't have to go up to Hamilton on Wednesday nights. I know Mrs. Summerville wouldn't mind another body about the place."

Lark grimaced. "Yeah, right, Prisma. You know you'd get sick of me around here after a while."

"Are you serious? One of my babies would be back home for good. This place is just too big and old for no one but me, Leslie, and Asil, who's over the garage and doesn't count anyway."

Truth be told, Lark staying here would mean she didn't learn a thing from the fire. But she needs to know she's welcome. That we love her.

Got a letter from my son, Sinclair, yesterday. If Mr. Percy had lived to see his son at this stage of manhood, I do believe he might have burst open with pride. As the new editor in chief at some publishing house in North Carolina, Sinclair's dreams have come true. And Charles Summerville didn't have to put one dime to that child's education, I'm proud to say. Not that he didn't offer. And offer. And offer. But Mr. Percy, he did well enough with our salaries and invested wisely. And with some low interest loans, we had the opportunity to put Sinclair through all of his schooling. Mother and child, both graduates of Johns Hopkins. Now that made me proud, and not in a bad way, more of a thankful way. God is good to those who let Him be. And He's good to those who don't. They just don't realize it.

Mrs. Summerville is going riding an awful lot this summer. I asked the others if they knew anything about it, and Lark just shrugged her shoulders. However, Baby Girl volunteered her services as the family private eye. Now there is a human being you can always count on. And I tell you the truth on that one.

Today I am thankful for Asil's flowers, Days of Summer, that my Duster only needed fifty dollars worth of repairs and not six hundred like they thought, that I'm only on one medication and those are eye drops. I'm most thankful for my son's announcement. January will welcome a new little Percy! Imagine me a grandma! I said, "Sinclair, it's about time, child. You're almost fifty."

And he just laughed and laughed. "Look at it this way, Mama. At least his old man will be able to write up the birth announcement."

Lark

HOW THEY EVER CONVINCED ME to go to Target, I'll never know. Of course, I soon realized the lengths some people go to set someone up. I swear Marsha called them after our dinner at Mick O'Shea's and said, "Hey, phase one of Operation Lark has been accomplished. Let's move forward!" Yesterday, tall and elegant as usual, Mother sidled into my "prayer den," as Prisma dubbed it. She hauled a wallpaper book and a set of fabric swatches on a big ring. After heaving them onto the sofa and catching her breath, she plopped open the large volume.

"Now I know you're going to blow a gasket, dear, but I thought maybe you'd want us to do this room over while you're here." She flipped through pages officiously, the general of good taste.

"I don't really think it will be worth it. I won't be here forever." Right?

She set the books on the desk. "Honestly, though, look at this place." My mother has a gorgeous shudder. "All this darkened wood, and just look at this sofa. It's been needing reupholstering for years now."

She flipped open the collection of swatches next. "You've always liked pink, haven't you?"

I love pink.

Yes. It's odd.

She pointed to a pink-and-lime-green plaid, a large print plaid. Next to it an accompanying floral fabric bloomed. "Don't you think a Laura Ashley look would lighten the walls up a bit in here?"

"Maybe we could paint them white."

"A wonderful idea! I'll have Prisma call the painter right away. We heard about the nicest young man last week. Fair pricing and you couldn't meet a nicer fellow, or so Mrs. Phillips next-door says. Why don't you just look through the rest of these to see if there's anything you like. Three fabrics would be nice. Sofa, drapery, pillows, and all."

Blah-blah-blahbity-blah. Yip, yip, yip. The general turned into an excited Chihuahua.

She arose from her seat and walked toward the doorway.

I breathed a sigh of relief and returned to my Barbara Cartland book, one that takes place in Russia. I love them. Especially *Fire and Ice,* where she decorates her white ball gown with star orchids that the prince sends her right from the palace hothouse.

"Larkspur?"

Oh no. Answer but don't look up.

"Yes, Mother?"

"Well," she rushed to say, "I know you'll die when you hear this, but you've been wearing the same three old outfits of mine since the fire. Why don't we go over to Cross Keys, and I'll get you some well-fitting clothes of your own. I really don't mind!"

The thought of sashaying over to Cross Keys almost brought on the bile. Such a snooty kind of place. "It's okay, Mom. I'm just waiting for the Flair catalog to get here. Flannery called for me, and it's on its way."

"But by the time you order, it could take weeks."

"I'm not in a hurry."

Flannery walked in then, and looking back now, I swear it was on cue. She handed my mother a cup of the Starbucks she'd made at work. "What's up?"

"Thank you, dear. What kind am I trying tonight?" Mother worked off the lid and sniffed.

"Caramel macchiato."

"Skim milk?"

"Of course, Grandy! Not that you need to worry."

She smiled at her granddaughter. "I only look like I don't need to worry because I do. Now you, dear, you really don't have to worry."

Oh brother. I hate female talk sometimes.

"So what's up?" Flannery asked again, to my delight because surely she'd be on my side when it came to shopping at hoity-toity old Cross Keys.

"Grandy's trying to get me to go to her ladies' shop for some new clothes."

Flannery guffawed. "You, at Cross Keys? See, Mom, I told you that you should have come to New York with us when you had the chance."

"Like there was a snowball's chance she would, dear." Mother sat back down on the old couch and sipped her drink.

"Thanks, Mother." I turned in my desk chair to face the others, both now sitting on the couch drinking warm, trendy drinks.

Flannery sure looked cute in her khaki pants and Starbucks shirt. She'd dyed a couple of her little ponytails red. Not many young women could pull such a style off. But Flannery isn't afraid of much.

Is that the grace of God, or what?

Flannery reached toward the side table for a Kleenex. Poor thing's allergies bother her year-round. "Well, I've got an idea." She blew her nose. "Have you ever been to a Target?"

And then she started in, and I knew I had been duped, had witnessed nothing less than a superb theatrical production by the other Summerville women.

So there I stood in the middle of the Saturday crowd with Flannery and Prisma shoving needless accents in front of the short-sleeved black shirtwaist I had chosen. On sale. Eleven dollars and ninety-nine cents.

As good as Flair prices.

Target surely surprised me. Great selection, good prices, and a lot of cotton. H'm.

"I think this scarf is what it needs to set it off, Mom." Silk hissed beneath my chin as Flannery fluttered a scarf dotted with tiny elephants against my neck.

"What it needs, Baby Girl, is this pin!" Prisma jiggled the card, a gaudy pin with rhinestone gardening tools jangling together.

I grimaced. "Prisma, I don't really know about that one."

Flannery nodded. "I hate to say it, but I agree with her, Miss Prisma. That pin is too much, and Mom doesn't garden so it would be sort of a lie." Flannery pulled out another scarf. "Look, this one is the small kind. See, you just knot it around the neck like in the fifties."

Like Audrey Hepburn?

I studied my own reflection, wanting to gag. Some days I wish I looked more like Leslie, who looked more like Audrey Hepburn. "I look like a rotten midget pear, and you two want to highlight that?"

Prisma reached behind her. "Some busyness up by your face will keep the focus off your lack of height."

"Prisma!" I hated the sight of myself in that mirror. I hated the fact that my frizzy hair, my sallow skin, everything about me deserved polyester pants and blouses, that even a black shirtwaist dress from Target lent me that "bag lady find of the year" air.

Prisma dislodged a card from which hung a gold chain with a sun face hanging at the bottom. "Well, baby, we all got our flaws. Just some are better than others at covering them up."

Well, Prisma knows. She must weigh at least 180 pounds and wears horizontal stripes when she gussies herself up for her dinner out with Asil twice a month, which she swears is not a date!

But we all know better.

The genius caramel woman no one can truly understand plus the Superfly gardener who still shuffles and bops like it's 1974. It's impossible not to love them. So why was I quibbling over a pin? They couldn't make me actually wear it.

"I'll take the pin and both scarves."

Prisma rested one hand on her hip and yanked one of Flannery's ponytails. "Baby—"

I pointed at her. "Don't even say it, Prisma. I know you've got my number."

Prisma pointed back at me. "Well, then at least buy a pin I like so someone will wear it."

Flannery said, "And there are two other scarves I'd wear more if you're going to buy two scarves you're not going to wear anyway."

"Throw them in the cart."

I'm telling you what. I hated hanging out with girls in high school because they acted like this. Scarves, pins. Good grief. And yet I watched them in awe as they fussed over which accessory to pick. Both of these women, butterflies in their own right, laughed and laid comfortable hands on each other's arms. My heart filled with love.

There is no fear in love. Yes, that was what John the Beloved meant. I liked that verse in the positive sense so much better.

We loaded up the cart with bras and underpants, socks, T-shirts, and some shorts for Flannery. I bought several boxes of tampons, thinking that when a woman's not sexually active she surely has a right to turn off the whole menstruation thing. I threw some VO5 conditioner and Head & Shoulders into the basket.

We hit the book aisle.

Two Barbara Cartlands for me, and Flannery chose one of those depressing artsy novels, the boring reading-group-type fare she insists broadens people's horizons.

Like I'm that deep.

Prisma thinks fiction wastes a woman's time. She threw in a book about do-it-yourself home decorating. Probably for Mother.

I dropped in a deck of playing cards, shoelaces, a pocket-sized word search game book, and a stick of Krazy Glue onto the conveyor belt. Flannery threw down a pack of gum packaged to look like chewing tobacco. "I've always wanted to try this stuff."

"Knock yourself out, sweetie."

The checkout girl rang us through. Gosh, what a sullen thing!

"Let's go to Friendly's for ice cream." Prisma eyed the candy bars.

"I'm in," said Flannery.

"Ice cream?" I cried. "Why? Why do we need ice cream at a time like this? Isn't a trip to Target enough?" I hefted the bags out of the cart and made for the parking lot and Flannery's little Toyota, leaving the others in my dust. I've always felt like an outsider in a way. Only one person met me in my world and not the other way around. That was Brad. Not that anyone else in this world could begin to understand that. And I no longer expected them to. I'd been waiting for another call from Brad, and it had yet to come. But it would. If I wanted it to come, prayed it would come, sent out all sorts of vibes Brad's way begging him to remember us, to acknowledge our existence, to glance our proverbial way—the call would never cross the country. Perhaps therein lay the answer!

Please call, please call, please call.

Nope. No Friendly's for me today. Queen Marsha could stick this little foray in her pipe and puff away till kingdom come!

I practically dove for the phone that night around ten. Thank God for a quiet prayer line.

"Lark?"

"Brad."

"We really need to talk."

"I know."

Boy, I knew. I knew my reverse-psychology plan had failed. I'd even gained five pounds in the bargain with all the lime sherbet I consumed, sitting there like an idiot night after night eating lime sherbet and consuming tea with Sweet'n Low. Trying to find a sugar-free lime sherbet, but no luck yet; I'd called around to all the stores.

"You mean you'll actually talk to me tonight?"

There it was over the coast-to-coast line. That boyish tone.

Help me, Lord.

"I'll talk to you for Flannery's sake," I said. "Where are you?"

"I'm still home in California."

Thank You, God.

"Still in San Francisco?"

"Yep. Never left here. Not even after I made it big."

"You made it big?"

He breathed in deeply. "You didn't know?"

"I've been out of the rock scene for years. I don't have a TV or even a radio. I play organ in a church."

"That suits you."

Now why would he say that?

He continued. "Your playing was too refined for the group anyway. Let's face it, you were just too good for me all around."

I really wanted to agree, to be mean, to take advantage of what he said. But the words stuck in my throat. I remembered Flannery. And how could I believe anything he said anyway? Did he think a little flattery would do squat?

Brave thoughts, Summerville woman.

Okay, Lark. Be Leslie now.

I trembled, gripping the phone more tightly.

"How is Flannery?" he asked.

"Flannery?" It gushed out of me. "She's beautiful, Brad. She has

Daddy's black hair and is willowy like my mother and refined looking. But she's so cool. She's an artist!"

"No way!"

"Yes. Can't carry a tune for anything and plays no musical instruments, but you should see her paintings!"

"Will I?"

My Flannery-high popped. My parental pride imploded. Oh man, I'd just ruined all my intentions with the Flannery gushing. Darn. Had I changed the tone of our discourses for good now? Did he expect a *truly* civilized, not remotely civilized, ex-wife?

"I don't know, Brad. You walked out on her." I tried desperately to leave myself out of this. If it became about me, who knew what I'd agree to? "And don't act like you've always cared. You could have tried to contact her at any time over the past twenty years."

"I know."

"Why didn't you?"

"My wife."

Oh man.

"So there you go, Brad. We all have our loyalties." I picked up the infernal Christmas stocking and set to work, thinking if I kept my hands calm my voice might stay the same course.

"You're right, Lark."

That's the thing about Brad. He is so agreeable. Always was. He never argued or fussed. He just avoided the issues by apologizing, by admitting guilt, and becoming prostrate with shame. And then, hello, he'd go and repeat it all over again. Flannery deserved better.

"Look, she thinks you're dead, Brad. Do you realize what kind of position you'll put me in if you appear on the scene?"

"But she's my daughter."

"You chose! You sat there on that parking lot and you chose to leave us. We talked about it at great length."

"All I'm asking you to do is think about it."

"Come on, Brad!"

"Please, Lark?"

Well, how could I not think about this?

"I'll call you soon."

"Okay, but if it isn't me that answers, promise you'll hang up."

Like his promises meant anything anyway.

"Okay. I promise."

Big, big problem, Larkspur! Big, big.

And this one wasn't going away on its own.

Listen, Lark!

THIS ONE ISN'T GOING AWAY ON ITS OWN.

I tried to jam that thought into my head like ground pork into a sausage skin. Push, push. Shove as much of that thought in as far as it will go, Lark.

Shoving the Christmas stocking back into the drawer, I sank far down beneath my comforter. As far as I could go. Did anybody ever die by suffocating beneath their covers?

Probably not.

PRISMA

YOU COULD SEE IT TEN MILES FROM YESTERDAY that Lark's emotions had been pickled by something. Lark's like this, she doesn't exactly wear her heart on her sleeve, more like just underneath the sleeve. Sometimes the sleeve is that of a wool sweater, sometimes it's cotton. But when she walked into my sitting room tonight, that sleeve consisted of fine gauze.

"Oh, baby," I said.

She just cried for a little while. She sat down on my love seat and folded herself up in a little ball right next to me, winding her coat-hanger arms around my neck. If she weren't forty-one years old, I would have lifted her right onto my lap. But being a woman, she needs to be afforded her dignity even in the midst of such pain.

Of course, my curiosity threatened to burst out like the innards of an unpricked baked potato, but I somehow managed to keep it in. Well, truth be told, I prayed like crazy and kept my eye on the clock because I had muffins in the oven. Not that I cared if they were going to bake themselves to extinction as food, but I didn't want the house to catch fire.

I patted her arm. "What is it, baby?"

"It's Brad, Prisma."

"Brad? You missing him after all these years?" How could that be possible? I hated that Archie Bunker, but Bradley and the term "meathead" fit together better than my feet and these Daniel Greens.

"No, it isn't that."

Thank You, Jesus! "What is it then?"

She sat up, pulled away from and reached for a Kleenex off my end table. "You promise you won't be mad at me?"

"You promise you won't say anything that could make me mad?"

"No."

"Then me neither."

Lark blew her nose. "I'll risk it then."

She sat back down close and rested her sock-covered heels on my coffee table. "I don't know how to even begin."

"Is he coming back to haunt you or something?" I figured maybe a joke might clear the black fog that settled in the room.

"I wish."

"You're confusing me, baby. Just be out with it. It's not going to get any easier."

"Bradley's in California." And she ducked her head beneath her arms like a shell-shocked doughboy in a trench.

Words failed, and in their place some kind of incredulous mist filled my brain, this swampy unbelief that he was actually alive, but even more of a mystery that this little insignificant skinny thing who was scared of her own shoelaces pulled off a two-decade long charade like this.

I stared at the blackened fireplace.

"Well, Prisma?" Her voice poked out from beneath her arms.

"Give me a minute."

She sat back up. I looked over and saw no tears coming out of her eyes now. That forced me back to my usual mode of caregiver.

"Were those tears before because you were afraid to tell me?"

She nodded. "You're the last person I wanted to keep this secret from, Prisma."

"Then why did you?"

"I guess if nobody else knew, it would be like it wasn't true."

I pulled her onto my lap anyway. "You were wrong, baby." And then I held her small face in my big, rough hands, and I said, "You are loved so well by so many, Lark. I wish you'd realize that."

The stars outside my window demanded little of me. I saw only the Lord.

"Jesus, we got us a big problem."

"I know, My girl."

"If I weren't so upset that that scoundrel is still alive, I'd be furious with Lark."

"Lies never solve a problem."

"I'm glad she could confide in me, Jesus. Although, what am I supposed to do now? Well, I suppose I'll just lean on You and hope against hope nobody gets hurt too badly."

"My yoke is easy, My girl."

"And You always show me the way."

"I always have. And then again, My girl, you've always listened to Me. People like Lark sometimes have stuffed-up ears. Stuffed up by fear or guilt or anger or even just plain selfishness."

"That's not Lark though, Lord. The selfishness one, I mean."

"Are you sure?"

"Well, maybe not, Lord. Not if You say so. But the other three... I've seen those for years now, Jesus."

"I know."

"The good thing is she came to me, Lord. She stepped out of her outer space and sought some help."

"Of course she did. It's time, you know."

I sighed. I can't wait for heaven someday.

"Be strong, My girl, and of a good courage."

"You got that right, Lord."

"Oh, I always do, Prisma. But you know that."

Prayer is a wonderful thing. To someday see Him face to face really keeps me going. Ever since I found out about Him, all I want to do is see fit to do good, just to make Him smile at me.

Tonight I am thankful for the happy home my Jimmy and I made for so many years. I am thankful that Lark doesn't have to face her troubles alone. I am thankful.

L a r k

Marsha and Father Charlie are the only people I really know here at St. Dominic's. Other than Babe, of course. Three people. After all these years. Four ball bearings in a five-pound coffee can. I don't fit in among the Catholics at large, and church shopping presents a problem because the only Protestant church in the area that's far enough removed from the Catholics is really a synagogue in disguise. No pork. No nothing. But I bless the day Marsha invited me to St. Dominic's after the Stride Rite incident. For so long I'd heard about "the Lord" at my parents' church, but He seemed so elusive. They didn't want to talk about the messy stuff, the blood down His back and face, the gore on the wood of the cross, what His robe, the only garment He had, must have looked and smelled like after days and days of wear. But the Catholics don't mind the mess. They don't sweep it under the carpet and pretend it never happened. So Jesus became very real to me, and the Bible that Prisma had given me for my twelfth birthday revealed even more.

The organist job followed a year later.

And I'm still just the organist. After ten years.

Did I really expect everyone to fall all over me, to invite me to bingo or something?

Well, maybe I did.

But Father Charlie reaches out. This week after Saturday's seven o'clock mass he convinced me to stroll down the street with him for some Chinese food at Fast Wok. Since it's on the way home, I agreed.

He walked hands-in-pocket up to the counter. "Kung Pao chicken, number ten on the spiciness."

I whispered to him that I wanted a vegetarian lo mein and an order of egg drop soup.

He ordered that too.

"I didn't realize priests ate spicy food," I said as we sat down in the Melamine booth.

He emitted a giant laugh. "Oh, Lark, you tickle me." And he slid in, telling me about his last trip back home and how ornery his father is getting. "But in a comical way."

Mo the Friendly Drunk walked by and waved.

We both waved back.

"What do you think about him, Father Charlie?"

"Mo?"

"You know his story?"

He shook his head. "But I should, being the priest around here."

"I don't know. How do you ask someone how they ever got to that point?"

"Numba foh-two-nine ready, eh?" the lady behind the counter called, and Father Charlie jumped to his feet. I watched his broad back as he paid for the order and then headed over to the condiment bar for the soy sauce. Dedication exudes a certain confidence, a true north. What happened in his life? What entered in, filled him enough to determine a set course? A holy wind? A miracle? God's voice?

"I got some tea, too." Placing a little stainless-steel pot and a tiny cup in front of my place, he winked one great deer eye. Then we bowed for a quick "Bless us, O Lord, and these thy gifts."

"So, tell me where you're at, Larkspur Summerville."

He forked a large bit of Kung Pao into his mouth.

Father Charlie proclaimed himself my spiritual mentor five years ago. He must think he's failing miserably is all I can say!

"Well, I guess I'm coming along as well as can be expected."

"See now, Lark, there's the problem!"

"What?"

"Low expectations. Remember that old Dickens book everybody has to read in junior high?"

"*Great Expectations?*"

"Exactly. Remember that old lady who lived in that big old house with the putrefied wedding feast? Remember her?"

"Of course I do, Father Charlie."

"Well?" He sipped his tea, a spice-induced sweat breaking out on his broad forehead.

"Well, what?"

"Who do you feel more of a kinship with, the old lady in the house or the young man going off to do all sorts of things?"

I remind myself of an overcooked pound cake at times like this. Guess I should read some of those books Flannery keeps trying to get me to read. "I guess I should have seen where you were going with that one right away."

"That's okay. Some are slower on the uptake than others."

"Gee, thanks. But if I'd been quicker, I might have said something like *A Christmas Carol.*"

"Oh, believe me, that one fits too."

"I am not an Ebenezer Scrooge!"

He raised his eyebrows. "You don't have to be nasty to be an Ebenezer Scrooge."

I pointed at him and allowed some uplift on the left side of my mouth. Father Charlie never once meant any harm to anybody during any part of his fifty-five years of life, I'm guessing. He grew up in the country, over on the Eastern Shore of Virginia.

After I finished my soup I said, "Flannery says God burned down my house. Do you think that?"

"Doesn't matter what I think. Besides, I don't think God does stuff like that much."

"Really, you don't? How come?" Guess Father Charlie and Prisma had theological differences.

"Well, Lark, let's face it, bad things are always waiting to happen, right around the corner. Your wiring needed attention, and you didn't give it."

"So it really is my fault."

"Well, sure. But now comes the God part. He could have made that wiring hold awhile longer, but He didn't. So He didn't burn your house down. He let things take their natural course."

"But why?"

I knew the answer to that, but I wanted to hear it from Father Charlie.

But he surprised me. "Because He knows you've got potential!"

I so love that man!

"But I'm serving Him, aren't I? Aren't the things I do good things?"

"Yep. They sure are."

"And Ebenezer Scrooge wouldn't have done those things."

"Got to agree with you there."

"Isn't God pleased with those things?"

"Yep. He is. As much as a musician is pleased with the instrument and some sheet music."

I sure followed that reasoning.

"So what you're saying is He's ready to start playing now?"

"Well, that's funny you should ask that, because while my analogy is good in some ways, it doesn't go all the way through. See, instruments don't usually have a choice whether they want to be played or not, do they?"

"No." I slurped another bit of tea. "Can we change the subject now, Father Charlie?"

"Sure, Lark. I've said everything I felt led to say anyway. Now it's up to you to mull for a while."

A few days ago before practice while getting my tea at the 3 B's, I ran into a man who started coming back to church this spring. Marsha introduced us, and that was pretty much it. But when he came into the restaurant he actually seemed happy to see me.

Odd.

"You're Lark, right?"

I nodded. "Uh-huh, yeah, uh-huh." I nodded more. I couldn't remember his name. I couldn't remember his name.

Think, Lark. Think.

"Hi-ya, Deke!" His attention turned away, praise God.

Think, Lark. Think.

"Hi-ya, Johnny."

Johnny. That's right. Okay. Okay.

Breathe in.

Johnny what?

He turned back. "Gotta tell you. You did a great job last week at church."

"Yeah?"

"Oh yeah. Love organ music!"

"You do?"

"Oh yeah."

"But you're under sixty!" I blurted.

He smiled. "Not much under, I hate to say."

That laugh was as good as a can of ant spray or something.

I'm not kidding.

Johnny shrugged. "Can't explain it myself, but hey, you like what you like, right?"

"Yeah, that's what I've always said."

I have? When have I ever said that?

Weird. So weird.

I looked around me. Had the rest of the world frozen in place? But there stood Babe at the head of a booth full of postconcert Sweet Adelines. Deke scratched his chin as he eyed himself in the mirror over the grill. And outside some giant boom box disguised as a blue car inched by.

And Johnny stood there and smiled at me.

He just smiled at me with this warm grin spread over crooked teeth surrounded by fuller lips and a curly beard and mustache with every color hair known to man growing there. A bright Berbered patch of graying facial hair that caught the sun coming in the window. He wore hospital scrubs, although "construction worker" oozed from his aura. Probably worked as a tech or something.

"How long have you been playing?" he asked and then caught Deke's eye. "A coffee to go? I've been on all night."

"You got it, Johnny." Deke turned away from the mirror.

"Thirty years." I gave that nervous little laugh I always do even though nothing comical lived inside that statement. I hate that chuckle. So self-conscious and pathetic. Somehow, those women wearing suits and perfect shoes on Monday through Friday and tights on Saturday when they zip through the country in those SUVs with bags of mulch and mums in the back don't at all strike me as the types that strangle out those stupid little laughs.

I deserved to have my house burned down if I couldn't even make decent chitchat at the 3 B's.

"Did you start when you were born, Lark?"

After examining his wrinkles, I could see he was probably close to sixty. Blueberry eyes recessed into the soft folds of age, Indian corn teeth, jowls blushed like an apple. All he needed was a cornucopia around his face and he'd make a darn nice centerpiece. Beautiful in its commonness, really. A living piece of Americana.

I still can't explain what happened next. I freaked at his compliment and my own close examination of his face. I just freaked. I snatched my plastic foam cup of tea and steamrolled out the door and up to the church without ever once looking behind me.

The organ cradled me, and I burst into Bach, thinking that a little Bach always cures what ails me. Or at least provides a Band-Aid.

And it did. I forgot about the world and lived within the music, plastering my heart and soul upon the page before me, grafting the run of notes onto my aching spirit.

Not until I arrived home did I realize the tea had sloshed over the edge of my cup and burned my hand.

"Hello. IPRAY4U."

"Hey, Prayer Lady, it's Gene."

"Gene! It's been awhile. You doing okay?"

"I sure am. You'll never guess what? I got the promotion!"

"I knew you would, Gene."

"Well, without your prayers, Prayer Lady, I don't know if it would've happened. There were three guys in the running for this position. One guy accepted another offer, and the other backed out for reasons unbeknown to me."

"Prayer sure can't hurt, I know that!"

"You're right."

"So when do you start?"

"Next week."

"Maybe you'll meet a nice girl there. I mean after all that happened with Christy…"

"I know. You prayed me through that, too."

"Hey, it's an honor. So what do you want me to pray about this week?"

"Just that I'll do a good job. It's hard starting all over again, you know? New floor. New people and all."

"Gene, you have no idea how much I understand!"

"Well, hey then, maybe I'll do some praying for you this week."

"I wouldn't say no to that."

"Okay, well, gotta go. Need to buy new loafers."

"Take care."

I called up Marsha that night.

"Do you know that Johnny guy from church all that well?" I asked.

"Johnny guy? This is Baltimore, hon. You need to be a little more specific."

"Big guy, bald on top, multicolored beard. He had on a set of scrubs when I saw him."

"Oh yeah, sure do. That's Johnny Josefowski. He's neat, isn't he? Why, do you like him?"

"Marsha!"

I swear all the women in my life are in cahoots.

"I saw him at the 3 B's today."

And so I got the scoop. Marsha dishes up some good scoop. I pictured her there on her waterbed with cotton balls splaying her brown-and-serve toes, a green exfoliating mask stuccoing her face. Definitely painting her toenails as we talked.

Johnny Josefowski. Doctor Johnny Josefowski.

Figures.

Someone capable of labeling me a certified nut case.

Oh, great.

"What kind of a doctor is he?"

"A cardiologist."

Praise God! Not a psychiatrist. "Oh yeah?"

"Real nice guy, isn't he?"

"Actually, yeah. Sure doesn't look like a doctor though."

"Nah. Not from your typical medical stock, I can tell you."

"Oh yeah?"

"Nope. Grew up next door to him right here in Hamilton."

"No kidding!"

"Nope. Heartbreaking story, Lark. Had this wigged-out mother who was in and out of institutions ever since I could remember…"

Oh, great.

"And his dad worked all the time trying to make ends meet. Johnny delivered the *Sunpaper,* groceries, you name it. He was on his bike from the time he woke up until well after suppertime. Except for school. He was a great student, which explains the doctor thing and all. Never married, if you can believe that. So did you get much of a chance to talk to him?"

"No. I got scared and ran out."

No use pretending with Marsha.

She sighed into the phone and said, "Oh, honey."

"I know."

"Well, if there's a more understanding soul in the world than Johnny Josefowski, I have yet to meet him."

Not that it would matter.

The next Sunday morning I closed up my organ after eleven o'clock mass. Johnny Josefowski sauntered up the aisle, right toward me.

Marsha, where are you when I need you? And what happened to Prisma? She picked a heck of a time to use the bathroom.

He hunched over and whispered. "Do you take requests?"

"I don't know…"

"Marsha says you can play anything by ear."

"And you believe everything Marsha says?"

"No. But I have a feeling she's right about this one."

"How? Men's intuition?"

He laughed. "Hardly."

"An ear for music?"

"Can't play a note. Can't sing on key."

Blue jeans covered his lower half. A Ravens World Champions T-shirt covered the upper half. A very big Raven. An XXL Raven, if I had to guess.

In fact, as I scrutinized him, I realized that he bassed my treble. Male, tall, heavyset, smart, nonmusical. Successful and altruistic if Marsha told the truth.

I breathed in.

Some men just smell good, you know? That clean, "I shower a lot" aroma wafts about them. No perfumes or scents, just soap and skin. His hair smelled fresh too. Johnny Josefowski sprouts that thick, porous kind of hair. Well, where it grows anyway. The top of his head reflected the lanterns overhead.

"So what do you want me to play?"

" 'I'll Be Down to Get You in a Taxi, Honey'?"

"The 'Darktown Strutters' Ball'?" My turn to smile arrived. "In church?"

"Why not?"

I spotted Marsha by the back door, this Howdy Doody grin threatening to split her Scots-Irish face in two. When she flipped me the double thumbs-up, I turned my face away as quickly as possible before this man beside me turned to see what had caught my attention.

A double thumbs-up!

Oh my word!

Suddenly the keys became real interesting, and I threw my fingers into a tailspin, playing the request.

Father Charlie veered out of the vestment room. " 'Better be ready 'bout a half past eight!' "

Oh my stars, as Mother would say! I suddenly found myself the organist for a circus! Right there at St. Dominic's. Oh my utter stars!

And then Prisma ran out of the ladies' rest room.

And then Marsha jiggled back up the aisle.

And they all swayed to the "Darktown Strutters' Ball," and for the first time in years I laughed so hard I could hardly play for the tears that squeezed out of a heart battered by a sudden abandon.

Leslie

"Newly?"

"Hello, Mother."

"You didn't have a date at all."

He chuckled. "It was Flannery; you found me out."

"Did you have a good time?"

"Of course. She's delightful. This family doesn't deserve that child."

"Isn't that the truth? She provides the only common ground we have. Now why is that?"

"I don't know, Mother. I think it must be genetics. You and Father were certainly perfect parents."

"Stop fooling around, Newly. Anyway, there is another reason I'm calling."

"And that is?"

"I was wondering if we might get together for lunch this week. Nothing huge. Just a shared lunch break near your building."

He hesitated.

Oh, Lord, let him say yes.

"How about Wednesday, Mother?"

"All right. You pick the place."

"Fine. I'll meet you in the lobby of my building."

"Noon?"

"Yes, Mother. Noon will be fine. Good night."

Click. Clickity. Click.

He gave me no chance to say good-bye.

I hung up my bedroom phone and slid between the sheets. This bed has supported me for years and years. I loved my life for so long. My dependable life, free of worries over money, thanks to Charles, and household issues, thanks to Prisma. Despite my world of charities and card clubs, the country club for drinks and dinner, the stables, I'm finding that I miss so much these days, cloistered with the same boring, sheltered people year after year. Especially since Charles died. Talk about a comfort zone!

And how much time remains to start living again, really living? I don't know. I just don't feel good anymore.

PRISMA

"OH, LORD, I CAN SEE MORE TROUBLE."

I pulled my quilt up to my chin. I didn't even feel like looking at the stars tonight.

No normal conversation with the Lord. I just talked to Him because sometimes He's quiet and simply listens and I'm too upset to go filling in His half of the conversation. But my heart ached for Lark.

He was up to something, that much was certain. I watched Lark closely all those years she examined her family as though shyly peering through bangs needing a good trim. And nothing ever changed. Yes, Lark asked Jesus into her heart, but He wants more from her now, I do believe. Nobody should be a babe in Christ for a decade. "Give her a deeper purpose, Jesus. Draw her in more intimately."

Although who am I to judge how intimate she is with her Savior?

Still, witnessing her having a good time at church did my heart good.

Maybe something there at St. Dominic's is the answer.

Maybe not.

But my sweet Lark cannot go on like this forever. To spread her wings again and really learn to fly, she needs a good plunge into the depths. She needs to get dirty and dusty and full of God's earth.

Flannery

I'VE ALWAYS WANTED TO BE LIKE PRISMA.

Prisma hauled me to church when I was growing up before Mom's faith blossomed, and sometimes on Sunday morning I still go with her down to Word of Faith Christian Center. There's more to the church's title, but I can never remember the rest. Me and Prisma are "standin' on the promises."

Not that Prisma is perfect. Mom told me how she had to hide her Easter and Halloween candy when she was a kid, or Prisma would eat it all up. She couldn't help herself, and I guess all that candy and cake and pie has gone a long way in making her sweet all the way to the bone. It really gets Grandy's goat that Prisma can eat all that stuff and have a subbasement cholesterol level, and Grandy eats dry toast for breakfast, clear broth for lunch, and small portions at dinner to stay a size six and keep her cholesterol from heavenly heights.

But it's like this, I think. More problems can come from starving yourself like Grandy does. At least that's what I think.

"Sweet Pea, Sweet Pea. Just wait until you get old like me," she says. "I ate all sorts of fatty things at your age and when I hit the age of forty-five, I started to balloon."

That did not encourage me, let me just say! And I'm not sure I believe her entirely either. Did balloon mean going from a size four to a size six?

Some calendars for next year came into B&N today, and I got a cool idea, so I called Prisma on my break and asked her if she could front me some money to buy a new camera since my old one was destroyed in the fire, and all I've got presently is one of those disposable wedding cameras. She said yes but wanted to know why, so I told her I was going to shoot pictures of the lighthouses on the Chesapeake and maybe even drive down to the Outer Banks. I want to start a new series of paintings about God. I'm always doing paintings about God, but people don't know that's what they're about, but God does, so that's all that matters to me. So anyway, Prisma's smile could be heard over the phone, and she said, "Baby Girl, I'll front you the money but only if you take me along on your shoots whenever it's possible." And so I said yes, and so we're going out on our first shoot tomorrow evening, down to the Inner Harbor to the old Hooper's Island Strait Lighthouse on display down there. We're going to shoot it at sunset with the harbor lights in the background.

Afterward, I know me and Prisma will head over to Little Italy for some ravioli at Chipparelli's.

July

Flannery

I CAN'T BELIEVE I AM DOING THIS! SPYING!

Just call me Flannery Bond or something stupid like that.

It's a beautiful Fourth of July evening, though, despite the day I had at work today.

Okay, so some of the grossest guys come into Starbucks. This one guy came in today as I was arranging travel mugs on the merchandise shelves, and he was pure yuck! Had at least ten earrings. And an eyebrow ring. No nose ring or lip ring or tongue ring, because I asked him when he started flirting with me as he waited for his triple Red Eye. I said, "You got a tongue ring, too? What's with this piercing stuff anyway? I mean two or three, okay. But I'll bet you've lost count."

He said, "No, I don't have a tongue ring!" Really snottylike.

And I said, "Prove it." But he just walked away, which was fine with me, because like I said, the guy was a total yuck, and let's face it, tongues are just gross, no matter whose tongue it is, so why adorn it with anything? Whoever did that French kissing scene in *Top Gun* sure missed the boat. Talk about nauseating. Saved my virtue in high school, though, let me tell you, so I guess I should thank the guy!

It's funny with guys. It seems the lower their drawers ride, the less I want to get to know them. Gag. The yuck guy, I have to say, however, did have normal jeans on, although he was wearing a Tommy Hilfiger jacket with the big flag on it, which is a definite point against him. There's no way I'd pay that much money to do someone else's advertising.

Anyway. Grandy refused to go over to Luskin's with us to watch the fireworks as usual, said she had a headache and didn't want to hear "those skull-cracking fireworks exploding like World War I. Not that I'd remember."

So Prisma and Asil in his white shoes grabbed the webbed lawn chairs Asil had hosed clean and went on out there. Mom said she wanted to watch the fireworks on PBS, and after the day I had at work, I shook my head and said, "Well, knock yourself out!"

Sometimes it's not worth it.

Prisma pulled me aside and said, "Find out where Mrs. Summerville is going."

And I said, "All right!"

So I'm taking my car and following Grandy out to the valley.

I pull behind some shed thingy (I'm not a horsy person, so don't expect any real horse-farm type terms here), put on a cowgirl hat, and watch her as she walks into the barn.

And there is my answer!

And it is a man!

Woo-hoo!

Somebody yells, "See ya next week, Jake!"

He gives one of those two-fingers-off-the-brim-of-the-hat-Robert-Redford salutes.

Grandy is actually blushing around that man Jake. My grandmother infatuated with a man named Jake! I never would have thought it in a million years. Although she'd say, "My dear Sweet Pea, must I remind you about John Jacob Astor? Jacob is a perfectly socially acceptable name." To which I would hurl back her own words she's hurled at me many times and I'd say, "That is twaddle and you know it!"

She's laughing and looking incredibly young.

Wow, what a beauty. Even in her condition.

Which makes me sad to watch her flirt with this man because I'm guessing she's a walking time bomb with this heart stuff she's downplaying. Oh yeah. If Grandy says it's a little thing, you can take it to the bank that it's humongous.

She was sort of cryptic about the doctor appointment she had yesterday. "Nothing to worry about, sweetheart. Just a routine checkup."

"Yeah, with a cardiologist!"

"At my age, a woman can't be too careful, you know."

And then she pulled out a magazine from the rack by her floral television chair in the den, flipped open to an article titled "Yes, It Is Your Problem!"

"See? Heart disease kills women more than we'd like to think. Those male doctors never take our chest pains seriously, and by the time they finally do something it's too late! Massive heart attack!"

"So you have chest pains, Grandy?"

"Did I say that?"

"No, but I thought—"

"I'm only doing what the article said I should do, Sweet Pea. Don't read anything more into it than that."

And she snapped the magazine shut and shoved it down into the holder. "And that's all I'm going to say about the matter."

All right, already! Yikes!

"So tell me about your day," she said and she hunched up her shoulders in that girl-to-girl way. "What did you wear?"

"Oh, Grandy, we have to wear the same thing every day."

"Isn't that a shame?"

"It sure is."

I'm so happy to be home on Greenway. It would be horrible to say I'm hoping some snag occurs in Mom's quest for alternate housing. But it would be true.

Jake helps her up onto her horse and off she goes!

I can't wait to tell Prisma!

Leslie

I CLIMBED THE STEPS UP TO JACOB MARLEY'S ROOM at the stables for a cup of coffee this afternoon. Truth to tell, upon reflection afterward, it was the worst cup of coffee I've ever had. Even worse than Midwest coffee, which is always the color of tea. If you're fortunate, that is. A twin bed, a rocking chair, and a small kitchen table with three chairs consumed the floor space. But it smells like him up there. Horsy and soapy. I haven't been this excited, in a womanly way, you see, since my Charles whisked me to Fiji, where we had our own stretch of beach. Even though Charles wasn't some Hollywood, choreographed lover, he practically worshiped me, and that made all the difference.

Jake barely knows I exist. Why, I claimed this fake caffeine headache, knowing Jake doesn't like to see anything in pain. Not surprisingly, he immediately offered to brew some coffee and get me an aspirin.

Mama is turning over in her grave, I just know it.

And truth to tell, this manipulation business is new to me. I'm not sure if I really like it after all.

Budding romances abound on Greenway though. That man from Lark's church, Johnny Josefowski, joined this newly formed study group meeting at Marsha's house once a week. That nice man Father Charlie is leading it, although I didn't know the Catholics planned that sort of thing. But that Father Charlie comes off as a visionary sort.

According to Flannery—of course Lark never tells me a thing—Johnny managed to sit next to her at the first meeting. He's a doctor, you know. Study group indeed. It seems to me a lot of those folks are singles.

Jake handed me the coffee.

"Thank you."

"You okay, Mrs. Summerville? You're looking a little pale."

"Just the headache."

"Hope the coffee helps."

"Oh, it will do just fine for what's ailing me."

Pathetic but sweet, he shuffled in his boots. A leather man with salt-and-pepper hair and stringy muscles.

"You miss home?" I imagined wide plains with mountains guarding them in the distance.

"Well, right here is home."

"Truly?"

"Yes ma'am. Was raised on this farm."

"Your parents owned it?"

He shook his head and leaned like a yardstick against the small counter. "Over in one of the smaller houses. My father was the stable master here for years."

"I don't recall meeting him."

"He died soon after I was born. I was a product of his old age."

"I'm sorry."

"Well, you've been riding a lot lately. Just enjoying the exercise?"

How anyone assigns the words *exercise* and *enjoy* to the same sentence stupefies me. "I just love horses."

"Me, too."

"And I always have."

"Me, too. They're something, aren't they?"

"My daddy used to call them velvet wind."

He nodded slowly. "That sort of sums them up right there, doesn't it?"

"It certainly does."

And Jacob smiled into my eyes, igniting a little pilot light down in a heart spot I never expected would burn again.

Flannery, who followed me out here on the Fourth of July and thinks she got away with it, thinks I'm in love. Twaddle. Not yet, at least, and probably not ever again. But even considering my defective heart, time deserted me long ago. And to make matters worse, the perfectly frightful news at the doctor's bit me like a mastiff on a Milk-Bone. I'm considering telling Prisma about it in case she comes and finds me in the middle of a heart attack. Having such confidence in a person is a wonderful thing. I shudder to think what I'd do without her. Maybe Lark's group will pray for an easy variety of death. But then I'd have to tell her about it all, and another worry may push her right over the edge this time. How much can one woman take? Besides, God has always blessed the Strawbridges with quick or quiet endings. It's our way. Best to just leave it at that.

Anyway, I scheduled the stress test for two weeks from tomorrow. Maybe Asil will drive us in the Bentley. Prisma should sit there in the backseat with me for moral support.

After I returned home from riding, Prisma and I sat at the dining room table and worked on my photo album.

My stars! I watched with the delight of a four-year-old as she slid out the new items she bought at the craft store. I never knew!

"They call it scrapbooking now, Mrs. Summerville, and you should see the huge sections of this stuff at the craft stores."

I picked up item after item, Prisma dutifully listing the possibilities of each one.

Die cuts for color and theme.

Wonderful things called gel pens!

Hole punches in the shapes of hearts and bears and other delightful things.

They've even developed scissors that cut a design instead of a straight edge!

My stars. Where have I been hiding all these years?

Then Prisma started a book of her own. I'd forgotten how cute Sinclair was when he was a baby.

Lark

MARSHA INFORMED ME ALL ABOUT JOHNNY JOSEFOWSKI.

Get this. Not only is he a cardiac surgeon, he's a cardiac surgeon's cardiac surgeon. He operates on a lot of doctors who need bypasses and whatnots. Too bad there's no such thing as an organist's organist, but at least it is possible to play without the whole anesthesia thing. People at least remember your work and never have to rely on me saying, "Yes, the music went fine. It was a textbook mass."

So where was Dr. Johnny Josefowski twenty years ago when Brad left and broke my heart? Does he repair that sort of thing?

I haven't heard from Brad for two weeks.

Figures. My strategy ended up working. What a relief. Imagine if I had blabbed the whole thing prematurely to Flannery. But I'd be lying if I said my world doesn't feel like it's hanging by wet toilet paper.

I'm not sure how I allowed Flannery to convince me, but we went out for lunch, just the two of us. And not at the 3 B's either. We chose Sanders, my childhood favorite. I had no idea they ruined the place over the last decade by upscaling it. Sure, business might be better for them, but rip out my heart, why don't they?

"You might have warned me, Flannery."

"Well, Mom, I think you need to see that you may think life isn't changing. But it is. And Sanders is only the beginning."

First Target. Now Sanders.

When I was a child, we'd take Sunday drives around Loch Raven. Sanders, just a little roadside store back then, sold homemade ice cream in flavors like peach and pumpkin, candy like Pixy Stix and edible neck-laces, and some handmade crafts from local ladies looking to make a little money from folks out for a day of relaxation around the water.

They showed us to a table on the new sun porch overlooking the water. This charming little restaurant should seem like an improvement.

But I miss the Pixy Stix and the smell of the place when scarred hardwood flooring and a fireplace burning against the left wall provided a rustic, camplike ambience. What was this sun porch supposed to prove? What did sun porches prove in general, in fact? Either one likes the outdoors or one doesn't. A sun porch just confuses things. It serves as some twilight zone, some faux outdoor experience. The imitation vanilla of outdoorsiness. Nature lite.

We gazed out over the road, our eyes resting on the Gunpowder River, the tributary that fed Loch Raven.

"So…" Flannery twisted her trunk in a little Chubby Checkers imi-tation, her silver bracelets jangling like the wind chimes on the front porch of the restaurant. "I saw your friend Marsha yesterday at work." She jiggled her eyebrows up and down. "You have anything you want to tell me about?"

Huh? I don't remember mentioning Bradley's reemergence to Marsha. Did I say something without realizing it? "What do you mean?"

"Oh, a certain cardiac surgeon?"

Whew. "Oh, Flannery! For heaven's sake! There's nothing to tell."

"That's not what I hear."

Marsha Fortenbaugh will die. I mean double thumbs-up and "Darktown Strutters' Ball" are one thing, but blabbing to Flannery? We'll, she's stepped on holy ground there.

Johnny Josefowski does have beautiful hands though. I failed to realize it until that moment. I mean, those are beautiful hands for some-one who looks like he gets paid by the piece.

"Look, Flannery. He's sat next to me in church a couple of times. He comes to the new study group if he's not in surgery or doing rounds or whatever else men of his esteem and brilliance, men I have no busi-ness attaching any sort of hope to, do all day and all night because they're so darned devoted to the good of humanity. If you didn't work

Sunday mornings and actually came to church with me once in a great while, you'd know that."

There, throw it back in her lap. Get off the defensive.

"Come off it, Mom. My church meets Saturday night."

"All those electric guitars."

Flannery waved me away with the mild disgust I deserved. "Don't try to change the subject. You're lucky to have a daughter who likes to be in church even if it does meet on Saturday night."

"The pastor's wife has blue hair and has a pierced eyebrow."

Good grief, did Leslie Summerville walk in and start speaking?

"So, tell me more about Dr. J. I can't believe you've had a crush on somebody and you didn't tell me!"

"I don't have a crush on him, Flannery! I'm too old for crushes."

"No you're not. You've been widowed since you were my age—"

And after that my eardrums closed up shop. I just gazed at Flannery in amazement as I watched her lips, her voice failing to register anything but "Waa, waa-waa, waaaah," like Charlie Brown's teacher.

My gosh! Divorced since Flannery's age! The thought abraded me like a million grains of sea salt on a bedsore the size of a dinner plate. For the first time I examined her youth and enthusiasm in contrast to my own state and realized I'd felt this age since I was Flannery's age. When Brad rode down that driveway, my youthfulness ran after him, screaming itself hoarse as it faded from my own view.

I've been middle-aged for years.

The waitress arrived, thank You, God, amid Flannery's chitchat.

"I'll take the tomato soup Florentine, please," I told her. A nice, bloody red soup. "And a tuna sandwich."

"I'll have the salad sampler," Flannery said. "Heavy on the tuna salad."

We smiled into each other's eyes, my maternal heart swelling and puffing, purring and bursting with a love so suddenly overwhelming I wanted to reach over and hold her in my arms like the baby she used to be. That smiling, chubby bear cub with sprouts of light brown hair fountaining from her tender scalp.

Loneliness, pain, the workaday world notwithstanding, we stood together in life, enjoying one another, one mother, one daughter.

Wow, had it all been worth it.

I breathed in and realized I deserved to feel relieved regarding Flannery. Worries never fade completely, of course, because motherhood never ends, but I'd completed the bulk of my work, and at least I'd succeeded at something in life. That's how I know God's grace really exists.

I crawled between my mint-and-yellow-floral sheets that night and focused on Prisma's stars.

I love my daughter so much, Lord. Thank you for giving her to me. What a lovely time we had at lunch. And supper tonight was so nice. Mother seemed…more settled than usual. When Prisma took me into her room tonight and showed me how well Days of Summer is doing under her care, I just cried. Daddy has so much to show for the life he lived. You can't judge people by their cocktails and sour onions, can you, Lord? When I first came to You, I scorned Daddy's society ways. But now…what have I got to show for anything? The house is gone. And I just keep hiding away in the gloom of St. Dominic's or here at Greenway. I'm missing some kind of boat. I feel it in my heart, and I'm sorry, Lord. Show me what to do. Show me where I'm going wrong. Amen.

If Jesus came down right now and sat on the end of my bed, He'd see me crying again, and He'd offer His sleeve, so I might lay my face on His forearm and let my tears soak into the white of His garment. It would be a river of tears. And the sleeve would never become heavy and sopping because no matter how many I cried, He could dry them with plenty of soft, dry comfort.

Flannery

TODAY WAS NOT A GOOD DAY. Man, it was so crowded at work, and there's this girl Ashley, who works the register. She always gets things out of order. Latte breve decaf grande. It's really hard to mark the cups, and she's such a snot in the bargain. She's so sullen and wears these shoes.

The cool thing is, though, that I was in pretty good spirits because the day before, Saturday afternoon, Prisma and I drove out to Concorde Point Lighthouse and took pictures. She even let me take some pictures of her, which she's never done before. Prisma has one of the most beautiful faces I've ever seen. Features you can't quite get a handle on, nationality-wise, and then this glowing skin! And I'm going to do a painting of her for Christmas. But then, like, who wants a portrait of herself? It's not like you're going to hang your own picture on your own wall. Now if Mr. Percy were living, he'd have hung it right there in their little parlor, and she'd have hated it for years. She would have walked by it every day, shaken a finger at it, lifted her eyes, and said, "Jesus, I'm only keeping that up there for You because You said for us to think more highly of others than ourselves."

Maybe I'll just keep it for myself then and enter it in a show or something. Maybe the Towsontowne Art Festival next spring.

So we were standing there where the Susquehanna River meets the Chesapeake Bay, and the skipjack that sails out of there came in, so Prisma and I took a ride on it. The water was so beautiful, I have to say I was tempted to paint a watercolor, the Lord help me.

A watercolor.

Gag me.

But the funny thing is, up comes that yuck guy that hangs out at

Starbucks, the one with the Tommy jacket and the regular size pants. And all those earrings. And I'm sort of thinking "What's a poophead like that doing on a skipjack?" But he walks right by me like he's never taken a triple Red Eye from my hands in his life. He didn't have the Tommy jacket on either, and he'd taken out all those earrings. Even that gag eyebrow one.

I finally figured out he actually works on the boat, and he was very respectful to his employer and everything. Now, I'm all for people who like to express themselves and stuff, but seeing this guy looking normal was very alluring. He's got a nice thick head of light brown hair that I'd never noticed before because of the little black weirdo hat he always has on, pulled down low on his brow like he's planning on robbing Bank of America or something.

So anyway, enough of that guy. But it's kind of nice to find out that people you think are total yuck may not be complete gag.

Prisma and I ended up having lunch at Fortino Brothers right in downtown Havre de Grace. White pizza loaded with fresh tomato slices, ricotta cheese, and broccoli. I don't know what it is with that woman and Italian food! Guess she's got an Italian ancestor as well. Then we walked around the antique stores and junk shops a little bit and she bought me a book about North Carolina.

"That's where I'm going to end up someday, Baby Girl."

"North Carolina?"

"Yep. It's where my roots are. Some of them at least. And I can run the foundation from there. Sinclair's there too."

So I started making our plans for the Outer Banks lighthouses trip. She said she'd take a long weekend off before I go back to school. Four days with Prisma Percy is just what I need to bolster me up before I head to grad school with a bunch of overpuffed, egomaniacal artists who think what they're doing is soooo original!

Like Prisma and King Solomon say, "There's nothing new under the sun." And believe me, in my line of work, the sooner you learn that, the less angst you'll have in the long run.

Grandy took us all out to eat tonight, except for Mom, naturally, which was pure, medieval torture because I'm always extra conscious of my manners around her. We went to Tio Pepe's, and everybody had a good meal but me, so I excused myself from the group before dessert and headed up to Mick O'Shea's for some bangers and mash. It was Irish folk music night or something, and this guy that played the uilleann pipes and the tin whistle asked me if I'd like to take a walk up to the monument on his break, so I went. He really is Irish and has that accent like Liam Neeson's. He's a really nice guy and sort of cute, but I couldn't help but compare his face to Tommy Boy's face, who, by the way, came into Starbucks today and totally ignored me.

Maybe I should dye my hair blond? Grandy loves it dark because she used to be a brunette, but I've got this feeling that Tommy Boy likes blondes. See, he was kind of smiling sideways at that Ashley girl, and she's a blonde, and a real blonde too.

She's definitely Puce.

And Tommy Boy? Don't ask me why I feel this way, but he's Golden Orange, like the middle tone of a sunset. My favorite color.

Not that he deserves to be a pretty color like that. No way.

He deserves to be Taupe.

I started looking through Mom's circus postcard collection last night before bed. She started the collection out with postcards of circus setups. Wagon trains. Circus trains. Tent raisings with the big elephants working hard.

I got to the animal acts next. Charley the Elephant balancing on a post. El Google, the twenty-five-hundred-pound seal.

Then there's these Clown Girls stuck right in the middle of the page, on top of the cellophane. Really freaky ladies standing next to a clown. What is up with that?

PRISMA

HONEST TO PETE, I DON'T KNOW what's gotten into the women on
Greenway! All three of these Summerville girls have gone completely
haywire. Mrs. Summerville making moon eyes at some man young
enough to be her son who looks, and I tell you the truth, like somebody
took my old brown leather pocketbook and stuck features on it. She still
has no idea I know about that man Jake. Not that he's all bad, because
Baby Girl says he's been working out there on that same farm in the valley his entire life. And you know I'm all for someone sticking with their
job. But Baby Girl and I spied out there just a few days ago. I know, I
know. We both have better things to do. But what's more important
than looking out after your own?

We left the house on the pretense of going to the Triple A for a map
and lodging book for North Carolina. And we did get our maps, just by
way of Dulaney Valley.

So she climbed out of my old Duster and went up to the fence
where this man was doing something with a horse and a rope, not that
a city girl like me would know his true intentions regarding that poor
beast who deserved to be running up some rocky slope with bushes
sticking out behind big boulders and all. And she leaned her arms on
the top rail, real Carole Lombard–like, and watched. Meanwhile, I sat
in the car trying to appear as normal as an old, toffee-colored woman
like me can in a gold '74 Duster in Dulaney Valley. The man never
noticed her, but some other equestrian sort walks over and strikes up a
friendly conversation. He asked what she was doing there, and she said
something and pointed to the car, and he nodded, and I waved self-
consciously, although by the time my hand was raised in a true gesture
he'd already turned around.

So I just scratched my head instead.

Baby Girl ran back to the car and said, "Hand me my camera quick, Prisma. I told him I was an art student and I wanted to take some pictures for drawing horse anatomy, and he said fine!"

So I did that, handing her the heavy old Nikkormat, same year as my Duster, she bought at a pawnshop a few days ago.

"Prisma, remind me to draw a horse picture when we get home so I can make sure I didn't lie!"

So Baby Girl took pictures, and now they're sitting at the developers waiting for pickup by none other than yours truly because, I tell you, these women around here have gone crazy! All of them interested in a man, and none of them admitting it. It's the truth. So my baby is going away to Ocean City for three days with some old high-school friends, and Mrs. Summerville decides to throw on the mantle of the overly concerned.

Last night at the supper table when I was scooping out the ice cream—caramel turtle fudge—and Baby Girl was pouring on the hot fudge, Mrs. Summerville officiated from her throne at the foot of the dining room table declaring all sorts of worrisome things about Ocean City like the yearly serial killers' convention met there in July, and wouldn't Flannery rather go up to Maine, or even down to Boca Raton?

That woman is out of touch! Imagine a group of youngsters heading to either of those places. But Baby Girl just kissed her cheek and said something like, "Grandy, you crack me up!"

So I'm left to pick up the film! Now what will Mrs. Summerville say if she discovers a roll of pictures of that man she's making a fool of herself over? That's something I don't want to think about. Asil suggested we hide them outside in the greenhouse or upstairs in his rooms over the garage, but it's too risky. The glove box of the Duster seems up to the task because Leslie Strawbridge Summerville wouldn't be caught dead in my car.

She goes riding almost every weekday now. Baking in that sun, even with those gaucho hats she wears, is a foolproof recipe for wrinkling that "magnolia skin" down to a walnut. Ha! If I weren't a Christian woman, that thought might be enjoyable. Oh well, I've got to be truthful; it already is enjoyable.

This one crept up on me, you know. Didn't see it coming at all. And a cowboy type at that. Where will this one end? The Lord only knows!

Let's just pray he never asks her out on a date, because, honest to Pete, if that happens, I may roll my eyes so far back into my head they'll never come down again.

That boy from our boat trip asked out Baby Girl. He still frequents Starbucks regularly and has always ignored her until yesterday. Then up out of the blue he saunters over and says, "How about dinner and a movie?"

"Miss Prisma," she told me later, "he just didn't seem like the dinner and a movie type to me at all."

"What type is he then?"

"Paintball and a big bucket of fries."

That child.

Today I am thankful for my son's fine marriage to Caprice. Poor baby is throwing up something awful with this pregnancy. I'm thankful for a cast-iron stomach and the spicy ribs I made Lark and me tonight! I'll get some color back in those cheeks yet. I hit the right chemical stock on the Dow Jones this month, and the tomatoes I found down at Lexington Market this afternoon...picture perfect! Got a card from my cousin in Chicago. Says the family out there is fine. They're the Italian branch. Praise God for family.

L a r k

"HELLO?"

"Is this that prayer line?"

"Yes. Can I help you?"

"I called about a year ago. Cancer."

Oh man. I could kick myself! My record book burned down with the house.

"Do you remember me?" the female voice asked.

"I'm sorry. All my records were destroyed in a fire a last month."

"Yeah, I guess you get a lot of calls, don't you?"

"Yes, I do."

"Do you want me to refresh your memory?"

"Please."

I adjusted my headset, sat down on the couch in my den, and rested my heels on the coffee table. It wasn't hard to remember her case as she went on about breast cancer and the fears of leaving three kids behind. Our personalities clicked last year, and we ended up talking about all sorts of things.

"I wanted you to know I made it through."

"Wonderful! I wondered so many times what happened."

"Yep. After I called you, it gave me the guts to ask my family and my friends to pray too."

"That's really good news. Do you have anything else you want me to pray for?"

"Do you pray for the littler things too?"

"Absolutely. I've prayed for warts before."

She laughed. "No kidding?"

"I kid you not."

"Wow. This a great thing you're doing."

"Call anytime. It's why I'm here."

"Okay. Well, if you could remember my daughter's spelling test tomorrow, I'd appreciate it. She's a little slow, it seems. Nothing major. Just has to work for it."

I sent up a prayer right away. "You know, some people just take longer to bloom than others."

"That's the truth. But prayer never hurts, right?"

"Absolutely not."

"Do you have kids?"

"A daughter."

"Will you tell me a little bit about her?"

Flannery

GET THIS! GAG GUY'S NAME IS QUIGLEY SMITH!

Quigley Smith!

I almost wet my pants when he tells me.

More surprising is the fact that I didn't even know his name when I accepted his invitation to dinner! He comes up to the bar at Starbucks as I finish my shift, looking freshly showered and shaved and smelling like Old Spice. Hey, the guy does work on a ship. He gives me this sort of lopsided grin. "I'm sorry, but I never quite got your name."

I thought, Yikes! I accepted a date with a guy whose name I don't even know? I'm losing it.

"Really."

He shakes his head. "Can you believe this? I don't think I've ever asked a girl out without knowing her name."

"So what's your name?"

"Quigley Smith. But most people call me Quig."

As I said.

Well, the Leslie Factor kicks in on some sort of etiquette autopilot. Not one mirthful sound flies out as I extend my hand. "I'm Flannery del Champ."

"Wow." He takes my hand.

"Tell me about it."

"What's your middle name then?"

"What's yours?"

"James."

"Strawbridge."

"Do you like your name?"

"Hate it."

"I hate mine."

We just stare at each other for about three seconds.

I thrust out my hand again. "Well then. Nice to meet you, James."

"It's nice to meet you...Strawbridge?" He looks more uncomfortable than the first day of Little League.

"Nah. Let's just go with Flannery."

"Okay. But you can still call me James."

"I like it," I say.

Now that, as Leslie would say, is a proper and fitting start.

"I changed my name when I was away at college," I tell him as we walked down York Road toward The Orient restaurant. "But after I graduated a few months ago, I realized that being called Fanny was worse than Flannery." I'm hoping we get on some other topic soon. The name thing is beginning to bore me, and my mind wanders. Thoughts of Grandy knitting out in her corner of the conservatory fill my head.

I have no earthly idea why she's so set on finishing that sweater so quickly. But I'll give her time. It's never fair to judge somebody's intent. It scares me though. Just a little bit. Like she's too driven regarding this thing. Why would it be so important? And the scrapbook? Oh my gosh! Never saw "scrapbook" in Grandy's repertoire!

The night has only begun as far as Quigley Smith is concerned though. There is a bucketload of hope on the horizon.

Lark

NOBODY IN THIS WORLD UNDERSTANDS how I felt about Brad. Nobody could begin to understand why it was easier for me to deny his existence than to proceed in the traditional divorced-couple manner. The first time we met I hated him. A bracy ninth grader, I accompanied my cousin to one of Mount St. Joseph's lacrosse games. My cousin, on Daddy's side of course, was a junior at that bastion of all-male Catholic secondary education. So despite Mother's disapproval of my job, I do have Catholic in my veins.

I felt like the big cheese that day.

Mother sighed her way through my first purchase of a pair of jeans with some of the Christmas money from my Summerville grandmother. One hundred dollars every Christmas. Crisp new bills. A little paper money holder decorated with snowflakes or poinsettias. The smell of fresh stationery wafting up. So I sat there in 1973, feeling spiffy and oh-so-up-to-the-minute in my flared jeans, sneakers, and a pullover orange sweater not knitted by my mother.

Never mind I had to buy them in the girls' department and not the juniors.

Mount St. Joe lagged so far behind when the second half began, no hope remained. But then, the comeback began. When one of the players scored the goal that zipped the Gaels ahead six to five, I went nuts! I jumped and cheered. I hugged my cousin. I hugged my aunt. I whirled and I whooped, because, honestly, living at Stoneleigh House, times like that happened more rarely than jazz on a harpsichord.

"Calm down. Calm down."

The voice picked at my ears from behind.

And I turned.

There a tall blond boy, wearing light blue eyes, Adidas shoes, and a brown suede fringe jacket, smirked. His good looks irked me. "Don't tell me what to do!" And words flowed like the juice from a quickly bitten, overripe peach. "Just because you think you're God's gift to women doesn't mean you can tell people what to do. Doesn't mean you can embarrass them like that especially when they finally got a stylish pair of jeans even if they did have to pay for them with their own Christmas money."

Did I say that? What a boob!

I felt my face flush.

The horn blew.

The pep band regurgitated the school song, and I sang it as loudly as I could. Daddy graduated from Mount St. Joe, so the fight song and I knew each other by the time I went to nursery school. "Purple and cream mean victory." I tried drowning out my own embarrassment.

"Oh see our colors in array."

He tapped me on the shoulder.

"Watch our team go down the field. For we are out to win today."

I ignored him. Or tried to make him think I ignored him.

"And if unto defeat we fall."

He tapped again. "Hey, girl."

"We'll be loyal just the same. And we'll fight fight team for the purple and the cream. Mount St. Joseph bless her naa-aaa-ame!"

He turned me around to face him, and he winked.

I scared myself to death.

So I turned and ran away pretending something was funny, and I laughed and laughed. Too loud. Too long. Too much like a braying ass.

"Hey!" the boy yelled.

But the more I ran, the more nauseous I became. My long ponytail swayed behind me, beating my back with the whipping it deserved.

"You have quite a singing voice!" he yelled, but I didn't turn around.

The most beautiful boy I'd ever seen had touched my shoulders.

Unfortunately, I needed a bath in Epsom salts that night as the fabric of those tight jeans had rubbed my inner thighs raw during my sprint.

"See, sweetie?" Mother said after my soak. Supported by a green, gold, and orange plaid cushion, I perched in my underwear at the edge of the window seat. "I told you tight jeans aren't a good idea."

"No, you didn't, Mother. You told me they made me look like a hoodlum."

"Same thing."

"It is not!"

"Larkspur. No back talk."

Her gentle fingers dabbed Neosporin on the rashes. Prisma, thirty pounds lighter at that time, haunted the doorway. "You all want some tea?"

"That would be lovely, Prisma." Mother finished up. "There, almost good as new."

"What about you, Lark?"

"Sure. Okay."

"I made some Congo bars."

"I'll have my tea in the den, Prisma."

Mother left. Prisma stared at me for several seconds, then swished back downstairs. And when I entered the den after shimmying into my nightshirt, there sat my tea on the coffee table in front of the couch. I picked it up with my left hand, grabbed the plate of Congo bars with my right and slipped off into the kitchen to sit with Prisma. Mother said nothing. She just reached for the remote and turned off *The Brady Bunch.*

Even now I can remember recalling Bradley's face and windblown ways. "I see the boys of summer in their ruin."

Johnny Josefowski drove me home from study group this week. In an old Jeep.

How unsafe is that?

Leslie

As if my pregnancy with Lark hadn't been exhausting enough, Newly's progressed into one of epic proportions! And poor little Lark, only four when I first became pregnant, just wandered around the house while I regurgitated in the bathroom from eight to noon. Every day for five months.

Five ghastly months!

Where did I go wrong with my daughter? I don't quite know. It's not that I'm not proud of her. She's such a good organist and did such a wonderful job raising Flannery. It's that she's not proud of me. That sounds self-centered, I know. The truth is that Lark couldn't care less whether I live or die. Why I've hidden that ridiculous heart attack of a few years ago mystifies me. For honestly, the fact that my charade remains intact speaks of a chasm split too wide for repair.

My own mama spent an hour a day with her children, you see. But Anna cared for us. Oh, how I loved Anna. Fresh off the boat from Ireland. Only seventeen when she joined our household in Charlottesville before Mama had me.

Her hair frizzed out from her head like a million wavy beams of autumn light, and her smile shone more brightly than her hair.

I never saw it coming.

Lark loves Prisma the way I loved Anna.

I never saw it coming until it was too late.

After all, Mama spent one hour a day with us. One hour. I took Lark and Newly to the park, shopping, movies, the club. I ran us all ragged on excursion after excursion. I'd have given anything for Mama to have given us that much thought.

And now that I'm old—yes, I'm old, although I'd never admit that out loud—now that I'm old, I look at my daughter and see someone lacking that indefinable essence of womanhood, that smooth confidence we should possess no matter our station. One foot in front of the other whether the path be down a golf course or the aisle of a convenience store, we wend our way through life, and though most times disquiet rests down inside, there are times we can forget about who we are and just...be.

Usually when we're trying to locate something no one else in the house can find.

Lark's never known how to just be.

Does my heart not ache? Truth to tell, it does.

I'm tired now though. More tired than when I was expecting Newly. Prisma found me asleep on the couch this morning.

"You slept here all night, Mrs. Summerville?"

"So what if I did?" I sat up, immediately ashamed of snapping at Prisma like that.

She shook her head and sat down next to me. She looked at me hard, like Daddy used to do when he caught me smoking Mama's cigarettes out the bathroom window.

She unpinned her braid from the bun at the back of her head. "If you don't tell me what's happening, Leslie, I'll start snooping."

One of the few times in my life Prisma addressed me by my first name, it snapped me to attention like an errant child. I knew I'd better confess, and honestly, who else would hear my confession?

"I've been scheduled for a stress test tomorrow."

"What else?" She wound the heavy rope of hair in a fresh knot down by the nape of her neck.

"My cholesterol is so high now, I'll bet Charles has tipped his hat to it up there."

Prisma laughed, but quickly sobered. "So the heart-smart diet hasn't helped? I'm sorry."

"I've never overeaten, Prisma. It's genetics, pure and simple."

"Still. Doesn't seem fair."

"You tell me! There you sit, more than fifty pounds overweight with arteries as slick and open as a new drainpipe, and then here I am!"

I might have sunk to the depths of self-pity just then, but Prisma patted my knee.

"Before we worry about it, let's just get the results of the test."

"I'm just so tired, Prisma."

"I know, Mrs. Summerville. I've known for a while now. I don't know how you go riding like you do."

"I make myself. To prove things."

And she took my hand.

And there we sat in my den on my floral couch for a long time, Prisma and me holding hands. Flannery's music thumped upstairs. Three ghastly songs later I said, "Prisma? I just wanted to say—"

"Don't say anything, Mrs. Summerville, 'cause you're going to be just fine."

But now I look in the mirror and I see a tired old soul staring back at me. I examine the lines that have spread like a creeping vine from the corners of my mouth and eyes to cover most of my face, and I examine the life lived inside this relaxing skin and I don't believe I've truly wasted it. But I've never really understood why I chaired charities, worked committees, and planned galas. It felt good at the time to help people. It still does.

But inside I still feel shallow and sore and filled with regret for having been alive and not really believed it. Our Anna used to quote religious sayings all the time. She'd look at us sitting in our buttons and bows, fighting and grumbling and snipping at each like mongrels as we waited for Mama to come for her hour.

"Whitewashed tombs ye are, right now! Whitewashed tombs!" And she'd waggle her finger in our faces.

Oh, Anna. Why did that take so long to sink in?

L a r k

"HELLO?"

"Lark?"

"Oh, sheesh, Bradley, I thought you'd given up."

"I just wanted to give you time to think about it all. Have you?"

"Yeah. And I thought you'd relieved me of the problem as only you could."

"It's not just going to go away, Lark."

It's not just going to go away.

IT'S NOT JUST GOING TO GO AWAY.

I squeezed the receiver. "I'll meet with you. If you can get permission from your wife, that is."

I winced. Man. And I'd been trying so hard.

"Rhonda's dead."

Feel sorry for him, Lark. At least try to act that way. "How long?"

"About a month ago."

"You didn't waste any time finding us again, did you?"

Now why say that? Why hand him that point in his favor?

"I don't know whether I've changed enough to suit you. But I can promise you I won't hurt Flannery."

"How did she die, Brad?"

"Diabetes. Her kidneys failed years ago. And the amputations started awhile back."

"And you stuck with her?"

"Yeah."

Oh my word. He wasn't making this easy.

"Did you have any kids?"

"No. She got the disease young. We didn't think it would be right to bring kids into the situation. Please, Lark. I have to see Flannery."

"What could you possibly have to offer her now, Brad?"

"Obviously nothing she hasn't been able to live without until now."

"You said that, not me."

"I won't just show up, Lark. You need to give me permission. I promise you. No surprises."

"How long were you and Rhonda married?"

"Nineteen years."

Maybe he really could keep a promise now.

And maybe I could become a supermodel.

"Can I think about it some more, Brad? Really think about it?"

"Yeah, Lark."

"Okay."

"I'm sorry it's like this."

"Yeah, me, too."

"Has it been hard, Lark?"

Oh, puh-leeze! "Sometimes. But Flannery's a great kid, Brad. She's amazing."

His silence broke my heart. Darn it.

The nausea began. "Call me in a week, okay, Brad?"

"I will. You can count on that, babe."

Yeah, somehow I knew that. I wished I didn't.

Flannery

"GUESS WHAT, UNCLE NEWLY?"

"What, Buddy?"

I adjust the handset of the phone higher up on my ear. I thought origami earrings from handmade paper would be a great idea. Not. "I've got a boyfriend. Well, at least I went out with a nice guy."

"That's lovely. His name?"

"James Smith."

"Sounds positively explorerish."

I laugh. "It does, doesn't it?"

"So what does your mother think about it?"

Mother? "Mother?"

"Yes, your mother."

"You know Mom. She tries not to micromanage."

He chuckles. "I'd best let you get back to work. Calling from Starbucks, are we?"

"Uh-huh. We is. I'm on my break."

"I'll pop in after work tomorrow night. Would you care to have supper with me?"

"Where?"

"You pick the place."

"Oh cool. Okay. I get off at six."

"See you sometime around six then."

"Cool."

Uncle Newly is so neat. Mom says he doesn't put much stock in things like faith and God, but it's like this. God puts stock in him, and you know how it is with God, you can run but you cannot hide! I hope I'm there on the day God jumps up in front of Uncle Newly and says,

"Boo!" Or maybe He'll just stroll alongside of him for a while, then tap him on the shoulder and say, "How long are you going to go on ignoring me?"

That will shock Uncle Newly. Either way, I hope I'm there when it happens because I've been praying for him for ten years now.

PRISMA

ASIL SMITZER HAS A NEW LADY LOVE!

After supper I caught him sneaking through the kitchen for some of my cold cream by the kitchen sink.

"Asil Smitzer, what on God's green earth do you think you're doing in my kitchen!" Let there be no mistake. Nobody at Stoneleigh House would dare to challenge the fact that after all these years, the kitchen belongs to me, lock, stock, and barrel, as somebody who must love guns once uttered. Maybe Mr. Eli Whitney himself! Always admired his resourcefulness.

Asil buttoned his plaid sports coat. "I ran out of hand cream is all, Mrs. Percy. You don't have to get all hot and bothered."

"Don't you be telling me what and what not to get upset about."

Let it not be mistaken that Asil Smitzer answers to me.

Then I smiled at him because any man wearing white patent-leather platform loafers and an autumn-toned plaid sports coat with brown pants, a rust-colored shirt and a white tie already has enough going against him.

"Get out of here before Mrs. Summerville finds you in the kitchen with mulch on your shoes."

He picked up a foot and looked.

"Gotcha!" I hooted. "Now, I'll walk you to the bus stop. I could use some exercise. Where you going?"

"Got a date."

I figured as much.

He pushed the kitchen door open and we walked onto the screened porch. It's been hot, even for July, and nobody but me wants to sit out here. Maybe I can entice Lark out here with some lemonade.

And some shortbread nibblers!

"So who's your date with?"

He pushed open the screen door and led me down into the courtyard in front of the garage that houses the Bentley, my Duster, and Mr. Summerville's Mercedes convertible and lawn equipment and supports Asil's apartment above. Asil and I have history. Good clean history.

He stooped down to deadhead a sweet little plant with pink balls of flowers. Never could keep up on flower names. "What's her name?"

"Jezzie."

"You going out with a woman named Jezebel?! I have heard it all!"

His warm chuckle oozed out as he stood up straight.

"And look, you got a green thumbnail now!

"Mrs. Percy, what am I gonna do with you?"

"Nothin' you'd like."

"Well, now, a man can't be blamed for admiring from afar."

"No, he can't."

"And I promised Mr. Percy before he died I'd look after you, which meant even from myself."

"You got that right."

"So you're safer than you may like to be!"

"In your dreams, Asil!"

We laughed together. Lark swears something's going on between Asil and me, and all I have to say to that is, the child isn't big on insight.

When I returned to my room after Asil hopped on the bus to pick up Jezebel, I sat down at my desk. I pulled my file box out from under the knee well and set to my Foundation work.

With Flannery seeing that James Quigley Smith again tonight, or "gag boy" as she now says with affection (don't ask me how), Lark locked in her prayer den, and Mrs. Summerville sacked out on the couch, plenty of time remains to get things done. Today I had to choose between helping the hungry in Oregon and rebuilding a burned church in South Carolina.

Lord, have mercy.

So much sin and suffering.

My shoulders feel so narrow at times like this.

I stood at my window for a while after that, waiting for the stars to appear, thinking it might just be nice to get a good view of Orion's Belt tonight. "Lord, have mercy."

"I do, Prisma. Through you."

"What should I do, Lord?"

"Pray about it, My girl."

"Pray even more, Lord?"

"You got that right. Pray even more."

So I knelt beside the bed, and I prayed, and a vision of a little church up in flames appeared behind my eyes, and within the flames children ran with Easter baskets, their many braids bouncing. Church suppers disintegrated in the heat, and a community was destroyed, leaving desolation—spiritual and physical.

"Do you see it's all the same, My girl?"

"Yes, Lord, I do."

"Feed My sheep."

And so I approved the check to Mount Zion Church of God in Christ for $100,000. And in the words of that white girl Scarlett O'Hara, I said to the sky, "Tomorrow is another day, Jesus."

I leaned on the Everlasting Arms for a while until Flannery pulled in at 1:00 A.M. hungry and tired and in need of a ham sandwich. I remembered the day Mr. Summerville told me he placed me in charge of the Foundation. He lay dying then.

Oh, God. If I remember too hard, I get sick. I said before that he was my best friend, but I want to say it again. Charles Summerville was my best friend. Let that never be mistaken.

"You're a wise woman, Prisma," he said that day.

"I try to listen to God, Mr. Summerville."

"I know. I wish I'd listened to you sooner about Jesus."

I waved my hand. "God was working on you even then. And working through you too. We can't begin to understand how and why He does what He does."

He chuckled and coughed painfully. Pneumonia had set in by then.

"Don't go trying to second-guess the past or God, Mr. Summerville. It's too late for that."

"You're right, Prisma. Would you hold my hand?"

So I did. Right away.

"I want you to take over the Foundation now. The paperwork is being drawn up."

Feed My sheep, Prisma. Feed My sheep.

"Mr. Summerville. I'm sure there are better people to run such an organization."

"Oh, financially speaking you'll have all the help you need. I want you to decide where the money goes."

"How do you know I'm the woman for the job, sir?"

He smiled again. And the nurse entered with his morphine shot.

"Will you stay until I fall asleep, Prisma?"

"You know I will, Mr. Summerville."

A simple woman with simple needs, I've been criticized by my own family for remaining here. But Stoneleigh House needs a shepherd. I'm feeding sheep, and, like the Good Shepherd, I love them and I know them by name.

And that's the truth.

Tomorrow is Leslie's stress test.

Lord, have mercy.

Lark

I'VE GIVEN UP TELEVISION. Not only does it waste time, it makes me feel horrible about myself and say all sorts of mean things about celebrity women.

I call them anorexic, which they just may be, but why throw the term around flippantly when so many regular people who will never be popular and thought beautiful suffer like that? Lollipop heads, my personal favorite (quite descriptive and heard on cable) is the second best. Then there are general adjectives like vapid, misguided, and lacking self-esteem. I can even get self-righteous and proclaim them responsible for leading teenage girls down a path to depression.

Judging?

Of course. Doomed to forever play the comparison game, though detrimental to my self-esteem, I am freed to at least realize that my nature demands it. And I have had enough of that. I want to live a life where I don't compare myself to a standard only achievable with lots of money, surgery, or expensive medications and supplements, or in those rare instances a metabolism with which King Nebuchadnezzar could have fueled the fiery furnace. So now I compare myself with the lady next to me in line at the CVS store, and usually I measure up just fine.

If on the short side.

Without the infernal tube feeding me these images, my radar screen only blips occasionally.

With these thoughts, I sat on my sofa with my craft bag. A CD played some soft piano jazz. But the shrill ring of the phone soon replaced the chuckling ivories.

I threw down my Christmas stocking and tripped over the coffee table getting to the phone.

"Hello?"

"Lark."

Drat him. Why would the man not give it up?! He jumped right into pleading his infernal case. And with his usual charm.

"Okay, Brad. I'll see you. But I'm not guaranteeing anything as far as Flannery is concerned. Do you hear me clearly?"

"That's all I ask for now."

"So will you fly over?"

"Yeah. I'm ready whenever you are."

"How about next week?"

"Okay."

"You need a ride from the airport?"

He laughed. "No. I can afford to rent a car."

I'd be seeing Bradley again. Dear Jesus.

"What band were you with anyway?"

"Feral Junket."

"No kidding? Flannery loves them."

"Really? No kidding?"

"No kidding."

"Did you have a stage name or something?"

"Yeah."

"Not a one-name thing, I hope."

"Yep, Babe. I'm known as Mole."

I wanted to laugh out loud. "How appropriate."

"Too true. Too true. Okay, well I'll see you next Friday. Would that be okay?"

"It has to be, right? Call me when you land. We'll arrange to meet somewhere. I definitely do not want you just showing up at Greenway."

"There's no telling what Leslie would do."

"I'd be more worried about Prisma if I were you."

"How is Prisma?"

God, why did You give him a voice like that?

"The same."

"That figures."

"It does, doesn't it?"

How we could suddenly be conversing like this mystified me.

"Twenty years is a long time, Lark."

Maybe that explained it. "Yeah, it is."

Good decision on the *Baywatch,* Lark, or you might have found yourself on a diet, trying to drop a few pounds before his arrival. Besides, yo-yo dieting can ruin a person's heart.

Daddy used to say, "You look just like your mother, Larkie." He was wrong. Leslie Lee Strawbridge Summerville still qualifies as a beautiful woman, one of those older beauties who nibbles on cucumber sand-wiches in high-class lunchrooms, displaying only a touch of makeup on her perfect face and understated polish on her clipped nails, one of the women who maintained good ankles, slender wrists, and the ability to wear a diamond pinkie ring on her right hand and slim gold bangles that tinkle but never clang. Women must stare at Mother and think— my gosh, if she's this pretty at that age, I can hardly *imagine* what she must have looked like at my age.

And then they stare down at their tummies and their thighs spread there on the seat and wonder how it ever came to this.

Although I do resemble my mother, somewhat, I'm a craft-fair ver-sion of her. Some kind of woodcarving of her, a carving the craftsman got a bit wrong—fashioning the torso too long for the general height, making the spread of the cheeks too wide, the legs too short, the nose a bit larger and somewhat rounder than necessary.

On their evenings out, she'd come into the playroom, clouded in diamonds and damask and French perfume. Her gentle scent preceded her shining, silken glory. The murmur of her and Daddy laughing or discussing their soon-to-be host or hostess that evening caressed my ears. My eyes anticipated their gratification as their footsteps continued down the hallway to where I sat on the floor playing with my Barbies.

My parents socialized at least two nights a week. Wearing his tuxedo, looking large and robust and pink, Daddy would usher her into the room. Not corpulent until well into his fifties, he had an almost Hollywood quality about him. Not the new Hollywood, but the old Hollywood, the smooth, suave, don't-mess-with-me Hollywood. Sport-ing a double-edged Martini. That was my father.

But I couldn't take my eyes from Mother. She always pulled her dark hair back in a braided chignon, or up in a French twist, and she applied a minimal amount of makeup, saving for the bright lipstick that embroidered her lips against the flawless velvet of her skin.

"Where you going tonight?" I asked on my sixth Christmas Eve. Newly was already down for the night.

Mother patted my shoulder and leaned down on her haunches to hug me. "To the Christmas Eve party at the Hendrickses' home."

"As usual." Daddy rolled his eyes. "I keep telling your mother we need to have our own celebration, Lark-honey."

"As soon as Newly's old enough." Mother stood straight to her feet. "I can't imagine him being around guests at this stage."

Daddy caught my gaze as Mother smoothed her hair by the mirror. The sadness in his eyes soothed my heart. "I'm sure Santa will still come even if we get home late."

"But it's sad to have Christmas Eve by myself."

"What about Prisma and Jimmy?" Mother asked.

I just shrugged. But inside I looked forward to decorating the Percy tree in their sitting room, drinking hot chocolate made with half-and-half, and singing Christmas carols to Asil's blues guitar. You should hear "Bring a Torch, Jeannette Isabella" spattered with major sevenths and flatted ninths.

The following year they hosted the party at Stoneleigh House.

Mother still casts the same general appearance, only the hair glints silver and the skin softly rests on her cheekbones now. She still wears perfectly fitting garments and freshly polished shoes. Never a hair out of place.

I'm sure she often wonders where I came from.

The front doorbell rang at half past eleven. I sprang from my sofa and almost collided with Prisma. "I'll get it, Prisma."

"Suit yourself. I'm pooped." And she spun around and disappeared back into her quarters.

I yanked open the door to find Johnny Josefowski standing there on the stoop.

Doctor Johnny Josefowski.

It horrified me.

There I stood in the doorway in a pair of Flannery's ragged sweat-pants, rolled up at my ankles, mind you, and a T-shirt proclaiming me a "Brat."

How humiliating, and why in the world would Flannery wear one of those Brat T-shirts anyway?

"Care to go for a walk?" he said, the yellow bulb of the door light illuminating him there in his scrubs.

"This late?"

He shrugged. "I was on my way home from the hospital and felt keyed up. Had an emergency surgery."

"I don't know. It's so late. And there are all sorts of things—"

"I'll protect you."

Our eyes locked.

"What kind of surgery?"

"Multiple bypass and valve stuff."

"Ever done a transplant?"

"Sure."

Well, I guess he deserved my trust. I guess he could get me around the block and back. "Only for a little bit though. I don't want to miss too many calls."

"Oh yeah. Marsha told me about your prayer line. I think that's great."

"I sure get some doozies."

"I'll bet."

"Let me get my shoes on. You want to come in for a sec?"

"Sure."

I escorted him into the living room. "Have a seat."

"No thanks. I'll just wait on my feet. That a picture of your parents?"

Mom smiled in Dad's arms at some party at the Belvedere. "Yeah."

"Your father passed away Marsha said."

"About ten years ago."

"You miss him?"

See, I rarely talk about my dad to anyone. I think about him all the time, but talking about him is an entirely different process. I

think my slow descent really began when Daddy died. "I really miss
him."

Suddenly Johnny's age seemed extremely appealing.

"I'll go put on my shoes."

"Okay."

I ran up to my room and tied on a pair of sneakers I bought at CVS
for $3.99. Then I hurried to Prisma's door and knocked. She cracked it
open. "Who was it?"

"That cardiologist."

"You're kidding!"

"Nope. We're going out for a walk."

"At this hour?"

"Just thought you'd want to know."

"You got that right."

And then she just shut the door. But as I walked away I heard her
mutter, "Thank you, Jesus!"

I walked in to find Johnny examining the other pictures on the
back of the piano. He had taken off his glasses and leaned over for closer
inspection. He popped back to a fully standing position and pointed to
the organ. "That's a beauty! Your parents bought that for you?"

"Uh-huh. When I was sixteen. A guy came over from Austria to set
it up and everything."

"H'm." He shook his head, looking confused.

"What?"

"Well. It just doesn't seem to fit."

"What do you mean?"

"Your parents look like charming people, loving parents."

"They were."

"H'm."

I felt a little bristly. "You're wondering how they could have sired a
nut case like me?"

"You are…unusual, but you're not a nut case, Lark."

"Yes, I am."

"No, you're not. I've seen bona fide nut cases."

Oh my word! I had forgotten about his mother! I'm such an idiot.
Such a self-centered moron! "I'll take your word for it."

"Ready to walk?"

Anything to get out of this room. "Uh-huh."

He opened the front door for me.

I had to admit I felt an attraction toward him. He possessed a confidence like Brad's. Only without Brad's innate cockiness. Although something about a bon vivant case of fun-loving arrogance such as Brad sported appealed to me as well.

Johnny maintained a quiet for a minute or two. The silence allowed me to compare him to Brad. How different this walk felt from anything I experienced with Brad. With Brad it was always go, go, go.

Well, one time it wasn't like that. Just one time. Stranded in a sudden, terrific storm, we sat under the side porch of an old historic mansion he'd taken me to see. Two frogs hid in the stream of a rushing rainspout, and he waxed eloquent about growing old with someone you could count on, someone as much of a frog as yourself. I fell in love with him.

After the St. Joe lacrosse game, I didn't see Brad again for a few years, despite my new status as a devoted Gaels fan. I had just finished the eleventh grade when his family joined our country club. There I swam in my sleek, red, racing-back Speedo swim-team suit with the white stripes down the sides, doing jackknife dives and flips and stupid poses off the high board with my then-best friend Elizabeth Waters, when I noticed him sitting by the pool in blue jeans and biker boots.

At a country club.

Cool.

Of course, at the peak of my swan dive, my eyes caught his for a split second and for some reason unknown to me I experienced enough presence of mind to flip over and pound down the best watermelon of my life in the exact direction of his chair, with a splash the trajectory of which surely soaked him clear through to his underwear.

And Bradley del Champ just laughed and laughed, whipped his shaggy wet hair out of his eyes and jumped into the deep end and dunked me good.

The lifeguard kicked him out of the compound. The guard's smug set to his jaw, the flash of his brown eyes told me that yes, indeed, weeks of sitting there twirling his whistle finally led to some real action. I saw "Security Guard" in his future.

I hurried to the fence to witness what transpired out in the parking lot.

"It was worth it!" he hollered to me as I stood there with my fingers bent at the first knuckle around the heavy wire chain link. I watched him climb into his little mustard MG—the only portion of him that bespoke his lineage.

And I just laughed and laughed.

"Sing for me again, pretty girl!" he cried.

And I waved him off.

And how many years ago was that?

And how different could Johnny and Brad be?

The silence swelled around the good doctor and me as if we'd suddenly been stuck inside a ham or something.

I turned to Johnny. "I'm sorry if this is awkward."

"Awkward?"

"Yeah. I mean I'm not much of a conversationalist."

"Lark, awkward is hardly this. You want awkward? You should see some of the surgeries I've performed. You'd be surprised at how many people actually wake up in the middle of an operation."

"Are you kidding me?"

"Yep."

"That was not nice."

"I know."

He smiled at me as we just walked along with our hands in our pockets, enjoying the breeze of nighttime. When he dropped me off twenty minutes later at the porch door, he said, "Hey, I'll say a prayer for your mom."

"Well, thanks."

"Yeah, well, I noticed she's on for a stress test tomorrow at the hospital, and I figured you must be worried too."

"Yeah."

Worried? A stress test? Oh my word! I'm going to kill her. But I tried to smile. "Thanks for the walk."

"Sure, Lark. I'll see ya."

"Yeah."

I hurried up to my room.

Leslie

I SNAPPED ON THE KITCHEN LIGHT around midnight. I just couldn't sleep with tomorrow looming so close. In a week August will hit. Where did the summer go? I wanted to do so much with Larkspur and Sweet Pea. At least I'm halfway to finishing Larkspur's sweater. So far she suspects nothing.

"Prisma?" I called. Voices ring so in dark kitchens.

She poked her head out of her door. "Yes, Mrs. Summerville?"

"You all set for tomorrow?"

"Of course. And Asil will bring the car around bright and early. If you want a snack you'd better eat one now."

"No thank you. Well, maybe a cup of tea."

"I'll get it for you."

"Oh no. I'll do it myself."

"Suit yourself, Mrs. Summerville."

She closed the door to her room and I stood in the kitchen, my gaze circling around the cabinetry that bordered the room. I had no idea where she kept the teacups. And what about the stove? Should I have to light it with a match first?

I clicked the switch and went upstairs to bed.

PRISMA

"I DIDN'T WANT TO DO THAT, LORD. We both know that woman cannot make a cup of tea."

"Don't take one to her, My girl. I've got plans for Leslie Summerville."

Hope filled my bosom. "You do, Lord?"

"I do. Did you think she was beyond hope?"

Shame on me.

Leslie

GOOD HEAVENS! I expected the Grim Reaper to walk in any minute! Is that any way to see if someone has heart problems, to try to kill them? Flannery volunteered her Nikes for the ordeal, but foolish me said, "Oh no, no. My Grasshoppers will be just fine."

Foolish, foolish woman.

And then I climbed down from the infernal contraption, changed back into my clothes, and thought to myself, "What's worse? Walking on that thing, or putting my nice pantsuit back on not having bathed first?"

I voiced that to Prisma, who sat there in the waiting room reading one of those corny religious digest things. "Well, Mrs. Summerville, I'd say the fact that you were capable of even thinking something like that shows you're not as bad off as you thought."

"Oh, really?"

"Yes, really."

"Well."

So Prisma says, "Let's go for a little drive, why don't we? It's still early."

I rummaged through my pocketbook for my lipstick. If I were really in such good shape I'd have remembered to retouch them in the changing room and not put on a makeup demonstration right there in the waiting room. "Where do you want to go?"

"I was thinking of going over the Bay Bridge."

"That's quite a drive."

"I know. The last thing you need is to go home and feel sorry for yourself."

I gave her my best glare, but inside, I knew she was exactly right. Not that I'd ever say that out loud! Good heavens, no. "That's twaddle, Prisma, but I'm too exhausted to argue."

We had a lovely time lunching together in a little inn overlooking the Bay. Asil smoked cigarettes out in the parking lot, which embarrassed me to no end for some reason. My emotions swim right up at the surface these days, and I hate it.

Tonight at supper Flannery forked up some of Prisma's sauerkraut and stabbed a bite of crown roast of pork with it. She knew about the test, somehow, but I determined to stay my course and say as little as possible. Prisma swore she hadn't said a thing, and I believe her. She hasn't lied to me yet.

"So what's next now that the treadmill thing is done?" Flannery asked.

I eyed my salad with an emaciated piece of grilled tuna placed on top. Bless Prisma's heart, she tried to arrange everything prettily, but it was still a salad. "What do you mean, Sweet Pea?"

"At the doctors'. What's next?"

"How should I know?"

"You mean you didn't ask?"

"Well, now, why should I?" I set down my fork. "We don't pay them so that we can take care of ourselves, now do we? I think I handled it all quite well, and I'm sure everything is just fine."

Prisma brought in a small boat of some thinned out, vinegary dressing. I'd never really cared for blue cheese, creamy varieties of dressing, but now that I can't have them...well! "Mrs. Summerville, the medical establishment isn't what it used to be."

"You said it, Miss Prisma!" Flannery sipped her water.

"They don't answer to the patient anymore; they answer to the insurance companies."

"Oh, fiddle!" I said. And then wondered where that word came from. I hadn't said "fiddle" in forty years!

Flannery and Prisma laughed themselves silly.

"I'll call the cardiologists tomorrow," said Prisma.

Lark entered the dining room and slid into her chair, placing her napkin on her lap just so. "Sorry I'm so late, Mother. Some lady called and was reaming me out because my prayers 'didn't work.'" Lark sighed, and my heart broke for her. "What do you say to that?" she said.

I huffed inside. Treating my daughter like that, when she gives of her time so faithfully! Who did that woman think she was? Probably some no-good from West Vir—

Oh, stop it, Leslie.

Fiddle, fiddle, fiddle!

Why I learned so little from Charles when he was alive is beyond me. Talk about a content person. That trip to the treadmill gave me a lot of food for thought as I stepped lively and waited for my life to flash before my eyes at any moment.

I lay on the couch, two sofa pillows beneath my head. *Law & Order,* my favorite show, aired, and I felt so mad at myself because I just couldn't seem to stay awake.

"Mother?"

Lark must have entered the room while I dozed. "Yes, Larkspur. Oh, that's a pretty shirt." She had changed into a blouse with poet sleeves.

"Thanks."

"Is that new?"

Oh my stars! The eleven o'clock news just ended?

"Uh-huh. Flannery picked it up for me at the mall today. They actually had a clearance rack, 80 percent off."

Inside my mama was screaming, Don't talk about prices and purchases.

"That's a good deal."

"Yeah. I feel a little silly in this thing though."

"Oh no! It suits your artistic nature, dear. You look like you did when you first started playing in that band."

Did I really say that?

She sat down on one of the plush chairs near the sofa, setting down her prayer-line phone headset. "I tried to catch you earlier today, but you were asleep. And then I went to practice at St. Dominic's. Prisma told me you were doing fine though."

"Yes. It was a lovely day."

"You feel all right?"

"Of course I do."

"Was it tiring? The stress test, I mean."

"Good heavens, Larkspur, stop asking so many questions. I'm fine! I still want to know how you found out about it."

Without another word she kissed my forehead and left the room.

I do my best to try to keep from worrying her. I think I am succeeding. But one never knows with Lark.

Truth to tell? More and more each day I feel like the dodo bird. The last of a dying breed. And you know, who really misses the dodo bird these days anyway?

Tomorrow I'm calling all my committees and telling them I'm taking a sabbatical from charity work until after the Christmas holidays. I'll blame it on Lark and Flannery and their move back home. The ladies will remember the fire and feel sorry for me. "Of course, dear. Your family needs you," they will say. And I'll say, "Yes, they do."

And I'll wish to goodness that was the truth.

L a r k

WELL, LORD, SHE'S SHUT ME OUT AGAIN. For a few days I've thought maybe we could come to some kind of understanding. I was even foolish enough to think these health difficulties might have been a vehicle to bring us closer. Guess not.

I can already hear You saying it's up to me to reach out. But she's the mother, Lord. She's the mother! I know, I know, she doesn't know You like I do, and I've got to remember to be compassionate.

I remember a sermon I heard on television once. The pastor said, "You're the only Bible some people will ever read." So, if that's the case, then things don't look good for my poor mother! If I'm her Bible, then...

Oh, God. Oh, God. I hate feeling so tortured all the time. I really do. A little peace, Jesus, a little peace. Help me not to worry so much about returning to my vomit. Help me to put it all behind me. But isn't that what I've done, put it all behind me? And now I'm back here. Back on Greenway.

And I have no idea if I'll ever garner the courage to leave.

Johnny Josefowski called me just as I turned on my CD player, gearing up for the evening calls. Just wanted to know how I was doing and said he was looking forward to study group next week and how about going out after mass one Sunday for lunch or something? I said, "Where to?"

"Someplace close. I promise."

"You sure you won't get me into the car and the drag me all the way down Route 40 or something?"

"I really do promise, Lark."

"Well, yeah then. Okay."

Gosh, I'd been doing so well. No ants for over a week. And now, they swarmed under every square inch of skin.

Help me, Jesus. Help me to do this.

I sat down at the organ and played and played. And after who knows how long, I turned around to find Mother and Prisma on the couch.

"Well, Prisma," Mother said. "I just got a little taste of heaven. You?"

"You know it, Mrs. Summerville. You know it."

"You feel better, dear?"

I nodded. "I do."

Flannery

I'M SITTING HERE IN THE QUIET OF ST. DOMINIC'S watching Mom play. To tell the truth, I did feel a little guilty when she said I never came to church with her. And, you know, she's always been supportive of my art, the least I can do is show up at church every once in a while to hear her play.

If she only knew what a special woman she is.

Get this! Grandy got a call from Jake the other day! I answered the phone, and it went like this.

"Hello?" That's me talking.

"Yes ma'am. Is Mrs. Summerville there?"

"Which one?"

"Well." And you could hear his discomfort. "Uh, the uh, the uh—"

"Older one?" I supplied, holding back guffaws.

"I suppose that might describe her, although…"

Weren't cowboys supposed to be men of few words?

Ha! This was great!

But I had mercy. "I'll get her for you."

"Thanks."

And do you know what? Grandy shooed me out of the room. Just shooed me right out! I loved it.

So the service is ending. I'm at the eleven o'clock mass, so I can try to convince her to go out for lunch.

She sure looks nice though. Her hair is actually back in a bun and not one of those puffball, Midwest ponytails she usually puts it in. And she's got that poet shirt on with a new black skirt. I said to her this morning when I gave it to her, I said, "Mom, I found this skirt the other day. It's no-iron too."

She took it from me. "You think? I mean I'm used to a fuller skirt."

I sat down on her window seat. "You know, a slim silhouette makes you seem taller. And black does too."

"Really?"

She pulled off her pajama bottoms, and I almost gasped at the sight of her in her underwear. I had no idea she'd gotten so thin. Oh, Lord, I prayed. You've got some work to do on this one!

She pulled it over her hips.

It's a size two. And that makes me, Miss Size Ten, absolutely sick. But hey, I'm healthy, right?

"Do you think that new blouse would go?"

"Absolutely."

And now, as she's finishing the postlude, I'm admiring my handiwork. She actually let me do that bun in her hair. Although when I tried to clip in one of my little butterfly barrettes, she drew the line.

She's closing up the organ now, and look, there's a man coming up to her. A really big, older guy, sort of a Santa Claus fellow wearing a polo shirt and jeans.

She's opening the organ back up, and he whispers something in her ear, and she starts playing "Charleston."

Well, what do you know!

I just sit and drink it all in. It's not like a lemonade on a cold day, this. It's like that first sip of hot chocolate after a day of chopping wood in the cold forest.

We sit together at the 3 B's. Me and Mom and her new friend Johnny Josefowski. See, I was right when I said earlier that she had a crush on him. She's blushing and this little curled piece of hair has escaped her bun and grazes her chin.

She looks like a woman. My gosh. My mother actually looks like a woman.

On the way home, she's apologetic. "I'm sorry if that bored you, Flannery."

"Are you kidding? I loved it."

"Really?"

"Oh, Mom. You really don't get it, do you?"

She looked out her car window and said, "I guess not."

Lark

TUESDAY MORNING I EXAMINED MY FACE in the bathroom mirror. I used to live such an exciting and different life, back before Brad left, not this boring, eccentric existence I inhabit now. Some eccentrics are labeled that due to their exciting, highly unusual lifestyles. Others are labeled that due to their static existence, their set-in-my-ways manners, their fears, their escapes into weird-dom, or religion, or string art.

Grabbing the scissors from out of the medicine cabinet, I pulled on an overgrown piece of hair. Why do I examine my face like I do? I remind myself of one of those gardening-type ladies with scraped-back hair, the kind who like herb farms, salt ware, and New England, and support the local children's theater.

"Mom!"

Flannery stood behind me.

"Don't!"

"Don't what?"

"Don't cut your own hair anymore."

"I do just fine at it."

She lifted a particularly shaggy portion. "You call this fine?"

Didn't she realize she was committing the unpardonable sin of the beauty world? "It's acceptable."

"Acceptable? Is that all you want from your hair? Acceptable?"

"Well, no, but—you know, you're getting a little disrespectful."

Let's nip this all right in the bud.

"Nice try. How about if I do it for you?"

"Flannery, you don't know how to cut hair."

"I did it for girls in the dorm all the time."

"Really?"

"Uh-huh. You'd be surprised at the spending money you can make doing stuff like that." She closed the lid on the toilet and reached under the sink for a pair of bona fide haircutting scissors.

"Where in the world did you get those?"

"Bought them at college. And I color hair too."

"But you don't have a license!" As a former nail artist, I knew you needed a license to do anything.

"Not at school, Mom. People are glad for a cheap haircut. It's not like they're going to report you to the state or something."

"But I don't want a real haircut."

"Look at how uneven it is."

I crossed my arms. "So you've been examining my head, I see."

"Ever since I got home from school. Now sit down and stop arguing. I know what I'm doing."

"How short are you going to cut it?"

"I'm just trimming, okay. Shoulder length would suit you. Long hair on short women makes them look even shorter."

How did she know all this stuff?

"And…it will still be long enough to put back in a bun."

"I usually wear it in a ponytail."

"It will be gorgeous if you used some gel and hair sparkles and pull it back, Spanish-like. I'll even make you a black snood."

"A snood?"

"Think of how much easier that will be."

"I don't care about easy, Flannery."

I lied. I hated any time I spent on doing hair. Why fight her like this?

"As Grandy would say, it looks quite 'ghastly' hanging around your face. Especially the way you wear it during the day with that grade-school headband."

"Ghastly? Oh, come off it, Flannery. Ghastly is a bit strong, isn't it?"

"If the description fits." Flannery raked her fingers through my hair, then began snipping at the ends. "Actually, I'll stop by the beauty supply place tonight, and I can give your hair a nice frosting to cover your gray. It would look beautiful with some lights running along the strands."

"Oh, Flannery."

"Come on, Mother—"

Mother. Crud. The formal M word. I had good as lost this one.

She combed from the front of my head to the back. "You really need to get with it here, Mom."

Where did she learn to be so headstrong?

Ha-ha!

"Okay. I know when I'm beat. Next thing you know, you'll be giving me a complete makeover."

"That's another thing. We've got to go shopping and get you some more clothes. You've hardly bought anything since the fire. And then there's the good doctor to consider."

I snatched the scissors out of her hand. "No thanks then. If I wanted a makeover, I'd have asked for one."

"But, Mom, you're so pretty! Why won't you let yourself look more attractive?"

"I don't have the time. And I don't have the time for this."

Not a bit put off, my daughter. "Everybody has time for a haircut. And getting some new clothes is something you need to do. Since you've got a clean slate, you might try wearing something other than those depressing polyester clothes the fire destroyed. Sheesh, I bet the flames literally sought out those gaggy clothes on behalf of the fashion world."

"Gaggy clothes?" Honestly, I don't know why I acted so offended. Of course they were gaggy clothes. They were 100 percent polyester, had elastic waistbands and fabric-covered buttons. I'd just never thought of them as gaggy before.

"Yes. Please, Mom? Please let me do your hair today. I'll run to Sally's right now and get the stuff. Let me help perk you up. Please?"

"I honestly don't have the time right now, Flannery. Let's do it this weekend, okay?"

"Promise?"

"I guess so." I was actually relieved she didn't ask what activity was so pressing today. Because I didn't have a good answer.

"No. Not I guess so, Mom. Either you promise or you don't."

I didn't quite know what to say. I guess I'd become used to life as the polyester Flair witch.

"Please?"

Oh, Flannery.

I nodded. "Okay."

"Saturday morning?"

"Okay."

"Maybe we can go even shopping for a Wonderbra next week."

"Now that is going too far, Flannery."

"Oh, Mom, you're such an easy target." She ran out of the bathroom. "I've got to go tell Prisma! She'll be so excited."

Oh, Jesus, my Jesus, what have I let myself get into? And am I really as dismal looking as my daughter suggests?

No woman wants the fact confirmed that they've let themselves go. But maybe Flannery made a valid point. Dressing plain and cheap all the time can't be good for a woman. We all need to live a little every once in a while.

Right?

PRISMA

I CAN'T BELIEVE MRS. SUMMERVILLE actually asked that horsefly over for a good home-cooked meal. On a Thursday night.

"You should see where he lives, Prisma. Horrible."

"You've seen it, Mrs. Summerville?"

"Well, I had a headache and he just took me up for some aspirin, and why in the world do I need to explain myself to you, Prisma Percy?"

"Oh, I'm not the one you need to explain anything to." And I swiveled back to the stove and grumbled. "Bringing a strange man to Greenway."

"It's my home and I'll bring anyone I like into it."

"H'm."

"M'm."

Leslie

OF COURSE LARK BEGGED OUT OF DINNER TONIGHT, and Flannery is working, so it will be just Jake and myself. But what to wear? Caught somewhere between dazzling him and not wanting to scare him off either, I finally decided on a black pantsuit that ties around the waist, with a cream-colored shirt. A simple ponytail with a tortoiseshell clip, and I deemed the reflection before me presentable. At my age it's all I can hope for.

Prisma outdid herself despite her disgust at the entire situation.

Leg of lamb, fresh peas, red bliss potatoes, and for dessert, this caramel truffle affair that sent me right over the moon. Earlier, when I saw Prisma preparing it, I gasped. "Can I eat that?"

"You shouldn't. But every once in a while won't hurt, will it, Mrs. Summerville? And let's face it, men love to see a woman with a healthy appetite."

"They do?"

"Oh yes. Nothing worse to a man then listening to a woman go on and on about her diets and all. Fork it in. That's what they like!"

"I never knew. And don't say, 'You don't know much, Mrs. Summerville,' or I'll pop you one!"

We laughed and laughed.

Jake and I drank more coffee out on the porch. Despite the heat. "You clean up real well," I laughed.

"Well, thanks, ma'am."

No Western accent here. He's a Maryland boy. They say ma'am here, too.

Then we discussed about the only thing I soon realized we had in common. Horses.

And after the stress test and all, I realized that a lot more important things in life defined me, and the rest of the evening bored me silly.

What had I been thinking? Honestly, if I was going to get that sweater for Lark finished by Christmas, the night would have been better spent knitting.

He left around nine, and I sauntered into the kitchen to sit with Prisma.

"Well?" She dried the sink. "Was I right?"

"I hate to admit it."

"You just liked his earthiness."

"You got that right." I rolled my tongue around Prisma's dialect for the first time in my life and loved it.

Prisma and I laughed together, shaking our heads.

Lark

JOHNNY JOSEFOWSKI, MD, KNOCKED ON MY DOOR around 10 P.M. looking wiped out. "Hello, Lark. How are you?"

What was he doing here again? Wow.

"Fine." Too bad I didn't let Flannery do my hair. What an idiot you are, Lark. "Are you okay? You look a little peaked. Can I get you a cup of tea or something?"

"I could use a cup of tea."

"Tough day in surgery?"

"Yes."

"Wow. I don't know how you do that, day after day."

"It's like playing the organ." He shrugged. "Just think of it as a different kind of performance."

"At least my songs don't draw blood."

"There is that."

"Come on back to the kitchen."

Prisma walked by. "My, my!" And kept on walking to her room.

What else could I say except, "How do you take your tea?"

"Milk and sugar."

For some reason that surprised me. Weren't heart surgeons Spartan people with little regard for those comfy extras? Although he was chubby. He must have seen my eyebrows rise as I held open the flip-flop door because he felt it necessary to explain. "My grandparents on my mother's side were from England. We all take our tea that way."

"Have a seat."

He scraped out a freshly painted red chair and sat down. "Wow, I like this kitchen!"

"Hasn't changed for years. Prisma won't let us do a thing in here."

"Was that Prisma who just walked by?"

"Uh-huh. Technically she's the housekeeper. But in all reality, she's the heartbeat of the Summervilles."

"You sure about that?"

"Oh, definitely."

"H'm."

"You and those 'h'ms,' Johnny."

I put a filled kettle on the stove. "You look nice."

"Staff meeting."

"So your surgery was earlier then?"

He eased his rear end down to a more comfy position. "Early. Emergency around 2 A.M. And then I just got busy and realized I should have come down earlier. I'm sorry I'm barging in so late."

An apologetic doctor. So was I on *Candid Camera* or something?

"So how's your mom coming along?" he asked.

"Fine, I guess. She hasn't said much. She's one of those private people. Who's her doctor, again?"

"Dr. Medina. He's in my group."

"Really? So then maybe you could keep an eye on things? Leslie never tells me anything."

"You call her Leslie?"

"Not to her face."

"I see."

I'm sure you do, I thought. The kettle screamed, and I poured the tea.

We sat in silence for a while, and then I asked if he wanted to watch a movie. He said sure, and so I turned on the television and found a movie called *Tremors,* and we laughed ourselves sick!

Two hours later I watched him go. He waved with a tired hand. You know something magical exudes from fingers like that. Fascinating in and of themselves, they perform miraculous wonders every day. Those fingers touch human hearts on a regular basis.

Human hearts!

Does he realize how blessed he is? I don't know. It took a lot of work for him to get there. Makes me wonder if his own accomplishments deprive him of the blessings of his very work.

He sure seems like a nice guy though.

Wonder why he never married?

There must be a major flaw tucked underneath there somewhere.

That thought actually encouraged me. Maybe there was hope for me yet. But Bradley was coming. In three days he'd fly into Baltimore, and then what?

I ran to the bathroom.

Flannery

I LOVE JAMES.

Is that like the weirdest thing or what? Here I'm thinking he is this total yuck, and he ends up really being anything but gag. I can hardly believe it.

He works on that skipjack on the weekends because he loves the sea! Is that romantic or what? He's already got his degree in marine biology and spent a bucketload of summers training dolphins ("Not dolphins, Flannery, porpoises") at amusement parks. Said he dated some of those variety-show dancers, but nothing serious since his freshman year of college.

He's twenty-four, and he works with the porpoises down at the National Aquarium.

"So what's with all the piercings?" I asked him during our second date when we finally got off the name thing and talked about our ambitions. We hadn't quite made it to family. I love my family, but let's face it, we're oddballs.

"Just stupid, I guess. You know how there are people like you artistic types who have a concrete way of expressing things? Then there's my type, who has so much inside trying to come out, and no good way to express it. So I do stupid things like piercing."

"A little does go a long way though."

"Tell me about it!"

"Do you ever feel kind of stupid? Like superficial or something?"

"Sometimes. But when you don't have talent, like you do, it's got to come out somewhere."

"Wow."

"Most people never think of it like that."

"I guess not. It wouldn't have dawned on me."

"And it might just be that way with me. I can't speak for everyone."

"Yeah. I know a lot of kids up at art school that look just like you."

"And here I thought I was unique." He gave me a slow wink.

Oh man! My stomach rolled in butter at the sight of that!

We sat in the food court at Towsontowne Centre drinking a cup of Gloria Jean's Kenya roast, and I kept hoping my boss wouldn't walk by. "Do you think you'll ever take some of those earrings out?"

He shrugged. "Give me a reason to."

Did he mean literally, right then and there, just fork out a reason? Or did he mean it figuratively, like, "I'd do it for you, you gorgeous hunk o' woman, if you take this relationship and run with it."

So I just said, "I think I need a little more cream."

When I sat back down, the sight of him sitting there, slouched low in the wooden chair, callous hand curled around the paper cup, touched me deeply. I can't describe it other than that feeling I got when Mom read me *I'll Love You Forever* for the first time.

We didn't talk much about our families then. But we did talk about God. I told him I loved Jesus, and he said he went to mass every Sunday morning.

"Wanna come with me to my church one night?" I asked. "The younger-type service is on Saturday evenings."

"You trying to convert me or something?"

"Nope. I'll go to mass with you the next morning just so you know I'm not."

He smiled. Oh man! There went my heart again.

Over the likes of pierced-boy.

I can't believe it. I'm telling you, this is just too weird!

Prisma caught us in the back garden tonight. She walked out with some food for the bird feeder, and I could see her out of the corner of my eye as James and I started to kiss.

And old Prisma turned right back around, waving a hand over her head. But she caught the screen door right before it hit her on the butt.

What do I say about this man? Well, I love him. Pure and simple. He does something to me, inside and out.

We sweetly kissed until the sun went down with the red rage of the star it really is.

I've been meaning to ask him about his sexual past and figure the conversation should be soon. If he's been all over town, I might want to call this thing quits before it goes too far. I mean, I'm not foolish enough to expect to go where no woman has gone before with this guy, but I'm hoping he's done it with no more than he can count on one hand.

Will he be shocked to find out I'm still a virgin! Mom's solitude after marrying young and then Daddy dying and all is enough to scare any girl away from frivolous sexual encounters! Not to mention that *Top Gun* scene too. Gag me.

But in all honesty, disappointing God like that means more than anything else. Jesus died for enough sins, unmarried sex included, but I try to do all I can to take care of some of them myself. A lot of people look at Christ's blood and say, "Well, it will cover this one too." And then jump right into whatever it is they want to do. And I do that too, sometimes. But this is a big one. This is one that matters to a lot of people, chiefly, the little ones I hope to come out of a clean womb someday.

The good thing is, if he's very promiscuous, and with my luck he will be, he'll dump me when he realizes I'm not an easy conquest.

And man, is that going to hurt.

Some girls think being a good girl is cowardly. But believe me—*believe* me—nothing is further from the truth. You have to learn to speak up, to speak out, to cull the jerks from the gems, and you have to do it year after year after year until the right one comes along and you decide you want to keep him around for good.

Lark

I located him on the Internet with Prisma.

Sitting next to me, her face lit up in the ray of morning sun piercing the window glass, Prisma cocked her head back to examine the picture through her reading glasses. "That's him all right, baby."

She took a sip of her morning coffee.

"I know."

I took a sip of my morning tea.

"He looks pretty much the same, doesn't he? Only older."

"Yeah."

"Lot more wrinkled than you are, baby."

"You think so?"

"Oh yes. Most definitely."

"Do you think he'll recognize me?"

"Uh-huh. You may have lost your curves, but your face looks just the same. Make sure you do up your hair and makeup though."

Even a wacko like me knows better than to evoke his pity, to tip him off as to my sorry existence, to let him think the years have been as hard on me as they really have.

"And wear something pretty. But not too fancy. You don't want him to think you went way out of your way."

"Don't worry, Prisma. I'm practicing before I meet him."

"He meeting you at the church?"

"Yeah."

"Well, all right then! I'd say you're putting the situation right where it should be. At God's house."

I shrugged. "I don't have too much to hang a hat on these days. I might as well make the most of what I've got."

"You've got more than you think you do, baby, so stop whining."

Yeah, yeah. She's right, of course. I've just been feeling sorry for myself for so long I'm not quite sure how to get out of it. "I know."

"No, you don't."

I pointed to the screen. "Click on that link. It shows those thumbnail pictures closer up."

She did.

"Hey, you're getting good with that mouse, Prisma."

"Don't I know it! Girl, I am a cyber queen!"

I'm sure Flannery's definition for "cyber queen" meant something quite different!

Bradley's face filled the monitor. Blue eyes pulsating with that life, that optimism that filled my heart years ago.

"He's still cute, isn't he?"

"Yeah, baby, he is."

My stomach soured. "I'm scared to death."

"I know you are. Do you have any idea what you're going to do with him?"

"None."

Prisma put an arm around me. "I didn't think you did, baby."

"Do I let him see Flannery?"

"That's the big question. And I don't have an answer for it."

"I guess I'll just have to wait and see, won't I?"

"You got that right."

Prisma flicked a glance at her wristwatch. "You want some breakfast?"

"That would be nice."

"Cereal with fruit?"

"Okay. Then I'd better get into the bath."

We shuffled into the kitchen together.

"Sort of like getting ready for the prom?" Prisma poured us both some tea.

"Oh my word, Prisma. Let's hope not!"

Sitting at the table, I pulled my Christmas stocking project out of the craft bag Prisma bought me to tote it around.

"Let me see, baby," she said.

I handed it to her.

"Pretty. You like it?"

"It's all right, I guess. I have to wonder if I'm going to get it done in time for Christmas though."

"Oh, you will. Especially if you want to give it as a gift."

"Now who am I going to give it to?"

"As if you don't know! I tell you the truth, Larkspur Summerville. You can be thick as a brick."

"Have you and Father Charlie been talking?"

"Why? Did he call you thick?"

"I think he might have used the word *dense.*"

"I knew I liked that man!"

Leslie

"MOTHER?"

"Newly?"

Newly?!

"Newly? Are you all right?"

He chuckled. "Yes, Mother. Flannery called me."

"Oh my stars."

"Were you ever going to tell me about the stress test?"

"No."

"Well, at least you're honest."

"Oh no. Not always. I lied and told you I was fine before."

"True."

"Now, I don't wish to hear anything more about this."

"Will you tell me the results?"

"Of course, Newly. As soon as I get them."

Another very big lie. They get back to you right away. I told no one that I have to schedule a heart catheterization.

"Will you tell me what they are?"

"When I'm good and ready."

"And not before."

"That's exactly right, dear. Now let me get some sleep. Good night, Newly."

And I hung up the phone. No clicks tonight! And if that wasn't a miracle, well, I don't know what the definition of one could possibly be! Perhaps it's too soon to tell.

Lark

OH, DEAR JESUS.

He sat near the church like he'd been there for hours. Settled on the cement schoolyard wall, reading the *Sunpaper*, he looked exactly the same. That baggy posture, that hayfield hair, that indifference to the goings-on around him, which included a huge bumblebee lumbering in flight by his right ear.

Did he not see the bee?

Did he not hear the bee?

I suspected he could even feel the bee at that proximity.

And then I remembered his many years as a hard rock musician. His hearing probably abdicated its drummy throne, retired its anvil, took its feet out of its stirrups years before.

At least he didn't hear me approach either, thank You, God.

A slow crawl began to mill beneath the surface of my exterior.

Breathe, Lark. Breathe.

And why, at times like this, does breathing through your nose help more than breathing through your mouth? I hadn't felt like this in weeks, I realized. I hadn't felt the ants like this, the fire beneath my brain, the breathlessness. The sensations almost felt foreign. Like echoes.

There is no fear in love. There is no fear in love.

Oh, God. Oh, Jesus. Please help me.

Think, Lark.

Prisma had prayed with me before I left. Thank goodness Johnny didn't call, or I might have blurted out the entire tale, and let's face it, I needed to keep my options open at this point. It was too soon to lift up my heavy baggage and say, "Oh, and by the way..."

I stood there, the July heat forcing its breath beneath my clothing. The humid jungle within met humid air without, and my hand automatically unbuttoned the top button of my blouse.

It won't get any easier, Lark. Just get your rear end over there.

Well before I preferred, I walked up to him.

I waved the bee away, and he looked up.

"Lark!"

And he jumped to his feet, and he towered over me, and he was blond and beautiful still, and now some age lines mellowed that sculptured face, and he pulled me into his arms.

Oh, God, he pulled me into his arms.

And twenty years melted away instantaneously, and I melted with them. And I hated myself even more in that instant than ever before.

I pulled back.

And I ran down to the 3 B's.

I heard his footsteps pounding behind me. "Lark! Stop!"

I skidded into the restaurant.

"Hey, doll!" My friend from the CVS, Rots DiMatti, called from his seat in one of the booths.

"A tea, please!" I whizzed past Deke.

Brad followed me in, skidding right into me.

"Babe!" he cried, trying to regain the embrace.

Babe Babachakos turned. "Yeah?"

And I ran into the bathroom, straight to the back, leaving old Bradley del Champ to sort everything out in the dining room.

I heaved into the toilet. Oh, God. This felt so wrong. Why couldn't I face life? Oh, Jesus. Please. Jesus. Please.

Please!

I sat on the dirty, octagon-tiled floor. And I cried. I checked my watch because despite my state, I wanted to make sure I didn't sit on a dirty bathroom floor all that long. I might be sick for weeks afterward.

Fifteen minutes later Babe came after me. She sat down in the next stall, right on the floor, and stuck her foot over on my side. "Come on out, hon."

"I know I should."

"He isn't so bad."

"What did he tell you?"

"That he's a louse. And he is. I mean, you wanted everyone to think he was dead."

"Yeah."

"That's the lowest of the low. I mean, I've had people that didn't want anything to do with me, but they didn't tell everyone I was dead or nothin'."

"No, I guess not."

"No wonder you're like you are."

"Okay, Babe! Sheesh!"

She reached her hand under, and I took it. "So that gives you the upper hand."

Leave it to Babe.

"And, Lark, I'm not mad at you for not telling us. I know there are some things people just can't air. And hey, the tea is on the house, okay? Come on, hon. Come on out. Your friends are all here to help. We won't let him get away with nothing."

"I guess I can't sit in here all day."

"Nope. We close in thirty minutes, and I'll kick your bony rear end out of here if you don't walk out on your own."

I laughed despite my blotched face and my tear-filled eyes. "Okay."

She scooted to her feet and waited for me on the other side of my door. "Wash your hands, hon. This place is filthy."

We cleaned up together.

Brad sat at the counter drinking a Coke or something when I walked over.

"Sorry," I said.

"Hey, I don't blame you."

I motioned to Deke. "How 'bout that tea?"

"You got it, hon."

Brad laid a hand on my arm. "It's good to see you, Lark."

"Yeah?"

"Yeah. You look good. Still as young as ever."

I shook my head. "Don't try to play me with your charm, Brad. There's too many years between us now."

He held up his hands. "All right, babe. You set the rules. I mean it."

"Yeah, right."

"You hungry?"

"No way."

"I am. Hey, Babe!" he called. "How about a BLT on rye toast?"

"You got it, sweet thing," she called back.

Sweet thing? Oh my word.

"So you're playing at St. Dominic's, huh?"

"Did Deke tell you that?"

"Nah, Rots did."

Cheer, cheer the gang's all here.

"How you doin' with the organ?"

"Pretty good."

Babe put down my tea. "She's great, hon. Don't let her fool you."

I waved the compliment away.

Shoo, Babe. Just shoo, why don't you?

"Let me look at you." He touched my shoulder. "You look great!"

"I look wind blasted, Brad. Let's be real."

"No, no, babe. You look distinguished, like a serious musician—"

"Who says she's in it for the music alone?" We'd had lots of passionate discussions on that in our younger days.

"Aren't you?"

I laughed. "Were you?"

"Heck no!"

"You know, Brad, I think I am now though. I'm finally in it for the music. Shoot, I wouldn't have stuck with it for this long if I wasn't."

And then safe ground lay beneath our feet. The thing that God has used to save my life for years.

It was always that way with us.

Some couples make love to make up after a fight. All Bradley or I had to do was spin a favorite album, and there we went, analyzing the daylights out of it. He'd look up at me and say, "Only you, Lark."

"I know," I'd say. "But don't you love this stuff?"

"Yeah, babe."

See, the sex really messed it up for me and Bradley. We should never have been married. Because between him and me it really had only been about the music. I should have seen that was all we were ever meant to share.

He smashed down the BLT on rye toast Babe set before him.

"How's your hearing these days?" I asked.

"Terrible. Look." He turned his head and pointed to his right ear. "Way down in there."

"Wow, a hearing aid?"

He nodded. "I've fried my ears. How about you?"

"Nothing major."

Rots came up as Brad took a giant bite of his sandwich. "How you doin', Lark?"

"Great, Rots. How 'bout you?"

"Oh, doin' fine."

"Your wife is home from Florida, right?"

"Oh, shoot, yeah. Didn't realize how much I enjoyed the quiet until she come home."

"I know what you mean." I thumbed at Brad.

Rots ran his large hand over his head. A lot of acne scars punctuate his face, and I wonder if he felt awkward growing up. I sure could relate.

"This is my ex-husband, Bradley del Champ."

"Pleased to meet you." Rots extended his hand, then looked at me. "Right, Lark?"

"Yeah. It's okay, Rots, thanks."

"'Cause you just say the word, doll."

"I promise, he's civilized."

Brad barked out a laugh. And I remembered again why I loved him so much. Why his desertion ruined me for two decades.

He followed me over to church, sitting right up front for all the world to see.

PRISMA

"Now, Mrs. Summerville, I have to give it to you. These scrap-books are the best idea you've ever come up with!"

"I agree, Prisma. Although it is taking time away from that sweater I'm trying to knit."

There we sat at the dining-room table, bits of paper, glue, scissors, and a hundred million stickers hiding the polished mahogany. "I don't know when I've enjoyed myself so much," I said. "Now look at this, Mrs. Summerville." I picked up a picture of Lark and Sinclair as small children, standing together in their Sunday clothes. "Is this the sweetest thing you've ever seen?"

Mrs. Summerville took the photo and held it at arm's length. "I do believe you're right. Look at those two. Sinclair in a white linen suit and Larkspur in a dark dress. They're positively negatives of each other!"

I laughed. "That's the truth. We had us a time here in the old days, didn't we?"

"Oh, we did, my friend, we really did."

"How about some tea?"

"I'd love that."

Mrs. Summerville found me in the kitchen just as I removed the tea ball from the pot. "You know, Prisma, lately I wish Sinclair was a little younger."

"Now what does that mean?"

She waved a hand. "I always thought that there wasn't a finer boy than your Sinclair. He would have been perfect for Lark. Don't look so shocked. You can't live around a person, watch them grow up so well, and not allow yourself a little indulgent thought."

My goodness. I never thought I'd ever hear Mrs. Summerville say anything like that. But honestly, as much as I love Lark, Sinclair deserved someone as strong and forthright as himself. Caprice was definitely the right woman for him. That girl is something!

"You want to keep working or take your tea upstairs and go to bed?"

"I am a little tired, I'll admit. Maybe it would be good to retire."

"All right then."

"Do you miss him, Prisma? Do you miss your son?"

I nodded. "Yes ma'am."

And for the first time in my life, I saw Leslie Summerville cry on my account. "I'm sorry then. I can't seem to do anything right these days. I should have fired you years ago."

We laughed through our tears.

But before I could really say anything, she retreated through the swinging door. I heard footsteps on the stairs as she made her way up to bed.

The fourth step creaked.

The ninth step groaned.

One, two, three.

And her bedroom door shut.

My heart broke. I know Jesus is up to something, but my, how it hurts my heart to watch Him stretching the proud Leslie Summerville. Yes, it certainly breaks my heart.

And then Lark's meeting with that no-good Bradley del Champ. I immediately knelt by my sitting-room couch.

"Lord Jesus, please don't let anything foolish happen over there in Hamilton."

No stars tonight. I was down on my knees and thankful for the extra padding.

Lark

BEFORE PRACTICE WITH MARSHA BEGAN, I found out a lot about Bradley's musical career firsthand. Of course I acted like I hadn't researched a thing on the Internet. I acted surprised and amazed, and down inside I remembered the sacrifice we'd made together all those years ago and the woman who accompanied him to the reward.

I played with soul that night. And I felt alive, even more alive than usual. My fingers felt blessed.

"Darn, girl!" said Father Charlie after the first couple of songs. "You are really something tonight!"

"You said it, Father." Marsha sat down next to me and opened a bottle of water. "You're hotter than a potato, Baby Doll."

"Thanks."

"I've got to use the ladies' room. Mind if we take a break?" Marsha asked.

I followed her to the back, mouthing "I'll be right back" to Bradley, who sat there smiling so simply.

Marsha hugged me in the bathroom. "If you had to play your best sometime, I am glad it was tonight! The creep."

"Don't say that, Marsha."

"Okay, then he's just a stupid-head for leaving you. I still can't believe you told everyone he was dead!"

"For Flannery's sake."

She blew slowly between her lips. "Oh man."

"Yeah. Is this all a nightmare or what?"

"You gonna let him see her?" Leave it to Marsha to add things up in a moment.

"I think so. He's her father. You know?"

"I loved my father a great deal."

"Me, too."

"Lark, do what you have to do, but take my advice—and you know I try not to give it too often—don't look at me like that, I really don't! But really, hon, don't make it overly easy for him."

"You're right."

She waggled a finger. "Now, you don't listen to me much. But take care you listen to this."

"I will."

We continued practicing, and when we finished up, Bradley offered to drive me home to Greenway.

I said, "Not on your life, babe. "

Father Charlie unlocked the church office. "I don't trust that fellow, Lark. I know he's your ex and all."

"Don't worry, Father Charlie. I don't either."

I gave Prisma a call. When I asked her to come pick me up she cried, "Hallelujah! Thank You, Jesus!"

I lay in bed that night staring up at Prisma's stars outside the bow window.

The last number of the evening swam in my brain.

Skylark? Have you seen a valley green? Father Charlie requested it.

Sitting up, I pulled the comforter off the bed, stood to my feet, and settled onto the window seat.

A green valley awaited me out there, I just knew that. But Greenway held me in check.

I whispered, "What are You doing, Lord? This is a situation that should have Your fingerprints all over it, but all I see are my own."

That's a thought capable of scaring anyone who knows me.

Tomorrow night Bradley would be waiting by St. Dominic's after Saturday's masses ended. He said we'd go out for a meal and talk some more.

I said, fine by me.

But it isn't fine. Suddenly I care more about my hair. And that's never a good sign.

What I wouldn't give for a walk with Dr. Josefowski right about now.

PRISMA

HONEST TO PETE! THESE WOMEN.

We made us a morning of the hairdressing. Even Mrs. Summerville got in on the action. She called into the kitchen from the lounger in her den. Yes, we bought a lounger yesterday. Now I know that woman must feel horrible!

"Sweet Pea! Why don't you put an old bedsheet down on the floor in here and set up shop?"

"Sounds good to me," Flannery said. "Miss Prisma, where can I find an old sheet?"

"Hold on." I set aside my coupon wallet on the kitchen counter. They're running a special on pickled onions at the Giant this week.

"I can get it!" she called.

I entered the den. "I'm sure you can. But you won't. You'll mess up the order of things."

On the face of things, these Summervilles appear as spoiled prima donnas because they do nothing for themselves. But truth be told, I don't let them. It makes twice as much work putting things back the way I like them when they try and take care of things on their own.

I still don't know how Lark and Baby Girl made it without me around. Of course, the inside of that house in Hamilton belonged in a hospital! Hardly a home. More like a place to stay in between the real living. Secondhand furniture. No pictures on the wall. Until Baby Girl got artistic.

So I opened the cabinet in the laundry room and pulled down a bedspread from the seventies when Mrs. Summerville took one of the guest rooms and made it look like "George Washington Slept Here." Those little bumps all over it hung like miniature nooses now, and the whole thing reminded me of a mangy sheep dog. The paint splatters didn't help any.

I spread it on the floor of the den and hightailed it back to the kitchen. I needed to get to the grocery store soon. Fresh spinach. We'd try out a new recipe I found on the Internet the night before. Parmesan spinach dip. And it called for fresh spinach. Not canned or frozen.

Must be a recipe by one of those snooty chefs.

Even made my own Melba toast to go with it real early this morning. Couldn't sleep last night. These girls worry me. I have to say Mrs. Summerville shocked me with that statement about my Sinclair. That encouraged me. Lark and Sinclair? An indulgent thought? Of course, Sinclair, who looks on Lark as a little sister will laugh himself silly when I tell him what she said.

Lark sat at the table finishing breakfast. "I'm crazy, Prisma."

"Yes, you are."

"I'm crazy to let you two do this to me."

"Well, now, as I see it, that is not the truth. As I see it, it's been long overdue. Now I don't like sitting around wasting my time talking about hair like most women do. Just get in there and let Baby Girl work her magic. I've got work to do."

"For some crazy reason, Miss Long Braid, I thought you'd be on my side here." Lark stood to her feet and gathered her plate and utensils. She made for the sink. "I mean, you've been wearing your hair like that ever since I can remember."

I just stared at her for a moment and wanted to cry. I thought about that buffoon Bradley and her crazy love for him. I thought of the early years after she came back from San Francisco, the way I'd go downtown sometimes to hear her practice with those awful rock bands. Then the nail salon. Then the church. And I'd place Baby Girl right there by her side to grow up beautiful, just like a Summerville should.

Do they begin to realize how good it would be if they let it? Do they realize how good life really is?

Well, Baby Girl does. I'd swear there are Percy genes in that child somewhere, for she's the only one with a lick of sense.

"Didn't you hear me, Prisma? I thought you'd be on my side."

"I am. Which is why I think it's high time you let somebody do something nice for you. You can't be your own savior forever."

"That's not fair, Prisma! You know I don't feel that way about myself."

"Well, maybe you don't feel that way, Lark, but you sure do act it."

"I've been trying to serve God for years. And then my house burns down after all I gave up to try and take responsibility for my life."

Poor baby. Oh well, Lord, I'll let her have it if You say so. "Maybe it's never been about giving things up, Lark."

"But the Bible says, 'Deny yourself, take up your cross and follow Me.'"

"And what does that mean exactly, Miss Smarty-pants?"

Lark's eyes filled with tears as Baby Girl hollered in from the den. "Come on, Mom! Grandy and I are waiting."

Quicker than a flash, Lark turned, pushed through the swinging door, and disappeared from view.

I turned on the water. "Well, Jesus, did I say it right?"

"She's forsaken her primary mission field, My girl."

"Mrs. Summerville, right? I figured as much. Don't know why I didn't see it sooner."

"So what're you gonna do about it, Prisma Ophelia Percy?"

"Pray."

"And?"

"Well, I don't know, Lord. I suppose You'll send Your Spirit to guide me."

And Jesus said, "You got that right."

Thing is, I don't know if my conversations with the Lord are real, but I hear Him guiding me, deep down inside. And there are things I know I'm supposed to do, and there are matters here at Stoneleigh House, matters He's put in my hands, that need tending.

"Lord," I prayed, "I know You're working. I just know it. Help me to know what to do."

Now, that is a prayer I know He'll answer.

Truth be told, Lark hasn't looked this good in years. Baby Girl used some kind of new gunk people use these days, and, honest to Pete, Lark's lost ten years off her looks. We all stood around the hall mirror, even Mrs. Summerville.

"You know, Larkspur, I might even get my hair colored, that looks so good!"

I sucked in my breath quietly.

"You really like it, Mother?" She ran her fingers through loose curls, curls that Baby Girl had coaxed with a curling iron as thick as a fence post.

"Of course. What's not to like? Sweet Pea sure knows hair."

"I'll do it whenever you want, Grandy."

Lark ran a hand over the soft blond streaks. "The color isn't too much?"

"Not at all," Leslie said, growing more and more tired. I could tell by the way she leaned heavily on the hall table.

"Well, let's celebrate!" I clapped my hands twice. "It's hors d'oeuvres for lunch! The Giant was just burgeoning this morning with all sorts of good things."

"Oh good!" Baby Girl made for the dining room, where I had arranged quite a spread while the beauty parlor had been in session. "Did you make any Li'l Smokies?"

"Sure did! And don't you worry, Mrs. Summerville, I did a low-fat version for you."

"My mama would die all over again if she knew how much her daughter loves cocktail weenies!" Leslie laughed and looked ten years younger, just like Lark.

Unfortunately, she only ate two before she said, "What a morning! Too much excitement for me. Would you all be upset if I went up and took a nap?"

"No, Mother, of course not."

"Are you okay, Grandy?"

"Of course! Now don't get worried. I just didn't sleep well last night is all."

Only 1:30. Too early for a nap.

The girls offered to help me clean up the kitchen, and I let them know the pantry needed a little rearranging. We shouted back and forth. Laughing. Joking. Just being the folks of the house.

I've lived here for fifty years, and I've always found it wonderful the way a new hairdo can perk up life in general.

Hours later I decided to sit in the garden with a cup of tea and my Bible. Lark left at four o'clock to go to play for mass, and Flannery said she'd drop her off on the way to work. Then comes her dinner with that Bradley. Mrs. Summerville is sleeping, and the quiet empties me, leaving waves of sadness licking at my toes.

How about your gold slippers for the afternoon, Prisma? It won't hurt just this once.

Live a little.

July is almost over, and this afternoon I am thankful for many things: the fact that nobody spilled hair goop where it has no business being, the last lemon bar in the freezer, Asil's new girlfriend. He hasn't been in my hair for a week now. I'm thankful most for the Holy Spirit's leading. And I'd be lying if I wasn't tickled about my computer at my desk. The Internet will never be the same now that Prisma Percy has a cable modem! Yesterday I sent a check to a local rescue mission here in Baltimore. What a work they do with men there! In fact, years and years ago they sent Asil our way. But I try not to bring that up. A man deserves to keep the dignity he's worked so hard to earn.

I looked up at the heavens, saw the breeze chasing clouds across the sky. I saw the sun, and I swear I heard Jimmy's voice saying, "Soon, Prissy, we'll get to be together again."

I'm hoping that "soon" is not the "thousand years is but a day in Your sight, O Lord" kind of soon. These knees aren't bad, but they sure won't hold up that long.

L a r k

I SHUT THE DOOR OF FLANNERY'S CAR and waved as she drove away from St. Dominic's. What is happening to me? My hands smoothed my black skirt, and I rubbed the fabric of the new silk blouse Flannery brought home.

"On sale, Mom! $10.99!"

Pale pink.

I showed it to Mother the night before and once again received her approval.

"I have just the thing, Larkspur." She hurried over to her jewel case, carefully pulled open the third drawer down, reached in, and turned around.

"Oh, Mother! Are you sure?"

"Positively. Here." And she extended a two-strand pearl choker with a diamond clasp. "It was my Mama's."

"I've never seen you wear this."

"I never have. I didn't get it until after she died. And by then..." She shrugged. "Well, your father had given me plenty of my own, and..."

And she was avoiding something to be sure.

"How come you don't talk much about your mother?"

Now, oddly enough, I never once met my maternal grandmother, Libby Lee Strawbridge. Mother and Daddy would visit Virginia, leaving Newly and me in the care of Prisma and Jimmy. But never once did they take me.

My mother's eyes filled with tears. "That story is for another day, Larkspur. You've got enough on your mind already."

I focused on my shoes, fighting my own tears. Would she never trust me with her heart? But I smiled bravely and lifted up the necklace. "Would you help me?" She never objected to that.

"Of course." Her cool fingers brushed the back of my neck beneath my new "signature" bun. Ha-ha. "And let's not forget the earrings!" She seemed almost girlish again as she scooted back to the case.

I threaded the simple drops in my ears and turned to face her. "What do you think?"

I waited, wincing inside.

"I think you're something, Larkspur Summerville. I think you look beautiful. But then I've always thought you were one of the prettiest things I'd ever seen."

And I think she really meant it. Even before my visit to Flannery's House of Hair.

In that ensemble I walked out of St. Dominic's to find a limousine waiting. Oh my word! Brad quickly jumped out of the car before the driver could circle. "Lark!"

"Hi, Brad." Oh man. How was I going to explain this to the denizens of the 3 B's?

"Get on in. We've got reservations for 8:30."

"Just as long as I'm back home by 10:30. That's when my calls really start coming in."

"No problem. I love your hairdo, babe."

"Flannery colored it."

"No kidding. She must be something."

And we zoomed away from the church, and I felt like I had on a going-away outfit, my groom smiling beside me.

Oh, Lark. I sighed within. Oh, baby. Don't do this to yourself. Now would be a really, really good time to get scared.

Flannery

"UNCLE NEWLY?"

"Hello, Buddy."

"Guess what?"

"What?"

"I know you've been holding out on me."

Silence.

"Aren't you going to ask about what, Uncle Newly?"

He chuckled. "Well, Buddy. I am sitting here wondering which portion of my very private life you've stumbled upon."

"You and that girlfriend are getting serious."

"No!"

I laughed.

"You don't say!" he tried unsuccessfully to sound shocked.

"You're a horrible actor!"

"Yes, you're exactly right. So how did you come to this stunning conclusion?"

"I saw you."

"You did? Where?"

"I was down by Maryland Institute just walking around the grounds, to get a feel of the place, you know. And I saw you go into the Lyric with her. You guys were holding hands in a very familiar, comfy way and you were smiling, Uncle Newly. And it wasn't your usual smile."

"How do you know it was me?"

"Oh, Uncle Newly, you crack me up! An albino wearing Brooks Brothers stuff? Who else would it be?"

He chuckled. "I talked to Grandy the other day. How does she look to you?"

"Tired, and I realize you're changing the subject. I think she looks very tired."

"That's what I thought. Too tired for me to take her out to dinner sometime soon?"

I pause. "Didn't you guys just go to lunch recently?"

"Yes. I wasn't in a good mood."

"Oh, Uncle Newly! Poor Grandy! And she was so excited."

Silence.

Oh brother. I hate when he does that. "So anyway, you trying to make amends?"

"Perhaps."

"Are you on something?"

"Not really, Buddy. Do you know how old I am?"

I calculated. Five years younger than Mom, who was forty-one.

"Thirty-six?"

"Yes. How long have I been thirty-six?"

Oh no. I had no idea. "I have no idea."

"Precisely."

"Okay. So I don't know your birthday."

"So typical it makes me want to puke."

"You sound like a Monty Python guy. They say *puke* all the time."

"It's a good word for this situation."

I gripped the phone. "Think of it this way, Uncle Newly. At least you've realized your neglect of the important things at thirty-six. I'd say that's pretty young."

"Well, Buddy, leave it to you to look at the bright side."

Yep, Uncle Newly was right about that. I'm definitely the keeper of the bright side in this family.

L a r k

I WANTED TO CRY. For Bradley. For me. For Flannery, and even for Rhonda.

We sat on the hood of the limousine. Before us, a vast pool in the night, rested Loch Raven Reservoir. Oaks and pines guarded the banks to our right and to our left, but where we sat, near the dam, the water moved before our eyes, sliding underneath the dome of stars before softly succumbing to concrete man's construction. The water hissed softly as it fell.

This wasn't Hoover Dam or Niagara Falls. It was just Loch Raven, a lovers' lane and the place I gave myself to Bradley twenty-three years earlier. Often I used to think about lovers' lanes and how lovers' lanes all over the country change lives for good. Create lives forever.

Yes, everyone looks back on their life and sees events, rolls them around in the years they've lived since, and longs for a fairy godmother to make it all right. Yet sometimes? Well, we can see our actions as ingredients, ingredients in and of themselves destined for nothing more than a mud pie or a worm sandwich. But what happens? God steps in. I know it sounds corny. But I realized, sitting there with my ex-husband, that even the messiest scenarios deserve redemption.

Deserve?

Well, maybe not. But that's what makes grace grace.

Already the story of a commitment I never knew possible flowed out of Bradley del Champ. About a marriage turned rockier than anything he and I ever experienced. "But by then she was pretty sick. I mean, how do you leave a dying person?"

"So the marriage was basically over?"

"Years ago. Well, the love part anyway."

He paused, fiddling with an amulet he wore around his neck. Ga-roo-vey.

"Actually, maybe that was really the part that stayed. I guess it was the passion, the infatuation and all, that left. You know what I mean?"

I nodded. Not from experience, mind you. When Bradley rode out of my life, I remembered thinking not a week before how unbelievably attractive he was, how talented, how amazing. But nevertheless, I knew what he meant. "So you stuck it out."

"Like I said, she was dying, Lark."

"Was there anybody else in the meantime, during her illness?"

"There could have been, believe me."

"Groupies?"

"Uh-huh."

"So, was there?"

He shook his head. "Once. It was horrible. Not the sex, but the next day after I went home and learned Rhonda was going to have part of her foot taken off."

"Oh my word."

"Yeah. The guys in the band, we have this running joke. 'Do nothing to make us prime candidates for Behind the Music!' "

I laughed. "Sex, drugs, and rock-'n'-roll."

"Yeah."

"So what you're saying is that it's really all about the music now?"

He let out a hoot. "No. It's still about the notoriety. But it's not about the chicks anymore, babe."

"Was it ever?"

"I hate to admit it, but yes."

"And I messed that up for you."

He shrugged. "Maybe you saved me. Who knows?"

"And then Rhonda picked up the baton."

"Sort of. In her own way."

The pool of darkness winked and waved, almost laughing at the years it had seen without mishap.

"Was it worth it?"

"No, babe. If I live to be a thousand, the memory of that drive out of our apartment complex will never stop beating me black and blue."

"But you stayed away."

"Yeah."

"Despite Flannery?"

He shrugged. "There's where I don't know, babe. If I'd have left Rhonda, I'd have been the same old scoundrel. Yet to stay…I was still a scoundrel to you all. It was a no-win situation."

"You can say that again."

He didn't. Thank the Lord.

"Have you ever driven around here when winter is fully bloomed?" I asked him.

He smiled, and I gazed at his profile. "Yeah. Pretty, isn't it?"

"Yes. And the water still flows over the dam."

"Yeah, it does. Those long wet streaks down the cement. But water won't ever be completely contained, will it?"

"No. It's like love, Bradley. Though frozen on top, there's always a little left to fall over the edge."

I wasn't sure what I meant exactly. I mean, I wasn't saying I was in love with him or anything. Because even if I was, time had done its marching and the band had moved from any field my feet would ever step across. But some form of love remained.

"This has everything to do with Flannery," I said. "She's the only reason I'd be sitting here with you, Brad."

"I know."

"And I know she's the only reason you're sitting here with me."

He said nothing. But then, Bradley never did say things that would outright hurt anyone.

"So will you let me see her?"

"Give me some time. I don't know how in the world I'm going to explain this one."

"How much time do you need?"

"Can you wait until the end of the summer?"

"Sure. I've got a couple of concerts overseas in August. But I'll be in touch, okay?"

Oh, Lord Jesus. Just when I thought life couldn't get any more complicated or stupid. Or scary.

"Okay."

And a mountain quickly collected before me. The volcanic kind. One I had no idea how to climb.

Someday I'm going to have to tell Flannery the truth about her father. But it won't be tonight. I am worn out. And tomorrow church begins early, three masses, and Johnny Josefowski promised to come to the eleven o'clock. And afterward he'll be taking me to lunch.

And, oh God, why now? Why all of this now?

Silly, Lark. Silly, silly, Lark. Why didn't you realize how good you had it?

I told him to drop me off two blocks from the house so Mother wouldn't see.

Flannery blow-dried my hair for me this morning before church. I didn't realize how much she looks like her father, not having seen Brad in so long. The way her nose snubs slightly at the end. The blue of her eyes, the way it sometimes shines green if the sun hits her face from the side. The certain blush along her jaw line when she feels deeply.

Had I made a mistake all those years ago in keeping her from him? Did I hold her for ransom? Who knows? What would happen now? And the fact that at the beginning of the summer I thought my life felt under control amazed me somehow. I didn't exactly feel like a deer suddenly caught in the headlights. I felt like a deer that had, in point of fact, been caught in the headlights for years and only just noticed it. I pushed thoughts of Bradley aside for the moment. The last thing I wanted was for them to adorn my face and then for Flannery to ask, "What's wrong, Mother?" And then I'd have to evade or downright lie, probably the latter, in an effort to beef up the evasion.

The blow-dryer soothed me even though I grumbled the whole time. Flannery assures me she'll be glad to do it every month. Prisma has already put it on the household calendar and declared that it will be monthly hors d'oeuvre night as well. That woman can make a tradition out of anything!

"Are you going to wear your black dress from Target today?" Flannery spritzed my hair with one of those new salon products she uses. Hair stuff smells so much better nowadays.

"I've worn it almost every Sunday for the past six weeks, sweetie."

"Will Dr. J be there?"

Oh, Johnny. My Great White Hope turned complication. In four hours I'd sit across the lunch table from this man and learn more about him. And meanwhile, Bradley, the new and improved, late-model Bradley, would be sitting on my shoulder whispering, "All men are just like me! Ha-ha-ha-ha-haaaaaah!"

"Yeah, he'll be there. He always is."

Flannery just smiled at herself in the bathroom mirror and said, "You're hiding something from me."

"What do you mean?"

But she just ran a light hand over the waves. "There. What do you think?"

"Looks even better than the last time."

Actually, I wasn't sure if it looked better, but it seemed the thing to say.

"Come into my bedroom, Mom. Maybe you can wear something of mine."

"Flannery, you're a different size than I am."

"I've got this dress though. Empire waist. One size fits all!"

We laughed. "I'll look at it, but I retain the right to refuse due to height deficiencies."

Besides, Flannery can get a little, well, a little too creative for a stick-in-the-mud like myself.

"It's kind of prairie-ish. Flowing and all. It will fit you fine."

More than a little skeptical, I followed her into Newly's old room, the walls now assaulted by blazing orange and fuchsia. She threw open the closet door. "I just got this on my trip to Saks with Grandy." And she drew out a soft pink, artsy dress. Sleeveless, drawstring neckline, folds of gauzy fabric falling from the bustline over an underdress of floral linen.

"This is made beautifully, Flannery."

"I thought you'd appreciate it."

"But you haven't worn it yet, have you?"

She shook her head. "I'm not going to. Grandy insisted I get a church dress, and when I tried to explain—"

"I understand. But you can wear it when you go with Prisma, can't you?"

"I like to wear white too. She always wears white to church."

I held it up against my body. "You think this goes with the lighter hair?"

"Even better than it would have."

"I don't have shoes."

She bent down and lifted up a new box. "Yes, you do. They may be a bit too big, but they're sandals so they should work."

At least I still had good feet and ankles. I hadn't worn anything like this since before Brad and I got married.

"Do you really think I can get away with it?" I asked.

"You can if you want to, Mom."

I stepped between the two sides of the opened zipper. I shivered as the cool metal touched my spine. Flannery zipped me in.

"Can I please apply a little makeup, Mom? Please? Just a touch."

"You promise you won't go overboard? I don't want to look like I'm trying to impress anyone."

"I promise."

I love my girly-girl girl.

So I reclined on her bed while she erased my dark circles and lines, bestowed a healthy glow on my cheeks, and lined my eyes with a soft gray. The softness of her fingertips against my skin almost put me to sleep even as they threw me back to her childhood when she'd drizzle me awake with the soft rain of her tiny hands and the kisses from her little mouth.

"Just a little bit of pink lipstick, and you're all set."

I opened my eyes. "You never wear pink lipstick, Flannery."

"I bought it last night."

I see.

I said nothing. Hopefully I could skip the unveiling ceremony, grab my music, and go. But not with good old Flannery.

She pulled me to my feet. "Okay! All finished!" And she ushered me to the old cheval glass in the corner. It used to be in my room, but as usual Leslie still liked to move things around.

"Oh." I caught my breath at the sight of my reflection.

"You like it?"

I shoved down the panic that threatened to engulf me, and I turned away from the reflection. Do this for Flannery, I commanded myself, and I smiled, hugging her. "I do, Flannery. You did a good job. Especially considering what you had to work with!"

"Oh, stop, Mom. You've still got it."

Whatever "it" was.

We heard a car door close. And we watched out the window as Asil circled around the Bentley to the driver's side. He folded himself inside, and he drove Mother to church.

"I'm worried about Grandy."

"Me, too."

"Is she going to be all right?"

"I don't know. I'll ask Dr. Josefowski about it at church."

"Isn't it funny how God worked through that fire?" Her eyes lit up. "I mean, we would never have been here for her if the house hadn't burned down."

I know Flannery never meant for her words to rip my heart to tiny shreds.

Marsha picked me up around a quarter past seven, in plenty of time to get to eight o'clock mass and warm up first. Now Marsha is not a morning person, despite her bubbles from noon onward. It wasn't until she'd finished her cup of Wawa coffee and we were climbing out of the car that she decided to notice Flannery's handiwork. She screamed, "You look wonderful!"

Oh my word, Marsha!

And several heads of early arrivers turned. Brother.

"And what's the occasion, Lark? Do tell!"

Scream a little louder, why don't you? I doubted if anyone even recognized me. "Flannery finally got sick of having a crone for a mother?"

Marsha hooted. "I love it! You look great."

No denying the crone statement. Huh.

"So, you and Johnny still on for lunch?" she asked.

"Yeah. I'm so nervous."

"Why? He's a gem!"

"I know. I'm scared I'll like him too much. You know?"

Marsha placed her hand on my arm. "You'll do okay, hon. You really will."

"Better get in there. I need to use the ladies' room first."

Flannery's words continued to haunt me, rattling battleship chains, then hanging them around my neck. We would never have been here for her if the house hadn't burned down.

Really?

Would God take away the little bit I owned to be gracious to a woman who had it all?

Flannery

JAMES MET ME AT THE HOUSE around 10:30. Grandy was still at church. Mom, looking fabulous, à la me, was long gone. I swear Miss Marsha saved her life when she got her that organist job. She's been good for Mom that way all around. Like her faith became more than just going through the motions when Miss Marsha began reaching out to her.

They'd been friends for a while, but then one day, about five years ago I think it was, 'cause I was a senior in high school, Miss Marsha began calling a lot. Just to shoot the breeze. As far as I know, she never made it plain that Mom was lonely and needed a friend and she figured she should do her Christian duty. She just called and talked Mom's ear off!

She'd call, and my mom would go, "Tell her I'm not home!"

But I'd just hand her the phone and get the evil eye in return. And because Mom is a Summerville, she'd act like she'd been sitting there all day waiting for Marsha to call.

So I figured Mom was sitting with Father Charlie in between the 9:15 and the 11:00 mass. Sometimes he brings a little bag of candy. I noticed Mom has been eating more sugar lately, surely a sign of something, and I say, "Oh yeah."

James pulled into the drive in his old Buick Century. Brown. Gag me. I watched him from the kitchen window, and I felt that little thrill all over again. There he was. My James!

My James. Is that mushy or what?

People say you can't ever call a person your own. They must be mental or something. It's like you belong to God because He loves you first. Same sort of thing with people, but without that perfection in the equation. I'm not quite that blind to either James's wrinkles or my own.

The doorbell rings, and I am ready. I've been ready for an hour, not that I'm going to tell him that. And you know what? I just hop right on up and get the door because it's okay. James won't get all cocky or think a thing.

I yank it open like it weighs eight thousand pounds.

James looks completely different than I thought he would. Like, he has respect for church, you know? Cool. You know? He wears a pair of gray pants, the kind with the pockets on the side, and a nice pullover shirt with thin stripes. I look down at my own outfit, a sheath dress in psychedelic tones, and feel kind of loud. "Come on in!"

He smiles.

Oh man!

Believe me—*believe* me—when only a smile can do that to you, you know it's really something!

"I think I'll go change," I say after he kisses me hello.

"Why?"

"Isn't this outfit kind of…well…"

"Artistic. Like, the nondepressing variety. I like it."

So I grab the little purse I wove last week, thanks to the class I signed up for at the craft store, tuck my hand around his arm, nice biceps by the way, and he shows me to the car.

See what I mean? This was gag boy from Starbucks. So you just never know. I've tried not to judge people hastily the way Grandy and Mom do, but I guess I'm more like them than I thought.

"Your earrings are out!"

"Yeah, well, we're meeting my parents there."

I don't know whether to shout hallelujah or break down in tears. So I just say, "Okay, that will be nice."

Nice. Like, is that an insipid response or what?

He smiles at me again, from the side, and starts up the car. And it squeaks out one of those grated, high pitched whines that I think comes from some kind of loose belt or something.

He's still smiling. I have this feeling I amuse James. Not in a bad way. And he admires me. He's told me that a lot.

Twenty minutes later and lots of handholding and talks about the movie we rented last night, *The Remains of the Day,* which I loved and he absolutely hated, we pull up to the Church of the Nativity out in Lutherville, one of those big, square buildings where the planes of the roof soar evenly up to an apex, crowned by a simple cross.

"I'll take you downtown to the Basilica next Sunday," he says as we walk up the concrete steps. "I'm thinking that will really inspire you with your artwork."

See what I mean about the Catholics and art and all?

And there are Mr. and Mrs. Smith waiting on the steps. I know this because he hollers out, "Hey, Mom!"

"Quig!" she calls and waves. "Over here!"

He gives a little wave and ushers me to where they stand near the set of glass doors farthest to the right. I smile broad and confidently, but I feel so scared underneath. Like ants are crawling beneath my skin or something stupid like that.

I mean, these might be my future in-laws.

Shy but pleasant is the way to go here. I am sure of it. And respectful. I sure don't want to become too familiar too soon, like an annoying waitress who tries to be your best friend when all you want is a BLT on rye toast with mayo on the side and maybe an ice tea with extra lemon.

Mrs. Smith grins at me and gives me one of those U-shaped hugs. Not a cranked down, staple-you-to-herself kind of hug like Prisma gives. But that's okay, 'cause you can tell with hugs right away. You can tell whether or not a faraway hug is because the other person thinks you're gross or beneath them, or they just want to go at your pace. Mrs. Smith was giving me the latter kind. She smells like peppermint and cigarette smoke. Not a cloying, old tobacco aroma, more of the cool, light variety. And some kind of green-apple shampoo scents her short, salt-and-pepper hair. Pulling away, she says, "Hi, babe! It's good to meet you. Quig's been talking about you like crazy the past month or so."

"Mom!"

"Well, you have. I've never seen him like this over a girl before. How about you, Lou?"

Mr. Smith just shrugs and says, "Heck, Anne, I don't know."

"And I think it's the cutest thing, the way he's changed his name. Quig is named after my brother. I should've had more foresight."

"Come on, Anne. Let's go. Mass is about to start." Mr. Smith looks up at me and gives me the same smile that James usually does, only with a few more wrinkles at the corners of his mouth and eyes. No wonder Anne and Lou are still together after all these years. I think my parents would have divorced eventually even if Daddy hadn't died. You can tell by their pictures they didn't have this type of connection.

So in we go. Passing through the lobby, Anne Smith says, "Do you want us to call you Flannery? Or should we think of our own name for you?"

"Whatever you want, Mrs. Smith. I'll answer to just about anything."

Lou Smith lets out a loud laugh, and we walk into the spare, modern sanctuary.

"I really like the name Flannery," says James.

"Me, too," says Mrs. Smith.

See, this is the thing. I read dark, literary books, and I don't know why, because my life has been a tale of grace. This should be the point where I find out that James is from some dysfunctional family where the mother relies too much on her son for support and therefore hates the girlfriend. Where the father sits alone no matter how many people are in the room—just as long as he has his beer.

But life hasn't been like that for me. God sends cool people my way all the time. I think He's making up for the fact that Daddy died before I could really know him. God is the only Father I've ever known, and I'd say He's done a wonderful job so far!

Leslie

I DO HOPE LARK REALIZES HOW LOVELY SHE LOOKS. That new hair color? Gorgeous! I had really begun to think she'd lost her looks for good. She looks so dreary normally. But then, life isn't easy for her. I do know this.

I can't contain this any longer. I heard Bradley's voice on the phone that first night. She's hiding so much from me and, truth to tell, has been doing so for years. But how does a woman sidle up to her daughter and say, "I know your ex is alive, and you've been lying to us for two decades"?

How?

Well, simply put, I just can't. I should. I'm the mother. But I just cannot do it.

Today Asil dropped me off at church, and I sat there in my spot all by myself. I began to doze during the sermon until the pastor said something I couldn't believe.

"The feeding of the five thousand can be interpreted many ways," he said.

What?

Even with my limited knowledge of the Bible, I knew that story and its simple message of how Jesus got the five loaves of bread and two fishes from a little boy and then He stood there and kept breaking off pieces. Although, how one breaks a fish in half I don't know. Perhaps they were smoked or some such ancient method of preservation. I'll have to ask Prisma. She knows about all that.

And then he offered up this ghastly, and I mean perfectly ghastly, explanation! "The miracle was in the hearts of the people. Suddenly they pulled out the meals they had been hiding in their robes and began to share."

What twaddle!

"So it was even more of a miracle than the Bible says. For it was a miracle of the heart!"

What?

Fiddle!

Fiddle, fiddle, fiddle!

You mean five thousand men had been afraid to pull out food and start chomping away? Talk about a miracle! I hardly believe men have changed that much over the past two thousand years.

So I pulled out that pew Bible, opened it up to the book of Matthew, and read for myself. I've never done that before because never has such a blatant denial of the facts filtered down from our pulpit! The nerve of that blowbag!

Yes, blowbag.

He's from some Northern seminary and stands there like a raven ruffling his self-important, pompous, asinine feathers.

I'm angry. And I wonder what else he's said over the past few years since we called him to our pulpit! I chaired the pulpit committee too! Did I not see what a conceited donkey he was? I wonder about myself at times like these.

Again, the dodo comes to mind. Have I outlived my usefulness?

After my salad at lunch I found Prisma in the kitchen. "What does your pastor say about the feeding of the multitude?"

Prisma finished drying the last fork. Why she keeps refusing a dishwasher, I'll never know. "He says that Jesus took one lunch and miraculously divided it enough to feed thousands and thousands of people."

"Do you believe that? That it happened just like that?"

"I sure do."

"What if the Bible is wrong?"

"Then it could be wrong about everything else. Either you can rely on it, or you can't, Mrs. Summerville. There's no middle ground, though some folk say there is. This pickin' and choosin' stuff is for the birds, if you ask me."

True. It was like learning only what you liked of French and then saying you spoke French.

But Prisma was just warming up. "I mean, if you don't want to believe it, that's your choice. Then just don't. That's between you and God. But to go driving around through the verses, just sightseeing what you want to see, I find that downright illogical, don't you?"

"I'd have to agree."

"Best of both worlds. That's what people want. They just want a big old magic book with spells and potions that tells them exactly what they want to hear, not what's really going to help what ails them."

"You're right, of course."

"They don't want to know God. They want some sugar daddy who's nice all the time. Not some fierce, mysterious, whirling dervish of a Creator whom we can't understand. No sirree, they want to make God just like themselves. That's it in a nutshell. 'Cause if God is just like them, then He's safe and wouldn't think about makin' them do anything their little hearts didn't want to do, He wouldn't think of takin' them out of their comfort zones and pushin' them out of the nests they made so they can soar! Soar among the eagles. And I'll tell you another thing."

As if I doubted she would.

"Nobody wants to talk about sin anymore! And I think it's the best news you can give somebody. They're feelin' it! They're feelin' the wrong they're doin.'"

She sure was slipping into her dialect now, getting fired up. Fascinated, I leaned against the counter.

"They're caught in a mire and somebody's tellin' them there's no such thing as sin, and they're feelin' stupid for feelin' guilty, for feelin' the effects of their God-given conscience, one of the very things that makes them human. And then you know what I say, Mrs. Summerville?"

I raised my eyebrows.

"I say, 'It's just that you're an old-fashioned sinner. Isn't that good news?'"

I shook my head. "I don't understand."

"Well, now, they don't usually either. So I say, 'And if sin's the only problem you've got, the answer is easy. Jesus is the answer. He'll see you through. There is hope.'"

"My, my."

She pointed at me. "You got that right." She blew out a shaky breath. "Well, that got me all fired up. M'm, m'm."

"Do you have an extra Bible, Prisma?"

"Sure do. What's this all about anyway, Mrs. Summerville?" She pulled a hanky out of her skirt pocket and wiped her bosom and neck.

So I told her what happened at church.

"Stuff like that's been going on for years," she said. "I'll admit the Bible can be uncomfortable at times, the parts about hell and the land of Canaan and all, but why take one of the more easy-to-digest passages and fool with it?"

"That's what I say. You know what I think, Prisma?" I leaned forward, placing my elbow on the counter for support and a little relief for my out-of-breath inhalations. "I think this man must be leading all sorts of people astray."

"Well, there's only one way you can find out. Read the Bible for yourself."

"And if I have any questions?"

"I'm always here, and my pastor will help if there's something I can't answer. He's a good man. Now let me go get you one of my Bibles. I think you'll like the New King James. Familiar enough but not obscure."

Mama always used the old King James, but now that I'm older I realize there were a lot of things Mama didn't know. "Whatever you think is best."

Her eyebrows lifted, and I admit my own words surprised me. "Well, why not, Prisma? I know I'm not as smart as you are."

"Are you all right, Mrs. Summerville?"

"No. I'm not."

Prisma hesitated.

"Just go get that Bible before I fall down. I'm very tired."

"Go on in the den, Mrs. Summerville. I'll bring it with a nice cup of tea."

"Are you going back to church tonight?"

"Sure am."

"Maybe one of these nights I'll go too." And I turned around and made for the den as Prisma laughed and laughed.

Yes, I know it is funny, the thought of me there with that hootenanny, multicultural crowd. But I'm tired, I'm old, and despite my wealth, my privilege, and my good taste and deeds, I'm agitated inside. That pastor was wrong! And I needed to find out why for myself. Big goings-on? Probably not. But to me a giant itch surfaced that just wouldn't go away.

Charles tried to talk to me about spiritual things before he died. Prisma "led him to the Lord." Whatever that means.

"You've got to become a Christian, Les," Charles said.

"I am a Christian, Charles! Our family has always been Methodist!"

"But do you really know who Jesus is, sweetheart?"

"Of course I do! Who doesn't?"

He just shook his head then. He prayed a lot as he lay dying. And when he slipped away, he smiled.

But where did he go? Prisma knows. Lark and Sweet Pea know. But I don't. That pastor said, "Heaven is in our hearts."

If that's the case, I'm in a peck of trouble, because a heaven like that may only feel like a roller coaster you can never get off.

Prisma found me in the den. "Here you go, Mrs. Summerville. The Bible and a cup of herb tea."

"Where should I start?"

"Why don't you read that account of the feeding of the multitude again? See if there's really room for maneuvering around the passage like that pastor did."

"All right. I will."

Prisma looked it up for me and went back into her room. But she left her door open, and I heard her clacking away at her new computer, and I longed to be Prisma just then. Beautiful Prisma. Kind Prisma. Smart Prisma.

"Say a prayer first, Mrs. Summerville!" she hollered.

"What for?"

"Ask God to speak to you!"

"He'll do that?"

"Yes, He will."

Well, all right then.

PRISMA

LORD, SHINE THE LIGHT ON MRS. SUMMERVILLE! I've been praying for her for years, Jesus! Shine the light!

Even as I prayed I remembered the day Jesus became my Savior and Lord. Daddy worked grinding lenses in the back room of an optometrist's office down on Light Street. He was a deacon at a Baptist church near our home by Patterson Park. The only white guy in the place. But you had to love my father. He was that kind of man.

Daddy arrived home from work one day while Mama was setting supper on the table. I can picture the meal to this day. Fried soft crabs my uncle had caught on the Magothy, homemade slaw, and corn bread. Mama cooked for a family on Charles Street. Even their parties. No caterers necessary for shindigs at the Brookses' house when Mama set her hand to the stove with such expertise.

Well, Daddy look tired. He ran a hand through his blond hair, and Mama kissed his forehead. "Revina, I'd swear all of Baltimore needs new glasses."

Mama laughed. It was Saturday. She had most weekends off during the summer because the Brookses stayed at their vacation home on Gibson Island from Friday afternoon until Sunday night. "Well, take a load off, Harold. Here's a good, tall glass of tea, and supper's almost ready."

"You didn't need to cook on your day off, Revina."

"I love to cook."

"But you do it all week."

"And I do what I love."

See where I get it from?

So we ate our meal after Daddy asked for God's blessing on the food. My younger brothers, Freddy and Harold Jr., asked if they could eat everything but the crabs.

"Don't eat it if you don't like it!" Daddy said quickly before Mama answered with her usual, "You need to try a bite of everything."

Daddy loved soft crabs more than anything.

Mama winked at him.

See, Harold and Revina Neubauer loved each other from the day they met down on the docks. He was unloading produce, his arms muscular and white, and she was trying to find a decent tomato, her brown fingers sensitive and smooth.

Daddy ate his fill and pushed away his plate. He watched while I nibbled on my corn bread. Mama'd sliced up a tomato at the last minute, and I constructed a crumbly sandwich. "Tomorrow's church, Prisma."

"Yes sir."

"Do you like church?"

"Yes sir."

"Do you know why we go to church?"

"Yes sir. To learn about the Lord."

"Who is God's Son, Prisma?"

"The Lord Jesus."

"Have you ever made Him your Savior?"

"No sir. At least I don't think I have."

"Do you think it's time?"

Mama put her towel on the counter and sat down next to me. "Let me, Harold. You can be a bull in a china shop about stuff like this."

"I'll put on some coffee."

"That'd be good." She gathered up my hand, and in her sweet, soft voice, her relaxed, ink-black hair falling over one shoulder, Mama took all of my Sunday-school lessons and bundled them in one package she called The Gospel.

I asked Jesus to be my Savior that very day!

The next day we learned a new song in Sunday school.

Oh, how I love Jesus. Because He first loved me. I was five years old.

Mrs. Summerville needs Jesus. We all need Jesus.

When Mr. Summerville lay dying, a nurse came in. One of Mama's people. She wore a pin that said "Jesus."

"I like that pin."

The light from her beautiful smile engulfed me, Mr. Summerville, the sickbed, the entire private room. "You gotta have Jesus," she said. "Everybody's gotta have Jesus."

I nodded.

"Does that man there have Jesus?" she asked me, as I sat there holding his hand, the morphine having taken him from his pain.

"He sure does."

"Amen, sister."

"Amen is right."

God's people are everywhere. In hospitals, the grocery stores, the houses we live in. They're everywhere.

Days of Summer sent a check to a man in California who takes kids off the streets and shows them how to dance. We're a nonprofit organization, so we don't just give to Christian organizations. But I can sniff out a brother or sister in Christ from clear across the country. When I called him last Friday and told him a check to put in a new heating system was on the way, he said, "Praise God!"

That's exactly right.

Praise God.

Lark

DR. J'S BEEPER TWITTERED in the middle of the homily. He waved to catch my eye, held up the wicked electronic device, shrugged in apology, and hurried down the aisle and out the door.

The pink getup was for nothing.

I should have known better than to step out like I did. Who did I think I was? Wearing a gauzy pink dress, pretty sandals, and blow-dried hair.

If God wanted me to date, He would have sent someone my way long ago.

Nevertheless, I let Marsha talk me into walking a few steps down to the 3 B's for lunch. Deke and Babe take Sundays off, and some odd guy who looked like a pumpkin with appendages worked the grill while this ancient woman with a topknot puttered back and forth from counter to booth like Tim Conway when he played that annoying old guy.

I hated that part of *The Carol Burnett Show*. Loved everything else though.

"So tell me all about Flannery's new boyfriend!" Marsha sipped her cup of boiling hot, winter-day coffee. Never mind it was 97 degrees outside and I had sweated clear through the linen of Flannery's nice dress.

Thank goodness the restaurant was air-conditioned. I can hardly imagine the days before air conditioning! I don't know how my mother always maintained her cool air of sophistication.

"I haven't met him yet. She doesn't say much, but she does call him her boyfriend already. Seems to be going pretty fast."

Marsha knew all about fast. She'd married Glen after three weeks of dating. "It could still work."

"He's Catholic."

"So? You're around Catholics all the time. I'm Catholic."

"But I'm really Methodist deep down."

"Oh, phooey, Lark. It's the same Jesus."

"I don't want to talk about theology. Anyway, she's gone to mass with him this morning. He went to church with her last night."

"Sounds good, doesn't it? Most kids their age couldn't care less about faith."

"Yeah, I suppose."

The waitress delivered our food. Overnight delivery, apparently. It was all I could do not to hop up and yank the plates out of her hands before she dropped them. I checked to make sure my burger was totally plain. Marsha picked up a chicken wing, not giving a rip about her beautiful, frosted manicure.

Hey, since when did the 3 B's start doing food like chicken wings? That sure wasn't nice for them to go contemporary on me like that.

We ate in silence for a while. She took a sip of her tea, then cleared her throat. "What happened to you, Lark, happens to very few people. Flannery deserves to fall in love."

"I know. I haven't said anything to her. I promise."

"It's more than about not saying anything, hon. Maybe you should encourage her to bring him down to St. Dominic's so you can meet him?"

"You think that would be a good idea?"

"I thought of it, didn't I?"

How do I describe Marsha? She sat there in her tight peach suit with coordinating blouse and scarf. Peach shoes too. Her calves, encased in fat-enhancing white hosiery, ballooned from off her shin bones. She ran at eighty miles per hour on love. Crowned with the worst of losses, Marsha knew suffering, pain. And she always had time for me.

"Tell you what. Why don't you all come over to my house for a crab feast next weekend? Glen'll put some hot dogs on the grill. We'll roast some corn, too. It'll be fun."

"I'll suggest it."

"And why don't you ask your mother to come, Lark?"

"Leslie? Oh, she'll never agree to that!"

"Just promise me you'll try."

"Okay. But only because it's you, Marsha."

Her smug grin easied her plump face even more.

I could hear her thinking, "Yes! Another step in the right direction!"

I wish I could be like her. I really do.

Flannery

I ALWAYS THOUGHT CATHOLIC PEOPLE HAD NO CLUE about what they believed. Like, religion was something you inherited, you know? I tell James exactly that. We are sitting around Loch Raven, a reservoir in the county, and there are some leftover hippie types (So give it up already. Jerry Garcia's dead. Dead. Dead, I tell you!) hanging around wearing tank tops, very droopy skin draped over emaciated health-food muscles. And lady, if you can't afford a bra, I'll be glad to buy you one before you start tucking them under your waistband.

James has his arm around me. "A lot of Catholics are like that. Religion has always been fascinating to me."

"Just religion?" Look at the green on that mallard duck's head. If that doesn't tell you there's a God, I don't know what does.

"Well, no. Christianity. You know. Jesus Christ."

"Yeah."

"Do you think you would convert ever?"

I shrug. "I've never thought about it."

"The Church is important to me, Flannery."

"Plain old Jesus is important to me."

"Me, too."

"How?"

And then he talks about Christ in very personal terms. Of course, I don't hear the usual Protestant buzz words like "asking Jesus in my heart" or "made Him my personal Savior." I just hear words like the crucifixion, the resurrection, a loving God who sent His Son to provide redemption to all mankind and how He believes all that. "Sure I fail at putting it into practice, Flannery. But if we didn't fail at it, we wouldn't need Jesus in the first place."

"Do you pray a lot? Or just do the candle-lighting thing every once in a while?"

"If you pulled up beside me in my car and looked over, you'd doubt my sanity."

"Then why the anger?"

"Who said I was angry?"

"Well, when we first met at Starbucks you seemed mad."

"I thought you were so pretty, I just acted like a jerk."

So. Okay.

I want to ask him the sexual habits question but can't just then. The major hurdle is crossed. He loves Jesus too.

Leslie

MY SCRAPBOOK IS COMING ALONG NICELY. Pages of color and texture. Events at a glance. Themes that bind otherwise nonconnected events. Like the party section. My stars, I had all these pictures of parties I'd attended with Charles, pictures that didn't even ring a bell!

Horrors!

I mean, surely one would remember a picture of herself in a sapphire blue Southern belle ball gown and her husband in a Rhett Butler getup?

Nothing. Absolutely nothing.

It truly is ghastly.

"Prisma!"

She'd remember.

She paddled in, wiping her hands on a tea towel.

"Do you recognize this?"

Taking the picture, she settled a pair of reading glasses onto her nose. Half-eyes the color of a tangerine.

"When did you get those glasses, Prisma? I didn't know you wore reading glasses?"

"I didn't before this afternoon."

"And you've already got them on a chain around your neck?"

"No sense in fighting it anymore, Mrs. Summerville. Fact is, my arm isn't going to get any longer."

"Charles said the exact same thing when he first got his."

And the look that passed over Prisma's face was so dear I wanted to cry and cry.

Oh, the years. The years.

Why, God? Why does time pass like this, leaving our arms too short, the nights too long, and the days speeding by and eating up the years we have left like hyenas over a rotting zebra corpse?

Or a rotting dodo bird.

She rested a hand on my shoulder and peered at the picture. "Well, let's see now. You're wearing that five-strand pearl necklace, which puts it in the late '50s I think. Remember?"

"Oh yes. I wore those pearls quite frequently then. And they were stolen in late '59, right? Is that right?"

"M'm, h'm. On that Nordic cruise."

"Well?"

"All I can think of is that costume party they had for the BSO. Was that it? I could have sworn you wore an emerald dress to that."

"I don't know."

She reached over and flipped through the few pages I'd completed while she went to church. "You've been quite busy."

"Pretty, aren't they?"

"They sure are. I like the party theme going here. No rhyme or reason as to chronology, but it works."

"Thank heavens! If I had to overorganize this thing I'd have quit long ago."

"Are you going to pass this down to Newly?" Prisma asked.

We laughed and laughed.

August

Flannery

PRISMA PATIENTLY LISTENS TO EVERY DETAIL as I tell her about my day. We sit at the kitchen table Monday morning drinking a cup of coffee, and we're talking about faith issues. Like, the whole Catholic-Protestant thing, and is Christianity really about Jesus or Jesus plus stuff? And if you believe in the "stuff" as well, won't Jesus still come through for you at the end despite the extras? Won't He say, "Well, you got the basic gist, and now you can rest and not worry about all that stuff. Not that you ever had to. So be free and live in My grace like you were always meant to live. Enter into your rest"?

And James too. We talk about James and what he said about faith.

"So what do you think?"

"Sounds like the real deal to me, Baby Girl."

"Me, too."

"So where did you have lunch?"

"Orchard Inn."

"Nice."

"With his parents?"

"Uh-huh."

"You didn't order the most expensive thing on the menu, now did you, Baby Girl?"

"You taught me better than that, Miss Prisma."

"You got that right."

She stands to her feet. "Now come into my room. I got to show you the funniest thing I found on the Internet this afternoon!"

Prisma and the Internet. Now who in the world would figure?

Looking at some bizarre picture of some person with at least a hundred piercings on his/her face, Prisma says, "See, it could be a whole lot worse with that boy James." Prisma and I played some games together on Boxerjam.

"I feel like drawing," I say without warning, even to me. The urge hits like that all the time, and my mouth just blurts like a cherry tomato bit unawares.

"Then go to it. Your grandmother's knitting in the conservatory today. It would be a nice place to go draw, and you know she'd love the company."

I gather my box of pencils and a pad and head in with Grandy.

Grandy gives me one of her usual, pretty smiles. "I'm happy to see you, Sweet Pea!"

I love her so much.

Lark

"HELLO?"

"Prayer Lady?"

"That's me!" I examined the Christmas stocking, proud of my progress. Those little roses are really easy once you get the hang of it. And the daisies are a snap.

"It's your musician friend."

"Huh?" I know lots of musicians. I pointed my toes there on the bed, trying to stretch my feet.

"You know, the guy that was about to get the record contract whose mother was all worried over it?"

"Oh yeah! How you doin'?"

"Great! I got the deal!"

"How's Mom?"

"Upset. Can you pray for her?"

"Sure. How about for you?"

"Well, things are going pretty good. I'll let you know when I need a leg up."

"We can always use a leg up."

"Yeah. Probably. But I hate to bother God if it isn't really necessary."

Leslie

I HAVEN'T GONE RIDING IN ALMOST TWO WEEKS. I wonder if Jacob Marley misses me? As Sweet Pea would say, "I crack myself up!"

Sweet Pea came home all sweet and blushed yesterday after her day out with her new boyfriend. This James has swashbuckled her heart. It dismays me a bit that he isn't Protestant, but nowadays, with life so precarious, I'll not complain. She tells me he's the scientific type, which encouraged me quite a bit. In my day, the scientific types seemed very unaware of "the latest." I like that. Flannery can be a bit trendy, or more to the point, worried about making a statement, as they call it these days. Perhaps this James fellow will influence her for the good along those lines.

Far be it from me to complain about her clothing though. Good girls like her deserve a little freedom. I remember my own days. It's too easy now to remember the good old days.

I swore I'd have better things to do when the geriatric phase settled on me.

Settled, did I say? Hardly.

No one prepared me for the walloping it delivers. I look in the mirror every now and again and say, "Where are you, Leslie?" Who is that old lady there? Who is that with the mouth corners that droop naturally into an expression of dissatisfaction? Who is that woman with the receding eyes? Who exchanged those sagging upper lids for my sculpted eye sockets? I look in the mirror every now and again, and I remember all the times Charles and I shared when I was young and fresh like Flannery, but tasteful. Dancing at the resorts, hopping on planes. The scarves I used to wear!

So I don't dream of uttering anything to her about her appearance! She's the prettiest one in the house. But I am the loneliest. How did this happen? How did a woman who surrounded herself with friends and acquaintances and causes end up haunting her own home, day after day?

I can't even fill up my schedule anymore. This tiredness has stolen even my paltry attempt at meaning. Mama always told me, "Don't rest on your laurels, Leslie Lee! Today is a new day. Measure your success by today only. The past is the past for the good and the bad."

Why does the woman continue to haunt me so? And who was she to talk, sitting up her room day after day with her friend Jack Daniel?

Once, when I was sixteen, I prayed for her to die.

She had no right to do that to me, to place all her failures upon me, to expect more than she ever gave. I've tried so hard to do the opposite with Larkspur. I've stepped back and watched her live her own life, a life hardly lived on the terms she ultimately wishes. But she's doing the best she can, and I admire her. I'd like to tell her that, but it would only come off as patronizing. She already thinks I take full credit for her general success as a decent human being. Which I do not! If anyone deserves the credit for it, it would be Charles and Prisma.

And you can take that to the bank!

Last night exhaustion overcame me completely. I'd read the Bible a bit but found my concentration sorely lacking. I did read the portion about the loaves and fishes and found that pastor to be all wet, just as I expected. The words are clear. He multiplied the little bit shared by a well-brought-up boy, and a multitude of people had the delight of a good lunch at just the right time.

I'm tired of that church anyway, truth to tell.

I'm thinking of going with Prisma to hers next weekend. I'm somewhat frightened of going into such a colorful congregation in such a poor section of town. Not because I think they'll harm me. Heavens, no! I'll just feel so out of place and either look like someone beset by noblesse oblige, or like some curious onlooker who doesn't care that my presence may or may not cause a disturbance. I don't know how to approach Prisma about it. I'm frightened that merely asking her these questions will sound condescending.

Last night after tea and Scripture, I retired to my bedroom. A few years ago I bought one of those walnut armoires that hold a television and VCR behind the door.

Why? Who knows?

Not much of a television viewer, really. I wondered even then at the purchase. But every so often of an evening I pad up there, change into my nightgown, and snuggle in with a nice, warm remote and a mug of whatever Prisma thinks I need.

How bad is television these days? Perfectly frightful.

Too tired to read, too worried to sleep, I slipped between the covers and clicked on a station they call VH-1. My stars. What in heaven's name is that supposed to mean? Very Honestly One Ghastly Scene of Gyrating Bodies and Ill-Fitting Streetwalker Clothing is my summation of it.

So I clicked from that station to one called TCM. Now, that was surely a pleasant surprise! There he smiled, my main squeeze from the silver screen, Cary Grant.

Oh my.

I saw him sit with the old grandmother on the French Riviera, Deborah Kerr looking on wistfully as she thought, "Well, this fellow is surely more than meets the eye." And then the poor thing gets in an accident and won't tell him she's paralyzed.

And I don't blame her one bit!

Frankly, I'd have said something horribly cruel to Nicky once he figured out the whole painting cover-up to have ensured his hasty retreat. I'd have said, "Get out of here, you playboy. It took an accident of this magnitude to keep me from meeting you as planned. And it took a recovery the likes of something you've never seen to show me what a mistake the entire cruise had been! So be gone! Shoo! And leave me alone. I've survived without you this long, and I'll continue to get along just fine!"

And then I would have found myself all alone. Just like now. But oh, sitting there, sitting there watching her and remembering how *An Affair to Remember* was one of the few movies Charles and I sat through in a theater—well, I felt young again. Alive and comforted that shows like this still find an audience. And I rejoiced for Larkspur and Flannery, whose lives still stretch ahead of them into an always pregnant if uncertain future.

Flannery arrived home just as *Flying Down to Rio* flared onto the screen.

"Who is that woman?" she asked, pointing at Delores del Rio.

I told her.

"Oh, Grandy! You've been right all these years! Look at that gorgeousness! A simple bun at the back of her head. And that dress."

"Clean lines, Sweet Pea. I've always said it, the cleaner the lines the better."

Flannery hurried back to her room and brought in a brown-paper bag of red licorice. "Here, Grandy. Take one. There's no fat, so it's not bad for your heart."

She ate hers as is, letting it hang from her mouth as she watched the show. I tied mine in a succession of knots, remembering the wonderful chokers and bracelets I used to make as a child.

"Too bad we've already gone to New York, Grandy. I would have gone with an entirely new angle. Guess it's too late now."

"It's never too late."

Tomorrow, I'm going to take her up to the attic and let her sift through all my old clothes from my younger days. That James will think he's the luckiest young man in the world. And I am thinking maybe I should take my own advice and believe it never really is too late.

On Friday I go in for a heart catheterization. I'm not even telling Prisma this time, or she'll have me traipsing who-knows-where afterward. I've already sworn Asil to secrecy.

Truth to tell, I'm frightened. I'm frightened again. I knew getting old meant aches and pains and even loneliness. But no one ever warned me about the fear.

Lark

"JOHNNY'S HERE, LARK!" Marsha yelled as she ushered down the steps into her club basement. An hour late, he wore an endearing blush.

I blushed back, darn it. And why did she have to yell it like that? Why single me out? Did the whole study group have to know?

So I flopped one of those annoying little waves. Hardly the greeting of an SUV woman with tweed miniskirts.

Johnny sat down next to me and whispered. "Sorry about Sunday. Had an emergency. Did you get my message on your machine yesterday?"

I nodded.

"So is that okay?" he asked.

"Yeah. But I don't eat much sugar. Can I go and just get a cup of tea?"

"I told you I'm safe, didn't I? We'll have dessert time without the dessert."

Dessert time. Not a "date." Oh my word.

Now I questioned the wisdom of accepting his invitation in the first place.

And then he turned, and a hint of his smell floated over to my little space, and I breathed it in. So fresh and nice. Just nice. I never noticed a big guy like him ever smelling that nice.

Strange.

Don't start worrying, Lark.

And what did dessert ever do to anyone? Just "dessert time" might prove the best thing for all concerned.

That's right. That's just what he had said.

Not a date. Just "dessert time."

Father Charlie prayed earnestly like he always does. See, he knows prayer isn't meaningless. And twenty minutes later we sat at the Double T Diner over on Bel Air Road waiting for the waitress to acknowledge our seemingly meaningless existence.

"This is a little far from Hamilton, isn't it?"

"I can have you home in twenty minutes."

I pulled out some hand cream Flannery dropped in my backpack and squeezed a kiss-sized portion on my hands.

He held out his hand. "Can I have some?"

"Sure. I guess you have to take care of your hands, don't you?"

"They're looking pretty bad. I've had to scrub a lot this week."

"I did nails for a while back in the early nineties. What you need is an extra-long massage."

"Sounds good."

He looked weary.

I asked, "Surgeries today?"

"Every day, it seems."

"I'm sure you were wonderful."

Who said that? Me?

Oh my word!

My overly chipper words hung in the air like a chant from a short-skirted cheerleader. Rah, rah! Sis-boom-bah! Cardiac surgeon! Rah, rah, rah! What in the world was I thinking? Me, a recluse organist, and a selfless, highly trained guy like him?

Selfless for sure. Why else would he be sitting here with me? That's most definitely altruism.

I hate myself.

Then he blushed as he extended his left hand. "Would you consider that hand rub right now?"

Uh, okay.

If I thought of this as an Exercise in Bravery, I might get through it.

"Uh…well, okay. Hold on." I dug through my bag for more moisturizing cream. "You want one here? Right here at the Double T Diner?"

He blushed. "Sorry. I'm still not used to this sort of thing."

"Me either."

"Was it too forward to ask?"

"Beats me, Johnny." All I knew is that Brad wouldn't have even asked for the hand rub. He'd have just stuck it right on out there, expecting me to know. His guitar calluses always made his fingertips look like he'd dipped them in hot wax.

But Johnny's hands belonged in another realm. I took his beautiful, lifesaving hand in mine, dolloped more cream in its palm, and got to work. "Is that good?"

"Yes. Very relaxing."

"Good."

He closed his eyes, peacefully settling into relaxation, his other arm resting on a belly shrouded in an ancient dark blue T-shirt with the words, "Maryland is for Crabs" stretched across its expanse. And I was happy for a moment.

My gosh. I was.

A soft breeze of exhilaration swirled through my sinuses and behind my eyes. Johnny Josefowski was used of God to heal. He performed miracles every day. And here he sat, tired and worn and silent and needing to be stolen from his own cares for a little while. I massaged his hands through the waitress's order taking, through the first round of coffee, and stopped when his pie arrived.

I was meeting a need.

Yes ma'am. A face-to-face need.

No wonder Prisma lived from strength to strength. For the first time in my life, I began to understand that her attitude of service didn't only benefit us, it fulfilled a basic human need inside of Prisma, it strengthened a vital emotional muscle I barely knew existed.

"Is your mom worried about the catheterization on Friday?"

What? Oh no. What catheterization? I'm going to kill that woman before her heart gets the chance! "Not really."

"Dr. Medina is great at caths, Lark. If there's any way he can put a balloon in, he will. Then she won't need surgery."

"Or you."

He laughed. "That's right. I like it if they never have to get to me."

"The last hope?"

"You could say that, although that's really up to God, isn't it?"

"Yeah."

So Mother was still trying to hide all this from me. Oh man, what now? I wanted to wake her up as soon as Johnny dropped me off at home and drag her over the coals. But if she wanted to shut us all out again, then so be it. At least I could check up on things through Johnny.

Later, Johnny walked me to the side porch door. "So you'll be playing this Sunday?"

"Uh-huh. I haven't missed a Sunday in years." I felt my skin deepen to red.

"What are you playing? Or do you want it to be a surprise?"

I laughed. "Hardly! No, I'm playing Mendelssohn.'"

"Do you know how special you are?" He tapped his fingers along the doorpost. "Oh, I don't know how to say this."

"Say what?" I feigned obliviousness. I refused to assume.

"You honestly don't know what I mean? About us?"

"Not really." That wasn't a lie.

"We've seen each other in church; since the beginning of summer I've been coming to small group; you've even asked me questions about your mother's condition. Well, I was wondering if maybe—"

He looked down at those hands. He stood before me a man swallowing his fear.

At least I hoped. Because I was swallowing mine.

Did he really understand me after all?

I wanted to say something to relieve his stress, but nothing came to mind that wouldn't totally embarrass us both, or worse, ruin what I believed to be his intentions.

"Well, I was wondering if maybe we could do something together after church on Sunday and if you'd consider this a real date and not just dessert time."

"Okay."

"I mean, I don't know why I called it dessert time back at Marsha's. That was stupid."

"Have you been cursing yourself for that all this time?"

"Yes."

"Sunday sounds fine."

Fine? Well, that certainly wasn't over the top.

But then I heard Leslie's voice. "Don't show an overeagerness, Larkspur. Men don't appreciate that sort of thing."

That sort of thing.

"So Sunday after church then?" He opened the screen door.

"Okay. I'll look forward to it."

"I will too. I'll look for you before the service. Unless an emergency comes up. You know how that can be."

Well, no. Not those kinds of emergencies. Not cardiac-arrest kinds of emergencies.

Cardiac arrest.

Scary enough though to throw one into the state itself. And the name. CARDIAC ARREST. And what about Mother? Is she due for that? Could it happen at any time?

"Lark?"

Will I come in one day and say, "Hello, Mother," and she'll say hello weakly, and then her heart will just stop? What do I do then?

"Lark?"

Do I call 911 first? Or begin CPR first and then call 911 between puffs? Does Prisma know CPR? I'd definitely holler for her first. Prisma would guide us through it right.

"Lark?"

I looked up.

"Wow. I felt like a fly buzzing around your head for a moment there!"

"Sorry."

And then a bright smile warmed his face. And those eyes! Those deep blue eyes crinkled at the corners. He backed away from the door. "See you Sunday then. I'll call you if I have to go into surgery." And I gave my stupid little self-conscious laugh and stupid little self-conscious wave. "Okay."

Then he poked his head back through the doorway. "By the way, I think your hair looks nice, Lark."

"Thanks. My daughter did it."

Now why did I say that? Makes me sound cheap.

You are cheap.

"She a beautician?"

"No, she's an artist."

"That explains it then."

Explains what, Johnny? I wasn't about to ask.

"Okay, I'll see you, Lark."

"Bye."

Bye. Bye. Bye. Bye. Bye. I really figured by the time a woman got to be my age, moments like this might not flow like a river of nuts, bolts, nails, and screws.

And what am I doing anyway? Going on a real date? With Bradley coming back around? With my relationship with Flannery hanging in the balance of my years of lies?

Am I crazy?

That night after Marsha called to find out what happened, I pulled the phone away from my ear she yelled so loudly at the news. "You should bring him to the cookout on Saturday!"

"No way!"

"Well, why not?"

"Because I'm not going to ask him to do something with me before the first date, Marsha! Please, be serious now."

"H'm. Well, okay. I can see your point."

One of Marsha's good qualities is that she sees my point every now and again. "I mean, I may have been out of the dating loop for a while now—"

"Two decades."

"Thank you, Mrs. Fortenbaugh."

"Sorry."

"That's okay. Anyway, I may have been out of the loop for a while, but I do know that calling him up beforehand reeks of desperation."

"I know. I said I could see your point."

"I was just making sure you knew what my point was exactly."

"Oh, Lark! You tickle me!"

I wasn't about to ask why. And you know, I really think I've lost my sense of humor. I really do. I haven't noticed it until now. Too busy. Too worried. Too busy being worried. Maybe underneath all that education and skill, Johnny Josefowski was a real yukster.

A regular stooge.

⌒

"So really, it's going to be fun, Mother. Marsha's husband says he'll even cook a chicken breast for you instead of a fatty burger."

Mother rolled her eyes. "I'm so sick of chicken I could lay an egg."

"Don't eat those much either, do you, Mrs. Summerville?" Prisma rocked back on her heels as she stood at the sink slicing up strawberries. I've often wondered about her feet. Compared to the rest of her they're just plain bony. But wide. Prisma's feet have always reminded me of a platypus.

Well, no wonder, Lark. She's stood on them all her adult years taking care of you and your mother!

"I don't think I should go, Larkspur. What do they want an old woman like me around for anyway?"

Flannery, home for supper before heading out with James to buy some art supplies, said, "You can wear that new pantsuit you got in New York. That cream-colored one."

I watched my mother sit there for several seconds. Her cool face never airs out her mind, but when she sits and thinks for a bit, she'll usually end up bowing to our whims.

"All right. But only if we can take two cars. Honestly, Larkspur, I don't think I can last all day out in the sun."

"Fine. That's fine."

Prisma turned around, bowl in hand. "I think it'll be fun, Mrs. Summerville."

"Well, what will you do all day, Prisma?"

"Oh, I think I can find something to keep busy."

I clapped my hand on my mouth. Don't laugh too loudly.

Mother just looked disgusted, as usual.

Always, always I thought she was disgusted at me. But now I had to wonder.

After the meal I looked up the word *panic* on the Internet on Prisma's computer. And lo and behold! I read all about myself all over the place.

The ants.

The heartbeat speeding up.

All that.

The nausea.

I am a wacko.

Okay. Not a real wacko. But definable at least. And that's good news.

But I had to admit life doesn't feel as paper-thin as before. That onion-skin crackle fades more and more each day. Greenway, so strong and solid, seems to dole out its own brand of courage. Maybe bravery goes along with the territory here on Greenway.

Or maybe it's just the bravery of the other women that's lifting me high above the flames of my own funeral pyre.

Marsha played this Irish music when we drove back to Greenway after the dinner at Denny's she had insisted on dragging me to the next night. "What in the world are you listening to now?"

She turned it up and sang with it.

My stars!

All these dips and twirls with her voice.

The song stopped. So did she. "I hear there's big money in Irish singing these days. Festivals and stuff."

"Yeah?"

"Yeah. Me and Glen, we're thinking about moving out to Carroll County, and we'll need the extra cash."

I began to sing "The Farmer in the Dell."

"You said it, Lark. Must be good farm cooks out there because 80 percent of the women are fatter than I am!"

"So you're thinking about moving out of Hamilton?"

She nodded. "I've only stayed here this long… Never mind."

Oh no. I wanted to finish the sentence for her. I knew the rest. A stronger person might have owned up to it and given Marsha credit for keeping up her end of a truly one-sided friendship.

"You think you'll ever come back to Hamilton to live, Lark?"

"I think so."

"Have you seen the lot since the fire?"

I shook my head.

She clicked the gearshift back into reverse.

When I first learned to drive, I forced myself to take difficult routes to the store or to school. I resisted going three blocks out of my way to make a left turn at a light instead of heading right up to the end of the street where the stop sign waited. I called these my Exercises in Bravery. I exercised my bravery several times a week.

They stretched out over the years. Once a week. Once a month. Only when absolutely necessary.

An Exercise in Bravery.

Yes.

There is no fear in love.

All right then.

Bayonne Avenue.

No ants, right? Be gone.

Shoo.

"You're taking me to Bayonne Avenue?"

"Uh-huh."

I sat back in my seat and began to pray. I'd survive this. Of course I would. I mean who never returned after viewing a long cold ruin of a fire?

It was almost like I was on a date. Marsha pulled up and came around to my side of the car. She opened my door.

"Ready, kiddo?"

"No."

"I know. How 'bout this then? Think you can get out of the car?"

"I'll try."

And so I tried to think about other things as I latched on to her hand. Any other thing. I thought of Mickey Mouse and Bugs Bunny, and I thought of the day Daddy showed me the new organ in the living room.

He'd been proud and almost like a kid, his excitement sizzled everything within two feet of him that Saturday afternoon. "Play me a good one, Larkie!"

"Oh, Daddy!"

Oh, Daddy!

Oh, Daddy! What a horrible, horrible sight!

Nothing left.

The late August sun shone down into the hole against the charred cinder blocks of the basement. The stairs had been ripped down and hauled off, and I thought, "I wonder if you could fill this thing with water and take a swim?"

And I fell to my knees.

Flannery

I'VE GOT TO SAY, MOM'S CIRCUS POSTCARD collection gets weirder and weirder. In the early days it was mostly setup scenes and animals. Then people acts like The Acrobat Family: G and K Bon-hair Truppe.

So, okay. Whatever a Truppe is.

Some of these cards are actually a linen variety. Is that cool or what? I'd like to paint on that.

There's Dr. Saw D. Po Min and his white elephant. That one's kind of cool. And then there's the garden-variety trapeze artists, tightrope walkers, and springboard leapers. Mademoiselle Cleo and her twenty-nine-foot python.

But I opened a new book today. Number three in her four-book collection. And I felt a chill run up and down my spine. See, this book was begun when I was three years old, after my father zoomed off and crashed on his motorcycle.

There's Zella the Frog Impersonator. He's a contortionist. Along with Marie Skitchen. She's one as well. And you know how today you see contortionists in lean gold or silver leotards? Well, there she sits on a chair, legs around her neck, and she's wearing a black gown and a white apron.

How strange is that?

But there's more! The Russian Giant and the Midget Policeman. Four hundred and fifty-seven pound Jolly Ray. Twins that weigh over eleven hundred pounds between them.

Even an albino! I wonder if Uncle Newly sent that one to her. Funny, but I've never thought of albinos as being all that strange.

Next week Prisma and I are going down to the Outer Banks for our photo trip. I can't wait. James and I went down to southern Maryland

and took pictures of the Hooper's Island Light. We held hands a lot. Not much kissing there, but handholding. James has those knuckly kind of hands, the kind where the fingers are real thin at the bottom, concaves where my fingers fit just right.

I love him.

I know I've said that before, but I'll just say it again.

I love him.

His mom invited me for dinner Saturday night. I'm going to wear one of Grandy's old outfits. It's from the '50s and looks very Audrey Hepburnish. Navy blue with a cinched waist, a silk belt out of the same fabric as the dress, and a crinoline like you see in those movies. I'm having it let out because I'm definitely not Grandy's old size. Okay, to be truthful, I added four-inch gussets on either side. Thank God for home ec and Prisma!

Remember Edith Head? I found a book on her at the store today. Now there was a woman who knew how to dress other women! I'd imagine Grandy has that sort of talent if she'd have been encouraged to go her own way like Mom and I have. She really is the frustrated, creative sort imprisoned by her own status.

So I try putting my hair up in a French twist today and it works. I trimmed little bangs, and let me just say, I'm excited about this new style. It will certainly make me stand out at Maryland Institute. And I even bought two pairs of pedal pushers and a twinset today! A pair of *Rear Window* sunglasses and a scarf, and I'm set for the trip.

James is excited about my new look. He said it's wonderful that I'm the type of person that's not afraid of reinventing her style, just so long as I don't expect him to do the same.

Of course, I wouldn't do that in a million years. Except for the Tommy jacket. Maybe one day, when we're older, I'll be able to lose it in the laundry with an odd sock or two.

We are standing by Hooper's Island Light watching the sunset. I love Thursdays because I don't have to go into work. Prisma helped me pack what she calls "a darned nice spread," as I love picnics so much.

As we stand there by the lighthouse, watching the pelicans and herons do their things, talking about all the spiritual metaphors one can come up with regarding lighthouses and getting, I must say, some pretty good ones, James says, "You're the only girl I've ever dated that I can show my spiritual side to."

"That's quite a compliment."

"It is. It really is. I feel free. Like I can really be all of me all the time."

That's how it is with us. All of me, all the time.

I like that.

The "promiscuous discussion" with him up is still on the shelf, so I just blurt out, "I'm a virgin!"

Well, he looks at me, examining me, then says, "Let's go sit down."

"I feel sick now."

"Don't."

So he leads me over to a bench by the water and sits me down. "Flannery, are you ashamed of that?"

"No. It's just that, well, I don't know what you expect. Or where you've been."

Then he looks out over the bay. "I've got regrets. I can tell you that."

Then I look out over the bay.

"Flannery, if I had known you were out there, I would have waited. In my heart I've been waiting for you all of my life."

Honest truth, that's just what he said!

"Are you willing to still wait for me?" I ask.

He reaches out and turns my face toward him. "Have I tried to put the make on you up to this point?"

"No."

"I won't. I promise you I won't. I knew you were different from the beginning, Flannery. You had virgin written all over you."

You know, there are times in life when you're in a snapshot. Here we are, sitting on the water's edge, his fingers wrapped around my chin as though he held a Ming vase. And I look up into his eyes. "I need to know how many girls you've slept with."

"Three. Why?"

Drat. Two would be better. But three is better than four or more. At least it's well within the one-hand criteria.

"This may sound a little hard, but I don't want to be picking up the pieces for somebody's mistakes, if you know what I mean."

I picture babies showing up on the hip of a strange woman, and all sorts of crawly viruses and crustaceans inside of James, which, as you can guess, really weirds me out.

"Flannery, do you still want to see me?"

I think for a few seconds. I think about judging and standards. I've always hoped my marriage bed would be completely free. But I love him.

I love him.

"Yes. I do."

See, sometimes love says, "It was a mistake. Everybody makes mistakes." And if love can't exactly forget it, it can certainly dismiss it as in the past.

And then he kisses me. He asks, "Can you forgive me?"

"Why do you ask me that?"

"I should have had more faith."

"We're all guilty of that, James."

"I know. But this is important."

"Did you love those girls?"

"One I did. The first girl. I was only fifteen."

A baby.

"Do you remember it?"

"Uh-huh. It was horrible. First times usually are, they say."

"I want mine to be wonderful."

"Oh, it will be, babe. It will be."

See what I mean about taking a stand? See how much harder it is to hold out? Because, back at the beginning of our day, I could have said, "Let's just go to a motel." And that would have been the day. But we'd said some important words, and made a wealth of good decisions in a single conversation.

"I'm glad you told me the truth," I say. "Because if you'd said you're a virgin, I would have known you were lying."

"I'm glad you asked."

"Really?"

"Yeah."

"Would you have slept with me if I had asked?"

"I don't honestly know. Let's just be thankful we don't have to find out."

That had to be good enough.

I always pictured myself marrying some church boy. Some khaki-panted guy with a fish on his car. But sometimes God has other things in mind. See, James has miles to go in his faith walk. Me, too. But he loves Jesus, and to my way of thinking, that's as good a start as any.

Leslie

TOMORROW MORNING, SEVEN O'CLOCK, Asil will pull the car around. Again, I'm frightened. Can you just imagine? Probing into someone's arteries? It's perfectly frightful, if you ask me. But nobody's asked me, because nobody knows.

Hurrah for me.

I picked up the Bible earlier tonight. Having come to complete disagreement with that upstart of a pastor, I decided to read the epistle my dear nurse Annie used to read on the sleeping porch in the summers. I hated the sleeping porch! So she'd lie out there with us until at least I slept. I'm the baby of the family, you see.

The book of First John.

Annie's voice came back to me all these years later. I read the epistle, but the voice in my head belonged to Annie. And I remembered her saying, "I'll pray for you all my life, Miss Leslie." She said that to me on my wedding day, and I said, "Fiddle!"

"Fiddle away, missy. But know my prayers are accompanying whatever music you make with your life from here on out."

Annie went away after I left. No more young people left to oversee, no more parties to give, no more dresses to make.

"I'll keep you in my heart," she whispered as Charles and I pulled away.

"And I'll keep you in mine," I whispered in return. But I don't think she heard. I've always regretted that.

"There is no fear in love. Perfect love casts out fear." That's what John wrote.

Perfect love? How on earth?

The more years I collect, the more I realize my imperfections. How many bad decisions I made over the years. How many good ones I made for all the wrong reasons.

Perfect love.

I need to ask Prisma just how one achieves something like that.

And so I turned off the light and prayed. I prayed for the women of Greenway, and even Asil. I prayed for Annie, though she must be dead and gone. No one knew what happened to her after she left our home. And with Mama's temperament, I was always afraid to ask.

PRISMA

I AM LEANING ON THE EVERLASTING ARMS! Pure and simple. No doubt about it. I look at those two women and think, "What more will it take?"

Something about being exposed to the ills of this world shucks all other problems right down to the cob, exposes the unnecessary, strips off the gilt and the polish, and gets you right down to the molecular.

And so you lean on the everlasting arms.

You lean on Jesus.

I take their troubles too much to heart. I have to tell the truth on that one. Ever since Lark visited the fire site, she's barely emerged from her room. Except for study group, where she sat beside that nice doctor. And here things were coming along so nicely with her. That Marsha! What was she thinking taking Lark out there like that?

Of course, Lark's totally avoiding the Bradley subject too, which is not good. I swear, if she puts this situation on the back burner like everything else, I'm going to knock her proverbially upside the head!

And there Mrs. Summerville sits, trying to smile and offer a suggestion or two when Lark does venture out of the room. "How about we go shopping today?" or "Look at what I found in this magazine!" And Lark shuts her out.

I'll admit, Mrs. Summerville could learn a thing or two about meeting somebody on their own turf, but she tries so hard.

Does Lark have any idea what she's doing to her mother? Does she know when she retreats like this it drives a knife into her mother's heart?

I'm glad Baby Girl is oblivious to all of this. She's loving her man and loving life! Way to go, Flannery Summerville del Champ. Greenway doesn't deserve you!

A good thing happened. Mrs. Summerville told me the stress test came out fine. And tomorrow she's shopping all day with Asil in tow.

Didn't see that one coming!

"I'm tired of my clothing, Prisma," she said. "I'm actually going to go to the mall."

"The mall?"

"Why, yes. Fall's coming, and I haven't done a thing. I'm heading to the Nordstrom Better Wear department at Towsontowne Mall, and I'll slum it. Life is too short these days. Off-the-rack is going to do from now on."

Well, I've got to say that made me chuckle inside. Nordstrom's Better Wear is slumming it? That is most definitely a hoot. But it's a hoot I'll take!

I looked up at the Great Bear tonight. Saw my Betelgeuse up there shining red. I tapped on my window. "Jesus? I got words to say."

"Yes, Prisma, My girl?"

"Something's not right here. I feel it."

"You tired?"

"No, it's Mrs. Summerville."

"She needs love, Prisma. A perfect love."

"But only You can give that."

"Exactly. Are you tired, My girl?"

"Yes, Lord. Although I don't like to admit it much."

"Lean on Me, My dearest child. You know you can."

"You got that right, Lord."

"I certainly do."

I'm going to strangle that man!

"Look, Mrs. Percy, she swore me to secrecy. The only reason I'm even saying one word is because when I dropped her off, I can say I've never seen Mrs. Summerville so frightened."

"Pale?"

"Yes ma'am, she was pale."

"A grayish pale?"

"As scared to death as you can imagine."

"You should have told me about this a lot sooner, Asil."

He drew himself up. "I answer first and foremost to Mrs. Summerville."

"The heck you do!" I felt my eyes bulge.

We were in for one of our yearly arguments if I didn't do something quickly. "Oh, forget it, Asil. I'm glad you told me when you did. I'm going to quick change out of this uniform and into my skirt and blouse. Would you bring my Duster out of the garage?"

He nodded. "All right. But I won't have you yelling at me any more today."

"That's a deal. And don't worry about coming back to pick her up. I'll bring her home in the Duster."

We shook hands, because that's just what Asil and I do.

"Well, that ride in the Duster should clear out her arteries," he said.

I hurried to my room and pulled down my green twill skirt and a gold blouse, redid my braid so it perched on top of my head like a cross-legged coronet, and clipped on my gold button earrings.

No Duster yet. That Asil puts King Syrup to shame. So I knelt by the bed.

"Lord, she's in there now. But so are You, and I'm trusting You to take care of her. Amen!"

Leslie Strawbridge Summerville is my best friend now. And I've never told that to a soul, not even to Leslie.

Oh, the years we waste in our foolishness.

Lark

FLANNERY CORNERED ME AS I GRABBED MY CRAFT BAG in the hallway near the back door. "Where you going, Mom?"

"I'm going shopping. A cab is coming." Oh man. What a lousy liar!

She crossed her arms over her bosomless chest and stared at me. "What about you, Flannery?"

"I've got the day off. So where you going?"

"I just said. Shopping."

"Really, Mom. With your craft bag? You've been Herman's Hermit for a week. Where are you going? It must be big."

"Grandy is up at St. Joe's for a heart catheterization."

"You're kidding me!"

"No. She was trying to keep it a secret, I think. Johnny Josefowski spilled the beans."

"She doesn't know you know?"

"No."

"Why does she have to be so darned secretive all the time?"

"I wish I knew, honey."

"If you ever get like that, I'll be so mad."

Get like that? I already was. I heard the ticking of the Bradley bomb as it steadily grew nuclear.

She scratched the small of her back. "If you give me two minutes, I'll throw on something and go with you."

"Don't you have to work?"

"Not until tonight."

"Okay. I'll go make a quick cup of tea."

"And cancel that cab! I'll drive."

Flannery ran back up the steps, the cadence of her feet on the hard-wood a lower-toned replacement for her childhood pitter-patter.

I hurried through the dining room and pushed open the swinging door. Prisma, standing there at the sink taking her vitamins, jumped a mile.

"Girl! You're enough to scare me to death!"

"Sorry, Prisma. I'm in a hurry."

"That'll be the day."

"Hey!" I put the kettle on and turned up the gas flame.

"Just speaking the truth. Well, as much as I'm intrigued, I've got errands of my own to run." As if on automatic pilot she fished a tea bag out of the canister and handed it to me.

"Oh yeah? Where to today?"

"Lots of places. Now I've got to go. Enjoy the tea, and for heaven's sake, don't go messing up my clean kitchen. I have no idea when I'll be back!" And she whirled out of the house, a caramel cyclone crowned in braids.

No idea when I'll be back? She really said that? That sure didn't sound like Prisma.

Almost true to her word, Flannery rushed into the kitchen five min-utes later, fresh and sweet in that Capri pants outfit she bought the week before. "Ready, Mom?"

Having already called to cancel the cab, I screwed the top on a travel mug. "Yep."

We drove north. St. Joe's was convenient, only about ten minutes away. Silence ruled, and if we gave it rein much longer, neither Flannery nor I would quite know how to handle it. Thank You, God, the traffic lights all shone green

Poor Mother. She must be so scared.

And boy, could I relate to that!

Leslie

OH, FOR HEAVEN'S SAKE, these dreadful gowns! I called for a blanket fifteen minutes ago, and here I lie freezing to death. Surely, I thought they'd perform this at Johns Hopkins, but here I lie in St. Joseph's, in an old ward they claim used to be the ICU. It reminds me of a progressive kindergarten building. Semicircular. Lots of linoleum and depressing, slick surfaces.

Why in the world did I think it was better to face this alone?

How foolish.

Oh, I can hear you, Charles. Loud and clear.

"Les, Les, Les. No man, or woman for that matter, is an island."

How many times did I hear you say that? I'll admit, it seemed awfully corny even though I know it hails from some great literary poem or other. No woman is an island indeed!

Indeed!

Indeed, my dear Charles, I bow to your wisdom.

Oh my stars! I must be frightened.

If I make it off this table and back out there feeling fine, I'm going to make some changes, let me tell you! I'm going to spread out like butter on a muffin and do a lot of things I never did, seep myself into the sweetness of the love I feel in my heart. And if that kills me, I will at least have died in the saddle, the way a Strawbridge should.

Strawbridge?

Oh, fiddle.

I am a Summerville. And now that I've finally got that into this hard head of mine, I'm going to start acting like one. I wonder how odd it would look if Asil and I had a sundae together at Friendly's?

Still freezing. I should have brought my knitting. I could have knitted an entire sweater by now, and I wouldn't be so cold.

Flannery

IT'S LIKE THIS: Greenway Avenue promotes stubborn women. If you could have seen the look on Prisma's face when we walked into the Cath Lab waiting room, you would have died laughing!

It is all I can do to hold it in.

"Well, hello, Miss Secretive!" Prisma says to Mom.

"I could say the same thing, Prisma."

They stare each other down. And well, I jump on in. "Speaking of secretive, how about Grandy?! She puts you all to utter shame."

Miss Prisma smiles with half her mouth and then decides to go whole hog with the thing. "You said it! Well, come on over and sit down. All they've got is business magazines, an issue of *Cycling World* and *Reader's Digest*s, which I normally love, but nothing seems particularly amusing today."

"Except perhaps this situation," I say, pointing to Mom and Prisma.

Mom sighs and sits down. "I'm glad you're here, Prisma."

"See?" I say. "Aren't we glad we're saved from doing the same thing to ourselves that Grandy is doing right now?"

And so I go over to the pay phone and call James, and he says right away, "Do you want me there?"

"Of course I do. But I think my mom and Prisma probably would rather it be just us."

"That's cool. Hey, how about if I pick you up later, when it's all over?"

"I've got my car here. Just keep your cell phone on. You at work?"

"Yeah."

"Okay, tell the porpoises I said hello."

"You got it."

I walk back over to the gang to find Prisma chatting up a storm with a middle-aged Baptist pastor wearing Baptist glasses and a Baptist belly. He also has a Baptist voice, but you've got to love those.

"Yep," he says, "my wife has already had angioplasty and open heart. They're not sure what's next."

He looks amazingly calm. And then Prisma says, "She's in God's hands for sure."

"Yes, she is. And the Lord knows I still need her."

"How old is she then?"

"Only forty-eight."

"My goodness! M'm, m'm, m'm. That's young for all that trouble."

He nods. "So who are you here for?"

Prisma tells him everything, then finishes up with, "You being a pastor and all, I can tell you the Lord isn't finished yet with Mrs. Summerville. He's still got plans to make her His child."

"Well, I'll be praying."

"And I'll be praying for you, Pastor. This reminds me of that song 'His Eye Is on the Sparrow.'"

"Amen, sister. I know He watches me."

And then they start talking about God's care, telling story after story of the gentle miracles of their own lives.

Now this is what it's all about. And then I wonder whether someday I will be out in the waiting room first, or will James?

Life sure is a funny thing, you know?

Lark

Dr. Medina came in around 2:30 to give us the findings. After the introductions, he sat down. I'd like to say he did so to seem more caring and concerned, but I think his feet hurt or something.

I felt the ants gathering, but I pushed them down as much as possible. This concerned Mother, not me.

"She's got a lot of blockage. I couldn't even do an angioplasty while I was in there. She's going to need bypass surgery, I'd say quadruple at least, or she'll have a heart attack. Her pick."

Her pick?

"So, there's nothing else she can do?"

"No."

Prisma said, "This can't be treated medically?"

"No, it can't. I'm sorry I don't have a better prognosis." And then he shook our hands, I suspected because that's what doctors are supposed to do, and he left the waiting room.

"Well how do you like that!" Flannery said. "What a jerk."

"You said it, Baby Girl." Prisma's feathers were clearly ruffled.

"Open-heart surgery," I said, and we sat back down on our chairs. "Do we risk going into the recovery area and letting her know we're here?"

We all thought about it for a moment.

Prisma tapped my knee. "It's your call this time, Lark. You're the daughter."

Yes, I was the daughter.

Gosh, you know, sometimes you realize you're sitting right in the middle of a possible situation totally in your care. And if you blow it, it's your own personal failure, your own bad call. And if you make the right decision, you make a lot of things right.

Easy, huh?

But usually those situations call for courage someone like me doesn't have. Chalk it up to another Exercise in Bravery.

"Oh, come on, Mom! Go in!" Flannery jumped to her feet. "It's just Grandy. She won't bite."

I sought Prisma's gaze, noticing a coating of tears on her irises. "Go on in, baby. We'll wait here until you tell us it's all right to see her."

"You're not making this easy for me, Prisma."

"That's never been my job, now has it?"

And so I picked up my craft bag, held it against my stomach, and entered the recovery room that might as well have been the Arctic Circle for all the foreignness and chill that surrounded me. Curtained compartments ensured a limited privacy for patients all around the room. Many reclined with a food-laden hospital tray hovering over their bed on one side, a loved one hovering on the other.

H'm. Mandarin oranges. Turkey sandwich. Salt substitute! There was the giveaway.

That pastor and his wife waved, and I guess he said, "I was talking to them out in the waiting room."

Oh, and she smiled so beautifully with her frosted, tousled hair and her sandwich tray there, and I prayed, I prayed, "Oh, God, show the doctors the way on this one. The world needs smiles like that. And if hers goes, I have a feeling his will too."

I turned my head and met the gaze of my mother, and I prayed some more. I didn't know what to expect other than the usual indignation, but she simply held out her hand and said, "Oh, Lark."

And I ran to the bed, sat alongside her, pulled her into my arms, and she wept, groaning as though giving birth to the world.

And so, therefore, did I.

Oh, Mommy. Mommy.

PRISMA

I'LL NEVER FORGET THE TIME we all traveled down to Greenville, South Carolina, one May for the dedication of a shelter for battered women that Days of Summer helped fund.

May down there blows warmer than May up here. Lark, still in high school, slipped on her little swimsuit and flip-flops and headed down to the pool. Of course it was just a Sheraton, and Mrs. Summerville was having a fit! But that's another story.

Lark and this other boy whose father worked for the organization just swam around in that outdoor kidney-shaped pool. Splashing, diving, doing those flips under the water, don't ask me how! She had that sleek seal head when she'd come up out of the water, and I admired that. My Jimmy and I sat by the pool, drinking ice tea and just conversing and making sure she was all right because that sign on the fence couldn't have been any clearer.

Swim at your own risk.

Now that's true pretty much wherever you find yourself.

Neither Jimmy nor I could swim, but letting Lark go down there all alone with that boy who, and I tell you the truth, had that womanizer-waiting-to-happen glint carousing in his hazel eyes, would well have fallen into that category of "knowing to do good and doing it not."

After about twenty minutes of this swimming, a hotel employee rushed through the glass door. "That's last year's water!" he cried. "The pool hasn't been cleaned yet this year!"

See what I mean?

One minute Lark was swimming in the muck, happy to be there, oblivious to the fact that it was muck, because, well, it seemed clean enough. It didn't stink. It didn't hurt. The next she was practically screaming she felt so "grossed out."

Well, it's happening to her again, I can say. Only God has chosen me to be that hotel employee screaming about uncleanness and last year's water. Let's just hope she has enough sense to get out of the water this time too.

I checked my watch, my dad's old watch. Five P.M.

They'd better let Mrs. Summerville out soon. I've got supper to make.

Bypass surgery scheduled soon. My goodness. I have no idea what to cook now. "Heart smart" sure bombed. Maybe we need to just throw in the low-cholesterol towel and have us an old-fashioned chicken barbecue like Mama's family on the Eastern Shore! Let me tell you that nothing compares to barbecued chicken from the Eastern Shore! None of that heavy, syrupy red sauce. It's light and just right.

That just about describes me, too.

Flannery

TONIGHT WE ARE SITTING around the kitchen table, all of us women of Greenway. It feels like it's been three days since the cath even though it was just this morning. Prisma stands at the stove brushing her sauce on the chicken halves. She's making twice as much because tomorrow night we're going to have chicken salad with hard-boiled eggs in it and real mayonnaise. "Honest to Pete, Mrs. Summerville," Prisma says as she glazes, "that heart-smart plan didn't do one thing. How much more can happen between now and your heart surgery in two weeks? I say let's live a little."

Grandy sits and pretends to work on that photo album. She's really just looking through pictures. But she's had a big day. "Why not, Prisma? I haven't eaten whatever I've wanted since…well, since even before I can remember."

What Grandy doesn't say was that her own mother was a real kook. She doesn't think anyone knows about Libby Lee Strawbridge, but my grandfather once told me that it took him five years after they got married to get Grandy to eat more than dry toast for breakfast.

Now she adds jam.

Woo-hoo!

I'm telling you, these Strawbridge-Summerville women are oddballs, Libby Lee, God rest her soul, as the leader of the pack.

Grandy nods. "Yes, that's it. I'm giving myself two weeks of dietary enjoyment."

"Well, Mother. Whatever weight you gain, you'll take off during your recovery from surgery." Mom darts her pencil like a flickering graphite sword at the *Sunpaper*'s crossword puzzle. When did she start doing those?

James is working the Mary Lewis skipjack for a private cruise, so it's no date for me. But that's okay. Like, we've come to the point where when you've gotta do what you've gotta do, the other misses you, but life is still moving all around us.

"What else are we having for dinner, Miss Prisma?" I lightly fork a bowl of Bisquick dough. I learned to make drop biscuits at college.

Prisma eyes my attempt at bread making. "As I am supremely wary of whatever it is you're making, Baby Girl, I believe another starch is definitely in order."

Mom loves potatoes more than any kind of food. "Mashed potatoes?" she asks.

"With barbecue chicken?!" Prisma looks as if someone suggested she walk nude down the middle of Patterson Park.

And Grandy sits there and smiles. "There's nothing like your potato salad, Prisma."

"The red bliss kind or the regular old-fashioned egg kind?" Prisma asks.

Grandy picks up the scissors. "Which one has the most calories?" She crops a picture of a cute photo of Mom wearing an Easter outfit.

"The old-fashioned kind."

"Then let's have that."

Prisma nods, smug. "Well, all right then. This jar of mayonnaise is almost done. Baby Girl, go to my pantry and get another jar while I get the water on and start peeling the potatoes. Yes ma'am, we're gonna have us an indoor picnic!"

Grandy looks up suddenly. "It's a nice day, Prisma. What do you say we pack up this food for dinner under the stars?"

Mom drops her pencil. Prisma turns around and says, "Are you sure you're feeling all right, Mrs. Summerville?"

"I am. I've never had a picnic dinner under the stars. Let's eat in the backyard, right by the little fishpond. There are still fish in there, aren't there?"

"Yes," all three of us say.

"Now, see there? I am the chief resident of this house, and you all know about the goldfish, and I don't."

"Well, there you go then, Mrs. Summerville, a picnic under the stars it is!" And Prisma starts humming "Victory in Jesus."

L a r k

THE PHONE RANG AT TEN THAT NIGHT, and I dove for it in my bedroom in case Bradley had decided to surface again.

"Lark?"

"Yes?"

"It's Newly."

No way!

"Oh, hello, Newly."

"It's been awhile."

"Yes, it sure has." I quickly calculated. "Has it really been two years since we've spoken?"

"That's what I figured too, so it must be the case."

Don't get into the whys, Lark. "Did you call to speak to Mother?"

"No, actually. I figured she'd be abed by now."

Abed? Who uses the term *abed* anymore? I doubt if people in England even use the word *abed* anymore. "You're right. She had the heart catheterization today."

"I know. Flannery called this afternoon."

"She did?"

"Oh yes. She keeps me posted on things."

Well, good for Flannery. I wish I were as mature as my daughter.

"And I do call Mother," he said.

"Does she know you know about her heart troubles?"

"No."

"Isn't it amazing, Newly?"

He sighed, and Newly rarely sighs. "Unfortunately, I understand all too well about keeping private."

I was about to say, "No kidding, Newly." But something stopped me. I immediately took stock of my own privacy pantry and found all sorts of moldy, dried-out, and tasteless items that nobody in my family knew about.

So keep quiet then.

"So is there something else you wanted to speak to me about?"

"Yes, as a matter of fact there is. I ran into your friend Marsha last week at this jazz club down on Lombard. The Eleven O'Clock."

My skin crawled. "My, you were slumming it."

"Oh yes. But at least I get out of the house."

Wow. Typical sibling exchange. I'd forgotten the joys. I could either go back and act like an adult or continue. If I continued, however, I might not find out why my brother had ventured a call. "You're right. So what happened at the Eleven O' Clock?"

"Marsha told me you had a visitor a few weeks back."

Oh no. That big mouth!

"Yes. I did."

And then, when Newly spoke, a note crept into his voice I'd never heard. He said, "Lark." And I heard regret and sadness and an apology and even admiration in that single syllable.

I inhaled, and he must have heard that and counted it as a response, for he said, "Flannery doesn't know, does she?"

"No."

"Are you going to tell her?"

"I have to."

"Yes. You're probably right."

"Bradley's coming back in three weeks to renew the relationship." He paused. "Do you think she'll want to?"

"Has Flannery ever turned away a needy human being?"

"Never. Most chief of them all being yours truly."

Now that was steak for thought.

"I'm not sure how to tell her, Newly."

"I don't know, Lark. I've thought about it many times since, and I've weighed it over and over, and I thought that maybe if you knew someone else knew, it might help."

"Oh, come on, Newly. What do you take me for? Why do you really care so much?"

"I know we haven't had an even passable relationship, Lark. But I do love you, you being my sister and all. And what happens to Flannery is of supreme import to me."

"I can't fault you in the uncle department."

"Well, good."

As good a start as any.

It's like this. You can go on for years and years and years, and life seems the same. But then one thing will happen, like your house burning to the ground, taking away almost everything you own, and it leaves you even more vulnerable, and you find yourself willing to look upon the same old vistas in a way you never allowed yourself to before.

Next week Flannery and Prisma leave for their lighthouse photo safari to the Outer Banks. Just Mother and me here on Greenway. Surprisingly enough, she said nothing like, "Oh, don't worry about me, Lark. I'll make do." She only said, "Well, let's make sure to order dinner in each night, Lark."

And I didn't blame her one bit. My cooking reminds me of a cheap vinyl chair. It doesn't look good, and it sticks to you so thoroughly the only way to separate you from it is under conditions of extreme discomfort.

The cookout at Marsha's house, first of all, bore no resemblance to what she originally proposed. That's Marsha for you. When she said hot dogs? Well, she actually meant kielbasa, bratwurst, knackwurst, and all those other wursts that people in Highlandtown still eat regularly.

And the crabs? I skipped the real food and zeroed in on the good stuff.

Johnny, having only arrived a few minutes before due to Marsha's invitation, not mine, sat down beside me at the picnic table, one of those piled-high plates threatening to buckle in his hand. Mother sat with her feet up on a lounger under the patio umbrella. A plate of food rested on her lap, and though she took a long time to eat it, she appeared to enjoy every bite. Marsha's husband, Glen, talked to her, and they nodded together about something. Don't ask me what. Mother has the talent of being a social chameleon. For all I knew, they discussed lawn mowers or motor oil.

Johnny smiled at me. "So, Lark. I'm surprised you're actually eating those bottom feeders."

"Gee, thanks. That's just what I needed to hear."

"Hey, the crabs haven't changed since I made that remark."

True. I pulled off a claw and dragged the meaty end between my teeth.

"Nice spread," he said. "Arranged pretty, too."

"Marsha does it right."

Please, God. Don't let him make the infernal Martha Stewart joke.

"What are you going to do with that lot in Hamilton, Lark? Seriously?"

I threw down the empty claw shell. "It's pretty much all I have in the world."

"I figured as much."

I wasn't about to ask him how.

"I have a suggestion."

"Okay." I mean, I love Babe and Deke, but so far they'd come up with nothing worth considering in the idea department.

"Why not hire a contractor to build a house there?"

"Maybe because I can't afford a house?"

"No. But once it's done, you can sell it right away."

"In Hamilton? Who's going to buy a new house in Hamilton?"

He picked up his corn on the cob. "You may be surprised."

"I'll think about it."

"Hey, it would give you something concrete to think about these days."

Oh my word! I didn't remember hiring him as my psychiatrist.

"Do you mind if I go over and meet your mother, Lark?"

I reached for the roll of paper towels and started wiping my spice-covered hands. "Why not?"

If I thought Mother would disdain this big, older guy in a medical supply T-shirt and old surfer shorts and flip-flops, I thought wrong.

"Mother, this is Dr. Johnny Josefowski."

Her eyes widened, and she stuck out her hand like a frog's tongue after a horsefly. "What a pleasure to meet you, Doctor."

"Oh, call me Johnny, please."

"All right then. And I'm Leslie."

"Lark's busy on the crabs. Care if I join you here under the umbrella?"

"I'd love it!"

She'd love it?

"Go ahead, Lark," Johnny said. "Finish up your crabs."

"That's right, dear. We'll keep each other company."

Yet another conspiracy seemingly begun. Marsha's web grew every week.

"Lark!" Marsha came out with a boom box blaring "In the Mood." "Get it? In the mood?"

I wanted to slide under the picnic table right down between that dark crack that bifurcated the patio.

Johnny and Mother just laughed.

Maybe the two of them should get together.

Leslie

I HAVEN'T ENJOYED MYSELF THIS MUCH IN YEARS!

So far this week Prisma has lived up to her word, and next week looks good with Lark and me planning to tiptoe night after night among the Take-Out Taxi's garden of delights.

We've enjoyed, of course, the barbecued chicken. And for breakfast the next morning, I ate Prisma's creamed eggs, a dish I've secretly longed for ever since Charles and I married.

I even nibbled on a piece of bacon.

The next five dinners, after the cookout, of course, were these:

Corned beef and cabbage, with potatoes, carrots, and Parker House rolls.

Rib-eye steaks, baked potatoes with butter, sour cream, and chives, steamed asparagus. Key lime pie for dessert. And my stomach surrendered before my taste buds.

Chicken à la King. Now, I know that reminds one of a TV dinner–type of offering. But it is truly one of Prisma's specialties. And she actually makes her own puff pastry. I watched her do it. "Prisma, don't you get tired of putting it in and out of the freezer?"

"Gotta be done, Mrs. Summerville."

The next night we enjoyed a slab of barbecued ribs, greens, and corn bread. Baked beans as well. And Prisma doctors them up with onions, brown sugar, a little extra ketchup, and bacon. She lays the bacon strips on the top, and by the time the timer dings, it's bubbling, and the bacon is cooked.

And here I took food preparation for granted all of these years. I'm having a lovely time.

Finally, last night we sat around the picnic table out on the screened porch and ate steamed crabs. Lark has been giving me grief all week because I failed to have some at Marsha's house. Which, of course, made Prisma start the ball rolling, traipsing up to the attic for the steamer.

Now, Charles tried and tried to get me to eat these spidery crustaceans, and I refused. How ghastly when you achieve seventy years of age and you realize you've deprived yourself of something as absolutely wonderful as steamed crabs because you had a mother with strange ideas about food and you let it color your habits for decades.

Not to mention those baked beans.

Extremely ghastly.

Now you may think I'm a foolish old thing. "What's this woman's problem? Getting excited over baked beans and such? I've been making baked beans like that ever since I was old enough to turn on a stove."

And you'd be exactly right.

I haven't lived.

But let the change begin! And it starts, first and foremost, with my daughter. And even Newly. In fact, I think that I've warmed the bench long enough.

Yes, yes, yes!

Baked beans are only the beginning!

Plannery

PRISMA SUGGESTED WE EXHUME Granddad's old convertible Mercedes out of storage for our drive down to the Outer Banks.

Well, cool.

Thanks to her foresight and keen planning prowess, she did it two weeks ago in plenty of time for the three-thousand-dollar repair bill. When Asil pulled it around the night before we left, Grandy cried. "I almost want to hug that old thing!" She cries a lot now, and it's a beautiful thing.

The drive is wonderful. I'm wearing a straw hat with a cherry silk scarf looped over it and tied under my neck. With my sunglasses and a neat little yellow cotton twinset, Capri pants, and espadrilles, the look is perfect.

Prisma sits next to me, the kinky gold and silver tendrils that escape her braid dancing like steel wool cartoon characters around her head. She smiles like a model for a cigarette ad, only she isn't trying to convince anyone of anything. "This is the life, Baby Girl!" she hollers.

I holler back. "You said it, Miss Prisma!"

"Why didn't we do this years ago?"

"Who knows!"

"Who cares?"

"That's right," I say, and we zoom past minivans and SUVs, campers and cars like my Toyota.

"Do you realize how much fun a trip to the beach in a convertible is, Baby Girl?" Prisma touches my arm. "Do you realize what a blessing you're living at this very moment?"

"I do, Miss Prisma."

"Good. Just making sure."

See, it's like this. Believe me—*believe* me—when I tell you that no matter what class of life you find yourself in, there is plenty of trouble to go around. People living hand to mouth have the majority of their troubles from without. Grandy's type find theirs from within.

And then there's Mom, who never does anything halfway and has both kinds.

Our second night we sit on the front deck right there on Whale-head Beach. To our left a group of bravehearts are setting off fireworks. Now, they aren't the big deal Fourth of July kind, but they aren't bad for a couple of beer-bellied guys in cutoffs.

All down the beach folks turn their gaze to the show of minute, man-made splendor. Mostly red and green starbursts exploding forty or so feet up in the sky.

But in front of us, right there over the waters of the Atlantic, the moon begins to rise.

"Look, Prisma," I say in the darkness.

"I already see, Baby Girl."

Just then a soft light rises from a heavy bank of clouds resting on the horizon. The moon is soon to follow. We know this, and we wait as the gentle silver light thickens. The moon, we know, is hefting itself upward, like a swimmer out of a pool, its hands reaching up to the edge of the cotton gloom of darkened cloud, pulling, pulling, and shining its light brighter for all its exertion. Come on, baby. Come on, baby. And then, that singular piercing blade of light as the moon gains over the clouds preparing to rise further in one small hole of sky.

Prisma sucks in a breath. "Oh, Lord Jesus!"

"What if it's now?" I ask. "What if He's coming now?"

In truth, it is a sight, as the moon rises higher, of such glory and power and honesty, more honest than fireworks could ever be, that I could see Him coming. And, Lord, is that You? Please let it be so.

And I am here with Prisma of all people! Prisma who showed me the Lord in the first place.

We hold our breath, and I reach for her hand while we watch and wait.

He doesn't come though. Not in that way.

⁓

Prisma brushes her teeth in her bathroom now as I slip into my night-shirt. I walk across the hall and stand at her doorway. "Do you think He'll come like that?"

She shrugs, spits, and drinks from a cup. Spits again, then rinses out her toothbrush. "At least we had it right as far as the eastern sky goes."

"I guess I never really figured it would be at night."

"I don't know why not. Of course, I imagine that when He descends, the sky, even the night sky, will be lit up like the daytime."

Pushing back the cuticles on my right index finger, I say, "I feel a little silly now. Getting all worked up over the moonrise."

"Now, don't go feeling anything about it, Baby Girl. You're just doing what He said to do, 'Keep looking at the eastern sky, for it is from there your redemption will come.'"

I can't wait for that day.

"It's Sunday night. You want to watch a little TV?" I ask.

"It's Gaither night." Prisma raises a holy hand. "I do love my Gaither night."

"I'll make the popcorn."

"I'll pour us some ginger ale!"

And Prisma and I have us a good old time listening to good old Southern gospel. That Guy Penrod is a hottie if you're into long hair and cowboy boots.

I lie there in my bed that night, the window open slightly to usher in the crash of the tide on the shore. I think about the fireworks and the moon and how the entire situation mirrored the world. There everyone was looking at the gaudy, sparkly work of men when just a little bit out of view lay a splendor, just a pure, truthful splendor. God's fireworks.

No wonder Prisma watches the stars. Maybe she's doing more than gazing at them. Maybe she's waiting to catch that first glimpse of Jesus.

James is like this too. He's not a fireworks guy, the kind that most people look at and go "Ooooh! Aaaaaah!" He's a moonrise. A gentle glow rising over the horizon to shed light in the darkness, a light nobody but the discerning soul might even notice.

Things are moving fast now.

And I can say this. I will be with this man for the rest of my life. I know that's true. And even if Christ came back tonight, it would be okay, for I've loved with a full heart.

Tomorrow we start at Currituck Light and work our way down. We just lazed on the beach today. I have to say, what with all the breast services plastic surgeons offer these days, the average bra size has certainly increased, and chests don't all lie down like they used to.

Lark

WE SAT ON THE SCREENED PORCH at the back of the house. The hibiscus, large salmon platters of flora, perfumed the darkness. A citronella candle twisted its flame in the breeze, and Mother's features looked twenty years younger in the candlelight. She knitted, and I embroidered more ribbon on that stocking.

"You know," she said, "I believe I miss smoking on screen porches more than anyplace else."

Mother and I, unbeknownst to each other before tonight, had fought the Battle of the Butt simultaneously ten years ago. "Me, too. With a cup of coffee, a breeze, and a fine companion, there's nothing better."

You know how some people say, "When I found the Lord, I tossed out my cigarette pack and never looked back" and all?

Well, good for you, mister. Not for me. I fight every single day against going to 7-Eleven and getting a pack of Marlboro Lights. Apparently Mother did too.

I was finding out a lot of things about Mother I never knew before. All those bridge clubs she attended? Well, it wasn't just for the socialization. Mother had actually earned Masters points. It was her sport.

Tonight, out at the screened porch, she shared an even more startling revelation.

I returned with refilled teacups and placed hers on the woven place mat in front of her when she said, "Mama disowned me after I married your father."

Just like that. She laid it bare.

"What?" I stood there, feeling too small and skinny for such a declaration, and quickly sat beside her.

"It's true. I lied to you all these years. Mama assumed incorrectly that your father was from an old family. And we hid it from her for a while, until you were five or so. But one day she was reading a Who's Who book, found your father, and for a reason known only to Libby Lee, researched it."

"And she found out he was from Highlandtown and that his parents were just regular people."

"That's right." Mother picked up her spoon and twirled it between finger and thumb, then placed it back on her saucer. "She wrote me a letter, Larkspur. A formal letter. She couldn't call me on the telephone or, heaven forbid, actually say it to my face."

"Oh, Mother."

She turned her face, the candle caressing but one side. "She was a strange bird, my mother."

"Why did you hide that all of these years? What difference did it make to keep it to yourself? Did Daddy know?"

Mother shook her head. "Heavens, no! Your father would have driven down there right away and tried to iron things out. He was like that."

"Well, he never did take no for an answer."

"Neither did my mother. And she would have beaten him at his own game. My mother, never once in her life that I knew her, did anything she didn't want to do."

"What did you tell Daddy?"

"That she was wasting away in a nursing home and I didn't want to remember her like that."

"She left a legacy, didn't she?"

Mother turned back to face me. "Larkspur, I'm sorry. We Summervilles sure know how to tell lies."

"I'm sorry too."

I had wanted to have this conversation all of my life. "But why do you always have to shut me out, Mother?"

"You've got enough troubles of your own, dear. I don't want you to worry about me."

"What if I want to?"

Mother drew in a quick breath. "You want more worry on your

shoulders? Larkspur, you've done your best to stay away from as much of life as possible. The good and the bad."

And I forgot about the candle and crafts, the wind, and the tea. I forgot about screened porches, woven place mats, and a delivered gourmet dinner. Instead I saw the face of a fair-haired boy. I saw a motorcycle, a parking lot, and a false death certificate. I saw a small little house, a 777 Prayer Line number, public transit, and a Spartan wardrobe. I saw one child, a little girl named Flannery, who—God, thank You—was never fooled.

"You're right." Why had I erected a monastery of self-imposed martyrdom around myself? If Mother shut me out of her ills, I'd closed the door on her as well. Only by the very nature of our relationship, I quit the castle and had gone on to build battlements against the relief forces, mistaking them for the enemy. Mother tried to protect the child she loved so much from more pain. I had no such excuse.

I had wanted her to read my mind.

"My mama always said one should keep one's problems to oneself as much as possible. But, honey, Mama was wrong." Mother's words blew between us like a scouring wind. "I was wrong."

"Me, too."

"We've got one week left, Larkspur. A week from tomorrow your Dr. Josefowski will cut me open—"

"Mother!"

"Well, it's true. And in light of that fact, I think we should renew each other's acquaintance."

"How?"

"Oh, I don't know. These suppers are a nice start. But I was thinking that maybe on Saturday night, you'd take me down to St. Dominic's. I never wanted to barge in before unannounced, and I knew if I asked to come…"

Barge! Barge away! "I'd like that."

Later that night, after I cleared away the dishes and made sure Mother was all set for the night, I picked up the phone and called Marsha. I related the conversation.

"Well, finally!" she cried.

"What do you mean?" I asked. "What's that for?"

"I've been praying for this, you know."

"No, I didn't know."

"God put you back home for a reason, Lark. I was just praying He'd show you what that reason was."

I laughed a little. "You mean it really wasn't just the faulty wiring?"

"Oh, hon, God works in the electrical business, too."

"I really thought He'd burned my house down to finally get me out of it for good."

"Well, you know how God is. He definitely is the type to kill two birds with one stone."

Birds?

Yep, that would be me and Mom. Thank goodness I didn't have to take the word *kill* literally. That would be bad.

"Hey, how was your date with Johnny?"

"We had to reschedule. He's coming over here for dinner."

"To meet your Mom?"

"He's already met her. At your place."

"Oh yeah, that's right."

"I figure the better he knows her, the better job he'll do."

"Good thinking, Lark!"

I agreed. I mean, my mother had finally opened her heart. And Dr. Johnny Josefowski needed to do all he could to keep it up and running for a long time to come.

Leslie

Lark invited that lovely man over tonight. Dr. Johnny Josefowski. A delightful man. Calm, quiet in demeanor, smart, and unpretentious. The perfect suitor. If Charles is looking down, he's thrilled. And to think he will be performing my surgery comforts me. I scheduled the preop visit for Friday afternoon.

"You're from Baltimore originally?" I asked as we sat down in the living room. I haven't sat in the living room in ages. And no wonder. It looks like something my mother thought of as a living room.

"Yes. I moved away for a little while to go to college though."

"Where did you go to college?"

"University of Virginia."

"UVA?" I sucked in my breath and glanced over at Lark. "UVA! Why, Johnny, I'm from Charlottesville!"

And then we talked about all the lovely countryside, the beautiful campus designed by Jefferson himself. "Of course, I wouldn't have been part of the society from which you came," he said. "But I did attend a party given in honor of the university president at the Strawbridge home, back in 1978. Your sister was the hostess, I believe."

"Caroline?"

"Yes, Caroline Farrow her name was."

"Precisely. She married one of the Farrow boys from the next county." I laughed. "It sounds like *Gone with the Wind* all over again!"

Lark smiled right at me, and we kept my family secret to ourselves. We raised our eyebrows at one another in conspiratorial joviality.

Through thick and thin and all that. A lovely thing.

"Have you been back there recently, Leslie?" he asked.

I waved a casual hand. "Not in years! Oh, it's so good to hear about all this again. Makes me feel decades younger. So, tell me what you do in your spare time."

He barked out that marvelous laugh, and I really am telling the truth when I say it visibly affected Larkspur.

What a wonderful man.

They took their leave to attend that study group thing, leaving me with an entire Thursday evening to myself. Truth to tell, the visit exhausted me after I'd worked on my photo album all day, so I poured a glass of water, grabbed that Bible that Prisma gave me, and climbed the steps to my bedroom. I wanted to read about the loaves-and-fishes matter again, and I wanted to be sure I asked Prisma if she could take me to church with her on Sunday. I refuse to go back to hear that pastor's viewpoint any longer. I can come up with my own if viewpoints are all I'm looking for.

Prisma and Flannery are coming back Saturday afternoon. It will be wonderful to see them. I've missed them. I never knew how much Stoneleigh House needed us all. Oh, that's twaddle. I never realized how much I needed all these women around me. No time remains for delusion, and there's not enough time to expect everyone else to shoulder my blame. I dropped the ball somewhere along the line. I'm not sure when or where, but I did. I was the mother. It was up to me.

My heart has swollen to three times its size. Not literally, mind you. And I am blessed.

Four more days until Johnny performs the surgery. At least I feel I can trust him. My goodness, if I can trust him with Lark, I can certainly place this old ticker in his hands with some confidence.

Lark

JOHNNY KISSED ME THAT NIGHT. After study group we drove to his house on White Avenue.

"Want to sit on the porch? I can put on a pot of tea."

"Thanks." A nice breeze blew that evening.

After escorting me out of the car, we climbed the steps up onto the wooden porch of his small home. Freshly painted obviously. Sunny yellow.

"I didn't expect you to have such a pristine little house."

"Why not? Don't let the T-shirts fool you. Be right back."

And then he leaned over and kissed my forehead. Just like that, really easy and natural. I froze.

He laughed and caressed my cheek. "Have a seat on the settee, Lark."

Then he disappeared.

Oh my word. The kiss seeped under my skin like brandy. I sat on the settee and allowed a small dream into my mind.

"I love the moon," I whispered to myself, settling my derriere further into the seat. Ooh, a glider rocker. I love those things.

"I do too."

I whirled around. "I didn't hear you come out."

"Just got the kettle on." He sat next to me.

"Do you ever find it hard to believe that at one time all of this didn't exist?"

"Yes. At times. And then at others I think it could only come from the mind of an artist."

"That's what Flannery says. It's one of the reasons she decided to make art her career. She says it makes her feel closer to God when she's drawing or painting or whatever."

I felt his arm settle across my shoulders, lightly as though he still bore most of its weight. "That's the way I feel during surgery."

"Really?"

"Well, God is in the business of mending broken hearts."

My smile warmed my own darkness. "Yeah, He is."

"Are you playing at church Saturday night?"

"Of course. And Mother is coming. To the five and the seven o'clock."

"Would you be jealous if I was her date?"

"No way! It would be a relief. I'm scared she'll get tired early on and have no way to get home."

"How are you getting home?"

"Flannery's coming to pick me up."

"Oh."

"Or you, if you want."

He captured my hand. "I want."

"You may have to take Mother home, then come back down."

"I really don't mind."

"Good."

I heard somebody laughing maniacally inside the house. "Who is that?"

"It's my sister Celine."

"What? I didn't know you still lived with your siblings."

"Just Celine. We're the only ones left after all of these years."

"Is she okay?"

He shook his head. "I've hired a full-time nurse. There's someone on shift here twenty-four hours a day."

Wow. No wonder my basic neuroses seemed like no big deal to Dr. J.

"What's her condition?"

"How much time do you have?"

I laughed. "No wonder you work so many hours."

He squeezed my hand. "You've got my number. Those who know

think I'm a saint for taking care of her. When in reality I just write checks on her behalf."

"Maybe. But where would she be if you didn't?"

"Who knows?"

"See?"

"I guess so."

It was nice to actually encourage somebody else instead of being encouraged. I've felt like the pathetic side of any conversation for so many years that I've come to think of it as part of my role. Like if people feel sorry for me, they'll become emotionally invested or something. I don't know.

I'm so messed up.

I hate that.

A light breeze ruffled the leaves of the maples and oaks in his front yard. Nature diminishes me sometimes, whispering that I've never measured up to my potential the way she herself does.

I think about that a lot. A tree becomes a tree, the exact kind of tree it was meant to be. A mountain is darned good at being a mountain. Rivers flow as expected.

And then there's me. I'm a woman, and I have no idea what that's supposed to look like for me. I'm a freak of nature, I think, searching for meaning even beyond my walk with Christ. I'm groaning for a purpose, a life beyond the walls of the house I've built around me.

But who wants to leave home? You know?

"Have you ever had any times of doubt, Johnny? About what you wanted to do?"

He shook his head, his wire-rimmed glasses twinkling in the moon-glow that spilled across us and onto the floorboard. "Not about what I do, but maybe where and how I do it."

"Well, at least you have that."

"So am I right in taking it you're doubtful about your own mission in life?"

"Yeah."

He sat in silence for a moment, parallel wrinkles nestling more deeply between his eyes. "So what you're saying is, the last twenty-two years raising your daughter was a waste of time?"

"No! Of course not."

"Because she's a neat kid."

"I know. I'm just thinking I'm pretty much through with that phase. Hands on, you know."

"Right. I know what you mean."

"And now I'm home with Mother, and there's so much catching up to do. But my life has to mean more than that, doesn't it?"

"Why?"

That startled me. "Well, because. Because there's a big world out there."

A really big world.

"And God's called you to save it?"

I laughed. "Hardly! And if He did, I'm doing such a lousy job He's definitely found another person for the job by now."

"Sh!" He held a finger up to his lips. "You'll alert the nurse I'm home. I've been sneaking around in there so I don't have to get the update yet."

"Sorry," I whispered.

He squeezed my hand again. "Still, Lark, I know what you mean about feeling more of a sense of purpose."

"You do?"

"Yes. I've been wondering about my own career."

"How so?"

"I've been thinking a lot about Third World countries and all the good I could do there."

"Not many people are willing to go over to places like that."

"My point exactly."

I thought about Johnny, serving people his whole life. "You'd be good at it."

"I really think I would. I hope that doesn't sound prideful."

"No, it doesn't. Just honest."

"Because, God knows, I'm as big a sinner as anybody."

"I wish you knew me better," I said, voicing the words as I thought them.

"I'd like to."

What a great guy.

"No, I mean, regarding a purpose. I wish you knew me better so you could tell me what to do."

He released my hand and touched my face. "Lark, I'm not the one to do that. You're a grown woman, a capable woman when you allow yourself to be. You don't need me to tell you that."

But, you see, I wanted that. I wanted a pep talk just then. I wanted my list of virtues to be called up and displayed within his words. I wanted him to tell me why, as a human being, I deserved his time and attention. "Yes, I do." There, I said it anyway.

"The big one is your playing. Now that's a talent directly from God."

"I play at church."

"Maybe God has a larger purpose for it?"

"You think so? Doing what, for heaven's sake?"

He shrugged. "I don't know, Lark. I'm just trying to do what you asked me to do."

"Well, you've given me food for thought." I shut down the conversation. He might have mentioned a host of better things. But he didn't. Just my playing.

Now, if I had been asked the same question by Prisma, I'd have said, "Oh, Prisma you have so much to give. And here's the list."

Kindness

Compassion

Sacrifice

Dedication

Service, no matter how big or small

Happiness

Contentment

Healing

Have I brought that into anybody's life but Flannery's? And let's face it, she's given more of that than I have.

Big deal. I can play the organ. I can pray on the phone.

Big deal.

And then Johnny kissed me again. Right out of the blue. Right on the lips. And I kissed him back. And that night in bed I cried and cried. So much work to be done, so many ties needing to be re-laid to keep my life from becoming the train wreck it was destined to become.

PRISMA

OH MY GOODNESS! That woman is much too hard on herself! Here she's raised a good girl. Goes to church. Plays for the Lord. And talks on the phone every night with strangers in need of hope.

Yet, if the Spirit is speaking to her about branching out, if He's itching about in places needing a good scratch, then who am I to question?

Here I was praying God would wake her up, and now that He's decided to do so, I just feel so sorry for her!

I laid out my clothes for the morning as Lark told me all about her discoveries over the week Flannery and I photographed all sorts of lighthouses—Ocracoke definitely being my favorite. It's this short little squat white lighthouse with a black bonnet. Reminds me of an old-time settler woman on her way out to gather wood.

So Lark went on and on about getting back to basics and trying to live more for others.

"By that, do you mean your mother?" I asked, dreading the answer because Lark can be a bit thick at times.

"Uh-huh."

Oh, Lord, she's seen the light! "I think that's good then."

"And I've also decided I'm going to go ahead and get my driver's license again. Flannery told me she'd help me."

I snorted. "Oh, Lark! That'll be a sight to see! Can I come too?"

"I guess so."

"Why the driving?"

"So I can take Mother around to her appointments and all."

"Do you think you've already begun weighing yourself down in the details?" That sure qualified as a zinger.

"Well, maybe. But—"

"Do you think maybe your mother just wants to be with you? Did you think that maybe you don't need to be cooped up in that den twenty-four hours a day? Did you think maybe you could seek her out once in a while and not have it always be the other way around?"

Now where did my special striped dress go? I turned to face my closet.

"Man, you're not pulling any punches, are you, Prisma?"

"You got that right." I waggled a finger at her, then continued to look for the dress. "The fact is, Lark, you have no good reason for behaving toward your mother the way you do."

"What about Bradley? What about all that?"

"What about him?" Ah, there it was, back between the blouses and the skirts. Now why in the world did I hang it there? I must be losing it.

"Well, how can anybody get over something like that?"

"They do it every single day, Lark. And you know it. Baby, I don't know why you can't get over all of this. I think you've been depressed for two decades, if you want to know the truth. I think you need to see a doctor and get some medication."

Did I say that? Oh my goodness!

Lark turned around and ran from the room.

A little while later she came back. "I'll make an appointment."

"Good for you! I think even Dr. J will think it's a good idea."

She nodded.

"Does he know about Bradley?"

"No."

"Think you ought to tell him?"

She shrugged and leaned up against the doorframe. "Yeah. But I need to tell Flannery first."

My heart broke for her. Lord have mercy, the child didn't deserve a situation like this. I threw my dress on the bed, crossed the room, and put my arms around her. "Baby," I whispered, "it really is time to get back to basics. You've just been talking about the wrong basics. It's time you own up to the truth. To your mother and to Flannery. Johnny Josefowski, and maybe even your hermit tendencies, is the least of it."

"I know." Lark began to cry. "I just don't know where to begin."

I would have offered to do it for her, but the Spirit was telling me no.

The truth shall set her free, Prisma.

That night I stood by my window looking at the stars.

"Jesus?"

"Yes, My girl?"

"Would You be working on Baby Girl's heart in advance to hear the news?"

"Are you asking Me to?"

"Yes, Jesus, in Your Name I am."

"All right then. And if it's My will that they be in for a little rough water for a spell, what is that to you, Prisma?"

"You know me, Lord. You know I can't stand to see anyone suffer."

"Even when I've got a plan?"

I closed my eyes. "I'll just pray for Your will to be done then, Lord."

"It's usually one prayer most of My children can live with."

"Although, sometimes it takes time to accept the answer, right, Jesus?"

"Sometimes it does."

I watched the night sky some more. "Prisma, My girl? You know I love you."

"I do, Lord."

"And you know I know what's best for all of My girls here on Greenway, don't you?"

"I do."

"Then rest well, My girl, and keep the faith."

I tell you the truth, Mrs. Summerville keeps knitting up a storm. It's a sight to see.

Flannery

GRANDY PULLS OUT HER ALBUM. The surgery's tomorrow. No one wants to leave the house. Even Asil's light burns in his window above the garage.

I mean, what if she dies on the table?

I'd like to think I have more time left with Grandy. A lot more. Especially now that she and Mom are at least trying to get along. Maybe I could even talk Uncle Newly into coming over for Thanksgiving this year.

Like that'll ever happen.

Stranger things have taken place though. Even here in the family. Prisma said Grandy actually walked the aisle at Prisma's church this morning. "Gave her heart to Jesus right then and there!"

See what I mean? And earlier this evening, when we saw Mom take Grandy a cup of tea and sit next to her on the couch, Prisma pulled me into the laundry room and said, "You see that there? We got our work cut out for us."

"What do you mean, Miss Prisma?"

"We're matchmakers of a different sort now."

And there they were, two women who were blessed enough to be given a clue before it was too late. Let's hope they didn't blow it.

Dear Jesus, please don't let them blow it.

See, with James and all, I know I can't be around for Mom the way I am much longer.

"I gotcha, Miss Prisma. I've felt sorry for Grandy for so long."

"Well, she never really handled either Lark or Newly the way they needed to be handled. But far be it from me to interfere."

We had ourselves a good laugh at that one.

Yep, this was a calling for sure. Prisma knew what she was talking about. Their feet were finally on the right road, and we weren't going to take any chances that they were capable of keeping them there on their own. "Yep, I gotcha."

So the four of us sit around the kitchen table looking at what Grandy has done that week on her album. "I'm only up to when you were in first grade, Larkspur. And I'm already almost finished with this album."

"I'll pick you up some more at the craft store, Mrs. Summerville," Prisma says. "This will be a nice thing to do while you're convalescing."

"Thank you, Prisma." She pats Prisma's hand, leaves it there for a moment and squeezes. Sometimes you just need a little vicarious strength from Prisma. "Now, see here"—she angles the book and slides it over to Mom—"this is your first day at school that year. And the other side is Easter Day."

Let me tell you, Mom was cute. A little yellow dress and coat. White Mary Janes, a tiny purse, and a boater with a yellow ribbon. Mom's finger points to a picture on the other side of the page. I have never seen this one. "What in the name of heaven are you wearing on your head, Mother?"

Grandy laughs. "That was my Easter bonnet that year."

"You're wearing it in front of the church, Grandy."

"I know. Your mother insisted I wear it all day. She made it that year at school."

Mom almost spits out her tea. "I made that? And you actually wore it to church?"

Grandy reddens under the memory. "Let's just say it was one of those moments you wished at the time wasn't happening to you. But looking back, I know it was worth it."

And Grandy has every right to be embarrassed. The sight of that literally makes me want to hoot with laughter. Take a paper plate, cut holes in either side, string bright purple gift ribbon through, and add lots of toilet paper roses and bows. Then tie it under a slender chin, and wear it with an ivory linen suit, pearl jewelry, and patent leather pumps and purse, and I'd call it an ensemble to die for. Die of mortification, that is.

Go, Grandy!

I turn to Mom. "Did you do anything like that?"

"Well, not quite to that extreme. I don't remember that at all, Mother. Wow."

I know. Wow. "So? Any embarrassing mother moments with me?" I'm not about to let the topic go. Mothers sacrifice their dignity for their children all the time. I am entitled to at least one such tale.

"Well, there was the time you pooped all over me as I was getting up to play in the band."

"Really?"

"Yep, before Daddy di—was gone. We were in some dive in San Francisco."

"What did you do?"

"I put on my winter coat and told the band, 'Winter Wonderland' in the key of C."

Grandy claps. "You didn't, Larkspur!"

"I did."

"How resourceful, dear. I love it."

Mom stirs her tea. "I was glad they could play it. They weren't the best of musicians back in those days."

"What did Daddy do?" I ask. I hope she remembers.

"Just smiled and did some amazing little licks on his guitar in between verses."

I'd give anything to have heard my father play. Even just once. I sigh. "I wish I remembered that stuff. I try so hard to recall him, but I just can't." I often think of all the nights I lay in bed as a kid and felt weird. The girl without a father. I mean, every kid wants to stand out some, but not like that! And my friends would complain about their "old man," and I'd sit there and stew because they had no idea how, deep down, I yearned to be held in big strong arms and to be admired by a set of blue eyes that crinkled inside worn, male skin.

"Well," says Prisma, in her change-the-subject-tone, but why we need to change it is beyond me. "Tomorrow's the big day, and, Mrs. Summerville, you need your rest."

Grandy sighs and flat-palms the table. "I know. I'd rather stay up and talk the night away. It's been years since I've done that."

And then Mom says, "We'll have scads of time for gabfests. And think how much better you'll feel after the surgery. You'll have so much energy we'll be able to talk for three days straight!"

Grandy inches to her feet. "Let's hope you're right."

Mom helps her to her feet and escorts her from the room.

I'm having another one of those life-is-changing-before-my-eyes moments. I've been having a lot of those lately. But tomorrow, things will be changed forever, one way or another.

Because she may die on the operating table.

Dear Lord, please don't let her die on the operating table!

Leslie

WELL, AT LEAST I'M MOSTLY READY TO DIE if I do go today. Jesus keeps my soul with "His perfect love," as Prisma calls it. Lark and I have stitched our wounds. And now the true healing can begin. Now there's my knitting, of course. I'm hardly done with my knitting plans.

It's dark outside. For some reason the streetlights dimmed earlier than usual. No sign of pink in the sky, and the lights closed their eyes, today of all days.

In my younger days I would have contacted the city about it, sputtering an earful.

I remember a verse my grandpa used to quote about the Spirit praying for you with "groanings which cannot be uttered." I'd rather not contemplate the kind of groanings the Holy Spirit groans. I'm just thankful He's doing it on my behalf, because right now I cannot pray on my own. I am stuck in this moment. Right here. And every moment after this, until I know whether I'm coming out of the anesthesia or stepping through heaven's gates, seems darker than the street outside.

Life or death.

The first scenario lends me Larkspur's face for yet more time on earth. The second gives me Charles for eternity.

As Newly says, that sounds like a win-win situation.

Larkspur gave a breathtaking performance at church. I understand her a bit more now, truth to tell. That amazing sound filling the church, her fluid arms and powerful renditions of songs I've always loved. And I'm proud of her. I do believe she achieved this in spite of me rather than because of me, and believe me—*believe* me, as Flannery says—that will change!

Oh, for goodness sake. It's only ten o'clock! And here I thought I had slept all night.

Fiddle.

PRISMA

WHEN I HEARD HIS VOICE ON THE OTHER END, I was glad I caught the phone on the first ring. Some voices you never forget.

"Is Lark there?" Bradley asked.

"Yes, but I have no intention of getting her at this hour, Bradley del Champ."

"Prisma Percy! Lark told me you're still on Greenway."

"And where else would I be?"

"The White House?"

Now even I had to chuckle at that. "Lark's told me everything, Bradley. I thought you were giving her until the end of the summer."

"I couldn't wait."

"You've got to. Mrs. Summerville is going in for bypass surgery early tomorrow morning."

"Is she gonna be okay?"

"Who knows? I'm praying she comes out of it all fine and feeling better than ever."

"I hope so."

And Bradley did. I could never fault him for being unkind in the general sense.

"Well, we'll see. Lark's a little nervous about it all and has already gone to bed. Plus, I don't think hearing from you *early* like this is something she needs right now."

"Has she told Flannery?"

"Nope. Not yet."

"Well, knowing Lark, she'll wait until the last minute."

"You got that right. Listen, I'd better get off the phone before someone wants to know who it is. Give her until after Labor Day, you hear?"

"I was thinking September the first."

"No. Let them have the whole summer. I think summer ends on Labor Day, unless you want to go with the real end of summer, which is September the twenty-first."

"No! No, that's okay, Miss Prisma, we'll do it your way."

Good boy. "I knew it wouldn't take long for you to see sense."

He breathed a sarcastic, "Hah. You'd be surprised how long it takes me to see sense. Okay, the day after Labor Day it is. Will you tell her I called?"

"Not a chance."

"That's what I figured."

After we hung up, I figured while difficult conversations ran amok, I might as well make another couple of calls. So I dialed down to the Inner Harbor.

"Newly!"

"Prisma? It's ten o'clock."

"Do you know tomorrow is your mother's bypass surgery?"

"Yes. Flannery told me."

"Are you going to be there?"

Silence. Oh, that pesky boy!

"Now, Newly, all she's got left is you and Lark."

"I know that."

"And family is family."

"That's what you keep telling me."

I wanted to reach through the phone and shake him by his white hair. "That's all I'm saying then. You be a good son, Newly. Please. Now good night."

Oh, my, goodness. These Summervilles!

Lord, I don't think I've done too good a job down here all of these years if improvement is this long in coming.

I dialed another number.

"Mama?" my son answered.

"Hi, baby. Just wanted to hear your voice."

"Mama."

"I love you, baby."

"I love you, too. When are you coming down?"

"Mrs. Summerville is having bypass surgery tomorrow, so it will be awhile. My heart is with you though. You know that."

He sighed, but said cheerfully, "We all have a job to do."

"Yes, we do, Son. How's that grandbaby cooking up?"

"With ingredients from me and Caprice and the recipe from a Master Chef, I'd say he's coming along just fine."

Oh, I ache for my family, and I tell you the truth on that one. Maybe I should heed my own advice and, instead of pointing fingers at Newly and Lark all the time, point some at me.

Lark

I SUPPOSE MOST WOMEN VIEW THEMSELVES more through the eyes of their mother than their own. If I truly viewed myself through my own eyes, I'd see a woman developing her talent, a woman who struggles but basically comes out okay in the end due to her faith and the love of those people she loves. I'd see a woman who took a bad situation and lived with it, and tried to do the best she could with what she had, tried to utilize the resources she alone possessed instead of begging off of anybody else.

And that's not so bad.

But instead, I've always seen Mother's view. Or what I perceived to be Mother's view. And now I'm wondering if I've been wrong about that too. Not only in trying to measure up to someone else's view, but has that view been false? Have I placed imagined expectations on myself and blamed my mother for them?

All this introspection because of faulty wiring and a burned-down home! I glided along for years on autopilot, only to come to this.

I couldn't get a doctor appointment until November. My whole life feels like a sleeping foot coming back to life.

So there I lay in the darkness of my own room. Midnight came and left and still no sleep. I heard Mother shuffling in her bed and got a novel idea to pray for her.

That's right, Lark. Put God to the test. See if He can handle granting a little bit of peace to a frightened old woman. See if He'll do that.

So I lay in the darkness, looking at the ceiling and asking God to give my mother some comfort or, at the very least, a good night's sleep.

The rustlings became less and less and died down entirely just as I myself slipped off into the luscious oblivion I had counted on for so many years to take me away.

Flannery

MAN, HOW COOL IS IT TO BE UP SO EARLY? I have to admit I am not a morning person, but I woke up at four and couldn't get back to sleep. That's okay though, because I wanted to pray for Grandy anyway, and I fell asleep before God and I could communicate much. James is lighting a candle for her at church this morning. I'm not exactly sure what that means to its fullest extent, but I do know it means he's praying, which is what counts anyway.

I decide to sit by the fishpond and listen to the gurgle of the little fountain. After about ten minutes I go back inside to get my fleece and a blanket. Autumn is right around the corner. And I've got a lot of hopes for this autumn, you know. Grad school, James, Mom and Grandy, the lighthouse calendar, and I saw Asil putting in a bunch of mums the other day. I asked if he knew what color they were, and he said he had no idea.

Isn't that fun?

This autumn should be the picture of predictability, and that is something I'm totally looking forward to. The world is my oyster, so to speak.

At six o'clock I decide to go on in and put the coffee on, but Prisma is already busy in the kitchen. She jumps a mile when I come through the porch doorway. And what a holler she lets out. "Baby Girl! What on earth?"

"Oh, sorry. I didn't mean to scare you."

"Well, you could have warned me you were out there."

"How? Anything I did would have scared you."

"H'm. Well, anyway, sit on down. Coffee's almost finished. And what in heaven's name are you doing up so early?"

"Do you need to ask?"

She slides a couple of slices of her homemade bread in the toaster. "Nope. Me, too."

"Are you making that for Grandy?"

Prisma shakes her head. "She's not allowed to eat anything after midnight. This toast is for you and me."

"Good. I don't think I could eat anything more than that."

"Me neither."

Wow, Prisma really is worried.

"Now, I'm going to go up at seven to make sure your grandmother is up and at 'em. We need to be at the hospital at nine for the eleven o'clock surgery."

"Is Asil driving?"

"Sure is."

"I was hoping I could drive her. With Mom."

"That's fine with me."

I eat my toast and head up to shower. As I dress in my bedroom, I hear the murmurs of Grandy and Prisma as they get her ready.

They are the only sounds in the house right now.

The soft scrape of their matching Daniel Greens, the whispers of their aged voices. The gravity of the day.

It all fills me with a sudden sorrow that time keeps passing and I'll be old one day too. I'm dying. I know this. Most people who live for heaven do.

So when I hear Grandy say, "They'd better let me wear my bra afterward!" I almost spit out my coffee it takes me by so much surprise.

"You're having open-heart surgery, Mrs. Summerville. The last thing you'll want on your chest is a bra."

"Put it in the overnight bag anyway. I'm counting on a quick recovery."

I finish dressing in my latest Hepburn getup of an ivory straight skirt and pale blue jewel-necked top, slip downstairs, and call James. When my heart is sore like this, he soothes.

I tie a scarf in my hair. "Tell me you love me, James."

"I love you, Flannery."

"You'll meet me at the hospital?"

"I'll be there by 10:30."

You gotta love this guy.

Lark

JOHNNY MET US IN THE FAMILY WAITING ROOM. And seeing him for the first time in his scrubs, with those crazy shoe covers on, offered me a calm reassurance. "She's almost prepped," he told us.

He actually looked like a doctor today. Like one of those heavy, studious type of doctors.

Prisma, Flannery, James, and I stood in a semicircle around him.

"You can come in for a couple of minutes before the anesthesiologist puts her under." He looked each of us in the eye. "You all doing okay?"

We nodded in unison. Somehow, you lose your identity at times like this. You become "a family member in the waiting room, worrying and fretting."

We visited Mother one by one, and I kissed her on the forehead, then on the cheek, and I held her hand. "Mother, I hope everything goes well."

"Me, too, Larkspur."

This might be my last moment with her. I felt sick, but I squeezed her hand and said, "I love you, Mom. We have a lot of good times ahead."

"You think so?"

"I really do."

She smiled a gentle *Madonna and Child* smile, her face void of cosmetics and looking touched by an old master. "I'll cling to that then. I really will."

"I'd better go."

"All right, dear. Larkspur, I love you, too. I'm very proud of you. I don't think I could have ever done the things you've done. You're very brave. Despite what you think."

"You be brave too now, Mother."

The nurse ushered me out.

Leslie

AND HERE I LIE IN THIS MOMENT, trapped in this moment. They wheel me in, and that nice Johnny Josefowski walks beside me holding my hand, though I'm not sure surgeons usually do that sort of thing. And won't he have to scrub soon?

I don't know.

I've never been under anesthesia before. I've never had surgery. Only two colds that I can remember have I suffered beneath.

And now I go straight from the picture of health to bypass surgery. Crack her open, crack open that rib cage.

My stars. Dear Lord.

They're going to crack me open like an egg, and there will be my heart exposed to the world at large. Just lying there pumping away like some piece of bloody meat that refuses to die. And then they'll put me on a respirator and something called a heart-lung machine that will pump blood through my body and keep air in my lungs while my heart is still. Some machine will become that spirit part of me that keeps sucking the air into my lungs, keeps my brain breathing and full of life.

A friend of mine had bypass surgery on her beating heart. No machine for her, she said. And I asked the doctor about it. Johnny Josefowski says, "I have better control when the heart is still."

And I said, "Then by all means, put me on the machine."

That was Friday.

It is Monday.

That surely happened years ago. Or was it five minutes ago? It's hard to tell when all you've got is this moment. I do hope they can jump-start me back to life.

Oh, God. Let them be able to jump-start me back to life.

Johnny Josefowski leaves my side, and a very nice anesthesiologist explains things to me. He's talking about counting to ten backward, which is downright silly. How can you count to ten backward? Now you can count backward *from* ten, but it's absolutely impossible to count *to* ten backward.

This moment is all I have. And so I will do as he asks because, as I said, he seems to be an awfully nice man. A doctor, not a mathematician, mind you.

"Ten."

If he were a mathematician…

"Nine."

I'd be in a pickle. A downright

"Is she going to be okay, Doctor?"

I heard the voice, but I couldn't move. The sounds seemed to filter through gelatin, slow and low and wet and thick and somehow sweetly buttery, although I can't explain that part of it. Newly's voice did the talking.

Newly?

I tried to open my eyes. I tried to say, "I'm all right, Son!" But nothing worked.

Dear God, I'm paralyzed. I'm a vegetable, and nobody knows it yet but me. Or maybe this is a coma.

"She's fine. She's just starting to come off the anesthetic."

Lots of stories circulate about people in comas and how they hear everything the people around them are saying.

"What are all those tubes for?" Newly asked.

Tubes?

Oh no. I'm going to be on a respirator for the rest of my life. Oh my. I'm just so *tired* I can't think anymore. Newly, I'm all right. I really am.

Am I?

"Those tubes are draining the fluid out of her chest."

"When will they come out?"

"Probably tomorrow. We'll sit her up in a chair later on tonight."

Up in a chair? Tonight?

Are these people crazy? I'm in a coma!

I felt Newly's lips on my forehead. "Don't tell anyone I was here," he said to the nurse.

"If that's what you'd like."

"Thank you."

I grunted just to let him know *I* knew.

Oh, good. A real grunt. That seemed like a good sign.

And then the scrape of ball bearings and curtain hooks told me that Newly had gone.

Well! I didn't die on the table!

Thank You, God!

Now, that's a thought that will make you sit up in a chair when they tell you! If I could only open my eyes, it would be a start.

Lark

THE VETERAN FAMILIES IN THE WAITING ROOM told us, "Prepare yourself for when you go in there. They look more horrible than you can begin to imagine."

What would I find?

I'd been doing so well. And now not only were the ants back, they literally swarmed beneath my skin.

When the nurse opened the door and said, "Is the family of Leslie Summerville here?" the four of us jumped to our feet. I actually squeaked out a little shout, darn me.

"You ready?" the nurse asked.

"Yes," said Prisma.

James hugged Flannery and said, "I'll wait here. This should just be family."

Prisma whispered, "Good boy," and followed the nurse into the sterile hall, through the electronic double doors and back into the semicircular cardiac recovery unit.

Not sure how I actually placed one shaky foot in front of the other, I somehow made it into the Cardiac Recovery Unit.

I scanned the beds quickly.

Big bald man.

African-American woman.

Really old, short-haired lady.

Silver-haired gentleman.

Pudgy little woman with her hair pulled back.

Backtrack. Wait. Pudgy? That was Mother?

I hurried over to her curtained-off area, quickly gaining the regal place right by her side.

"What in the world is that hose thing for coming out of the bottom of the bed?" Flannery asked as she stood beside me.

It looked like the hose of a vacuum cleaner! And there Mother lay, all swollen up to twice her size. What was wrong? Did this mean she was going to die?

The nurse entered. "I'm Janet. I'll be with your mom all night. In this unit she's my only patient."

"So she'll get good care," Prisma said, looking whiter than I'd ever seen her and now standing on the other side of the bed, as close to Mother's head as the equipment would allow.

"She'll have my undivided attention."

Flannery began to cry. "Is she going to be okay?"

"Oh yes. She had a rough time coming out of the anesthesia, and we sedated her. It's not uncommon."

I felt scared. "Are you sure she's going to be okay?"

This horrible bunch of multicolored wires stuck out of her neck like some space-age, alien medical treatment or some obscure part of a car engine.

"She's actually doing quite well." The nurse adjusted one of the many boxes on the IV pole. "Her vitals are wonderful."

How much medication was she on anyway? I counted down. Five different units. "And all these drips?"

"Standard for after surgery. Really, she's doing wonderfully. I know that's hard to believe."

I decided I'd take her word for it. "Is Dr. Josefowski around?"

She shook her head. "He went right into another surgery. He'll be in to check on her around five. But Dr. Boniczek is right over there at the desk if she needs him."

Even swollen, Mother looked so small and battered there in the bed. "Is that a respirator?"

"Yes. We'll start weaning her from it this evening. She's already taking some breaths on her own."

It was just plain creepy with that tube down her throat, stretching her mouth down to the side, revealing her tongue. Oh, Mother, Mother!

God, this all had better work. She had better be up and at 'em, or I'm going to be so ticked.

Extreme anger enveloped me for the first time in my life. It's hard to believe, but before, I had always felt scared. Not now.

I mean it, God! You've got to bring her through.

And I cried.

Flannery still cried, so I put my arm around her and squeezed. "Is that swelling normal?" I asked several minutes later after we'd calmed down a bit.

"Oh yes," Janet said. "They give them a lot of fluid during surgery."

Prisma, still resembling a plus-sized mannequin, clutched her purse more tightly. "Okay then. That's good that it's normal."

The nurse began washing her hands at the sink. "The visiting time is up. It's quite short in this unit. But you can come back tonight from 8:00 to 8:30."

Prisma kept hold of that purse and nodded decisively. "We'll be here."

At eight o'clock Prisma and I stood by Mother's bedside. Thank You, God, she had awakened, her hazel eyes brighter than her bodily form otherwise implied.

Prisma gathered her hand. "How are you feeling, Mrs. Summerville?"

She shook her head and shrugged, unable to say anything due to the ventilator.

I smiled at her. "Well, you should be glad you didn't get your hair cut like mine, Mother, or you'd be a human hairball like everyone else in these other beds. Instead you look neat as a pin."

Mother smiled and rolled her eyes.

We laughed.

"Are you sore? In pain?" Prisma asked. "Because if you are, just say the word! I'll make sure they give you something."

She shook her head and lifted a graceful hand as if to say, "I'm fine."

Prisma nodded once. "Good."

I held her other hand. "Flannery was so upset by the sight of you out cold this afternoon she couldn't bring herself to come in. She said to tell you she's sorry."

Mother grimaced and waved my statement away.

"You understand?" I asked.

She nodded.

"I knew you would, Mother. But I'll tell her you're looking more like your old self, and I'm sure she'll be in tomorrow."

Johnny entered the ward as we walked back through the automatic door. "I'm glad I caught you."

"How's she doing, Doctor?" Prisma asked.

"Fine. We're about to take her off the respirator. She should be moved back up to the fifth floor tomorrow. A lot more visiting hours up there, of course, and then further upstairs to rehab. She's in good shape. That will stand her in good stead."

The sight of him thrilled me. So stable and sure. And as foreign as all this felt to me, it was an everyday occurrence to him.

He reached out and squeezed my arm. "I'll take good care of her tonight, Lark."

When we left that evening, Prisma navigating the old Duster back down Charles Street, I said a silent prayer of thanks for second chances and for Johnny Josefowski. Sometimes God gives us exactly what we don't deserve. Obviously, He decided to lend me an extra hand, to extend a heaping portion of grace to me and Mother.

So take a big bite, Lark. Take a giant mouthful, savor the flavor and enjoy the rest of the meal because you don't know how much time will pass before this particular plate gets whisked away.

"Did you get more of those albums for Mother yet, Prisma?"

"Not yet, baby."

"Why don't we swing by the craft store on the way home?"

"You got it."

"Hello?"

"Prayer Lady?"

"Hi, Gene."

Hi, Gene. Hygiene. I wanted to laugh myself silly.

"Guess what, Gene?"

"What?"

"My mother made it fine through her bypass today."

"Great. Let me tell you what happened at work!"

Wow. They really don't give a fig about me, do they?

"Hello?"

"Lark?"

"Johnny?"

"Yeah."

"How you doing? Long day?"

"Very. Just wanted to let you know your mom's doing fine. They had her walking the hall about a half an hour ago."

"No kidding!"

"Nope. Par for the course for the healthier patients. She's obviously taken good care of herself over the years."

"She has."

"Well, I just wanted you to know all that."

"Thanks." Should I do it? Should I invite him over for a walk and a cup of coffee?

"Would you like to come on down and take a walk?"

He hesitated, and I froze.

Oh man!

Darn.

He cleared his throat. "I think that would be great."

"Good! See you in a little bit."

"Okay."

And I jumped up from my desk, turned on the answering machine for the prayer line, and ran upstairs to get ready. This was almost like being in love.

Oh yeah?

Really, Lark?

H'm. I guess I'll have to think about that one a little more.

September

Flannery

WHEN IT'S RIGHT, YOU KNOW IT.

So get this. James and I are going to get married! It's a small, quiet surprise sort of thing. "Let's get it over and done with," I tell James as we go up to a coffee shop in Bel Air to listen to some live music. "I just want to be with you."

He grins at that, and then he kisses me. "You wanna get married at Stoneleigh House?"

"Of course. With Father Charlie presiding, and Miss Marsha can sing. And we'll just walk Grandy in from her bed at the den. Although maybe she'll want to dress for the occasion. And Prisma will plan some kind of little party afterward."

He squeezes me. "You sure you want to do it this way?"

"I am, James. If we wait, I might let you do something I regret."

"Thanks for the vote of confidence."

I cross my arms and stare up through my lashes. "Well, am I right or am I right?"

"Even if there's the most remote chance you are, I say let's go for it."

"Me, too."

And we kiss again.

We go down and get the license, and it's quick because Maryland doesn't require a blood test. And Father Charlie is all smiles as we sit with him in the sanctuary at St. Dominic's.

"A surprise wedding, Flannery? Are you sure?"

"Definitely."

"Why?"

"Can you imagine what it would be like planning a long, drawn-out thing with those women?"

"Not really. No."

"And it could take away all the progress they've made these past couple of months."

"You think so?"

"Maybe not. But it's not worth the risk. Besides, Father Charlie, it's different. I like to be different."

"Well, okay, but it's the first surprise wedding I've ever done." And he runs one of his hands over his head.

Miss Marsha is at her real estate office over in Timonium, and she starts shouting and says, "Of course I'll sing!"

And it's tomorrow!

Mrs. Quigley James Smith.

Flannery del Champ Smith.

Flannery Smith.

Yeah, just plain old Flannery Smith. That suits me fine. Flannery plus del Champ is way too much name for one person.

Yesterday Grandy said, "This is the first time I've had a good appetite in years!" Is that cool or what? You should see her and Mom going at it for afternoon snacks. The two of them remind me of comic strip girl Cathy and her mother now. Yep, I can get married and move out with a very clear conscience.

L a r k

JOHNNY AND I SAT ON THE BENCH by the fishpond. Twilight purpled the sky, and the September breeze scented the air with the first tinge of dying leaves.

"She's looking pretty good, Lark, don't you think?"

"Yeah, definitely."

"It was a clear-cut surgery. No surprises going in. And her recovery has been textbook."

"Really?"

"Sure."

Johnny never tries to impress me with medical jargon. He just tells me what I need to know the way I need to know it. I like that.

Bradley called the day after Labor Day. I told him I needed until the end of the week. And tonight is Thursday, which means I'd better tell Johnny because tomorrow, we might all find ourselves in the midst of another Pompeii.

"I need to talk about something important, Johnny."

"Okay. It sounds scary by the tone of your voice."

"It might be." How to do this? Just plow on forward. "I'm divorced. My husband didn't die like everyone thinks. I've been lying for years."

I concentrated on the bubbling fountain on the outskirts of the pond. Fish swam within their simple surroundings, just swimming away, not married fish, not divorced fish, just fish. Why couldn't it be like that for us?

Johnny cleared his throat. "Well, I guess I should feel complimented by the fact that you feel the need to tell me."

Definitely not the answer I expected. Now why didn't I have that kind of outlook?

"I guess so."

He took my hand. "Do you want to expand on that thought?"

"Yeah, I do."

So I told him everything. Even the mess I was about to get myself into with Flannery.

He whistled low and long. "Oh, Lark. How in the world are you going to tell her?"

"I have no idea. If you think of anything, let me know."

He looked up into the darkening sky. "I have a small suggestion if you want to hear it."

"I sure do."

"Why don't you ask your mother?"

"Mother? What would she know about it? She had the perfect marriage. I don't know if she would begin to understand what I'm up against."

Johnny shook his head. "I don't think it's so much that she understands from a personal point of view, Lark. It's just that she loves you and she's a pretty wise lady. We've had some neat conversations since the surgery."

"Really?"

"Oh yeah. I call her every day to see how she is."

"She hasn't said a thing about it."

He shrugged. "Funny, isn't it? Your mother actually has a life of her own."

H'm. Well.

"Talk to her, Lark."

Prisma called from the screen door, "You all want some ice tea?"

"We'll be in in just a minute!" I hollered back. Then I turned toward Johnny. "So, what about it? Do you still want to date a divorcée?"

"It was infidelity. You had grounds."

"I didn't have a choice. He left me. I would have forgiven that man anything."

"Do you forgive him now though, Lark? He's put you in a real predicament."

The fish swam before my gaze in happy circles. "I haven't decided. I guess the talk with Flannery will decide that for me."

Even as the words came out of my mouth, I knew I erred. Forgiveness was something you decided for yourself despite the circumstances or the offense. Johnny knew that too but was kind enough to leave it alone.

PRISMA

I TELL YOU THE TRUTH, sometimes in life the word *bittersweet* fits with such perfection you don't know whether to laugh or cry or to somehow do both at the same time.

My time on Greenway is coming to a close after all of these years. Half a century I've lived my life behind these stones. We weathered the Korean War and Truman's H-bomb and rejoiced over the polio vaccine. Mr. Summerville and I shook hands when we heard Stalin had passed on. I cheered on Rosa Parks and the Hungarians who gave it their best shot. The USSR launched *Sputnik*. NASA was founded, men made their way to the moon, and yet I stayed on here in Stoneleigh House, our own milestones achieved with the birth of Lark.

Poor Marilyn Monroe died a year after the Bay of Pigs, only to be followed by JFK a year later. And Lark started nursery school that year and sang her first solo, "Jolly Old St. Nicholas," at the school pageant. Newly arrived a year later, howling and screaming, affronted by his removal from the womb. Vietnam, the Six-Day War, all sorts of history going on even as we made our own. Dr. Martin Luther King Jr. assassinated. Man walking on the moon.

So if anybody says I should be ready to go, I can honestly say, it just isn't that easy. And yet, I'm so happy for Mrs. Summerville. Yesterday when I helped her into the guest room for her afternoon nap, she said, "Prisma, you're my best friend."

"Well, Mrs. Summerville, you're mine."

And I can tell you, that is the truth.

Mr. Charles, you're dead and gone, and you can't be my best friend anymore.

Yesterday I okayed a large check to help with the new wing of a children's hospital in Birmingham. I love it when Days of Summer helps children. So much ahead of them, so much history painting the backdrop of their lives.

Who is going to take over for me when I leave? I'll just leave it in the hands of the Lord, for now. I'm sure He's got plans of His own. Better plans than mine, too.

My list of thankful things stretches a mile tonight, so I just want to leave it at this: Thank You, God!

Leslie

ONE OF THE MORE AMUSING THINGS about my stay in the hospital was the way Lark, Prisma, and Sweet Pea snuck decent food up to my room.

One night, on my fourth night in the hospital, Lark came in with a bowl of Prisma's cream of crab soup. When the tech arrived to take my vitals, Lark thought it was the nurse and threw the entire bowl into her purse.

I haven't laughed that much in years!

I honestly don't know who I'm trying to stay so thin for anymore. I've been positively thrilled at being away from the country club, the horse farm, and Jacob Marley (I have no idea what that little foray was all about). I've been piddling away at little charity functions when right before me Days of Summer goes on without any sort of attention from me. I could have been helping thousands.

Breakfast seemed like a good idea now that I was back home on Greenway, but I didn't feel like getting up yet. Lying in my bed talking to God in the mornings is a wonderful thing. I was in the guest bedroom on the main floor, and I had decided to redecorate and make it mine. No, I didn't share it with Charles. But it was time to get on with my life in ways that I'm sure Charles himself could have hardly imagined. And yet he'd be proud.

Are you looking down, Charles? Do you see what God has done?

As I imagined him in heavenly form, his portliness gone, a light knock vibrated my door. "Come in."

"Mother?"

"Come in, Larkspur. I've been awake. I'm just lying here in the quiet."

Larkspur hadn't looked this relaxed in years. But something bothered her this morning. "Are you all right, Larkspur?"

"Not really, Mother. I need to ask you something. I need some good advice."

Well, miracles never cease! But, my stars! Was I ready for this kind of responsibility again? Out of the blue?

I suddenly hoped and prayed I wouldn't fall short.

I held out my hand. "Come and sit on the bed, dear, and tell me everything."

"Mother, Bradley is still alive. I've been lying to you all these years."

I smiled, sat up, and pulled her into my arms. "I know, Lark."

Tears erupted from deep within my daughter's soul, and I cried with her, wishing as always that I could bear the pain for her.

After several minutes she surfaced. "Why didn't you tell me you knew?"

"I was afraid you'd get mad at me. I ran into Bunky del Champ years ago in Boca Raton. Your father wanted to confront you, but I told him you must have had your reasons. And then I overheard that phone call that first night, and I prayed I was just imagining things. That it wasn't really Bradley."

Larkspur reached across me to the bedside table where she plucked out a Kleenex.

"Larkspur, I need to say something, and it's not easy. But I've done a lot of thinking over the past month. Actually, ever since you've moved back." Libby Lee Strawbridge reared her ugly head for an instant saying, *Mothers should never apologize; it weakens them!* Oh, stuff it, Libby! "I need to apologize. For some reason the lines between us frayed. I don't know where or when it happened, but I sort of gave up on you."

"Oh, Mother, you didn't."

"Yes, I did. I figured you'd come around when you'd want to, and I'd be there. But you really didn't come around, and I'm sorry. I should have followed your father's advice. I should have been there more for you."

"You were there."

"Only when you wanted me, but not when I knew you really needed me. So, I'm sorry."

And we cried some more. Oh, we did, and my heart puffed up like a warmed pastry filled with the sweetest things life could offer a woman. My arms circled my baby once more.

And we cried even more. It certainly hurt my incision. But that didn't matter one whit. Oh, Larkspur. Oh, my sweet Lark.

"I was so scared you were going to die, Mother."

"Me, too!"

"Just when things were going so well."

"I know."

And then the moment ended. But not with a finality. The moment itself ended, yes, but its vibrations would power our hearts for years.

When Lark pulled away, she asked, "So what should I do about Bradley?"

I shrugged. "You have to tell Flannery."

"How?"

"I don't know. Let's just pray God clears the path for you."

"He's calling Friday night."

"Well then, God doesn't have much time, does He?" I felt strange as the next words, foreign, slipped out of my mouth. "I'll be praying for you, Lark."

She looked at me quizzically and shook her head as though releasing marbles that had stuck together in a pile inside her brain, and then a smile stretched her lips, and I caught my breath. She looked so beautiful to me just then.

Now you may think this is all just a little too neat. Mother and daughter learn to get along. And isn't that just so nice? But I do believe the world deserves to know that sometimes God is afoot and He's able to heal broken hearts, bind wounds, and breathe new life into deadened souls who walked the lonely halls of their own making. And He can do it without cardiac arrests or big car accidents. Sometimes our most defining moments are the most still.

And I am thankful.

Now, the question remains, what is next for the women at Greenway? Change dances in the air. I feel it in my old bones, and for the first time in years I find myself extremely excited.

Flannery

"YOU BRING THE LICENSE?" I ask as James and his parents slip into the back door of the house at 10 A.M. Friday. "Hi, Mom." I kiss Anne's cheek.

"I did."

"Oh, hon," Anne says. "You look beautiful."

"Thanks for the phone call."

"Just wanted to reassure you." She turns to Lou. "Didn't we, Lou?"

"Heck, Anne. Sure." Mr. Smith leans forward and hugs me, with lots of pats on my shoulder blades.

Prisma paddles over, handkerchief at the ready. "The living room is all set. The flowers arrived as directed at seven this morning. Father Charlie is here, and so is Marsha."

"Cool." I just can't believe this! I want to scream like the girls in *Clueless*. "Are Mom and Grandy dressed?"

"They are and mad as hornets," Prisma says. "Your grandmother says, 'Why on earth am I lying on this hospital bed in the den in a silk suit?' And I'm doing my best to look like the Cheshire Cat and feeling like a fool! I still don't know why you had to make this a surprise wedding, Flannery. Sometimes you can be the strangest child!"

We all laugh.

Prisma tucks something white inside my hand. "This was your grandmother's wedding hanky."

"But it looks like a baby hat."

"It sure does. I made it into one. Your mother wore that home from the hospital. Wrap it around the handle of your bouquet and remember that family means everything, Baby Girl." Prisma waves her hanky, then smiles. "Okay, I'll bring in those two."

"How's Mom?" I ask.

"Mystified and uncomfortable."

"That's pretty much par for the course, isn't it, Miss Prisma?"

Father Charlie and Marsha tiptoe into the kitchen, hug me and James and everybody with a pulse, and wait for the cue.

Prisma takes her cue. "Pray for me. This one is going to be a stretch."

We hear her take on her tasks through the flip-flop door.

"Come on, baby. I just want you to go sit at the organ and play some Bach. Give your poor sick Mama a concert. That should cheer her up."

Mom mumbles something, which is a shame because I love to eavesdrop.

"I'm not asking you to drive a bus down I-95, Lark. I just want you to play a little Bach!"

"Mumble, mumble…sheesh, Prisma!"

"Well, all right then!"

Go, Miss Prisma!

Soon the strains of a fugue or something blow out of the pipe organ. I arrange my ecru, gauzy gown that I found in an antique store and smell the small bouquet of larkspur and daisies.

James grabs my hand and squeezes.

I don't know how Prisma accomplished the next feat of mountain moving, but somehow she got Grandy in there because she pokes her head in the flip-flop door and says, "They're ready. Now just hold on a minute while I get your mother to play 'The Wedding March.'"

" 'The Wedding March'? Miss Prisma you're good, but you're not *that* good."

"Oh, you just watch and see, Baby Girl!"

Sure enough, the fugue stops. I open the flip-flop door and hear Mom say, "What on earth for, Prisma?"

"Just because I like it! Does the woman who's cooked and cleaned for years around here need any other reason than that?"

Whoa. She sure used up all her chips on that one!

And then the strains begin. I'd say tenderly and beautifully, but Mom is attacking the keyboard, a loud staccato sound coming from the pipes. It sounds horrible.

We all laugh as we file out of the kitchen and into the living room.

Leslie

OH, MY UTTER CONFOUNDED STARS! That child!

I should have been furious, but she looked so beautiful, like a fairy princess bride. Prisma handed me an extra hanky she had tucked in the pocket of that striped dress of hers.

Thank goodness she made me change into that outfit and put on a little makeup. Larkspur looked nice sitting there at the organ, banging away, oblivious for the first few seconds.

Prisma cleared her throat and then walked over and tapped Lark on the shoulder. "Look around, but don't stop playing."

So Lark did exactly the opposite. And there stood Sweet Pea, with that bouquet and a wreath of flowers around her head and the most gorgeous pair of little antique boots. Her dark curls spilled over the flowers, and the sunlight shone along them.

Of course, Larkspur stopped playing right away and ran over to her. I do believe I saw all the questions play across her face as she discarded them one by one. You see I knew what the questions were because I asked them myself.

A surprise *wedding?*

Are you sure about this?

Do you love him?

Does he love you?

Why now?

Aren't you rushing things?

Are you making the same mistake I did?

Are you PREGNANT?

Oh, Flannery, are you *sure* about this?

And her eyes darted over to James and to his parents, who beamed and shone like the steady suburbanites they were. And her eyes darted over to me, and I gave a shrug and a smile and an "it's okay" nod all at once. Or I tried to anyway.

Flannery

I SAY, "I DO"; HE SAYS, "I DO"; and well, we do!

We are getting married! And we hold on tightly the entire time.

Mom stands behind me holding back tears, and just before the vows I say, "Father Charlie, hold on a minute."

"Sure, Flannery."

I turn and take Mom's hand. "Excuse me, everyone. I'll be just a minute."

James taps my shoulder, leans down, and whispers in my ear. "Good going, babe. I'm not going anywhere." Then he stands back up to his full height. "Marsha, how about an a cappella version of…"

"'Oh, Promise Me'!" Anne Smith says. "I love that one."

"Good idea."

I wink at Grandy there on the couch as I lead a very pale mother to sit with me on the steps out in the foyer. Marsha's clear strains follow us.

"I know you're probably mad at me, Mom."

"Not mad. Just confused. Why couldn't you tell me?"

I hold both her hands now. "Are you happy for me?"

"If you love him and if he's good to you, I am."

"Well I do, and he is."

"Are you pregnant?"

"No! Mother!"

And the left corner of her mouth creeps up. "Have you…?"

"No!"

Her chest deflates, and her eyes close. And she says nothing.

"Mom, do you really, honestly feel you would have been up to all this at this time in your life?"

She shakes her head. And I notice how pretty she looks in that pink dress Grandy bought me. "Your makeup looks nice, Mom."

"I'm sorry I'm never there for you, Flannery. I wasn't even at the house with you when it caught fire."

I decide to do something seemingly cruel. "Mom, let's make this day about me and not about you, okay?"

Her eyes tear up. "Is that why you did this?"

And I nod. I hadn't really known exactly why I was compelled to do this until that moment.

She rests her hand on my cheek, pulls my face forward, and kisses me on the mouth like she used to do. "I'm sorry, Flannery."

Some kids are raised, and others just grow up.

"Mom, it's a day for joy. Let's just be happy today. That's all I want from you. Make it my wedding present, okay?"

"Okay."

"Now, walk me back in. We'll pretend it's the processional all over again, the way it should have been if we were a normal sort of family."

That makes her laugh, and I am glad.

PRISMA

"It's done! We did it!" that James boy hollered and held up a victorious fist.

The Smiths cheered, and I clapped, and Mrs. Summerville jumped to her feet. Even Lark got into the swing of things, and soon with James and Baby Girl in the middle we made up a big huddle of jiggling and patting arms there in the middle of the living room floor.

Flannery yelled. "Love you, Mom. Love you, New Mom and Dad!"

"Love you, Flannery!" Anne yelled. "Don't we, Lou?"

"Sure, Anne." Only Lou doesn't yell.

And James kissed Baby Girl, and we cheered some more, and the huddle broke off its appendages one by one. What a morning!

James grinned, and I do have to say there is a real charm about the boy. "Well, guys, we're off to our one-day honeymoon."

"You sure it's safe to go on that skipjack?" Anne Smith asks.

"I sure am. Mom, I've been on boats for years, you know that."

Anne raised her hands in easy defense and turned to Lark. "A mother never stops worrying, does she, Lark?"

"No, I guess you're right."

Then Lark pulled Baby Girl into a tight embrace. "I'm sorry," I heard her whisper because I still have ears like a bat.

"No, Mom. It's okay."

"I promise to try harder."

"It's okay."

"You'll see a real change when you get back."

Flannery kissed her cheek and pulled away, entwining her arm in James's.

Oh, Baby, Baby, Baby Girl. Be free! Just go on and forget about all this. Slough off those scales. Be your butterfly self.

Flannery

AND OFF WE GO! We sail out far into the Chesapeake Bay, and I give myself to James, and he gives himself to me. And it's that simple and that right. That evening, about three times later, a wonderful meal and a walk by the lighthouse, a sorrow for my mother quiets me, for all she has lost. And I vow to lick every square centimeter of this wonderful bowl God has placed me inside of, because I know that some things aren't forever. Please, God, let this be, I pray as James puts his arm around me there by the water. Please let us grow old together, forever and ever. Amen.

Lark

I COULDN'T TELL BRAD ABOUT THE WEDDING because he didn't deserve to know, and even thinking about it reduced me to a blubbering mass. "Honestly, Brad. She left this morning and isn't back yet. She won't be back home until tomorrow."

"Come on, babe, you said you'd do it by the end of the week."

"I know. I'm sorry."

"Look, Lark, I have this feeling you're not going to tell her without some help."

"No! That's not true. I will!"

"I'm coming to Baltimore on Sunday."

"Oh, come on, Bradley. Please!"

"I've got to."

For some strange reason I began seeing things from his perspective. But he still upset me. "I guess once again I don't have a choice."

"Yes, you did. Past tense."

What could I say to that except, "You said you wouldn't force it, but you did, Bradley. You said you wouldn't up and surprise her."

The silence stretched from here to California.

And Bradley's voice became tender. "Lark. Please. It's time to mend things. Please."

"But why now? Things are starting to shape up for me."

"And they'll go even better with a clean slate."

Gosh, I hated his logic.

The truth will set you free.

There is no fear in love.

"Okay, Sunday then. Call me when you get into town."

"Oh no, babe. I'll see you on Greenway at 7 P.M."

I sure was glad Mother was praying. Because only God could work within the parameters of Bradley del Champ's timing.

"I've got to go, Bradley."

"You playing tonight?"

"Practicing with Marsha. And I've got a wedding to play for Saturday afternoon. At a different church than St. Dominic's." I could hardly believe I'd accepted the job.

"You're doing good, Lark."

I sighed. "Well, let's hope you don't come along and change all that."

That night I wore a mint green dress I found in Mother's old stuff. Good old Johnny sat at the back of the church listening to us practice, and the dream I dared to dream had not one chance of coming true.

I cried myself to sleep, womanly regrets filling me with such pain, such a heavy pain only tears could break it apart.

PRISMA

WHEN I SAW MRS. SUMMERVILLE standing at the door to my room, I couldn't believe it. "Are you okay, Mrs. Summerville?"

"Never better, Prisma."

Still weak, truth be told, but improving every day. Almost two weeks from the surgery, and my goodness, her color is positively pink again!

And she swears she's still knitting on the same sweater she's been working on since the beginning of the summer. But I know better. This one sports a rolled collar, the other a mock turtle.

"Is there something you need?"

"Yes, as a matter of fact there is. I want you to tell me all you know about Days of Summer."

I laughed. "Well, that's quite a bit."

"Then we'll need to get started right away."

Bittersweet, yes ma'am, bittersweet.

One by one they are throwing me into obsolescence.

Well, I'd better make the most of it. "Come on over to the computer. First thing I'll do is take you on our Web site."

Her fine brows arched even further. "We have a Web site?"

"We sure do. Snazzy, too."

"My stars."

"Here, sit in my desk chair. It's more comfy. I'll get a chair from the kitchen."

Two hours later, I stopped the tutoring session. "You're exhausted, Mrs. Summerville. Let's get you into your den, and I'll make you a nice cup of tea."

"Make *us* a nice cup of tea, Prisma. I have a thousand more questions."

"You Summervilles," I said. "You don't know when to quit!"

"You got that right," she said with a smirk.

I hooted a laugh and clapped my hands.

She stood to her feet, gathered her cane, and walked on her own into the den. "You won't be needing that thing much longer," I called as I put some water in the kettle.

"Let's hope not."

Actually, the longer it takes, the longer I have here at Greenway. I'm apprehensive about the next stage of my life, but I called my son after Leslie went to bed, and I told him to start looking for sweet little white houses, front porches, and picket fences for me.

"We can add on the fence and the porch if we need to, Mama."

"I want a front porch and a picket fence before I move in and no trees outside my bedroom window, Son."

He didn't ask why, only said, "I'll take care of everything."

How many times have I uttered those words myself?

I looked out at my stars last night and said, "Jesus, I'm sure glad You are with us wherever we go."

"I sure am, My girl."

You see, Jesus loves me. This I know. And not just because the Bible tells me so. He's been guiding me each step of the way for a lot of years now, and He's never steered me wrong.

Fear not, for lo! I am with You always.

I couldn't wait to hear about the honeymoon!

Leslie

"NEWLY?"

"Mother! How are you feeling?"

"Fine. I'm sure Flannery invited you to the surprise wedding, didn't she?"

He sighed. "She called me Thursday and left a message. I was already on a flight to Boston."

"All right. I can handle that excuse."

"Besides, I'm not ready to face Lark yet."

"Why, Newly?"

"Honestly, Mother, I don't quite know. I feel so sorry for her I'm afraid my pity will show, and she'll get her hackles up."

"Oh, so it's for her dignity."

"In a way."

"Fiddle."

"Fiddle?"

"Yes, fiddle, Newly. We don't pull away from people to preserve their dignity. That makes no sense."

"I beg your pardon? I learned that from you."

"Well, it didn't make sense then, and it doesn't make sense now. It just took me awhile to realize how important it is to involve yourself in the lives of the people you love."

He chuckled. "You are something, Leslie Summerville."

"Yes, I am. And don't you forget it. Now, you're coming for Thanksgiving this year, and that's that."

"Right then. Can I bring someone with me?"

"That girlfriend Sweet Pea told me about?"

"Precisely."

"Do you want to tell me about her?"

And to my supreme shock and amazement, Newly did. She waits tables in the lunchroom in the lobby of his building.

"She's not your type, Mother."

"Why not?"

"She works hard."

I thought of what lay ahead of me with Days of Summer. "Well, then, Son, maybe I can learn a thing or two from this lady."

Newly's speech must have skedaddled because it took a good ten seconds for him to respond, and then he only said, "Huh."

And that most certainly is not British!

Is it?

Lark

AFTER MUSIC PRACTICE WE SAT ALONE at the 3 B's, Johnny and I, and only the tube of fluorescence over the mirror glowed behind the counter. Deke left an hour before. "Lock up before you go." And he zoomed off in his gold-trimmed Lincoln.

"There's something I have to tell you about." Johnny's eyes glowed in the darkness. "I haven't been this excited in years."

"What happened?"

The Flannery news would have to wait.

He peeled a napkin from the metal holder and began shredding it with his beautiful fingers. "I've been looking into how doctors are really needed in Third World countries. Did I mention that?"

"Uh-huh."

"So, like I said, I've been looking into it. I can go for a couple of years to Kenya. It's nothing I have to sign on for for the rest of my life."

"What about your practice here?"

"I can take a sabbatical. Physicians do it all the time."

"I've never heard of one doing that."

He smiled. "So what do you think?"

"About medical missions in general? About you going specifically? About how I feel about that in regard to us in particular?"

"All three."

I sat back against the black vinyl of the booth. I blew out air. I tried to think. "I guess I need to know first how *you* feel about all this regarding us?"

There was no way I was going to say or suggest anything first.

"My feelings are deepening. I'm wondering if you feel the same. If you regard me as more than just a guy you go out with."

"I do feel the same." Did I? Or was he just so nice, a great catch, and somebody comfortable to grow old with? Was he insurance against loneliness? Easy prescriptions when I would start needing them?

Oh, that's horrible, Lark. I can't believe you even thought that!

"I'm not sure I'd want to go it alone."

I inhaled, held it, then ventured to say, "You want me to go with you?"

He smiled, nodded and squeezed my hand. "What do you think?"

"Well, my first reaction is to think, What in the world good would I be to anybody over there?"

"That's not true. Look how great you've been at caring for your mother."

True.

"And don't forget the power of a song."

Very true.

"Music has a healing quality, you know. But you don't have to answer yet, Lark. Just tell me you'll think about things for a while."

"Have you put in an application yet?"

"Yes."

"When do you expect to have a departure date?"

"I can set my own. I can go anytime I want. The need is that great."

Not surprising. But I needed more time. I was figuring on months and months for Johnny and me to build a relationship, much less a future.

"Listen. Bradley is coming into town Sunday, and I still haven't told Flannery about him. Can we talk about all this next Thursday night? I'll at least be a little less sidetracked."

"Sure. That's fine. I guess I was so excited about it that I didn't think about the timing of springing it on you. I'm sorry."

"That's okay. I wish I could be more excited for you."

He looked at me with eyes of understanding that wounded me. He deserved somebody better than me. But didn't I say that when we first started getting interested in each other?

"I think we'd make a great team, Lark," he said. "I'm not asking you to marry me. There's time for that. You've been talking about serving God in a tangible way. This could be it. And we'd make a great team."

That fact starched up the situation even more.

"Just think about it, okay?"

"Okay. I will."

And then I told him about Flannery and James. I could hardly believe how the words slipped out slow yet slick, and every feeling I felt, every word I thought slipped out as well. The guilt, the shame, the anger at myself mostly. The disappointment. The fear of life without her, of a life where a husband should and would take first place.

Johnny just listened, asking questions every so often.

Finally I looked at my watch. "It's 2 A.M."

"I'll run you home then."

"You don't have surgery in the morning, do you?"

He shook his head. "Not usually on Saturday. Unless it's an emergency or something."

"Your beeper's been awfully quiet tonight."

"Yeah."

I wondered if he pictured a beeperless life in Africa. I think he did.

We rode home with little to say.

It was too much, too soon. I hadn't expected this move from Johnny. Not at all.

No Africa for me, thanks. I knew that when he pulled up in the driveway. Too much existed on Greenway now. I had a tangible mission from God. Matters that needed attending to by me and only me. I refused to put anything off anymore. And I was unwilling to string Johnny along, no matter how much I cared.

I turned to him. "Johnny?"

"Yes."

"I won't go to Africa. I'll have a better answer for you later as to why, but right now, I can only say I know I won't go."

I was so thankful I couldn't see his face clearly in the dim interior of the car. So thankful.

"Would you still like to see each other though?"

"I'd like that a lot."

"I'd hoped…"

"Me, too. But my life is too complicated, don't you see? Between Mother and Flannery and now Bradley returning on the scene, I have matters to attend to."

"Many of them." He gripped the wheel and shook his head. "I don't know what I was thinking. I was a fool for asking."

I reached out and touched his face. "No, you weren't. I'm honored that you wanted me to be with you."

"Well, chalk it up to enthusiasm then."

That was it.

Johnny didn't bare his soul. Not that I thought he would. "I'll see you in church on Sunday?"

"I hope so. We'll see how Flannery accepts the news."

"Would you…"

"Like to go out for waffles afterward?" I asked.

"Waffles?"

"Yeah, there's a new Waffle House in Riverside. We can go eat together."

"All the way out in Harford County?"

"Believe it or not."

"Sounds good."

I watched him drive away, saddened that someone like Johnny, so smart and talented, nice and caring, and all those things women are supposed to adore was too good for every single one of us.

He was positively beating himself over the head right now.

I walked by Flannery's room, turned, and headed into the darkness. She'd escaped Greenway. She had the guts to do the right thing for a happy future.

I have to say that I realized in that moment there was nobody on earth I admired more than my daughter.

Flannery

THEY SIT IN THE KITCHEN eating breakfast when we walk in Saturday morning.

Prisma throws down her dishtowel. "Well if it isn't the honeymooners!"

Mom rushes over and hugs me, and there are no tears. She just beams.

Grandy sips her coffee. "Welcome back to the funny farm."

Prisma lets out a hoot.

Mom stands up. "Call it what you will, Mother. I'm just glad to see she made it off that boat."

We laugh. And I hold James's hand up, bend my elbow, and bring it up right next to my breast, our fingers intertwined. It's so intimate and married-like, and I realize that I've never been happier in my life, right here with James and the women of Greenway.

"Now this is exactly right!" I say.

"You got that right, Baby Girl. How 'bout some coffee and one of my cinnamon buns?"

Lark

HOW COULD I TELL HER NOW?

The joy in her eyes shone exactly as it should have...bridal. She sat there before me wearing one of Mother's old suits, a white one. Her hair was pulled back, and she looked so perfect, blushing and womanly.

She'd always done the right things.

How could I tell her now? How could I destroy that joy and drive a wedge between us now that she was finally on her own? Where would that leave me?

Well, that little piece of selfish pity decided it for me. "Let's go into the garden, Flannery."

She turned to James.

"Go on, babe. I'm going to eat another cinnamon roll."

Prisma picked up the plate and stuck it in front of him. "I do like this boy, Baby Girl."

Flannery stopped me by the door to the screened porch. "Are you at least happy for me, Mom?"

"I really am, sweetie. I was afraid you were going to make the same mistake I did."

Flannery shook her head, confusion in her eyes. "What do you mean?"

The phone rang on the wall to her left.

"I'm expecting a call from Starbucks." She picked it up. "You go on outside, and I'll be there in a minute."

I sat myself by the fishpond and waited, deciding that I'd call Bradley when they left and beg for more time. We couldn't destroy this joy. She deserved at least a month of pure happiness. Surely I'd be able to convince him of this.

Flannery slammed out of the kitchen and marched over to me, tears streaming down her face. "Why didn't you tell me Daddy was alive?"

"That was your father on the phone?"

My mouth dropped open.

"Yes. He called to say he was taking the earlier flight tomorrow." Her voice sounded dead and thick. Oh, baby.

Think, Lark, think.

No answer came. Heat ignited my face. My throat closed.

Do this!

"And he asked for you, not me?"

"Of course."

"Flannery, I was going to tell you."

"Well, Mom, now is not the right day to find this out, is it? Good grief! I can't even have two days in a row without you and your stupid problems haunting them!"

"Do you want me to tell you now, or do you want me to wait?"

"Tell me now. But I've got to tell you, Mom. I've been mad at you before but never anything like this."

I could think of no appropriate response.

"Come on, Mom! Tell me! Just get it over with."

Amid the mums, purple, white, and yellow with barely opening buds, I told her all of it. Stone faced. The circumstances of her conception. The disastrous marriage. My crazy love for her father. The infidelity. Bradley's promise to stay away.

She said nothing. Looked down at her hands.

"Flannery, look at me."

"No."

"Please."

"No!"

I told her of years of struggle and pain and disappointment. Bradley's marriage to a diabetic. His career. A whole life lived without us.

"His wife died this summer. He called me after that."

"Oh."

"I thought he'd come for us, sweetie. Years ago, I did. I made him promise not to find us. But I didn't think he'd take me seriously. I don't know why I even did that! I've always wondered if I asked him to promise to disappear so he'd realize how important we were to him. Right then. Right there. I thought he'd say, 'Oh, babe. I'm sorry. I can't bear to be without you two.' But he didn't bite, Flannery. He didn't bite, and I knew I'd done the wrong thing. And then as the months wore on, I realized that maybe he really didn't care, because what kind of father would keep a promise like that?"

She kept her face down.

"He wants to see you again, Flannery."

"I gathered that, Mom!" Flannery jerked her head back and looked at me. I tried so hard to gauge her feelings but couldn't. I could only see tumult in her eyes.

She ran away then.

I called after her, but I knew she wouldn't turn around. I don't think I would have either.

A minute later I watched her and James back the old Buick out of the garage. Prisma waved them off, and James waved back, but Flannery sat close to her new, sweet husband and wept on his shoulder.

When people say life isn't fair, they're exactly right.

So I went in and cried on Mother's shoulder, and she held me for a long time. When I pulled back, she slid a hand over my hair and said, "Whatever happens, Larkspur, we're in it together. I really mean that."

"Do you think she'll come around?"

"Yes."

"What about her father?"

"Now you can leave it in his hands."

I reached out for a cup of tea Prisma placed there during my spell of tears. "That's not comforting."

"Well, I know. And all you can do is wait awhile for her to come back to you."

I sipped. "What if she never does?"

"Then you'll seek her out. Because that's what mothers *should* do."

"Mother, would you think poorly of me if I told you I feel relieved?"

She put a hand on my knee. "You've been carrying this secret for a long time."

"And now it's out."

"It was going to come out someday."

"The funny thing is, I wondered if that was true. The last few years I thought I might have just pulled it off."

"That's when it really gets dangerous, dear."

"You said it, Mother."

"That Bradley's a rat," she said.

"He gave me enough time. But I figured I could stall him. It didn't work."

She sighed. "I'll have to try to be nice, I suppose."

"It would be best."

She kissed my cheek. "You did the best you could, Larkspur."

Flannery

IT WOULD BE EASY TO WONDER what I was thinking when I ran out on Mom like that. Truth was, so many thoughts whizzed around in my head, so many questions, I couldn't focus on even one of them. All I could do was cry.

We went over to James's apartment, well, my apartment too, and he fixed me a glass of milk and put me to bed. "Sleep, babe. You'll be able to think about it better when you wake up."

And then he curled up beside me until I slept. When I woke up a few hours later, he was studying his oceanography stuff at the table in the kitchen. It's an old kitchen and an old table, and it's on the second floor of the house his grandparents used to own. Which means I can really paint and stuff. It's thoughts about stuff like that that are keeping me sane right now.

I'd say "My whole life has been a lie." But not only is that melodramatic, it's just not true. I believed a lie all of my life. That is more to the point.

I sit down across from James. "So what do you think about all of this?"

Believe it or not, earlier I was able to get out Mom's story in fits and starts. And James listens and says, "Oh, babe," like, a thousand times or so.

"I can see why you're so bummed."

"Yeah."

"But I've been thinking a lot about it while you were asleep. Trying to come at it from your mom's perspective, you know?"

I nod and reach for a McDonald's sugar packet that sits next to the salt. "I guess. But it's never right to lie."

"No, I didn't say it was. I just can't imagine how hurt she was at the time."

It is the only thing that keeps me from hating her.

"My father is coming into Baltimore tomorrow."

"Are you going to see him?"

"I don't know."

Now isn't that the strangest thing? All my life I thought of how much I'd give to spend even a little bit of time with my father. And now the opportunity stands before me, and I don't know if I want to grab it or not.

He hurt Mom badly. Just as James said. He flew down that driveway and left me behind without an argument. Believe me—*believe me*—when I say that it was easier when I thought he was dead.

I can't even recall his voice now that I've heard it.

Leslie

I'M FEELING QUITE WELL THESE DAYS. Prisma drove me to the mall to walk around. After what happened with Flannery, we both needed to get out of the house.

"You need to be exercising now," she said.

"Well, so do you, Prisma."

"So let's do it where it's flat for now."

That made sense. Truth to tell, Prisma makes sense most of the time.

So Saturday evening, while Lark, heartbroken to be sure, played her first wedding gig at a different church, Prisma and I went up to Towsontowne Mall.

My goodness.

I could hardly believe the variety nowadays. "Now this is the way to window-shop!"

"It sure is."

"Look at that Bombay place. I love that picture."

It was of a bride getting ready for her wedding.

"I do too. Makes me think of the church."

We continued our slow stroll. "Now what is that supposed to mean?"

"We're called the bride of Christ in Scripture."

"Well, isn't that perfectly beautiful!"

"It sure is."

"My, you're agreeable this afternoon, Prisma."

"M'm h'm. It's a good evening to be window-shopping with your friend."

What a lovely thing to say.

"Have you talked to Sweet Pea since she found out?"

"Called her before we left." Prisma nodded. "She's taking it hard."

"So is Lark."

"And there Mister Bradley is sailing clear and free."

But I wasn't so sure. "You really think so, Prisma?"

She thought as we passed about five storefronts. "I guess not."

"So he's coming tomorrow."

"I know."

"I know. Let's roll out the red carpet!"

"What? Have you gone crazy, Mrs. Summerville?"

"Absolutely. Stark raving mad, as my mama used to say."

Prisma stopped. "Why do you want to do this?"

"Well, think about it, Prisma. Bradley is the key. If we can get Flannery to love him, and Lark to accept him, that's the answer."

"One big happy family, is that it?"

"Sort of. Is that an impossible task?"

"Probably."

I tucked my hand in her arm. "But it's worth a try, right?"

"I'm game. I guess. Although I'm not so sure about him and Lark getting back together."

"Not back together like that. Just good friends."

Prisma hooted. "Good friends? Oh, Mrs. Summerville, you've been watching too much TV before bed!"

"Oh, come on. It will be fun." Excitement filled me. "What time will he be at the house tomorrow?"

"Seven o'clock."

"Do we have enough in for a nice meal?"

Prisma rolled her eyes. "Now what do you think, Mrs. Summerville?"

I rolled mine back at her. "Let's finish our stroll and go home, Prisma."

A hard night lay ahead for all of us.

Lark

I REMOVED THE PRAYER PHONE off the hook that night after I returned home from playing at the wedding. So proud of myself for even taking the gig, I felt like a traitor to love, sitting there at the organ. Who was I to take part in wedding festivities? I'd fouled up the institution of marriage so thoroughly I didn't deserve to play "The Wedding March." I didn't.

It wasn't that I was feeling sorry for myself, really. I ached so deeply for Flannery I had no idea what to do.

PRISMA

"Now, Mrs. Summerville, I think this is going too far! He could have taken a cab from the airport. He can afford it."

I'm telling you the truth, they've gone crazier than ever around this place!

But when she pulled a sign out of her purse and unfolded it, that crossed the line. With Asil at the wheel of the Bentley, we'd ridden all the way down to BWI where Asil dropped us off at ticketing, walked all the way to the security checkpoint—huffing and puffing I hate to say—and to make sure we made it on time we left an hour earlier than we needed to.

And now a sign?

"Mrs. Summerville, I will walk out of this terminal and get in that car without you and have Asil drive on home if you do not put that sign away."

"But I spent an hour on it. It looks cute, don't you think, with the heart stickers? I'm so glad we had those scrapbook supplies."

"Yes. It's cute all right but not for that rock star. Remember what he did to your daughter!"

There, that might convince her to put it away.

But Mrs. Summerville got quiet. "Believe me, Prisma Percy, I've never forgotten what he did to Larkspur."

Oh, for heaven's sake. Why do I do these things? Why don't I just keep my mouth shut?

"And that's why I'm trying to help here, to maybe give Lark a little peace, Prisma. She deserves it. You're right about the sign though. As Newly would say, 'It's a bit over the top, Mother.'"

I laughed. "That was a good impersonation."

"It's one of my secret talents."

So I walked back to the Starbucks cart and bought us each a cappuccino. We sat for an hour, and when Bradley del Champ walked up the ramp at three, Leslie took my hand, breathed in, and said, "I've never meddled before, Prisma. Let's hope we don't mess this up."

And I said, "Amen to that."

Lark

WATCHING THE GANG PULL UP IN THE BENTLEY with Bradley sitting among them, it was all I could do not to put my hand through the wall. Not that I'm strong enough for such tantrums or anything, but I felt like it.

What was this all about?

And boy, did this anger feel good!

Yet a girl shouldn't feel this mad on a Sunday.

Still, I pasted on a somewhat-smile and opened the side door and yelled, "Come on in, and be quick about it. It smells like something's burning!"

Prisma shot out of the car and ran across the courtyard and through the door. She yanked open the oven door, examined the perfect roast underneath its tinfoil tent, then glanced over at me with a raised eyebrow.

"You deserved that, Prisma."

"I still work for your mother, baby. I'm not any more happy about this than you are."

Bradley came inside. "Wow! It looks just like I remembered."

Mother followed. "I don't know whether that's a compliment or an indictment." She set her purse on the kitchen counter. "Well! I'm exhausted. I'm going up for a nap. Supper's at seven, Prisma?"

"Yes, Mrs. Summerville."

I stood there observing this well-oiled machine before me. Mother, so tired, yet smooth and gracious. Prisma fussing over the food. Asil out hosing off the car.

"Lark," he said and held out his arms. And I went into them just like always. I hugged him back and watched as Prisma retreated into her apartment.

I shook my head at my ex-husband. "I guess it's just you and me, Brad." And I pulled away.

"I know this is a hassle for you, babe. Listen, I told them to just take me to a hotel, but they wouldn't listen."

"I hope they didn't convince you to stay here!"

"No. Now that I could refuse graciously. Whoa, look at you! I love that dress."

I'd unearthed a light pink tulle creation at the thrift store. "Thanks. Your daughter is wearing off on me. You want to sit in the den or on the porch?"

"The porch sounds nice."

So we sat there on the stodgy cedar chairs, him in his rock-'n'-roll jeans and me in my thrift-store regalia, and I told him about Flannery's reaction. "I have no idea what she's thinking, Brad. She's upset at me, I'm sure, and probably at you."

"She shouldn't be upset at you."

Hah, like that was even remotely true. "Anyway, I don't envy you. Suddenly up and appearing like this all these years later. Are you just going to show up on her doorstep?"

"Well, I was kind of hoping you could help me out."

"No way, Brad. You are on your own."

"Lark—"

"How does it feel?"

And then he started to weep.

Oh man! Can't I even have one small moment of triumph?

With a sigh I reached out to comfort him.

Oh man!

"Do we even have James's number?" I asked Prisma after Asil left to cart Bradley to the hotel. "I'm assuming that's where they went."

Prisma sat at her desk. She pointed to the screen where an e-mail with financial figures hovered. "Look at that. Do you see there? Days of Summer is doing better than ever."

"How come?"

"Newly. He does the investing. Or heads that up anyway."

"He does? I didn't know that."

"There's lots you don't know, baby."

"Obviously."

"Pull up a seat."

So I did.

Prisma took a sip from a teacup near the mouse pad. "So you're not going to let this thing with Baby Girl rest? You're going to do something about it?"

"I have to."

In a rare display Prisma reached out her hand and caressed my cheek. "Good for you, baby. You're learning."

"Oh, Prisma. You think so?"

She nodded. And a look of sadness melted her features. But a smile quickly replaced it. "Let me get that number for you."

A few minutes later I rested on my window seat and dialed the portable phone. It rang only twice before I heard James's voice.

"James? It's Lark Summerville."

"Hey, Mrs. Summerville. How you doing?"

"The question is, how's Flannery?"

"Coping pretty well considering the circumstances. But she's the type, you know?"

"I know. Can I speak with her?"

"She's at work."

I thought for a moment. "When does she get off?"

"She's usually done by 10:30. I was going to pick her up then." He coughed. "Unless, of course, you want to."

I gripped the phone. "You think I should?" Could I drive all by myself?

"Yeah. Can I be, like, totally honest with you, Mrs. Summerville?"

"Yeah, but please call me Lark first, okay? Mrs. Summerville is my mother."

He chuckled. "Sure. Look, it's like this. Flannery feels like the adult in her relationship with you."

Ouch.

"I know it may be hard to hear that. But the way I see it, you might as well know."

"I appreciate it."

"So you gonna go pick her up?"

"I haven't driven in years."

He said nothing.

"I haven't even kept my license up. I thought I'd get it renewed, but I haven't gotten up the guts."

"The traffic won't be bad that time of night," he said with optimism.

"Okay then. Don't worry about her. I'll bring her home."

"And all you have to do is get there," he said. "She can drive home."

"After what you just told me? Not a chance."

"Well, I'll talk to you later then."

I needed to not blow this. "James, congratulations. If this conversation is any indication, I think you'll make a fine husband for my daughter."

"I'm sure going to try…" And then he sounded like he wanted to say my name, but all the available choices felt uncomfortable.

"Mom?" I supplied, thinking, *My gosh, I'm only forty-one!*

He laughed. "Okay, why not?"

We said more uncomfortable good-byes, then I hung up the phone and went to find my mother.

Leslie

I WATCHED LARK PULL PRISMA'S DUSTER out on the road, stepping on the brakes every other second, the car dry heaving itself out of sight.

Oh, heavenly Father.

Standing by the window a moment longer, I prayed like I had never prayed before. A crucial moment faced all of us, and it lay completely in the hands of my daughter.

A few months ago that thought would have frightened me silly.

Lark

THE ONLY GOOD THING I CAN SAY about getting in that car and driving off is that it kept my mind from dwelling too intently on my mission. I might have gone and turned around.

But I didn't.

I stopped at red lights, green lights, stop signs, yield signs, oncoming cars, parked cars.

With the horns blaring all around me, it was the loudest night going north on Charles for a very long time.

Where did Bradley go? Did he go back to his hotel?

Oh, it makes me sick the way he still puts butterflies into my stomach.

The creep.

Because of him I was driving the Duster hoping and praying my daughter didn't hate me.

Whoa! Almost didn't see that turn!

Towson already? I'm already here?

God help me. Please tell me what to say.

Flannery

OH, WOW! I CAN HARDLY BELIEVE IT when I see Prisma's Duster at the curb and Mom at the wheel. Sometimes, a small thing will tell it to you like it is.

The only way I can describe what came over me is Divine Compassion. Sometimes I think Jesus lets you view people the way He does.

I see a woman with a shattered heart sitting there behind the wheel of that car. And I see somebody who does the best she can. Is Mom perfect? Far from it. But that is not my problem. My problem is how I accept her knowing she's lied to me all those years.

That is my problem.

As usual, I need to be the adult.

But I love Mom, don't you see?

As soon as she sees me, she jumps out of the car.

The shock of the situation hits me. This is totally not my mom.

"Flannery!" she yells.

I walk over. Something inside me makes me want to at least make her sweat. I cross my arms. "Mom. What are you doing here?"

"I called your apartment to talk to you, and James suggested I come pick you up."

That rat. "But you don't drive anymore."

"I know. But I didn't know what else to do."

"Actually, it's a good thing."

"It is?"

"Yeah. Let's go before you get a ticket for being in a no-stopping zone."

"Oh no!"

"And, Mom, I'm driving. I really am."

She doesn't argue. But once we are in the car she says, "I told myself I wasn't going to let you, but then after the drive over here, I realized that a mother tries to keep her child safe and happy as much as possible, so if you offered, I'd say yes."

Safe and happy. That's all she was really trying to do, wasn't it?

We make up. Say all the right things, hug, and cry. And she apologizes. In a really heartfelt way. I don't realize that's what I have been looking for until the words are out of her mouth. When we sit in the drive of the apartment house, she says, "So are you going to see your father?"

"Someday. But I've decided I'm not going to make it easy on him, Mom. He's got to know he can't just mess with people like that."

"He's asking for your phone number."

"Go ahead and give it to him. But don't tell him where we live, okay?"

She nods.

That night after James and I have some lovin' time, and let me tell you, it is all so totally worth the wait, I ask him, "Should I just forgive him and be done with it?"

He pulls me close to his chest. "Don't know, babe. I'd make him sweat a little, but I wouldn't take it too far."

"I want to see if he's really changed though."

"The last thing you need is for him to tire of the situation."

I kiss his chest. "See? That's exactly right. What if he shreds my heart like he did Mom's?"

"He already has, babe."

"Yeah. I guess I don't want those threads snipped into smaller pieces."

James kisses my hair. "But you know you have me to fall back on, babe."

And Mom had no one all those years ago. Man, I am glad I forgave her!

"I saw the final book in her postcard collection the other night," I told James.

"Yeah? How far downhill could it go from Zelda the Frog Impersonator?"

"Lots."

"Really?"

"Yeah."

And I told him about three-legged men, two-headed people. "Not your garden-variety midgets," I said.

"I guess not."

Bearded women, human horns. Elastic skin, impervious skin, exaggerated curvature of the spine. Then there was some guy named Coffey, The Living Skeleton.

"I kid you not, James. The guy was in perfect health and looked like a skeleton. But then there were the others, victims of severe muscular atrophy, the whole nine yards. It was horrible."

"Why do you think her collection took that turn, babe?"

"Maybe because she felt sorry for them? You know? I mean, maybe it helped her realize she wasn't in the worst straits. Maybe it kept her going to know those people still made it somewhere, despite their shortcomings."

"In a freak show?"

"Okay, maybe that's a stretch."

I know James thinks it's all weird. And I do too. But I know my mom, and I know she didn't collect them to make fun of them. Maybe she wanted to preserve their memory somehow. Maybe she wanted to somehow show that she understood. But I can't even say that to James.

PRISMA

"Hello, Son."

"Mama!"

"How's Caprice doing?"

"Pretty good. Five months to go."

"Are you having one of those ultrasounds done?"

"We want to be surprised."

I slapped my thigh. "Good for you! Me, too."

"How are things on Greenway, Mama?"

"Busy as usual. I'm tutoring Mrs. Summerville on the goings-on in Days of Summer."

"Oh? Interesting."

"Yes it is." And sad. I felt so sad, and yet so much stood before me. "So, you found me a house yet?"

Sinclair laughed. "Almost. I've narrowed it down to two."

"Send me pictures."

"Good idea. I'll do it over the Internet. And remember, we can add the porch and the fence."

H'm. "So they don't have porches and fences?"

"No, Mama."

"I'm not moving down until I have a porch and a fence."

"I know that, Mama."

"Good. Just so long as we understand one another."

Sinclair chuckled. "Mama, you never change."

"Some people never do."

"Mama, speaking of people that never change, what's happening with Bradley del Champ? Caprice saw on *Entertainment Tonight* that he cancelled several engagements for his group this month. He still in Baltimore?"

"Yep. Sure is. Trying hard."

"H'm. You think he'll win Baby Girl over?"

"He'd better!"

"That's what I say. Gotta run, there's a deacons' meeting at church Tuesday night and I've got to get my agenda ready."

Oh, my son! I'm so proud of that boy. Head deacon.

Now Bradley del Champ could learn a few lessons from my son. Sure, he learned loyalty with that woman he abandoned Lark and Baby Girl for. But can Lark really forgive him? I sure don't know. Because, to tell you the truth, I'm having a hard time forgiving him myself.

October

Lark

I LIVED FOR YEARS IN LONELINESS, and now two men vie for my affection. The autumn wears on. Bradley swears he will wear Flannery down and get her to see him. "I spent twenty years trying to forget about her—which I never could—and I'll spend however long it takes to win her back."

The problem is, he's trying to win me back too.

We sat together on the screen porch in late September.

"I'll tell you what would go a long way in proving yourself to us again, Brad."

He sat forward. We were at the redwood table playing gin rummy. "I'm all ears."

"You could buy my lot from me."

"What?"

"The lot in Hamilton."

He set down his cards. "You mean, set up a residence here?"

"Yeah. Don't you think that would prove a lot to Flannery?"

He relaxed against the cushions and stared up at the beamed ceiling where a tin star with cutouts shed light on our game. "Wow, babe. Let me call my financial guy and see about it."

"Oh, cut the garbage, Brad. We both know you can afford a hundred of these houses. It's Hamilton, for pity's sake. It would be a haven for you when you're here in the area."

"A nice change from California," he admitted, his mouth turning down as he nodded. "H'm. Can I see it first?"

I laughed and threw my cards at him. "Of course, silly." Why does he have to go and be cute all the time?

He dealt another hand. "I'm thinking of going in another direction with my music. I'm tired of the rock-'n'-roll scene."

"I don't blame you."

Tapping his finger on the tabletop, he cleared his throat. Before he could speak, I said, "No *way*, Bradley. No way. I'm not going to join back up with you. I set the contemporary music scene behind me years ago."

"What about jazz?"

"What about it?"

"Oh, come on Lark. I've got all the connections. It would be a sure-fire way to finally make it."

Indignation rose within me. And it was luscious. Rich and sweet, because I realized something, praise God. "I have made it, Bradley del Champ."

"No, Lark, I didn't mean—"

"It doesn't matter what you meant. I'm happier than I've ever been. I did a fine job raising our daughter. I'm playing music with people I love, and Mother and I are working together now. We're totally assuming the helm of Days of Summer in a couple of months. My life is mapped out beautifully. And for the first time in years, I am at peace. I feel God's pleasure now, *babe*, in a way I've never felt it before. I am accepted in the Beloved. Do you even know what that means?"

He shook his head. "You know me and religion, babe."

"Well, maybe you should try some."

He looked up at the tin star again. "Whew. Sorry for bringing that up. I was only trying to help."

I reached out and put my hand over his. "I don't need your help. And that's okay."

The left corner of his mouth lifted. "You're something, babe. You know that?"

"Yeah, for the first time in a lot of years, I do."

Three weeks later Bradley closed on the lot. He threw a costume party there in the burned out basement to celebrate. Neighbors came by, trick-or-treaters. It was a hoot. Flannery promised me she and James would show. Mother, Prisma, Bradley, and I spent the entire day getting ready.

Johnny was coming. Marsha and Glen. Babe and Deke, and Rots, too. Father Charlie said he'd come dressed as a priest.

I love that man!

"I want a neutral setting to see Daddy in for the first time," Flannery told me. "Make sure of that. Invite as many people as you can."

Of course, I'd had a phone call with Newly.

"Come on, Newly, come to the party."

"What in the world would I come as, Lark?"

"I don't care. Put a sheet over your head. Flannery can use all the support she can get."

"I'll think about it."

The good thing is, when I told Mother I had totally given up hope on mending things with Newly, she told me he had visited her at the hospital. That went a long way.

"Anyway, we'd be glad to see you. And you can bring your girl-friend."

He chuckled. "Did Flannery tell you about her?"

"Yes. I still can't believe you'd have dinner over there at the apart-ment and won't come to the party."

"Lark, I don't know if I can hold my temper around Bradley yet."

Wow. "Really?"

"Yes."

"Well, if that's the reason, then don't come, with my blessing."

"You see, dearest, I do have my reasons for things."

"Newly, we have to see each other sometime. I know I wasn't always the best sister."

He sighed. "It was years ago, Lark."

"But it carved a gully between us."

"That's the way it is with siblings sometimes."

"But does it have to be forever?"

Silence.

"I'd better go."

I felt desperate. "Well, let's shoot for Thanksgiving."

"Maybe."

I left it at that. Pushing it would be stupid.

Leslie

I DID A FINE JOB arranging the crudités platter. The baby carrots lined up in a yin-and-yang pattern. The broccoli and cauliflower stood on their trunks, close together, like a field of daisies. We even carved out cucumber boats and loaded them with cream cheese and sprinkled them with chives.

The chives were my idea.

Prisma cooked beef stew in two large pumpkins. The spread also included corn bread and some kind of autumn fruit salad. Pears and apples and walnuts. Grapes too. They called it Waldorf salad in my day, but now, as in everything, it's been casualized. The recipe in the paper simply said, Autumn Fruit Medley. Which isn't a bad alternative as it lets the reader know right away what they're in for.

"That looks pretty, Mother," Lark said, floating over in a fairy outfit. She'd overhauled that pink tulle thrift-store number she'd bought a couple of months ago, added wings and sprinkled sparkles over her skin.

Oh, and the extra ten pounds becomes her greatly.

"Not as pretty as you, dear."

And I was rewarded with a soft kiss on the cheek.

"You look pretty fine yourself, Mother."

"I know!"

We laughed. Lark flew off to set out the napkins and cutlery, and I realized the pillows on the futons we brought in for the occasion needed a bit of fluffing. I caught a picture of myself in the punch bowl. A size eight now, rosy cheeks, and the picture of health. Prisma and I walk around the neighborhood these days. Truly, I have never felt this good in my life.

They say these procedures last about ten years.

I patted the folds of my costume into a neater arrangement. What a fine Queen of Hearts you make, Leslie Summerville.

Seven o'clock, the time of Flannery's arrival drew near. All of us arrived early to help, and we congregated in the basement trying desperately not to brush up against the blackened walls. Marsha and Glen as the Blues Brothers, Johnny as a doctor (as he did not have time to find a good costume), and Prisma, her hair in cornrows now, saying she was Bo Derek in the movie *10*. Father Charlie came as a priest. Deke and Babe arrived as Count and Lady Dracula. And finally, Bradley.

In a cardboard box painted silver he awaited his daughter. Spangles and buttons sparkled, and the words painted on the back screamed his uncertainty. "If I could go back and do it all over again differently, I would."

"Like it, Mom?" he asked me.

"I take it you're a time machine."

"What do you think?"

"If I could get my arms around that thing, I'd hug you."

The revelation astounded me.

At seven, the headlights of the old brown Buick skimmed the upper cinder blocks. We all waited. As they descended the steps, my ex-son-in-law became so ill he ran to the far, darkened corner.

"Flannery!" Lark waved from beside the chiminea that threw out heat in the other corner. "Come on over."

Sweet Pea's brows furrowed. "Where is he?"

"Over there, throwing up in the trash can."

Marsha chirped, "He's that nervous."

"Good," Sweet Pea said.

I laid a hand on her shoulder. "I like your style."

She turned to her new husband. "It's now or never, James. I might as well get it over with. And if I go to him, it will give me the upper hand."

Sweet Pea? A diplomat?

Well, with her growing up around her mother and me, it wasn't surprising.

We all busied ourselves quickly as she walked into the darkened area of the basement, careful to keep one eye flitting back to the scene. But only a quick flit, mind you.

Flannery

SO HE WAS RETCHING over the trash can, and I got a clear view of his message. I met it with skepticism, and to be honest, I sort of thought the whole getup a little childish and goofy, but he was my father. And you know what settled it all for me? James. Earlier today I was in the spare bedroom working on a painting, and he sat reading in the corner in an old recliner we bought at a yard sale for twenty bucks.

"You know I don't know the Bible all that well, but I did learn the Ten Commandments."

I looked over from my painting. "Wow. That was random."

He laughed. "I was thinking about your father."

"Yeah, *do not commit adultery*. That's his commandment need all right."

"Actually I was thinking of your commandment need."

My commandment need? "A specific one?"

"Right. And it may help you a little if you get that chip off your shoulder, babe."

"James!" He didn't have to say it like that.

Then he got to his feet, walked over and stood behind me, arms around my shoulders, hands on my rib cage. "I just love you, Flannery. That's all."

Oh, what a sweet man. "I know."

It's so wonderful to be in love at times like this. "So what commandment is it?"

" 'Honor your father and mother.' "

I kissed his arm. "You would have to bring that up."

"Well, babe, as I see it, if you don't really have a choice, not if you live what you believe and all, that sort of takes some of the pressure off."

Wow. Is this guy something or what?

And I remember that conversation in vivid detail as I lay a hand on his costume. Exodus 20 doesn't say "Honor your father as long as he's a great father." Or "Honor your father unless he's one of those man-children you can't really trust more than you can throw." It doesn't even say "Honor your father except if he deserts you and doesn't begin to deserve your honor, the creep."

It just says "Honor your father," which means that even if he's wearing a stupid costume that is not working its intended magic, you don't have a choice.

See? Some people think that having a choice about everything is so great. But that's why I love following Christ. If you're truly living in Him, well, the choices aren't so many, and life isn't nearly as confusing.

"Dad."

He turns, and the uncertainty in his eyes endears him to me right away. Sort of like when you feel sorry for a frightened alley cat. This will be no normal father-daughter relationship. I know that. In fact, now that Mom is finally tucked away where she should be, I guess I have a job to do on my father.

"Flannery? My gosh, you're beautiful!"

And he breaks down in tears, but, like, that's okay, because it gives me something to do. You know?

I take off my cowgirl hat and help him out of his box. And I let him hug me, and I feel nothing but pity. But I pretend I am happy to see him when he says he's dreamed about this day for years.

It is as good a start as we are going to get. And that is okay. I look over his shoulder into the basement, all lit up with glowing pumpkins, scented candles, twinkling lights, and brightly colored leaf garlands. All these nice people who love me or Mom enough to be here look up at once and smile. But my mom gives me a double thumbs-up and a smile that says, "You know, sweetheart, you're really something."

See it's like this, we all have regrets. Some of us more than others. And those of us who are blessed enough to have them slim and few are also blessed to be able to even things out for the others.

I smile at Mom and pull away from my father. "So how are we going to begin this thing?"

"Play it by ear?"

Sounds like something a musician would say. "Sounds like a plan to me."

What parents don't realize when they break off their relationships is that someday, in some way, it will all be up to the child. I can't pretend it isn't a burden, but I can't pretend that honoring my father and mother can be translated any other way.

November

L a r k

I took Johnny to Dulles Airport in mid-November.

I drove there.

Yes.

We stood by the security check.

"I'll see you in April, right?" he said.

"Yep."

"I know I'll be looking forward to it even more then than I am now."

"We will too."

His flight was called. "I can't believe Leslie will be coming."

"Are you kidding? She's taking Days of Summer very seriously now. She's never been to Africa either, and she's using the mission as an excuse to go. 'Just to make sure the funds are going to a real place, Larkspur.'"

He laughed at the imitation. "You're quite a mimic."

I shrugged. "It's one of my hidden talents."

"I've got to go."

"I know." I put my arms around him and hugged him. "It's better this way, Johnny."

He pushed his glasses up on his nose. "I'm not so sure about that. But I enjoyed our times together, Lark. I won't pretend I didn't."

"You're a good man. Do well."

He raised a finger. "With a little help."

"Amen."

There hadn't been kisses on the mouth between Johnny and me for several weeks. Sometimes relationships take a lovely turn all on their own.

Before he disappeared at the curve of the ramp, he turned and waved. I returned the gesture.

Good for you, Johnny Josefowski, M.D.

Dr. J.

I returned to find Mother and Prisma sitting in the kitchen, initial plans for an extension to Days of Summer's headquarters splayed out on the kitchen table.

I poured myself a cup of tea and sat down. "Wow. I love it. You did a great job with the architect, Mother."

"Yes, I did."

Prisma laid a hand on the plans. "When your mama wants something, she knows how to get it."

I sat down. "What amazes me is that we can all live in this house, this big monstrosity on Greenway, and get along."

"Oh, fiddle!" Mother waved a hand. "It's even more than amazing. It's a miracle."

PRISMA

"JESUS? THE PORCH IS DONE. The fence will be ready next week."

"Perfect timing, My girl."

I gazed up into the heavens. "My work is done here, isn't it?"

"You got that right."

"So I'm guessing You and I are off on another adventure?"

"There's people that need you. People that love you and they need you."

I gripped the window sill, absorbing the indigo of the sky into my being. "Will I ever rest, Lord?"

"Someday, My girl. Someday."

The good news is this. When Lark, Greenway's own Sleeping Beauty, was kissed awake by the Lover of Her Soul, she opened her eyes and asked only to sleep for five more minutes. But she's awake now.

Honest to Pete, that's the truth.

December

Newly

Contrary to popular opinion, I'm not just a voice on the phone. And I came home for Christmas for the first time in years. I would have brought my girlfriend, Brenda, but she's a real family sort and stayed in Dundalk with all her nieces and nephews, sisters and brothers, parents and grandparents, aunts and uncles. I've received quite an education from Brenda. Prisma already moved south. Lark cooked the turkey and dressing. Buddy and James brought some casseroles, and for the first time Mother gave only two gifts each. Picture frames.

And matching sweaters.

Good heavens.

Bradley del Champ popped in for a brief while to give Buddy her present. They nabbed him to take a picture of all the family to go into the frame.

My gosh, a family portrait, all in our hand-knitted sweaters. And we sat for hours laughing over Mother's scrapbooks.

"I'm going to make one each year. I'm not going to miss a thing."

If I didn't love them, I'd want to regurgitate.

Nevertheless, I found I didn't wish to leave at four as I told them I would. I stayed well into the evening. I would say we got along just as we used to in the old days.

Truth be told, however, the old days were never this good.

Is my family perfect? Heavens, no! With Prisma now in North Carolina, you should hear the two of them argue about what to have for dinner.

But I wouldn't have them any other way.

Strange, isn't it?

So I'm back in the family.

And with the way they're planning on traveling all over the world, those two, it's a mighty good thing. Somebody needs to hold down the fort.

Flannery told me the other day, "I'm glad you'll still be here in town full time."

"And why is that, Buddy?"

"Because you're such a crackup, Uncle Newly."

We're all insane to some extent, we Summervilles. And as my father would have said, "Isn't it grand?"

I'm thinking about keeping my new Christmas stocking up all year long.

About the Author

Lisa Samson, author of twelve published novels, changes her hairstyle and hair color almost every year, but the love of her family—husband, Will, and three children—never grows old. She makes her home in Maryland, where she cuts her own grass on her new, orange riding mower. She ran it into a tree the second week she had it.